MICHAEL WEBB

The Last Shadow Knight

First published by Whatup Publishing LLC 2021

Cover design by jeffbrowngraphics.com.

First edition

ISBN: 978-1-7375788-0-2

This book was professionally typeset on Reedsy.
Find out more at reedsy.com

This book is dedicated to all of my friends and family who . . .

. . . thought that my writing a book was one of the coolest things they'd ever heard.

. . . said they couldn't wait to buy it without even knowing what the book was about.

. . . promised to read it, even though they didn't have any indication of whether it would be good or not.

. . . asked constantly how long it would be until it was ready.

Contents

Land of Terrenor

North Sea

Bryveld

Nortris

Notaverre River

Daratill

Norshewa

Rydland

Korob Mountains

Gap of Thardor

Molyaigh

Kyrd Forest

Westfale Ocean

Karad

Kironail

Bromhill

Nasco

Tienn

Feldor

Kandis

Fenaverre River

Felting

Rynor

Strailh Mountains

Lorranis

Felaverre River

Palenting

Isle of Paratill

Tarving

Tesaverre River

Tarphan

Searis

Portris

Marris

Gulf of Tartis

Parthe Mountains

N

Parathan Ocean

City of Karad

North Gate

Benevorre River

Prinvestor

Gate St

West Fairren

Castle

Farrier St

High St

Karad Square

East Fairren

Market St

Merchants Row

Archibald St (Split)

East Gate

The Bottoms

Kulling Square

Gate St

Upper Sherry

Dock St

The Docks

South Gate

Prologue

Moonlight bounced off the rooftops and spires, creating a glowing veil over the city. Merrick Ryd paced the balcony, waiting. By the end of the night, the King of Feldor would be dead, and he would be the one to kill him.

Merrick appreciated his perch from atop his tower of stone. Lanterns illuminated the stone streets of Felting, and the Felavorre River shimmered in the distance. The bustle of the day had settled to a trickle of people making their way through the city at night. He stood tall, like a ruler surveying his domain, untouchable in his walled fortress.

He looked across the city to the castle. Soon, the king would receive an urgent message. After reading it, the man with more compassion than brains would get in his carriage and ride through the streets to his cousin, the one who would desperately need his help. Merrick and his men would be waiting.

What a fool, he thought with a smirk. He felt at his hip to make sure his sword was there—it always was. *Time to begin.*

Merrick walked through the open doorway, and a blanket of silence fell over the men inside. A lone candle burned on a table, but the light from the moon outside illuminated the room where eleven men waited. Some worked for him at the Ryd Shipyard. Others had similar business interests. All would willingly give their lives for him. He looked through the crowd, taking his time to lock eyes with each of them.

"I'm sure most of you are curious as to why I called you here. Tonight, the king will die, and I will take his place." Merrick spoke in a calm voice as he let each word stand in the silence. Evil grins formed as heads nodded around the room and Merrick began to pace. "For years, King Wesley has held us back. He doesn't want us to prosper. He doesn't think it's right for us to work hard and enjoy the fruits of our labor. Last season, his minimum wage edict took away our ability to pay our workers an amount that reflected the work they did. Now, these unskilled laborers are using *our* rightful money to buy nice clothes and bigger houses to live in." He stopped and looked around as a low grumble flowed through the room.

"I didn't burn down Felavorre Shipping or kill the Lord of Trade to allow this to happen. Wesley and his charity are a stain on this city. For the sake of our businesses and everyone in this city who doesn't have the guts to stand up to him, we will do it for them." He looked to a short man with thick arms on the far left. "Adriel, are your men in place with the roadblock?"

"Yes, sir," Adriel replied, standing rigidly.

Merrick nodded as he scanned the crowd. "Let's go."

He walked past his men to the stairs at the far end of the room, but no one followed or even pivoted their heads. When he turned to see what held their attention, his face froze along with the others.

Standing in the balcony doorway, silhouetted by the moonlight, were three figures wearing hooded cloaks. Merrick couldn't see their faces obscured by shadows, but all three held swords and stood ready to fight.

"Merrick Ryd?" said a female voice coming from a slender figure with long hair escaping her hood.

"Who are you?" Merrick puffed out his chest, masking his unease. *How did they get past my walls and guards? How did they get up here?*

The figures moved toward him, but Merrick's men stepped in the way, drawing their swords.

The intruders halted, and the tallest one with broad shoulders said in a deep voice, "Our issue is not with you men. Leave now if you do not wish to die."

Ryd's men laughed. The mocking response echoed off the walls of the stone room and settled Merrick's disquiet. His men fanned out and surrounded the intruders while Merrick watched from outside the circle.

"Very well," the tall man said. The three figures stood back-to-back, crouched with their swords pointed outward above their heads.

Adriel moved first, swinging to knock the woman's sword out of the way. Expecting to hear the clash of steel, Merrick gasped as the weapon hit nothing but air, and the woman's blade already stuck into Adriel's chest.

How did she do that? Merrick inched his way backward. As he tried to understand what happened, all three figures moved like blurred shadows. Before his men could react, they fell victim to the intruders' lightning-fast swords, receiving fatal wounds one by one. Cries of anguish erupted as blood sprayed through the air. Merrick blinked in time to see the woman pull her sword from the neck of the last of his defenders. The entire fight was over before Adriel's short body even hit the ground.

Blood pooled together from the eleven bodies strewn across the floor as the three figures turned and strode to where Merrick cowered in the corner.

"Who are you? Wh—what do you want?" he asked, holding his shaking sword in front of him.

The hooded figures glanced at each other. The third man spoke in an aged voice as he nodded at the man next to him. Wrinkles on his face were barely visible in the moonlight. "William?"

"We are the Shadow Knights, and we serve the kingdom," the tall man said as he moved his arm slightly.

A glint of candlelight reflected off something fast and metallic. A flash of pain ran through Merrick's body before he felt no more.

I

The Beginning

Ten years later

1

The Tailor's Shop

Veron stood on the roof and looked at the city surrounding him. A collection of buildings in various shapes and heights jutted up unevenly. He imagined the streets and alleys below that flowed together like a collection of streams. Lanterns lit in the main streets gave Karad a glow as if a muted serpent of fire snaked its way through the city's wealthy areas. Behind him, the Bottoms where he called home was completely dark.

"What's the worst that could happen?" Fend asked.

"Seriously?" Veron replied, looking at his friend. "That's your pitch? Getting me to imagine the worst that could happen?"

Veron peered over the edge of the building at the long drop to the empty street below. The wind picked up and whipped his hair, causing him to feel unsteady.

"Come on!" Fend said. "This place'll be the best we ever hit! You seen all the fancy outfits he sells from his shop. You can't find fabric like he sells anywhere south of Split. He's gotta be loaded. Plus, neither of us ate in days. You know you want this!"

As if on cue, Veron's stomach growled. He was hungry. He did want this.

"We'll watch our backs like we always do," Fend continued. "If anythin' goes wrong, we get out of there."

"You 'member the lender's office we hit after we ran away?" Veron asked.

"Yeah. What about it?"

"That was sposta be the best ever, and we left there with nuthin'!"

"That's 'cause we had to run. Your shaggy hair stuck out from behind the wall and gave us away!" Fend punched him on the arm. "Look, Veron, you're thirteen and aren't gettin' any younger. We can't count on people pityin' us and givin' handouts anymore. We need to take care of ourselves."

A gust of wind sent a chill through Veron. His tattered clothing did little to keep him warm, especially during the frigid season of wiether. "What if someone's there?" he asked.

"I told you, no one's home. I saw the tailor and his family pack their wagon this mornin'. I even talked with the girl and asked her where they was goin'. She said they're headin' down to Felting to buy supplies—fabric or somethin'. Won't be back to Karad for three days."

Veron surveyed the city again, trying to avoid deciding.

Under every one of these rooftops is someone with money and food, Veron thought. *I'm tired of bein' hungry. I'm sick of this city gettin' the best of me.*

He looked back to Fend and nodded. "Okay, let's do it."

Fend set down the sack of supplies he had been carrying and took out a metal wire. "Hold my legs while I get the latch on the window," he said as he crouched at the edge.

Veron sat on his legs, letting the older boy dangle upside down from the second-story roof.

"Got it!" Fend whispered after a moment from over the edge. His hand appeared at the edge of the roof, and Veron pulled him up.

After looping a frayed piece of rope around a nearby chimney, Fend held onto it as he made his way over the edge, feet first. Although he tried to appear confident, his breath quickened as his body lowered. Soon, he disappeared.

Veron waited and listened. For several seconds, all he could hear was his heart beating and the sound of the wind. He tapped absently at the medallion hanging beneath his shirt as he strained his ear forward. Finally, a whisper confirmed it was his turn.

Even though Fend made it look easy and Veron had done it countless times before, he was still nervous. *What if the rope breaks? What if I slip and fall? What if someone's in the house?* Despite the fear, Veron grabbed the rope and worked his feet over the edge. When his foot rested on the wrought-iron sign below, his nerves settled a bit, but only when he made it through the window and landed inside the building did he feel in control again.

The two boys stood at the end of a short hall. A sliver of moonlight revealed one door frame on the right and two on the left. The staircase at the end would lead down to the shop below. Fend had his ear against the first door on the left, listening. So far, everything was silent.

After a seemingly endless wait, Fend motioned for them to go. The first room was an office with a full bookcase and desk. Veron rifled through the ledgers and papers, but nothing looked valuable. In the far corner, he spotted a chest, and his heart raced. He tried to open it, but it didn't budge. A keyhole on the front stared at him, taunting him.

With a grin on his face, Fend handed him a small pry bar and whispered, "Your turn."

Veron took the pry bar and worked on the chest, doing his best to be silent. The wood groaned as the chest fought back. The sound was quiet, but it felt like an alarm bell to him. Sweat beaded on his forehead from both the noise and the effort as he strained to open it. He was about to pass the bar to Fend when the lock broke with a loud crack. Veron froze, his ears strained for the slightest noise. The silence soon returned, and they each let out their breath.

Veron's heart raced as he opened the chest, but his smile disappeared and shoulders slumped when he saw it was packed full of papers. Both boys rummaged through the stacks of official-looking documents and maps. The scent of dried parchment clung to Veron's nose—the smell of disappointment and squandered hope.

"What a waste," Fend said as he threw a handful of papers down.

Why would a tailor have so many documents locked away? Veron thought.

Hoping for something more, he continued to dig through the chest until he found a velvet bag at the bottom. A clink sounded as he picked it up. Opening the bag, he emptied it into his hand. Coins—six copper tid and four copper pintid.

"Whoa!" Veron exclaimed, forgetting the need to be quiet.

Fend looked over his shoulder. "Nice!"

Veron had never held that much money in his life. *We could live for almost a season on this. We could buy supplies, bread, fruit—meat even. Maybe we could get real beds and blankets?* Not wanting to hang around any longer than necessary, he put the coins back in the bag and stuffed it in his pocket.

"Let's keep lookin'," Fend said.

The next door down the hall creaked when opened to reveal a kitchen, including shelves with food. There wasn't a lot, but to the starving boys, it was a feast. Veron's stomach growled as if calling out to it.

"Jackpot!" Fend said.

Both boys grabbed what they could, gorging on bread, salted pork, and carrots. They laughed at the unexpected bounty as they took turns shushing each other between bites. After their eating slowed, they stuffed their pockets with as much as they could carry. The pocket space ran out long before the food did.

"If they're gonna be gone three days, why don't we take what we can, then come back tomorrow and get more?" Veron asked as he chewed on a tough piece of pork.

"Yeah, that's a great idea," Fend said with a grin. "Let's get out of here."

They went back into the hall, and Veron grabbed the rope dangling outside the window. Fend remained in the hallway, standing by the remaining door.

"Whatcha doin'?" Veron whispered.

"I wanna see what's in here first."

"We can't carry any more. Let's go."

Fend eased the door open, and Veron sighed as he let go of the rope and joined his friend. The room was dark, with the only bit of light coming in from the window. Shadows covered the floor from the outline of two beds. One bed was bare, and the other held a pile of blankets. A bookshelf stood at the end of the room with what looked like two bronze candlesticks on top.

"Whoa!" Fend said as the boys crossed the room. "Those hafta be worth a silver argen apiece!"

With one foot on the edge of the bed and the other on one of the shelves, Fend extended his arm, but the first candlestick was barely out of reach.

"What do you think you're doing?" a deep, unfamiliar voice asked.

Veron spun around and froze. A body stood behind them—a body shaped like a pile of blankets. Veron cursed himself for not being more careful when they came in.

"What are you doing?" the bundle of blankets repeated with growing intensity.

7

"I—I saw the tailor leave this mornin'. I thought the house was empty," Fend said with a wavering voice.

"The tailor?" the other man said. "His shop is next door. You thought you could take his stuff while he was out?"

Veron glared at Fend. "You got the wrong house?" he muttered.

Before Veron could think of what to do, Fend yelled as he ran at the man and collided with his body square in the midsection, knocking him backward over the bed. Veron's heart raced as he and Fend ran for the stairs.

Desks, books, papers, and files filled the shop below. *We must be in the tax assessor's shop next door to the tailor's. That explains the chest full of documents.*

Veron reached the door first, and his stomach dropped—locked. He frantically looked around. They were trapped. He froze, unable to think as fear set in. His paralysis shattered along with the window as Fend threw a chair through it, spraying glass and splinters of wood into the street.

"Let's go!" Fend said, motioning.

The boys scurried through the broken window. Glass shards tugged on Veron's clothing, hands, and legs. He ignored the pain as they stumbled onto Market Street at the edge of Karad Square.

"Thieves! Stop them! Thieves!" a voice shouted from above.

Veron looked up. The tax assessor leaned out the upstairs window where their rope dangled limply. He pointed at them but looked across the square to where three soldiers stood staring back. Veron's heart sank as he recognized the tallest soldier. Captain Mortinson—the last man he wanted to see.

The boys took off. Running from soldiers, shopkeepers, or anybody he tried to steal from was nothing new to Veron. He was fast and able to climb up and squeeze through places few people could. They turned left at the first alley, but the soldiers had already

8

closed half the distance. Futile calls for them to stop echoed off the stone walls and streets.

Fend led the way with Veron on his heels, fighting to keep up. The bulk of the food stuffed in their pockets made running difficult, but they didn't slow, even when items began falling out.

Veron glanced back as they left the alley and crossed Split Street. To his dismay, the soldiers still pursued and were even closer. *Why do they hafta be so persistent?*

On the other side of Split started the Bottoms—a labyrinth of passages and alleyways. Buildings grew on top of buildings, many of which were falling over and unsafe to inhabit. Veron and Fend knew the neighborhood better than anyone, and in seconds, they would disappear in the maze of dark streets and buildings.

Fend ducked down a narrow passage as they entered the neighborhood, dodging between buildings. After emerging onto a larger street, a crumbling stone staircase led to the third floor of an abandoned building. Veron followed Fend up, taking two steps at a time. Many years ago, the building and those around it made up the Benevorre Lumber Mill. Years before, the Great Fire destroyed much of the city, including most of the mill, which was never rebuilt and left to fall into ruins.

The rickety door at the top of the stairs was off its hinges, revealing a decrepit room inside. Much of the walls had crumbled. The roof eroded long ago, and the rains had done their damage to the rest of the structure. Holes dotted the floor, which looked and smelled of rot. On the opposite side of the room through a busted window stood the remains of a stone wall.

Veron panted, trying to catch his breath as he peeked around the doorway to see if they'd lost their pursuers. Fend joined him in the opening as Mortinson and the others emerged from the tight passage on the street below.

Before the boys had a chance to duck back, one of the soldiers pointed at them. "Up there!"

"This is no good, Fend. They won't stop," Veron said, voice shaking.

Fend's mouth twisted in a smirk. "Let's see 'em follow us here!" The older boy laughed as he crossed the room, dodging the holes, and stepped through the window frame to walk the precarious path on top of the wall outside.

Veron wasn't about to be left behind, so he forced himself to step out after him. The wind picked up, and he held out his arms to keep balance. Blood from the shop window cuts dripped down his arms as he walked. The stone wall consisted of rocks and mortar jutting out in no regular pattern, making balancing difficult. On the left, the ground was barely visible in the darkness below. On the right, across a small alley, was the roof of another building. When he was only a few steps onto the narrow wall, the soldiers arrived at the window behind him.

"Stop! Come back!" one of them yelled.

Veron kept moving. "Uh . . . Fend? Where we goin'?" he asked as he looked ahead. "This wall doesn't go much more."

"Just keep movin'," Fend told him.

After a dozen more steps, the wall ended abruptly. Fend stopped and peered over the end, muttering a curse to himself. Veron turned around to look for other escape options. The roof to their right was not far away. Made of slate, it held up against time better than the others around it and appeared stable. The soldiers remained at the window behind them. Mortinson's formidable frame in the opening caused Veron's legs to wobble.

Veron looked to Fend. "The roof?"

"The roof," Fend replied, his usual jovial state replaced with a grim expression.

One of the soldiers stepped onto the wall. Veron's pulse raced, and he suddenly felt dizzy from the height. Steeling his jittery legs, he leaped.

Clearing the gap, he landed hard on the slate and fell to his knees. The impact was jarring, but the roof held. Fend came next, effortlessly covering the distance, but as he landed, a slate tile shifted from the sudden impact. He staggered and cried out as his body fell backward. Out of instinct, Veron reached out and caught his flailing arm.

Fend leaned precariously over the edge while Veron held tight. The two boys froze, and for a moment, Veron thought he had saved his friend until his grip began to slip. The blood covering his hand was too slick for him to hold on. Fend's eyes pleaded with him. The uncharacteristic fear he showed unnerved Veron. He tried to hold on with all his strength until Fend's arm slipped from his grasp. Their eyes locked in terror as the older boy tumbled backward over the edge.

"Fend!" Veron yelled into the darkness. "Fend!" He listened for a moment but heard nothing. Using a drainpipe on the far side of the building, he scurried to the ground.

The alley was dim, lit only by the moon high in the sky. The stone walls, blanketed in a mossy green, smelled damp from years of water and neglect. Fend lay at the base of the wall, looking at Veron in anguish. He lay on his side, breathing fast, shallow breaths.

Veron knelt next to him and put his hand on his shoulder. "Fend! You okay? Can ya get up?" he asked.

Halfway down the lower part of Fend's leg, the torn, light-colored fabric was dark and glistening where a smooth stick impaled his calf. Veron grimaced. He put his hands under Fend's arms to try to lift him, but Fend yelled and grabbed at his leg. Veron paled as his stomach turned. The object wasn't a stick. It was a snapped bone.

Veron fought back the urge to retch. *No! I have to be strong for*

Fend! Suddenly, he remembered their pursuers and looked up to the abandoned window. *Where are they?* He glanced around, finding nothing but empty passageways. *They could be here any second!*

"We hafta go!" Veron said, trying to lift Fend again.

"Just go!" Fend said, pushing him away. "I can't move anywhere. Just leave!"

He wouldn't leave me, and I'm not 'bout to leave him. I need a plan. The empty alley offered no help, but he could check the building.

"Hold on! I'll be right back," Veron said before darting into the building. "There's a cart here!" he whispered forcefully over his shoulder. His arms ached as he wheeled a heavy wooden cart across the room. "Fend, I think we can—" Veron stopped when he looked up.

Fend lay by the wall, but something was wrong. His eyes were wide, and there was a slight but definite shaking of his head.

"Well, well, look who we have here," said a voice, coming down the alley. "I guess jumping off a roof to get away isn't such a good idea, huh?" The three soldiers came into view through the open doorway.

"Where's your friend?" Captain Mortinson's deep voice cut through the darkness as he stood over Fend.

The sight of the captain turned Veron's blood to ice. His trimmed beard framed a face as hard as flint. Veron set the cart down and crept to the edge of the building behind some crates. In the shadows of the building, the soldiers wouldn't be able to spot him.

What are they gonna do? Maybe if I run up from behind and grab their swords . . . ?

Mortinson leaned close to Fend, speaking in a calm, ominous voice. "I said"—he put pressure on Fend's leg—"where is your friend?"

Fend screamed, tears running down his face. His head shook from side to side, but he refused to answer or even look at the soldiers.

Veron shook with rage. *How can they treat him like that?*

"Do you find it amusing to steal?" Mortinson asked as he straightened. "This city is defined by people who contribute. They do what they're told and follow the rules. And you? You do nothing but contribute to its filth and decay. One day, if I get my way, I'll run all of your kind out the gates."

The captain looked at the other two soldiers and nodded before turning and walking back up the alley. The two soldiers didn't follow.

They're gonna look for me!

Where he hid was dark, but they would find him if they looked. Another doorway on the opposite side of the room gave Veron hope. He inched his way in that direction as he glanced back at the soldiers, ready to spring into action. They hadn't moved. *Somethin's wrong. They're not searchin' at all.*

Suddenly, he stopped. His heart beat rapidly again as his hands grew clammy. The world slowed as one of the soldiers drew a sword from its sheath. The metallic shriek sounded like screaming in his ears.

No, they can't! His chest convulsed as he watched the soldier run Fend through the chest with his sword, drawing a cry of anguish from him. Veron tried to scream, but no sound emerged. He grabbed his own chest to numb the pain while his arm shook uncontrollably. He covered his mouth with the other hand.

The soldier put his sword away, and the two of them left. Rocks skittered off the walls of the alley as their laughter grew distant.

When they were gone, Veron ran to his friend. "Fend! Are you—?" He choked back the next words.

Fend held the wound on his chest, but the pool of blood was already too large. He looked at Veron with sad eyes that knew what came soon.

"I'm so sorry," Veron said. "If only I'd . . . I could've . . ." He shook his head, unable to find the right words. He fought tears as Fend shook his head with him.

"Not your fault," Fend said before a fit of coughing took over. Blood stained his lips from the effort. "I shoulda got the right shop." He managed a weak smile. "Promise me . . ." Fend took several labored breaths. "Promise me you'll be more than this."

Veron leaned back. *More than what?*

"Don't be a thief. You're better than this. Don't end up like me. Promise!" Fend said before coughing up blood again.

Veron sniffed and wiped his eyes. "I—I promise." He took Fend's free hand and held it tightly. They both managed a weak smile. After a moment, Fend's chest stopped moving. "Fend?" Veron gently shook him by the shoulder—no response.

Sobs racked Veron's body as he sat on the ground. He no longer felt the chill of the cold night, and he couldn't smell the must of the decaying alleyway. All he thought of was wishing he could have held on. Veron had no idea what to do next. His only friend in the world was dead.

2

The Streets of Karad

Fend deserved better than his body rotting away in some alley, but Veron didn't have the means for a proper burial. The next best option was the river.

His arms shook as he labored to carry the body down the dark street toward the water. Thankfully, it was close. He choked back tears as reality set in. *What am I goin' to do on my own?* he thought. As his friend's blood stained his own clothes, Veron struggled to keep him from slipping.

Arriving at the water's edge, he set Fend's body in the river and gently pushed him away from the shore. Veron sat on the bank and watched through blurry tears as the body caught the current and disappeared, downstream. He wiped his eyes, but the loss he felt remained.

Veron wanted to do anything *but* go back to the abandoned building they'd made their home over the last few years. It would feel too empty without Fend, so he aimlessly wandered the dark streets in a daze. All he could think about was Fend's body on the ground . . . the sound of the sword . . . his bloody handprint on Fend's arm.

If only I held on, or fought 'em off, or called for help. In all his life, he'd never felt so alone.

Veron walked up Gate Street as the sky began to lighten and people started to get up and around. Due to the high traffic of the main road, eager shopkeepers lived along the way and set up goods outside in the street to tempt those passing. Being the first day of the workweek, shop owners opened early on Marketday. They were eager to get started after being closed Weekterm the day before. The clatter of vendors assembling wooden stands and calling out exuberant greetings to each other bounced off the stone street.

After meandering for a while, Veron arrived back at Karad Square and turned left down Market Street as if some force pulled him there. The square was mostly empty so early in the morning. Veron shuffled along with no real destination, passing the baker, grocer, butcher shop, and empty benches in the square. He stopped for a moment outside the window of the cobbler's shop, the older man already hard at work by the light of a lantern.

I wish I could do that. I could wake up early and work hard makin' shoes . . . if I knew how to do it.

He continued along the road a few more steps until he was stopped suddenly by the sight of the tailor's shop. Seeing it made his stomach turn. Veron hated the shop. The door was closed, and all the lights were off. As if taunting him, a sign hung in the window. Although he couldn't read, he knew enough to tell it said they were closed.

Above the sign was a window on the second floor. To the right of it was the one he went through the previous night. Beside that window, a wrought-iron sign hung flapping in the light breeze with a picture of coins, identifying it as the tax assessor's office. The tax office window on the ground floor was already boarded up, but broken glass and wood still littered the street.

Veron wasn't worried about being noticed because of the darkness

16

of the previous night. The real truth was he didn't even care if they did. The longer he stood there, the more the memory hurt. A cramp developed in his side, and his chest tightened. As his eyes watered, he knew he was losing control and had to leave.

Veron backtracked the way he came, past the market. Smelling the scent of the bakery, he wished he hadn't lost his bread as he ran. *I have money!* he thought suddenly, perking up slightly.

Veron entered the bakery, and the owner gave him a suspicious look.

"One loaf of bread," he said, standing up tall, acting as if the blood staining his clothes was normal.

The baker scowled and grabbed a loaf to hand to Veron. "Two pintid."

Veron laughed to himself. *I could buy thirty-two loaves if I wanted!* He reached in his pocket to pull out the bag of money. *Oh no!* His heart sank as he realized it wasn't there. He patted his pockets and looked at the baker with wide eyes.

The man immediately pulled back the bread he was extending toward him. "No money, no bread."

Veron's heart sank as his face flushed. He kicked the counter in frustration. The feeling of shame was familiar. He had grown accustomed to it over the years. But this, on top of being hunted by soldiers and losing his friend, was too much to handle.

"Yeah, well, I didn't want your stupid bread anyway!" he snapped.

Veron went back to the tax office and retraced his steps from the night before, looking to see if the coin bag lay on the ground somewhere. *Six tid and four pintid. How could I lose that?*

As he searched, he kept looking over his shoulder, expecting a soldier to appear with a sword at any moment, but there were none. He found the remains of the bread that had dropped from their pockets surrounded by a swarm of mice. He looked everywhere they ran but found no trace of the money. He was once again a coinless street kid. A strained laugh trickled out as Veron shook his head and wiped the corners of his eyes.

Everything is lost. Fend died for nothing.

Knowing he couldn't avoid it forever, Veron finally returned to the rundown room where he stayed. The one-room building had been empty for many years before he and Fend discovered it. To get to it, they had to climb through the remains of another collapsed building. A roof covered only some of the room, and weeds grew as tall as trees through the spaces where windows used to be. Plaster was missing from most of the walls, but they remained standing. On each side of the dusty floor was a pallet of straw where each boy slept with threadbare blankets. Their prized possession sat in the middle of the room—one rickety chair.

Other than the clothes on his back and his chair, the only possession he valued was his father's medallion. Made of pewter, the round medallion displayed the letters SK and a sword pointing downward. It hung around his neck on a leather cord, nestled against his chest. Veron didn't know his father's name but assumed SK were his initials. When he sat in thought, he often traced the line of the sword absently with his finger.

Veron never knew his mother and only had a vague memory of his father who would visit him monthly at the orphanage when he was young. He was the only kid who had any parent visit, so it made him feel special until it ended suddenly many years ago. He assumed his father either died or forgot about him, which was part of the reason he ran away.

Veron sat in his chair and stared across the room at the empty straw pallet where Fend had slept. He didn't want to go near it. He pictured Fend sitting there as they recounted their adventure.

"Fend, that was a crazy night, last night, huh?"

"Sure was, Veron. We showed those soldiers we could run, didn't we? I can't believe I got the wrong house, haha. Maybe next time I should let you pick the job?"

Veron smiled at his friend until a bird outside the window drew his attention away. When he looked back, Fend was gone, and he remembered he was alone.

How am I sposta provide for myself? I don't know how to decide what places to hit. Fend had always been the driving force behind their team, coming up with plans and ideas.

His hands started to shake. His chest hurt as he tried to fight back the tears.

I hate this city.

* * *

Veron perched atop a roof, looking out on Kulling Square on an unseasonably warm afternoon for the fourth week of wiether. Usually, the thirty-week season was well into frigid temperatures by this point, but Veron didn't complain. He always counted the weeks down until the warmth of suether returned.

One of Veron's favorite things to do was to climb buildings and check out the area from up high. From the rooftops, not only could he look for potential places to rob, but he also simply enjoyed the peace and solitude. In the crowded city, it was a land all to himself. Walking through the streets surrounded by people, he felt alone and inconsequential. When on a building, even though he was the only one there, he felt like he belonged to something. He was the most important person around.

Fend had been gone for several weeks, but the pain was still fresh. For the moment, Veron was content to rest and observe the city. Pigeons chased each other while people came and went in the square below. Children ran around, laughing, watched by adults who sat together and talked. Although the Bottoms was a poor neighborhood, people still carved out a meager living for themselves.

A woman emerged from an alley and walked up to a man by a vegetable cart. She gave him a box of food, and he gave her a small pouch that she put in her pocket. After a quick kiss, she turned and walked away.

A wife bringin' her husband fresh food from a garden, Veron thought. No one else saw the interaction, and he smiled, feeling part of it in a small way.

The woman walked back down the alley the way she came, but before she turned out of sight around the corner, two men jumped her, causing Veron to flinch. He couldn't hear because of the distance, but he could see it all. One grabbed her from behind, and the other punched her in the stomach. When she fell to the ground, the men wrestled with her to take the pouch in her pocket. Veron tensed out of instinct. The sight of conflict made his pulse race and body freeze as unpleasant memories came to mind. He assured himself he was too far away to help the lady, but he wouldn't have even if he were close.

As he watched the scene, two soldiers walked up the alley. The tall bearded one he could recognize anywhere. Captain Mortinson. Veron's blood boiled. The soldiers spotted the lady and ran to her, chasing away the thieves, who fled empty-handed before they could be caught.

After helping the lady back to her feet, the soldiers talked with her. Although Veron couldn't hear, he could tell the conversation was heating up from the animated gestures. Mortinson slapped the lady across the face and took the pouch out of her pocket after a brief struggle. She bent over, holding her face as the soldiers walked away around the corner.

Veron shook his head, disgusted, but he wasn't surprised. *They would've thrown those men in prison had they been caught, but the soldiers are no better.*

That was normal for life in Karad. No one trusted those in charge. Given a chance, they cheated because they were selfish. As a result, people learned to depend on themselves. If they didn't make something good happen, it never would.

A life devoted to stealing wasn't without consequences, and the city provided regular reminders of it. A week before, another street kid named Reed tried to steal money from a merchant in East Fairren and got caught. The soldier who caught him took him directly to Karad Square and, to the horror of everyone watching, proceeded to chop off his hands as penance. Veron also knew of several street beggars who simply disappeared. No one knew exactly where they went, but most assumed they were forced into slavery. For someone who lived on the streets, the choice was either to give up and die or keep begging and stealing to survive.

I'm tired of this, Veron thought, exhaling heavily. He gazed across the rooftops of the city. *Somethin' needs to change. I need to be more than this. I can't grow up bein' a thief. But what can I do? I don't have any skills or abilities. What I need is money. If I had money, I could stop bein' a thief. But how can I get enough money?* If he kept stealing small things, he would eventually be caught. His heart started beating faster as he formed an idea. He needed a big job—something he could do once and be done. Then he could start an honest life.

Veron smiled at the thought as he got up and dusted off his pants to head home. *Tomorrow, I'll start lookin', and I have an idea of just where to begin.*

3

Young Lord of Commerce

Anyone who saw him knew Brixton Fiero was from an affluent family. His clothes were richly colored, clean, and well pressed. His straight blond hair was perfectly kept and trimmed. When he walked, he stood tall, projecting confidence. Despite the refined outward appearance, being a fourteen-year-old boy, he had an unpolished excitement to him—a sparkle in his eye.

It was late in the morning, and the sun had risen well above the city wall to the east, taking the morning chill away. Brixton stood on the edge of Karad Square, bouncing on the balls of his feet, waiting. The smell of warm bread from the bakery wafted through the air, causing his mouth to water even though he had already eaten. He watched his father, standing next to him, surveying the square, and waited on the instruction he knew was to come.

His father, Raynor Fiero, had been Karad's Lord of Commerce for the last five years. In appearance, his hair and features were similar to Brixton, but the years had taken a toll on him. Lines recently began to cover his face, and his shoulders had started to sag, but the slowly fading exterior did not embody who he was on the inside. Raynor was not a man to be crossed or even questioned. He

23

got where he was by being ruthless and would not stand for being second-guessed.

Brixton spent most of his young life learning with private tutors—math, science, economics, reading, writing, even sword fighting. When he wasn't learning elsewhere, Brixton often shadowed his father.

Raynor pointed to a man with a cart in the middle of Karad Square. "Do you see the vendor selling candied nuts over there?" he asked, and Brixton nodded. "Why do you think he's selling from a cart rather than from inside a store?"

His father frequently asked him questions. They often made him feel stupid as if he should already know the answer, but he was eager to try on the chance that his father would be impressed. "Um . . . I don't know. Maybe he couldn't afford a store?" Brixton replied.

His father huffed in response. "No, the rent for a storefront *would* be higher, but there are a lot of advantages to offset that cost. Higher security, less hassle to set up, and you don't need a place to keep a cart. If someone wanted a store, there are some cheap ones out there they could find."

Brixton thought again but couldn't come up with anything else. He shrugged.

Raynor exhaled in frustration. Brixton didn't share his father's natural intelligence in the area of commerce, so to make up for it, his father pushed him extra hard. "Think about it. Why does anyone go to a store?" Raynor asked.

"Because they need to buy something?"

"Yes. They *need* something, so they go to the store that has it. No one ever has candied nuts on their list of needs. Rather, as they walk across the square to do something else and see the candy in front of them, they may want to buy some. Consider how that works if they hide their store down a back alley. How many people go out of their way to buy candied nuts?"

"No one?" Brixton asked.

"So, why do you think he sells from that cart?"

"Well, with a cart, I guess he can set up where he wants—along the busiest streets, or by the docks when boats arrive, or in the middle of the square on festival days. He'll probably want to set up where he'll be noticed and could get people to buy when they weren't planning on it."

"Finally!" Raynor shook his head as he turned to head up High Street.

Brixton did his best to remember each time he learned something new. He tried never to make the same mistake twice.

An older lady walked by them going in the opposite direction, carrying a flat of turnips. Her clothes were ratty and face dirty. Brixton could smell her even before she passed. Having just turned around, Raynor collided with the turnip vendor, knocking her over and sending the vegetables rolling across the ground.

"Watch where you're walking, you imbecile!" his father shouted.

"I'm so sorry, sir," the lady mumbled. "I'll try to be more careful."

Brixton bent down to help the lady gather her turnips.

"Thank you, son," the lady said with a smile as Brixton finished.

Brixton smiled back while the lady walked away. As he turned around, his gaze met the scowl of his father.

"If that's the way you want to live, so be it," Raynor said. "But remember this well, son. Elevating yourself in life will require someone else to fall. If you help others up when they need it, they'll either pull you down with them or pass you up altogether. You need to consider what status you want to attain in life."

Why would it hurt for me to help that lady? That's not going to bring me down. I like helping people . . . but I also want to be successful. Brixton grinned as an idea grew. *I'm going to prove to him that I can do both!*

His eyes lit up, and feet felt light as he followed his father up the street.

It didn't take long for them to make their way up High Street. Halfway between the square and the castle stood the office of the Department of Commerce. Like all the other buildings on High Street, the old stone structure was well maintained. The shutters on the windows were black in contrast to the light gray stone. The angles of the door and windows were sharp, giving it an imposing look. For someone who lacked confidence, the building would be intimidating to enter.

Brixton entered with his father to the familiar smell of the office, ink and paper. The large room contained several desks where the commerce clerks worked, keeping track of all commercial information in the city. The job was a busy one and was well suited to those proficient in keeping detailed records and working with numbers.

"Brix, it's good to see you!" the man at the first desk said as they entered the office.

Tucker Waystone was a somewhat heavyset man in his mid-thirties who had served as head clerk for sixteen years. The other two clerks, Roland and Heath, both acknowledged the Fieros' presence with a nod.

"Tucker, write up a fixed price declaration on iron ore to take effect in two weeks," Raynor said, pausing beside the clerk's desk.

"Sure, at what cost?" Tucker asked as he began to write.

"Three tid per pound."

Tucker's head shot up. "It's currently trading around 1.7 tid. Are you sure you want to go up that much?"

"Why do you think I said it?" Raynor said with force, drawing the attention of everyone in the office. Silence hung awkwardly until he offered further explanation—his voice noticeably softer.

"The market has been soft due to competition, and suppliers aren't even covering their procurement costs. As it is now, iron is set for a massive supply emergency unless we can bring prices up."

Tucker nodded and turned back to his work while Brixton followed his father to his separate office in the back of the building. Compared to the clerks, his father was seldom in the office. It seemed to Brixton that most of his work was simply to tell the others what to do. He got involved with disputes or when pricing needed regulating, but he usually just spent his time looking over reports.

"So, what'll you work on today, Father?" Brixton asked as they sat down.

"I have some new license applications to review. I'll spend some time checking tax records. Later today, I have a meeting with Charles Marshall."

Brixton squirmed in his seat at the mention of the Lord of Treasury's name. *Maybe I can skip that meeting somehow? That guy gives me the creeps.*

"I also need to choose the Gold Crown winner for this year," Raynor added.

The Gold Crown Award was what all shopkeepers in Karad desired, but only one shop per year earned it. The winners received a seal to mount over their door, which they kept as long as they lived. Once awarded, their taxes dropped, and sales usually increased due to the prestige. At the time, only seven businesses in Karad held the honor out of almost 300 licensed shops.

Brixton's father handed him two stacks of papers. "Here, check out these applications for new business licenses and let me know what you think."

All right! A chance for me to prove I can make decisions! "Cheel Lovingood . . . applying for a blacksmith shop in the Docks . . . requested building unoccupied," Brixton said aloud as he reviewed the documents. "No personal business experience but apprenticed under a master in Karondir. Wants to make horseshoes along with weapons and armor. Starting assets are iron, steel, vise, anvil, hammers. Only one other blacksmith in the Docks currently." He looked up from the papers. "Sure, I think this looks good."

"Anything there give you pause?"

"Not having business experience isn't the best, but I imagine that's the case for a lot of people. Plus, apprenticing could make up for that. With only one other in the area, there shouldn't be an issue of there being enough work to support him. Yeah, I'd say it should be fine."

"What would you post his seasonal license fee at?" Raynor asked.

Every business owed the Department of Commerce a license fee, which varied depending on their size, due the premweek—the first week—of each of the two seasons, wiether and suether.

Brixton rechecked the papers. "It's a single-story shop, small, in the Docks . . . maybe five silver argen?"

"Not bad," Raynor said, nodding his head. He took the top sheet from Brixton and scribbled a few words on it before giving it back. "Hand that stack to Tucker. Tell him, six argen fee."

Pretty close! Brixton beamed with pride as he left the room to pass the message on to Tucker and give him the papers.

Sitting back in his father's office, Brixton looked to the second stack. "Muriel Dalstrom, applying to operate a clock shop on Market Street. Ran one in Felting for five years and has just moved to Karad. Starting inventory is good. Shop recently vacated. Two-room living space above the shop. This one definitely looks good."

"Really? Nothing stands out as a flag?" his father asked with a raised eyebrow as he leaned back in his chair and fingered his chin absently.

Brixton had a sinking feeling in his stomach. *I'm missing something!*

But what?

"What about the fact that she's a woman?" his father asked.

Brixton pursed his lips and tilted his head. *I don't get it. Why does that matter? Maybe I'm about to learn something important!*

"Take your mother, for example. She takes care of us—me, you, and your sister. We need her to do the things she does." Brixton leaned forward and nodded. "And I work and earn money. You need me to work, and you need your mother at home. So, can you see how it might be a problem to allow a woman to operate a clock shop?"

"I guess, but"—Brixton shuffled back through the papers—"it says here her husband died, which is why she moved to Karad—to be near her son. She'll need to be able to make money somehow, right?"

"But what sort of message does it send if we allow her to have a shop?" Raynor asked. "Then, other women will want to have their own shops, and who knows where it'll stop? Her son can take care of her."

"So, you're going to deny her for being a woman?" Brixton fought back a laugh. "That's ridiculous, Father!"

Raynor leaned his head back and stared down his nose at Brixton without responding. The clock on the wall marked the seconds as they passed, each tick making Brixton more uncomfortable.

"No," Raynor said. "Of course not." He snatched the sheet from Brixton's hand and wrote on it, the scratching of the pen drowning out the clock. "I'll approve her application," he said with tight lips. "Maybe she'll be successful. Tell Tucker to approve—four gold sol for the fee."

Brixton's head popped up from watching the paper, his face screwed in confusion. "What? She'd never be able to pay that much."

His father smirked. "Well, if that's the case, then that solves our issue, doesn't it? And if she somehow *is* able to pay, that's more income for our department."

The treasury office was nearby on the other side of the street four buildings down. Its facade was unique in that it was the shape of a large coin—impossible to miss. Brixton and his father entered the small space inside. Two clerks sat at their desks facing the door, but Raynor ignored them as he walked directly to Marshall's office in the back. Brixton followed.

Lord Charles Marshall was intimidating to Brixton—not in the way a soldier was because of their size and strength but rather because he always seemed to be up to one scheme or another. His wrinkled skin made him appear much older than he actually was. Brixton hated shaking his bony hand. When he stood up straight, a defined crook to his back left him short in stature. Being in his presence made Brixton feel uneasy.

Although he was supposed to gain experience through listening, when the men droned on about rates, caps, and lenders, Brixton rarely paid attention. He sat in the office, staring at the walls while the men talked. He counted the seams in the boards and read the titles of the books on the shelf—all of which looked boring. The sound of children laughing penetrated the walls, and Brixton found himself longing to be out of the stuffy room.

I can't see myself doing what Father does every day, Brixton thought. *What do I want to do?* He thought back to the variety of people in the square, all with different jobs. His mouth watered as he remembered the smell of the bread. *I can learn to knead dough and bake bread and pastries to sell in the square! I could eat whatever I wanted and have the biggest and fanciest bakery in Karad! What would Father think though? Would he be disappointed if I became a baker?* He pictured the rows of goods to sell. He imagined his wife with flour covering her baby bump, helping him take trays out of the oven. Customers waited in a line that went out the door. *Yeah, I could do that.*

He opened his eyes with a start when he realized they were closed.

I must have drifted off. I don't even remember falling asleep.

The men were still engrossed in conversation and appeared oblivious to his presence or lack thereof. They talked in hushed tones. "Do you think it'll hold?" Marshall asked.

"Of course, that's what we do. It'll be fixed at three in two weeks," said Raynor.

Marshall had a wicked grin on his face. "Excellent."

"When will your mine start producing?"

"We started shipments last week."

Raynor nodded. "And the coins?"

"Next week."

Both men smirked in an odd way. Marshall's eyes flicked to an awake Brixton, causing him to fidget in his seat.

"Brixton, you're awake, I see," his father said, glaring at him. "I think it's time to go."

Brixton followed his father out of the office, nodding at Marshall as he left. He was relieved to go but nervous about how his father would make him regret falling asleep. A smile came back as his mind returned to his imaginary bakery.

4

Walls of Opportunity

The opportunity to steal much of value was rare in the Bottoms and Upper Sherry. Veron often found himself wandering the alleys on the other side of Split, looking for scraps, loose coins, or anyone who would take pity on him.

Other than Gate Street, Split Street was the largest in the city. It ran from the East Gate straight to the river. Its official name was Archibald Street, named after some baron from long ago, but everyone called it Split because it split the city both physically and economically. The wealthy merchants, nobles, bankers, and anyone with money lived north of the road. Dockworkers, laborers, beggars, and thieves lived to the south.

Although he usually avoided looking for food south of Split, the place in front of him with its tall stone wall and solid gate in Upper Sherry had been on his mind for a while. *Maybe this could be the job?* he thought. *With a wall like this, surely there are plenty of valuables inside.* He paced the alley, evaluating the barrier for weakness. The wall was in disrepair and had chunks falling out of it, but it had been enough to keep him out so far.

At one of the corners, he used the cracks in the stones to raise himself high enough to see inside the complex. A wooden house stood two stories tall with several windows on both floors. Almost double the size of most places in the south of the city, it appeared well kept. To the house's right, a garden filled with heads of lettuce, green verquash hanging from their stalks, carrots, and several other foods made his mouth water. The garden alone looked worth a visit, but what he imagined was inside the house excited him more.

A house that large has gotta have treasures inside. Coins. Gold. Silver. I could be rich! This is it. This'll be my job!

Several hours after darkness fell, Veron walked the alley a couple of times. The moon was almost full, lighting up the street and the wall. The luminous space left him feeling vulnerable, but no one was around. After climbing the wall, he paused to scan the area. Everything seemed dark and quiet, so he dropped to the other side.

The garden tempted him. He smelled the freshly turned dirt and saw the plant stalks with vegetables ripe for harvest. His hunger begged him to take some beans and verquash and run, but he stopped himself. He wanted money and could come back for the food later.

Veron crept to the house and peeked through a window. The wooden shutters that neatly framed it stood wide-open, but nothing was lit inside. He tried the front door. *Unlocked!*

Inside, the house smelled crisp and clean without the odor of mold. On the right, an empty sitting room held three chairs and a short table. A bookshelf stacked with books leaned against the back wall. He walked through the room quickly but didn't see anything of interest. On the left side of the house, opposite the stairwell, a kitchen held some food, which Veron would pilfer as he left. The far side of the kitchen led to a room at the back of the house. As Veron walked into it, his mouth dropped.

The room was enormous. It ran the width of the house and had an impressively high ceiling. A window sat at each end as well as two more on the long side. At the far right, a door led back out toward the garden. The only furniture was a long narrow table against the back wall. In the back right corner, chains suspended a large log from the ceiling that looked like it had been beaten to death from years of abuse.

What held Veron's attention was the various weapons that covered the walls. Swords, daggers, shields, a battle-ax, several wooden poles, and clubs. He had never seen so many weapons all in one place. One sword was particularly stunning. It had a ruby in the hilt and ornate scrolling along the blade.

Wow, should I take this and leave? He quickly dismissed the thought. He needed to find coins or something easier to sell. *What type of person lives here? Either a collector of weapons or some sort of warrior.* The consideration gave him pause. *Maybe this isn't the best house to be stealin' from?* Veron looked around as sweat beaded on his forehead. He took a deep breath and shook his head. *I don't have a choice. I have to try.*

Veron returned to the front part of the house and crept up the stairs. A few of the steps creaked, but when he paused, nothing stirred. Two closed doors greeted him at the top. He opened the one on the left, revealing a small room with nothing but an empty bed and a small table. Over the bed hung an old painting of a castle, which sat by a calm lake that reflected it like a mirror. He wasn't interested in taking artwork, so he quickly left.

Whoever lives here must be in this last room, Veron thought as he turned the handle of the final door and pushed it open a bit at a time. Visions of a warrior in full armor, carrying a sword and waiting for him flashed into his mind. His arms felt weak as he moved the door, which didn't make a sound.

The open doorway revealed a bedroom similar to the other.

Moonlight slanted into the room, lighting up the center of the floor. No warrior stood waiting, but someone was in the bed. Most of their body was covered by a blanket, but the face revealed a bald head and wrinkles—an elderly man. Rhythmic breathing confirmed he was asleep. Veron smirked.

To the left of the bed was just what Veron looked for—a chest. His heart raced at the sight. *This could be what I need!* The wooden box was mostly black with a silver trim. The front contained intricate designs. It was the most ornate chest he'd ever seen.

Veron kept an eye on the sleeping man while he attempted to open it, but the lid held fast. Locked. A cold shudder ran through him as he flashed back to the last locked chest he opened. Unbidden, thoughts of Fend falling from the roof and being killed by the soldiers came to his mind.

No, that was different. It's not gonna be that way this time.

He tested its weight with his thin arms, straining from the effort. Giving up, he stared at the obstacle and frowned. *I couldn't get this out of here without bangin' it around. Maybe I should give up on the chest and just take what food I can from the kitchen and garden?* The more he thought about food, the hungrier he grew, and the more content he became with the idea.

As Veron reached the door, he paused, glancing back at the sleeping old man. *This guy has plenty of food and money. He'll probably be dead soon anyway, so it wouldn't really matter if I took what's in that chest. What'd this guy do to deserve living in a nice house while I live on the street? It's not fair! I need that money to be able to start a regular life like I promised Fend.*

He would take what was in the chest one way or another.

The weapons! If he wakes up, I can knock him back out. Then, I'd be free to take whatever I want!

Veron snuck back down the stairs to the room with the weapons and stood in front of the swords, weighing his options. He settled on a wooden staff that was longer than his body.

He lifted it off the holder on the wall. It was heavier than he expected. The smooth surface and number of marks and dings along the wood proved it had seen some action. Resolved to do what he must, he turned to leave the room. Before he even took a step, Veron froze.

The old man stood in the doorway, watching him. He wasn't much taller than Veron even though he stood up straight with a posture that belied whatever age he must be.

"What do you plan to do with that staff?" the man asked.

From years of instinct, Veron turned toward the door to run but then stopped.

He's the only thing standin' in the way between livin' on the street and freedom. He's the reason I'm hungry every day. He's the one who forces me to be poor. He's why Fend is dead.

Veron's breath grew rapid. He tightened his grip on the staff as he stared down the old man. Yelling, he ran and swung the staff at the man's head, but he deftly ducked. Veron's momentum threw him off balance and carried him into the wall. He spun around and jabbed at the man who dodged to the side. Frustrated by his misses, Veron swung again with all of his might at the man's chest. To his surprise, his opponent caught the staff with both hands and pushed down at the end. Veron lost his grip as the opposite end of the staff flew up and caught him under the chin. The force of the blow knocked him down, stunned.

The old man stood above him, holding the staff like a walking stick. "What is it that you want?" he asked.

Veron scrambled backward into the wall of weapons and grabbed the closest thing to him—the ruby sword. He stood up and pointed it at the man.

"I'll use this!" Veron yelled. The sword trembled as he held it out. The man smiled and chuckled, his shoulders bouncing. He took one swing with the staff, knocking the sword out of Veron's hands and across the room. The man hit Veron in the stomach with the end of the staff, causing him to double over in pain. Another heavy blow slammed into the left side of his chest and next on the right. Veron struggled to take a breath or even stand up. Pain exploded through his skull as the man hit him on the side of the head.

The final blow sent Veron sprawling onto his back. The room spun as the man walked up and stood over him. He held the staff out and pointed it at Veron's chest. Veron flinched, closing his eyes, but a blow never came. When he opened them, the man was frozen in place, staring at his chest with wide eyes. Veron looked to see what he was staring at and found the end of the staff under the leather cord of his medallion.

"No!" Veron said and hit the staff away with his hand, rolling out of reach. *He's not takin' this!*

He jumped to his feet and ran outside into the cold night air. He scaled the cracked wall with difficulty. Veron's chest and head hurt, but he forced himself to ignore the pain as he climbed. Before he turned to drop down the other side, he glanced back. The old man stood in the doorway. He leaned on his staff, watching Veron go with a puzzled look on his face.

Back at his abandoned building, Veron ached as he lay on the straw. His sides were bruised, and his head hurt. *How embarrassin'. I got beat up by an old man.* While he traced the outline of his father's medallion, all he could think about was the disappointment of losing whatever was in that chest. *Gems, jewelry, rare artifacts . . . could be anythin'!* His stomach hurt from the beating he took and the hunger that was always there—a bitter reminder of another failure.

***

Veron slept fitfully. Aches from his injuries woke him throughout the night, and the next day, he hurt even worse. Early morning sunlight pestered him as it peeked through the missing windows. He longed to stay in bed, but the pain of hunger and ache of cold demanded he move. His inadequate clothing and blankets did little to fight the chill.

Although the city didn't care about the poor, it did operate a food dispensary in Upper Sherry, which gave food out once a week on Prefinday. Commonly known as the Trough, the offerings were always meager. It wasn't nearly enough to live by, but it allowed the city officials to claim generosity. Even though they often had no more than a moldy scrap of bread, Veron fought through his aches to crawl out of his shelter and see what they had to offer.

Dock Street connected the Bottoms, the Docks, and Upper Sherry—the three poorest neighborhoods in Karad—and was not a pleasant road to walk down. The heavy foot traffic meant there were shops with food and goods for sale, but the atmosphere was grim. People were dirty, and buildings were streaked with black where the rain had run down the sides for ages. Weathered traders hawked black market wares from their seedy-looking storefronts. After years of neglect, the paved street was more dirt and filth than stone. The smell of mud, trash, and animal waste was offensive to anyone unaccustomed to it. Veron didn't even notice it as he walked along.

When he arrived at the heart of Upper Sherry, a line of people already stood outside of the Trough. Usually, a line meant they actually had food that day, so he was hopeful. The boy ahead looked slightly younger than him and was in a talkative mood. He was short and thin with blond scraggly hair.

"Cold night last night, huh?" the boy said, turning to Veron. "I hear they have boiled chicken today! I'm excited cause I haven't eaten a thing in four days! My name's Tatum, what's yours?"

"Veron," he mumbled as he avoided eye contact, looking up at the buildings around them.

"Veron, I like that name. It reminds me of my uncle Geron. Maybe you know him? He lives across Gate Street from the docks."

Veron shook his head. *Just leave me be, kid. Go talk to someone else.*

"He's a great guy. You'd love him!" the boy went on. "I sure hope they don't run out of food. I'm literally starving. Did you know I haven't eaten anything in four days?"

"Would ya shut up?" Veron snapped, glaring.

Tatum's eyes widened, and he stopped talking. "I'm sorry," he said before turning around and facing the rest of the line.

Veron felt a little bad for snapping at the boy, but the beautiful silence that came after was worth it.

The line shuffled forward as the day warmed up. After about an hour of waiting, Veron made it inside. They didn't have chicken, but they did have bread, cheese, and apples served by a gruff looking man.

Ahead of him, Tatum resumed his upbeat attitude. "I heard you had boiled chicken today, but I guess not, huh? That's okay. This bread looks great! I haven't eaten an apple in half a season. Thanks for being here. I really appreciate you!" he said.

The man snorted but refused to smile as Tatum left the room. Veron took his food without saying a word and left. With the sun out and the air warming, he decided to find a quiet place to eat. He put the food in his pockets and headed to one of his favorite rooftop locations where he could watch the entire city.

Walking along Porter Way, a commotion caught his eye down an alley. Three older men surrounded something on the ground, and one was kicking an unseen object. Veron stepped closer to get a better look. It was Tatum, and he clutched a piece of bread in his hands. An image of Fend helpless on the ground in front of the soldiers flashed in his mind.

"Hey! Leave him alone!" Veron shouted before he had a moment to think.

The three men stopped and looked at him, and Veron regretted speaking up once he recognized them.

Coffin was tall with greasy hair and scars on his arms and the back of his neck. He held an apple—presumably one he took from Tatum. Bruiser was the largest of their group. His arms and shoulders were as massive as his thick beard. Veron knew what it felt like to be on the other end of one of his blows. Slash, the unofficial leader, stood back and watched the other two. Being the shortest of the three, he was not as physically intimidating, but he made up for it by his ability to instill fear in his targets. Veron was more scared of Slash than even Captain Mortinson simply because he never knew what the man was capable of doing.

"Veron," Slash said with a sneer, his voice raspy and harsh. "We haven't seen your ugly face in a while."

"Look, he got some too," Bruiser said, pointing at the bread sticking out of Veron's pocket.

Veron backed up as the men approached. Before he had a chance to turn around, Coffin was already pushing him into the wall. Between the men's bodies, Veron saw Tatum stand to his feet. The boys locked eyes for a second before Tatum turned and limped away in the opposite direction.

"Give us your food," Slash said.

Veron saw what they did to Tatum, and he knew he would not be able to get away. "Here, take it." He handed them his bread and apple but kept the cheese hidden.

"What else ya have?" Bruiser asked, snatching the food, and putting it in his pockets.

"Nothin'. That's it," Veron told them.

"He's lyin'," Coffin said.

Bruiser grabbed Veron as Slash stepped up in his face and pulled out a dagger. "Are you lying to us, street trash?" Slash asked, holding the dagger up to his cheek.

Veron felt the edge of the steel and smelled Slash's noxious breath as tears came to his eyes. Coffin rifled through his pockets and found the cheese, handing it to Slash.

"Nothin', huh?" Coffin said with a sneer. He took a bite from his apple before punching Veron in the stomach, making him double over in pain.

"That's whatcha get for not listenin' to your elders," Bruiser said. "And this is whatcha get for bein' scum!" He punched him again in the stomach, followed by a hit to the face.

Veron's nose broke, and blood gushed down his face. The pain was sharp and blinding. He fell to the ground with his face in his hands. Slash's laughter bounced off the walls as an unseen kick caught him in the side. He writhed in pain but couldn't get away. The metallic tang of blood in his mouth made him gag. The blows and laughter kept coming as his senses grew duller. Finally, he passed out.

* * *

All Veron could feel was the pain. His body hurt all over, his nose and jaw throbbing with each breath. The ground beneath him felt different—softer. A pungent smell filled the air, which he couldn't place—like some of the herbs they sold at the market. He heard nothing except the steady beat of his heart and blood rushing in his ears.

41

After much effort, he cracked an eye halfway open. Through swollen eyes and blurry vision, the edges of a small room came into view. He lay on an unfamiliar bed. A window confirmed it was night, and a lit candle rested on a table next to him, burned almost to the end. Veron tried to sit up but couldn't. His side felt like it was being stabbed with a knife.

As he lay back, something on the wall above his head caught his eye. He turned as much as the pain would allow him, and his stomach dropped. *I know that paintin',* Veron thought.

His heart raced. His legs felt like cold water ran through them. He could not forget the old painting of a castle from the house he tried to rob.

5

Artimus

hat am I doin' here? Veron thought. *How'd I get here? What's the old man gonna do to me?* He wanted to run, but he couldn't even sit up.

Footsteps echoed outside the room, and the door swung open. Veron's heart pounded as the old man stood in the doorway.

"How are you feeling?" the man asked, carrying a lantern with a hint of a smile on his face.

Veron stared with a slack jaw, caught off guard. "My face hurts," he replied.

The man entered the room. "I'm sure it does. That was quite a beating you took." He carried a bowl with some liquid and a rag in it, which he set down on the table. "Here, let me see your face." He grabbed the rag to wipe Veron's wounds.

Veron recoiled as it touched his nose. The pain was sharp and radiated through his nose and jaw. "Argh, that stings!" he said through clenched teeth.

"Yes, but it will help. It's my magic water," the man said with a chuckle. "It's a special mix of water, sage, turnfoil root and antispurn petals."

Antispurn. That's the smell, Veron thought, remembering it in the market but never knowing what it was used for.

The man spent the next few minutes soaking the rag and wiping Veron's face, chest, and arms. The bowl turned from clear to a shade of red. The pain of Veron's injuries slowly changed from a sharp pain to a mild tingle to where he eventually felt nothing.

"Why'm I here?" Veron asked.

The man cocked his head. "You were hurt, and I'm helping you get better."

"But why? Why d'you care?"

"You need to rest. I'll bring you some food in a little while," the man said before leaving the room and closing the door.

As much as Veron wanted to know how and why he was there, all his body really wanted was rest and food. His head spun. *Why is this man takin' care of me? He doesn't even know me! I don't have anythin' to give him, so what does he want?* Veron clutched his medallion. *I hope he's not thinkin' of takin' this as payment.*

As the pain lessened, he soon fell asleep again.

* * *

Light shone through the window when Veron woke. His nose told him something warm and salty was near, and he quickly discovered the steaming bowl of soup on the table next to the bed. The pain in his side was dull enough to where he could sit up. He downed the soup, ignoring how hot it was. It was mostly broth but had carrots, beans, and a small amount of chicken along with herbs in it. As he finished, the door opened, and the man came back in.

"Feeling any better?"

"Yeah. A lot."

"I thought you might be. That magic water can work wonders."

The man winked.

"How'd I end up here?"

The man took a slow deep breath. "I brought you here."

Veron looked at him, expecting something more—something that would fill in the gaps. *How'd he know I was attacked?*

The man took the empty bowl and got up to leave. "Get some more rest."

"Wait, but—" The door closed, cutting Veron off. Outside the window, Veron heard people walking down the alley. *If I yell, maybe they'll come and rescue me?* he thought but quickly ruled it out. *I was in trouble the other day, and it seems this man is the one who saved me already.*

He lay in bed for a few hours alone with his thoughts. Lying still made him anxious, so he decided to try getting up. Sitting up was more manageable than before since the pain in his sides had lessened. Standing took a moment, but once up, he felt strong enough to walk.

Veron opened the door to find himself at the top of the stairs he snuck up the other night. His thoughts went to the chest he knew sat in the other room, but he shook the image away.

The motion of going down the steps hurt more than he anticipated. He inhaled sharply at the pain to his ribs and legs, causing him to second-guess his decision to get up. He kept going, using the walls to help support him.

Downstairs, the sitting room and kitchen were empty. Veron recognized the smell of herbs and chicken and saw a large pot cooling over the stove. He shuffled his way into the room with the weapons. The staff and sword were back on the wall in their places as if they'd never been touched.

Walking through the outside door, he found the old man on his knees in the garden, pulling weeds. His back, stained with sweat, faced Veron as he worked. As Veron shuffled closer, the man turned and stood. "Finally awake, I see. And you made it downstairs on your own!" he said, dusting off his knees. "I'm Artimus. How about you?"

Should I give him my name? Maybe I shouldn't say anythin'? "Veron," he said after a pause.

Artimus nodded. He indicated toward a wooden bench looking out onto the garden. "Would you like to sit, Veron?"

Tired from the effort of coming down the stairs, he winced as he sat. Pain had returned from the movement, so he was happy to rest again.

"I 'preciate what you're doin' for me, but . . ." Veron hesitated. "I was here to rob you the other night. I even tried to attack you. Why are you helpin' me?"

Veron watched Artimus' face for a reaction, but it gave away nothing. The man walked over and sat next to him on the bench. He pointed at Veron's chest, touching his ratty shirt and pressing the medallion against his skin. "That's why."

My father's medallion? he thought. "What do you mean?"

Artimus' gaze wandered over the garden. "Many years ago, I joined a group in service to the king. Our job was simple—to protect the realm. When a threat required . . . special skills to address it, we acted. Known for our stealth, speed, strength, and intelligence, we got where others couldn't and accomplished things they weren't able to. We called ourselves the Shadow Knights."

Veron's eyes grew wide. "I've heard of the Shadow Knights. They're supposed to be the most fearsome warriors in all of Terrenor. I heard they live forever and can conquer entire armies with only one man! And they can walk up walls and even fly!"

Artimus raised his eyebrows and laughed. "Unfortunately, I have to admit none of that is true, but we were pretty fearsome warriors." He looked at Veron with a glint in his eye. "There were ten of us,

46

including me. We weren't used during battles, but rather, we helped prevent them. For almost thirty years, I lived in Felting, trained with the Knights, and served the realm. As my skill and experience increased, eventually, the group chose me as the Shadow Master. I was in charge of training, discipline, and the well-being of all members. Do you know the name Edmund Bale?"

Veron's blood ran cold at the mention of the name. "Yeah, of course. Bale, King of Norshewa?"

"Yes, the same one, but he wasn't always their king. Many years ago, he was commander of their army. Bale led Norshewa in war with both Feldor and Rynor to the south. It was no secret that Bale had aspirations. He wasn't content to just lead their army—he wanted to rule. Bale used the army to take the crown of Norshewa in a bloody coup. Once he became king, he declared his goal to take over all of Terrenor."

Veron shuddered at the thought, having heard plenty of stories about the brutal ruler. *I can't imagine someone like Edmund Bale takin' over Feldor.*

"One day, Bale led a company of soldiers in attacking a small town in the north of Rynor. After the town surrendered, a woman approached him and said he'd never rule Terrenor. She had seen it in a Dream."

Veron's eyes widened. He had heard of people having Dreams, which were predictions of things to come. In the mornings, he often racked his brain to remember if he had Dreamed. He wanted to be able to see things while sleeping, but it never happened.

"Her Dream foresaw that Bale would be killed . . . by a shadow knight." Artimus stopped for a moment as a pained expression crossed his face. "Bale was furious at the prophecy and sent spies across the land to search out this shadow knight. That search led him to us. One night seven years ago, thirty of his best men attacked our compound while we slept. They killed most of us before we even woke. A few put up a fight, but the element of surprise and their sheer numbers were too much. I don't know that the prophecy was anything more than gibberish, but Bale believed in it so much that he was willing to kill because of it."

Artimus hung his head and stopped talking. Tears formed at the corners of his eyes.

"So, how'd you survive?" Veron asked after a moment of silence.

"Oh, they killed me—at least they thought they did," Artimus said, looking Veron in the eye and forcing a half-smile. "It's not easy to kill a shadow knight." He sniffed and wiped the edges of his eyes. "The other nine weren't so lucky. With our group destroyed and realizing it was no longer safe to be known as a shadow knight, I spoke with Wesley. We decided—"

"Wesley? You mean King Wesley?" Veron shook his head. *That's just crazy.*

"Yes, King Wesley and I decided I should go into hiding, so he gave me money to make it happen. I moved up the river to Karad, bought this place, and have lived in obscurity ever since. After the Shadow Knights were gone, Feldor turned on itself. Wesley is still king, but his influence wanes, especially outside of the capital. Greed rules now. It's only a matter a time before Bale shows up and finds the land ready for the taking."

That sounds too wild to be true! Still, why would he make it up? It has to be true. But the Shadow Knights? I was sure they were only stories. Wait . . . The king gave him money? "So, you're rich? All your money is from the king?" Veron asked.

"Oh no, that money ran out long ago. Now that I have a place to live, my garden provides most of my food. I make some money selling what I don't eat, but I don't need much anymore."

Veron frowned as the image of piles of coins disappeared. "So, what does all this hafta do with why I'm here?"

Artimus took a deep breath and exhaled before continuing. "The Shadow Knights had a rule that you must remain unmarried. Since we served the realm, there could be no other attachments that competed with our loyalty. One young knight named William Stormbridge fell in love with a woman of Felting named Julia, the only child of a stonemason in town whose wife had died several years earlier. One day, her father was killed in an accident on a job, and she was left alone.

"William knew he was not allowed to marry, but since he couldn't stand the thought of the girl he loved being left on her own, they wed in secret. I learned of their marriage while Julia was alive. Although William tried to be secretive, he was too honest of a person to be convincingly deceptive." He laughed softly as he shook his head. "It was my job to punish him, but . . . I loved someone once who I lost. I couldn't do it to William." He sighed. "I allowed it to continue as long as they kept it quiet.

"A couple of years later, she became pregnant with a child but, due to complications, died in childbirth. William couldn't care for the child on his own, so he did the only thing he knew to do—give the child to the orphanage along with whatever money he could scrounge up.

"As the boy grew, William kept asking me if he could bring his son back to live with him and the other knights, but I kept putting him off. 'One more year,' I always said. William loved him dearly. I went with him occasionally to visit. I remember being there on his fifth birthday when William gave his son a gift—his Shadow Knights medallion."

Veron's throat went dry as Artimus turned and looked him in the eyes. His heart pounded, and his hands felt clammy.

Artimus pointed at Veron's chest. "And that medallion is hanging around your neck."

Veron stopped breathing. His mind scrambled but felt empty at the same time. Visions flashed in his mind. He saw his father handing him a gift, wrapped in cloth. He beamed as he put it on even though it hung below his waist. His father stood tall as he left, promising to be back soon.

SK—Shadow Knights. William was my father. My father was a shadow knight! "What happened to him? What happened to . . . my father?" Veron almost choked on the words.

Artimus hung his head and spoke softly. "William was killed by Bale's men in the attack, three days after we last visited you."

Veron was stunned. He stared ahead, unsure of how he should feel. For a moment, neither Veron nor Artimus said a word.

"We have plenty more to talk about," Artimus said, finally. "But I need to go out for a bit to run some errands, and you need to go back upstairs and rest. We can chat more when I get back."

Veron felt separated from his body. He wanted to continue talking, but his ribs were in pain, and most of his aches had returned. Exhaustion hit him as the weight of everything settled on his shoulders. He allowed Artimus to help him upstairs, remaining quiet as he wrestled with the questions in his head about his past, about the Shadow Knights, and about his father.

Lying on the bed, Veron felt his chest tighten. He covered his face with his hands and barely managed to not fall apart. He always figured his father had died but hearing what happened affected him more than he expected.

So that's why he stopped visitin'. I wasn't abandoned! He smiled and wiped away the moisture from his eyes. *I had a father who loved me and would still love me if only . . .* Veron's smile melted away into a hard line. *Bale. Bale did this. I wish I could make him pay.*

* * *

Veron didn't know how long he slept, but when he woke, he was hungry again. As he sat up, he found his ribs hurt less, and his nose no longer ached. He made his way downstairs, where Artimus sat in the kitchen.

"There you are! Are you hungry?" Artimus asked as he grabbed two bowls from the counter.

"Yeah, starvin'!" Veron said.

They sat at the small table in the kitchen, and Veron made quick work of the soup. The warmth comforted him on the inside. He looked longingly at the pot on the stove as he licked the last drops of soup from his lips. Artimus chuckled as he took the empty bowl and refilled it.

For a while, they ate in silence until Artimus spoke. "I'm sure you have questions."

Veron nodded as he swallowed a spoonful. His eyes were wide, eager to hear more. "Can you tell me more about my father?"

"I knew William Stormbridge well—since he was around your age. Even though you've grown, I have no doubt you're his son. Your eyes and nose look like his, and your hair is identical."

Veron couldn't help but smile as he ran a hand through his hair. He'd always hated the bushy, unkempt brown hair, but now he relished it. All his life, he'd felt alone, with no connection to anyone. *Veron Stormbridge . . . with the bushy hair . . . like his father.*

"Growing up, he was brash and arrogant," Artimus said, causing Veron to adjust his head back and blink. "He learned things quickly and couldn't stop himself from making sure everyone else knew it. He annoyed me to death, always making up ridiculous songs that got stuck in your head. When he sat, he bounced his leg constantly, which drove me crazy." Artimus laughed softly and smirked. "Still

. . . William was my favorite. He settled as he grew older and more mature. I never heard him say a bad word about anyone. He encouraged everyone around him, and when we went on a mission, he always volunteered for the most dangerous part but never showed fear. William saw every day as a new opportunity—a new adventure. It was rare to see him without a smile on his face.

"Most of the other men in the Shadow Knights were crass and crude. Don't get me wrong, they all were great men who did their job well, but when they were off duty, they spent most of their time at the tavern—throwing dice, drinking ale, and chasing after women. That wasn't your father though. I never saw William drunk, and he didn't have eyes for any woman but your mother. He never apologized for being different and wouldn't compromise who he was."

"How'd he die?" Veron asked. "I figure it was Bale's attack, but what happened?"

Artimus' smile vanished, and he shook his head. "We don't need to discuss that."

"Please! I've spent all my life not even knowin' who my father was." He paused. "I wanna know."

Artimus paused. Eventually, his eyes drifted to the floor as he spoke. "William was on guard duty that night. While we slept, he would've been at his post outside when the men arrived. After Bale's men believed me to be dead and left, I stumbled away to get help. I came across your father's body in the hallway outside the common room. He had five arrows sticking out of his chest and legs, and his throat had been slit. In the hallway around him were the bodies of nine of Bale's men, all dead."

"Are Dreams always predictors of the future?" Veron asked. "Are they ever wrong?"

"Sometimes they're a vision of the past. As far as whether or not they're always true . . . I can't say. I've never had one, myself."

"If you're the only shadow knight who survived, does that mean you'll have to be the person to kill Bale like the prophecy said?"

Artimus stared at him with a grim expression. "I don't know. I guess we'll see."

I can't imagine someone as old as Artimus defeatin' anyone like that. Veron's mind spun from all he had learned. His father, the Shadow Knights, who Artimus was. "I'm sorry I tried to steal from you," Veron said.

"Ha! I'm glad you did. If you didn't, I don't think I'd have found you." He put his hand on Veron's arm and looked him in the eye. "And I forgive you."

Veron felt a weight lift off him. Although he had only known Artimus briefly, he felt safe in a way he hadn't his whole life. Other than Fend, this was the first time Veron felt anyone cared about him.

"So . . . your job was to teach people to be warriors or somethin' like that, right?" Veron asked. "Can you teach me to fight?" He imagined himself walking up walls and flying as he faced off in a sword fight against Edmund Bale.

Artimus stroked his chin and gazed at the ceiling. "I *am* the Shadow Master . . ." The corners of his mouth broke into a crooked grin. "Come here."

Veron stood, and Artimus led him into the large room at the end of the house. The table at the far end now held two hourglasses, a large one and a small one. In the corner of the room, the suspended, beaten-up log had been replaced with a brand new one. Veron also noticed a pile of stones outside the door leading to the garden that he couldn't remember seeing before.

"This is my training room," Artimus said as he walked over to a pile of clothes on the table and handed them to Veron. "And these are for you."

Veron's eyes opened wide, and he looked at Artimus. "Really?"

What he currently wore was given to him by a lady in the Bottoms whose son grew out of them. They were tattered, stained, and falling apart. Tears came to his eyes as he grabbed Artimus and hugged him. "Thank you. So, you'll teach me to be a shadow knight?"

"No!" Artimus said, pulling away as Veron recoiled. The old man's face was stern until he sighed. "I'm sorry." He lowered his voice. "No, I won't teach you to be a shadow knight. As long as Edmund Bale is alive, that title isn't safe, but I *will* teach you to fight."

Veron smiled, relieved.

"But that's not all you'll learn. You'll also learn about finance, politics, and commerce, which are even more important. You'll learn—"

"To read?" Veron asked.

Artimus stopped and cocked his head. "Yes. You'll learn to read *and* write." He stared at Veron. "This won't be easy. You'll need to work hard every day, and I won't accept anything less than your best. Do you agree to give me this?"

I've never thought I'd be able to learn so much, but I'm willin' to try. Veron nodded. "Yeah, I do."

"When I tell you to do something, you do it. When you're tired, and I tell you to keep going, you go. When your muscles hurt, and you want to stay in bed longer, and I tell you to get up, you get up. Agreed?"

Veron's eye caught on the sword with the ruby hilt. The gem glistened, tempting him to revert to the only life he had ever known. His heart rate increased. *Can I do this?* he thought. *Can I actually change? It would be easy to take that sword and leave in the night. Maybe I should stick with what I know?* Fend lying on the ground flashed into his mind. *No. I don't want to be that anymore.*

"Agreed?" Artimus reiterated.

Veron swallowed hard. "Agreed."

"How does your body feel?"

"Good—still sore, but the worst is gone."

"Good," Artimus said. "Keep resting. We'll start in a few days. Before we do, I want to do some tests so we know where you're starting from."

"What sort of tests?" Veron asked.

"Balance, agility, strength . . . a variety of things. Don't worry. It will be painless."

* * *

Artimus always woke early. It was a habit he'd developed over many years of discipline. That morning was different though. For the first time in as long as he could remember, his nerves were on edge. He hadn't trained anyone in years.

Do I still have the ability, or am I too old? Guilt weighed on him from living when William did not. He rubbed his shoulder, where a coarse scar marred his skin. *I'm doing this for William.*

He peeked out of the window and saw the faintest hint of light peeking in the east—time to start. He looked forward to the shock on the boy's face. After giving him a few extra days to rest and let his body recover, it was time to begin training.

Artimus left his room and opened the door across the landing. "Time to get up!"

Not hearing any grumbling, he sensed something was wrong. "Veron?" He walked to the bed and felt it. Empty. *Is he already up and waiting for me?* he thought.

Artimus walked downstairs and looked around. "Veron?"

His stomach sank when he noticed food missing from his kitchen shelves. He continued into the training room. No one. The hair on the back of his neck stood up before he saw the blank spot on the wall. His sword with the ruby hilt was gone, and so was the boy.

Artimus hung his head as he shook it. *I just wanted to help. I thought I could fill in where William couldn't.* Suddenly his body jolted as a thought came to him. *No, he couldn't have—*

Artimus raced back to the steps and ran up as fast as he could. Back in his room, he knelt in front of his chest with the silver trim and examined it. *Nothing looks broken.* He removed a cord from around his neck and grasped the key that hung from the end. The familiar feeling of the lock catching as it turned in the keyhole was reassuring. He slowly lifted the lid as his heart raced, afraid of what he may find.

Artimus stared into the chest as the lid sat open. A long sigh of relief escaped his lips as he lowered his chin to his chest. Closing the lid and relocking it, he went back downstairs. The beat of his heart settled as he considered what to do next.

6

Trapped in Privilege

Chelci grabbed the branch above her. "Come on, quickly!" she said to Emma. She climbed higher into the sugar maple tree with her friend right behind.

The early afternoon sun beat down on the garden below them, but the colorful leaves shaded them. Being the fourth week of wiether, some of the leaves had fallen, but enough remained to shield them from view. The red velvet dress she wore was streaked with dirt, and her brown hair, ruffled from the branches, blended in nicely. When they couldn't climb any higher, the choreman, Jensen, appeared in the garden below. The two girls giggled as they hid amongst the leaves.

"Chelci!" Jensen shouted as he searched. "Chelci, where are you? Your mother will be furious!"

The old tree in the garden behind her house was Chelci's favorite place in the world. Nothing could touch her there. Even if found, no one could make her come down if she didn't want to.

Chelci held Mr. Butters under the crook of her arm. The stuffed cow was never far from her ever since her father had given it to her on her fifth birthday. Even though no other girls her age kept stuffed animals, she refused to say goodbye to him. Originally stark white, now that she was twelve, his color was closer to brown. His tail and one of his horns went missing long ago, but both stitched on button eyes remained. No matter how hard the servants tried to keep him clean, he found a way to get dirty again. After all, her stuffed friend loved adventure as much as Chelci did.

Below the girls, Jensen gave up looking in the garden and exited through the eastern stone gate that led back to the manor.

Chelci breathed a sigh of relief. "I'm so tired of those classes! They make me practice stupid things over and over, like how to hold my teacup and what things I can say at dinners. It's so dumb!" She readjusted her feet on a thin limb.

"Well, at least you get classes at all," Emma said. "My parents don't even care. I'll probably end up marrying a butcher's son or some ugly boy with warts all over his face." Both girls laughed. "I wish I could learn all that you do."

Emma smoothed her dress as she sat on a branch. The fabric was green and dull and cheaper than Chelci's, lacking the ornamentation typically found on expensive clothing. Tears at the edges that were never mended grew whenever she followed Chelci on her adventures.

"Trust me. It's not that exciting," Chelci said. "When I get married, all I'll care about is that he's rich, so we can have servants because I'm not about to cook or clean anything. Well, I'd probably be happy either way—as long as he didn't have warts all over his face." She nudged Emma, and both girls laughed again.

Emmalyn Barton was Chelci's closest human friend, and they spent nearly all of their time together. The daughter of a lawyer who lived nearby, Emma's family was only barely of a high enough class for Chelci's mother to allow the friendship. Although her clothes weren't as nice, Chelci was jealous of Emma's curly blond hair.

With Jensen gone, they made their way down the tree and snuck inside the house. The girls crept through the large manor, trying to get back to Chelci's room without being spotted. The sitting room was empty, so they dashed through it to the stairs on the other side. Mr. Butters helped Chelci peek around the corners to make sure the path was clear.

"There you are!" A female voice boomed down the corridor as they stepped into the upstairs hallway.

Oh no!

The girls turned to see Luciana Marlow storming toward them, her long face set in a sharp line as her lean legs carried her down the corridor. Chelci froze at the grim look on her mother's face, immediately regretting the moments of fun.

Chelci's mother grabbed her by the arm. "Where have you been?" she asked. "Your lessons were supposed to start an hour ago! Emma, it's time for you to go home."

Emma hung her head and waved before shuffling back down the stairs with drooped shoulders. Chelci dragged her feet as her mother pulled her down the hallway. They paused in the doorway to the room where all of her lessons occurred. She hated it there. The room was large with high ceilings, but she felt confined. A window looked out onto the garden below, displaying her sugar maple on the far side, reminding her of what she was missing.

"If I find you skipping lessons again, I promise you'll be sorry," her mother said as she pushed Chelci into the room and closed the door behind her.

Chelci clutched Mr. Butters and grumbled to herself. *One day, I'm gonna do what I wanna do, and she's not gonna push me around anymore.*

"There you are," said her teacher, Margaret.

Chelci sat down and prepared herself for the upcoming lecture on poise and posture or some such nonsense. Margaret traveled the city, tutoring young upper-class girls whose families could afford it. Chelci didn't like her because she was mean and always had her doing stupid things she didn't want to do.

"Go and grab your notebook," Margaret said, pointing to the shelf of supplies against the wall.

"No. If you want me to use it, you get it," Chelci replied, crossing her arms and leaning back in her chair.

Margaret raised an eyebrow and stared.

"My parents pay you to teach me. Do you want me to tell *Luciana* you won't?" Chelci asked with a smirk. "I'm sure she'd love to know about that."

After staring for a moment, Margaret walked over, grabbed the notebook, and brought it back to her before launching into her lecture. Chelci smirked. She loved getting people to do what she wanted, especially annoying, old teachers.

The lecture was boring, as expected. Chelci did her best to appear attentive, but it was difficult. As time went on, her gaze drifted to the leaves blowing outside, calling to her. She loved being outdoors. She enjoyed leaving the city and exploring the woods beyond, but she could only do that when her parents were gone.

Chelci was the only daughter of Darcius and Luciana Marlow. Her father was the High Lord of Commerce in Felting—one of the most prominent positions in the kingdom of Feldor. Although her father held the title, the real authority in their family was her mother. If Luciana Marlow set her mind to something, it happened. Darcius, weak-willed by nature, was helpless to resist anything she wanted him to do.

Being in such an esteemed family, they frequently entertained wealthy guests, so they expected her to be on her best behavior at all times. Half of her life involved lessons on how to become a proper woman. The other half was being a showpiece for her family. She hated the lectures and resented being shown off.

"Chelci? Hello?" Margaret waved her hand in front of Chelci's face, forcing her to blink.

She'd been staring out the window and didn't remember anything her tutor had said. "I was lost in my thoughts, I guess," Chelci replied.

Margaret shook her head. "Well, that's it for today. I'll see you next week," the teacher said with a sigh.

Chelci squealed with joy as she jumped up and left the room to head downstairs. Every Postday and Prefinday, her older brother, Jackson, received fighting lessons in the afternoon. Her mother didn't like her to watch, but she didn't care about her mother's opinion. It was exhilarating.

The sparring room was outside, at the opposite end of the garden. After exiting the back door, Chelci hiked up her dress as she ran through the winding path between the foliage.

"Chelci?"

The voice brought her to a halt. She turned to see her father, sitting on a bench among a circle of trees. She often found him there and suspected he used it to escape from the hubbub of the house. He had been reading from a thick book, but Chelci held his attention.

"Where are you going?" he asked.

"Hello, Father." Chelci tried to shrink her shoulders as she looked down, unwilling to admit her destination.

He motioned for her to come to him. "Are you heading to watch your brother?" His eyebrows were raised as she stepped toward him.

She glanced down the garden path toward the building at the end. "Um . . . I . . . I was just walking through the garden."

"It seemed to me that you were *running*," Darcius said while tilting his head. Chelci adjusted her weight on her feet as she looked down. "Your mother doesn't want you spending time watching his lessons, you know."

"I know, Father."

"We better make sure we forget to tell her."

She looked up to see him wink with a smirk on his face.

"What do you say about you and I spending some time together this Weekterm?" he asked. Chelci's eyes lit up as a broad smile covered her face. "Maybe we could take a walk through the woods. I could probably even sneak some practice swords along with us and show you a thing or two."

"Yeah, that would be great!" she said, bouncing on her feet.

Her father motioned with his head in the direction of the sparring room. "Go on now. I think they're just getting started." After she turned to leave, Darcius called her name. "I love you," he said with a comforting smile.

The words warmed her inside as her smile grew. "I love you too."

After skipping the remainder of the way through the garden, she arrived on the side of the building where a small tree grew that Chelci could climb. She stepped onto the roof from the branches and entered through a window that led to a small loft they used for storage. From there, she watched without being seen.

The sparring room was large and open, with high ceilings and plenty of space. The wooden flooring was rich mahogany, but large windows kept the space well-lit and airy. Jackson would never be in the army because of their family's status, but her mother thought it was vital for him to learn how to fight. He practiced various disciplines, but Chelci liked watching when they used swords the most. Her brother got hit a lot, which made her laugh.

She tried to get Emma to sword fight with her using sticks, but her friend didn't want anything to do with it. One day, her mother found her fighting on her own against a tree with a stick, and she was furious, insisting a lady didn't do such things. Chelci went to bed without eating dinner that night.

Chelci curled up behind the slotted loft railing as Jackson and Barlan, the fight master, sparred. Barlan had retired from the army many years ago. In his older years, he trained young men from upper-class families. Even with age, he was fast, strong, and strict.

While Chelci watched, she mimicked their moves with Mr. Butters, moving his arms and legs as if he had a sword. *I wish I could learn to fight with Barlan every week! I know I'd be great.*

In addition to learning to fight, Jackson also was taught about mathematics and the sciences. Chelci loved the idea of using numbers and learning about systems—like how plants and animals worked and what the parts of the human body were—but she was never allowed.

It's not fair that he gets to learn interesting things while all my lessons are stupid!

That night, the Marlow family sat around the table for dinner while servers bustled in and out, bringing dishes. Chelci's father sat at the head of the table. She always wondered how and why he and her mother ended up marrying. Darcius was kind and loving, traits she never witnessed in her mother. Luciana pushed him to have political aspirations, but to Chelci, it seemed like he probably would have been content to be a farmer or a merchant. Stress had eroded her father away over the years, but her mother seemed to thrive in it.

Chelci picked at her food as she bounced her foot under the table. Biting the side of her lip, she mentally rehearsed what to say before taking a deep breath and sitting up straight. "Father, I know I have a lot of different areas that I'm trained in, but I would like to sit in with Jackson during his lessons about science and mathematics . . . if that would be okay?"

Darcius's head drew back suddenly at the request. "I guess that should be fine," he said, glancing at Luciana before continuing. "I'll speak to his teacher about it."

Her mother held her fork frozen in mid-bite as she stared at Darcius with her mouth fixed in a hard line.

Chelci smiled, but the churning feeling inside only increased at the thought of what came next. After looking at Mr. Butters on her lap for courage, she cleared her throat. "I'd like to have weekly lessons in sword fighting as well."

"Absolutely not!" her mother said as her fork clattered against her plate. "Sword fighting has no place in the life of a lady." Darcius didn't try to interject.

"Why not?" Chelci asked, scowling.

"Because I said so!" Luciana's face was tight as she glared across the table. Her voice grew even louder as she projected herself to anyone listening in that half of the house. "If I find anyone has been practicing sword fighting with my daughter, they will find themselves with an appointment at the whipping post." She looked around at the servants dotting the room. "Do I make myself clear?"

Chelci assumed the servants nodded or bowed, but she only stared at her father, watching him swallow hard and bury his attention in his food. *So much for him showing me a thing or two.*

Chelci ground her teeth as she fumed. Her boldness grew, and she stood to her feet, trying to make herself as tall as possible. Her hands clenched in fists by her side, but her legs shook. Chelci lifted her chin and stretched her neck as far as it would go. "I *will* participate in sword fighting." She tried to sound strong, but a waver in her voice betrayed her fear.

The chair scraped on the floor as Luciana stood. She moved around the end of the table, her eyes shooting daggers, and stood in front of her daughter. Pain exploded from the side of Chelci's face as her mother's hand struck. Chelci cried out as she grabbed her cheek to lessen the pain and Mr. Butters fell to the ground.

"You will not speak back to me. You don't even realize how good you have it," Luciana said with a twisted face and a low, menacing voice.

Chelci stood as still as a stone, not daring to move. Tears formed at the corner of her eyes from the pain and humiliation.

Her mother bent down and picked up the stuffed cow. "If you insist on growing up, then it's time to put childish things behind you."

Chelci's eyes grew wide as her mother grabbed Mr. Butters' head. Her breath caught in her throat. *No, she wouldn't!*

Chelci screamed as her mother tore off his head, the seams popping one at a time. Once the head was off and the stuffing visible, she strode toward the fireplace, carrying the torn parts in each hand. "No! No!" Chelci yelled.

She ran after her mother, hitting her with her arms. Luciana didn't look back as she tossed the remains of Mr. Butters into the fireplace. Chelci fell to her knees, sobbing. Through blurry eyes, she watched as the flames consumed her friend until he was nothing but a gritty, black lump among the logs. The sulfurous odor stung her nose and made her feel nauseous. She wiped her face with her long velvet sleeve and sniffed to clear her runny nose. She looked helplessly back at her family, eyes red and puffy.

Her mother had sat back down and wore a smug look of satisfaction on her face as she chewed on a roll. Her father watched her with sadness, unable to do anything. Jackson sat quietly, looking down at his food.

"You're excused to your room for the rest of the night," Luciana said.

Chelci knew better than to argue and turned to leave. As she passed her seat at the table, she picked up her plate and threw it against the stone wall, scattering the food and breaking the dish.

Immediately, servants appeared to clean it up as she stomped away.

Upstairs in her room, Chelci curled up against the headboard of her bed. She wrapped her arms around her legs, tucking them tightly to her chest. The tears returned once she stopped moving. She had often considered running away from home, but now she wanted to more than ever.

She sat in her bed for hours, waiting for someone to come. *Maybe Father will say how much he loves me?* she thought. *Perhaps he'll promise to get me a new stuffed animal? Maybe Mother will apologize for burning Mr. Butters or will rethink letting me train to fight?*

Muffled conversations and shuffling feet sounded up and down the hall. "Luciana, I want to go and make sure she's okay." It was her father's voice, barely audible through the wall. Knowing he was there and wanted to come to her made her smile. More mumbles followed as two people talked, but Chelci couldn't make out what was said. She leaned forward on the bed and watched the door.

Father, where are you? Her hands tightened around her blanket until her fingers hurt, but no one ever came in. *That's the last straw.* The tears were finished, and so was she.

After wiping her eyes, Chelci got up and gathered a few of her things—an extra dress, a warm green cloak, her favorite comb, and a handheld mirror. She carried them in her arms as she opened the door, peered into the empty hallway, and left her room.

Chelci snuck downstairs to the empty kitchen in the basement. She found a burlap bag in the storeroom and stuffed her things in it. Food lay everywhere, so she gathered enough to last her a few days—bread, cheese, apples, and dried meat. She decided to wear her cloak and was about to leave when a knife on a cutting board caught her eye. Not sure what she might need it for, she wrapped it in a cloth and put it inside a pocket of her cloak before slipping out the servants' entrance to their house.

Tap, tap, tap. Chelci knocked on the window.

The window creaked open, and Emma popped her head out, rubbing her eyes, her hair tousled. "Chelci? What's wrong?" she asked.

"I'm doing it, Emma. I'm running away!" Chelci replied. Butterflies fluttered in her stomach as she said it out loud.

Emma's eyes widened. "What? You—You can't just run away! Your mother would kill you!"

"Shhh," Chelci said, finger to her lips as she looked up and down the street to make sure no one was around.

Emma continued in a loud whisper. "You're the daughter of a high lord! You have everything you could ever want!"

Chelci's face grew serious. *I don't have the one thing I want more than anything—freedom.* "I feel trapped. I can't stay there anymore."

"Chelci—"

"Come with me!" Chelci said, eyes pleading. "You and me, we can do it! We can live in the woods. We can build our own lives and be whoever we want to be!"

"Um . . . I don't know, Chelci," Emma said. "I don't know how to live in the woods."

"I brought some food, and we can build a house!"

"I don't think I *want* to live in the woods," Emma told her as she shrugged. "And I doubt it's that easy. I don't think you can just . . . *build* a house."

Chelci fixed her jaw. "I don't care—I'm going with or without you."

"Think of all the snakes and spiders. You could run into a bear or even a valcor!" Emma said.

The thought of creatures in the woods made Chelci shudder but didn't deter her.

"Please, Chelci, don't do this! Don't leave!" They stared at each other in silence until Emma shook her head, tears forming. "I'm sorry. I can't. I can't go with you."

Chelci stared at her, hoping she would change her mind, but she didn't. "Fine," she said with a tinge of bitterness. "Have a good life then."

The emptiness of the city surrounded Chelci as she walked away from the Barton house, hearing her name called behind her. She didn't even look back.

"Some friend she is," she muttered as she walked the darkened streets. *I need to do this for myself, whether Emma is with me or not. Nothing is going to stop me now.*

Passing through the gate out of Felting, Chelci left behind fear and pain, taking nothing with her but hope.

7

Into the Woods

The flat, dusty road made putting distance between her and the city easy. Chelci followed the moonlit path north out of Felting, walking as quickly as she could. The Benevorre River flowed on her left, and to the right lay the woods. During daylight, the trees were inviting and magical, but they were a black wall of the unknown at night. Her stomach churned as she considered entering it.

As soon as they find I'm gone, they'll send riders out to search, so I need to get off the road soon, she thought.

Before long, her legs grew heavy, and her steps stumbled as her eyelids drooped. When the fatigue was too much to handle, she took a deep breath and stepped off the road to find a place to sleep.

Traveling through the trees was difficult in the dark. Chelci's clothes snagged on invisible branches and briars as unknown sounds surrounded her. The smell of the woods felt foreboding. Her steps crunched on fallen leaves and discarded branches. The uneven ground caused her to trip and fall several times.

Deciding she was far enough off the road, Chelci cleared some sticks away and lay down, covering herself with the cloak. The ground was hard and cold. Rocks embedded in the dirt poked into her back at odd angles. She rested her head on her bag of clothes and stared at the bright stars peeking through the trees. Even though it was a far cry from her bed back home, she was so exhausted that as soon as her eyelids closed, she fell fast asleep.

* * *

Chelci woke to the sound of a horse whinnying. Her heart skipped a beat as she opened her eyes and sat up. It was light out, and she could finally see the woods around her. She heard the horse again, but the sound was far away. Looking in the direction of the noise, she realized she had not traveled as far through the woods as she imagined. The road was still visible, and on it were two soldiers on horseback, riding away from the city. She ducked, holding her breath. When she checked again, the road was empty.

Feeling safe, she stood and stretched. Her back and right leg hurt from the way the ground had poked into her. Her body was stiff and exhausted from the uncomfortable night, but between the brisk morning air, the sun on her face, and the hope of what was to come, she had never felt so alive. After fishing a chunk of bread out of her bag to eat, she continued into the woods with a spring in her step.

Progress was much easier during the daytime. Chelci walked up rolling hills and down into valleys on the opposite side. She jumped over streams and clambered over rocks. Trees taller than anything she'd ever seen littered the forest with limbs contorted into curious shapes.

I wish I had those back in my garden at home. They would have made great climbing trees.

With her legs tired and her stomach growling, she stopped to rest at a stream to eat some food and take a drink. She kicked herself for not grabbing some sort of container for storing water when she left home as she licked her dry lips. Using her hands to scoop the cold water, she drank her fill.

When I settle on a location to build my house, it'll need to be by a stream or a lake so that I can have water.

Rather than leave the water source, Chelci continued her journey uphill along the stream. Scrambling over a large boulder, she spotted two bunnies munching on grass and wished Emma were there to help her chase them.

I can't believe Emma tried to talk me out of going! If only she had come and seen how amazing it is, then she wouldn't be afraid. I wonder if Mother and Father think I'm afraid . . . because I'm not. I hope Mother is sorry for how she treated me. She smiled as she imagined the look on her face after discovering she was gone.

* * *

On her third night in the woods, Chelci woke, not to the sun or a horse, but to the pitter-patter of rain falling on her face. It began lightly but steadily grew in intensity. The drops were disorienting as they dragged her from sleep, leaving her tired, irritated, and wet. It was still dark out, and it took her a moment to fumble around and gather her stuff.

There wasn't a roof she could stand under or a cave she could hide in. Her cloak was on, and her bag was packed, but she had nowhere to go. Tired, discouraged, and waiting for daylight, she stood underneath a tree. It didn't wholly keep her from getting wet, but the drops were lighter. She dug another apple and some bread out of the bag. No matter how much she ate, she was always hungry, and it seemed to grow stronger each day.

I could go for some roasted meat about now.

When the daylight broke, the shower increased its intensity. Realizing she would get wet under the tree or not, she hiked the bag over her shoulder and walked into the rain.

Every layer of clothing was soon soaked. She stayed warm enough when moving, but whenever she stopped, a chill caused her to shiver. Her shoes were soggy, and blisters covered her feet.

When she first set out on her journey, she didn't have a destination in mind—all she wanted was to get away. Now that she was "away," she considered what it was she sought. *The perfect piece of land to build a house? A small village looking for a girl to teach them about etiquette? A magical castle to live in with parents that love me? I'll know the right place when I find it.*

Around midday, she opened her bag to get food but couldn't find anything. She dumped her dress, mirror, and comb onto the muddy ground in hopes of finding the bread or dried meat hiding at the bottom, but there was nothing. Her breath started to quicken. *I'm sure I haven't eaten it all.*

Chelci glanced around the woods for something to eat. Plants grew everywhere, but she had no idea what was edible. She hadn't seen an animal all day, but even if she had, she wouldn't know how to catch anything—much less cook it. Her stomach growled and twisted uncomfortably.

It would be nice here if I had some food and a house to rest in out of the rain. The idea struck her. *This is it! I can build my home here! The ground is flat and clear. The stream is close, and that clearing ahead could hold a garden.*

She wasn't sure where she would find servants to take care of things, but she imagined that would come in time. The idea perked her spirits, but it only lasted a moment as her thoughts turned.

I have no idea how to build a house. She wrinkled her brow as she looked around. *Where can I get polished stone blocks to make the walls? How do I create a roof? Where can I find a bed and chairs in the middle of nowhere, and what would I even buy them with?*

Her heart raced again as a sinking feeling grew in her stomach. *I'm in trouble. I can't build a house or gather food, and no one is here to help me.* She swallowed hard as a dizzying thought hit her. *Unless something changes quickly, I could die out here!*

Emma was right. Living in the woods was not easy.

Chelci hated her mother and resented so much about how she grew up, but given a choice, she would rather live at home with her family rather than die alone in the cold. *I don't want to but . . . I guess it's time to go home. At least there it's dry and I have food and a comfortable bed. Plus, I'm sure Father misses me. I miss him too.* She turned around, her feet dragging and shoulders slumped in defeat, and headed back the way she came.

Soon after turning around, the rain strengthened. The pelting drops were distracting to the point of madness.

I can't take this anymore, she thought.

A shallow rocky outcropping came into view on the side of a hill. Rather than trudging through the rain, she decided to wait it out. Chelci sat under the rocks, wiped the water off her face, and hugged her knees to her chest in an attempt to stop her body from shivering. Her heavy cloak did little to keep her warm after it became soaking wet, but at least the rocks above her kept the rain off her head. The excitement of the new adventure was long gone now that she was cold, wet, and starving.

If I follow the same route back, a full three days of walking should get me to Felting.

Her stomach writhed in pain with intense hunger, but she had nothing to feed it. She lay back against the rock to keep the faint feeling at bay as her hands shook.

I miss my servants. I used to give them an order, and they would bring me anything I wanted. She squirmed in her rocky seat. *I can't believe how I used to send food back when it was cold or even slightly overcooked. What I wouldn't give for that food now . . . and some dry clothes.*

As she sat thinking, her feelings toward her mother began to soften. *Maybe I was too rash in my decision to leave. Father really is kind, and Mother means well, even if she is harsh. I wonder if I could just talk with her, maybe she'll listen to how I feel?*

The gray clouds began to recede, taking the rain with them. Gold and pink streaks from the setting sun painted the sky through the trees. *Great! Now it stops!* Chelci thought, sneering at the beauty taunting her. *I can't sleep now. If I follow the sound of the stream, maybe I can keep moving at night? That would get me back home a day sooner!* Willing to take the chance, she grabbed her stuff and left.

Within an hour, the sunlight was gone, replaced with a partial moon that provided only a faint light. Stumbling over rocks, Chelci's progress was slow as she followed the stream. Even so, she was thankful to be moving, knowing that each step brought her closer to home and safety.

I was so stupid to run away—thinking I could build my own house in the woods. I wish I were back home already.

Chelci walked all night, stopping only to drink from the stream. Tired and disoriented, she could barely form a thought. She continued marching in a daze, stumbling and scraping her legs and arms on rocks.

By the time the sun returned, her legs were weak from exertion and lack of food, and her feet ached from water-logged blisters. The pain caused her to limp. The progress she made gave her the motivation to keep going through the next day despite her condition.

When dusk arrived, Chelci came across a small waterfall. Something important nibbled at her tired mind, and she frowned. *I don't remember seeing this. I didn't walk past where I started, did I?*

Staring at the rushing water, she watched it fall with her head tilted. Suddenly, her heart raced, and sweat beaded across her forehead.

I went the wrong way! I was supposed to follow the water downstream, not up! Now I'm further away from home instead of closer. Her breaths came quickly, and her legs wobbled as she fell to her knees. *What am I going to do now? I'll never make it home!*

She clutched her stomach as it painfully rumbled, and she began to cry. As if cued by the falling tears, thunder boomed, and drops of water fell from the sky, landing in her tangled hair.

Chelci considered how things couldn't possibly get any worse when a howl cut through the air over the sound of the waterfall and the patter of rain. Her head shot up. She stood and stepped tentatively forward but couldn't see anything through the woods. Another howl sounded behind her. She spun around but saw nothing. Chelci continued to circle.

Finally, she saw them—three sets of glowing yellow eyes visible through the trees in the dim light. Shaking, she reached into her pocket and fumbled around in search of her small knife. Her heart beat wildly as she found the hilt and pulled it out, holding the blade in front of her with white knuckles. Chelci backed up until a low growl rumbled behind her. She whirled around and saw another set of yellow slits just on the other side of the stream. This set was even closer and belonged to a large gray wolf.

Chelci dropped her bag and ran as fast as she could. Her feet hurt, and her body felt stiff and weak, but she pushed on, having no idea where to go. Several howls sounded at once as the animals gave chase. Her foot caught on a root, twisting it sideways and sending her sprawling headfirst onto the muddy ground. She cried out in pain as her hands scraped on the rocks. Chelci scrambled to her feet, her leg screaming at her as she glanced back. The wolves were still coming. She tried to keep running, but her knee couldn't bear her weight without buckling.

Something collided into her back as she limped away, its claws ripping through her clothes. She was on the ground again with a wolf on top of her, snarling and snapping. Its hot breath covered the back of her neck as she thrashed, trying to escape. The weight of the animal pushed the breath out of her lungs, and she struggled to breathe.

Chelci stabbed blindly behind her with the knife and managed to catch the animal in the leg. It yelped and dashed away for a brief moment, giving her the chance to turn around on her knees. Before she could stand, the wolf sprang at her. Holding her free arm in front of her, white-hot pain seared through her as the wolf's jaws found her forearm. Her flesh tore as the beast locked on and shook its body.

Desperately holding on to the knife with her other arm, she managed to plunge the blade deep into the animal's neck. Its jaws loosened as the animal collapsed with its full weight on her. She screamed as warm blood spurted on her body. The wolf was silent but spasmed as Chelci used all her strength to roll it off of her.

Free from the animal, she stood up and winced from the pain shooting through her leg and the throbbing sensation in her bleeding arm. Three other wolves emerged from the woods, crouched and growling as they surrounded her. The rain fell heavily as she held the knife, slippery with blood, out as far as her shaky arm would reach, glancing between the three. Her eyes were wide, and she limped as she pivoted.

"Back! Stay back!" she shouted.

The wolves took turns, darting and snapping at her as she waved her knife. While fending off one in front, another grabbed her leg with its jaws from behind. The pain was excruciating as the teeth clamped down. She spun toward the animal and tried to kick it off, but it wouldn't let go. To the side, the other two animals approached.

As they were about to leap onto her, a long scratchy howl pierced the darkness from deep in the woods. The sound was powerful and unnatural. The pressure on her leg lessened as all three wolves froze and stood up straight. The animals glanced at each other before backing up. A moment later, they turned and slunk off away from the new sound.

Where are they going? What was that noise?

Chelci kept spinning and looking, waiting for more to attack, but they never came. Her cuts were deep and bled heavily. The trees spun around her, and her legs wobbled as she stumbled. Exhaustion took over, and she sunk to the ground. Her vision blurred. She tried to stay awake, but the pull of oblivion was too strong.

Trapped on the edge of sleep, Chelci felt weightless, like she was floating on a cloud. While her body urged her to rest, her mind fought to wake. The blurry image of a man's face hovered over her when she managed to open an eye. As she wondered whether she was dead or alive, the desire of her body slowly won, and she drifted back into darkness.

8

Dinner at the Castle

While the servant finished straightening his collar, Brixton admired himself in the mirror, leaving the sleek black coat unbuttoned so his green tunic of finely woven wool and white puffy shirt were visible underneath. His leggings were uncomfortably tight, but his mother always insisted he wear them for formal occasions. His belt was straight, and the buttons were polished. He looked sharp. Brixton went downstairs to the lounge, ready and excited.

Baron Rycroft had invited each of the four lords of Karad and their families to a dinner at the castle in celebration of his wife Eliana's 52nd birthday. Brixton looked forward to what was sure to be a fine feast. For events like this, it seemed his family spent half the day getting ready. They had to make sure they were washed and cleaned, and their clothes were perfect down to the last button.

Arriving in the lounge, he found his father sitting in his chair, dressed in his nicest purple and black silk tunic. "How do I look, Father?" Brixton asked as he spun with a smile.

"You look like a slob. Fix that scuff on your shoe," Raynor said.

Brixton's smile faded as he glanced at his shoes. The right one contained a mark on the leather. A servant appeared shortly with a rag to buff it out.

"Where's Mother?" Brixton asked as the servant worked.

"She insisted on re-doing her hair," Raynor said, leaning back in his chair and tapping repetitively with his fingers.

Elenor Fiero, Brixton's mother, was the perfect foil to his father. Calm and loving, she tried to spread peace wherever she was. She never raised her voice, and she never spoke poorly of Raynor even when he worked himself into a fit.

Sensing his father wasn't pleased to wait, Brixton walked with spotless shoes to the window to avoid confrontation. Out in front of their house, Mila, his younger sister, was already dressed and running around the courtyard with one of the servant's kids.

Brixton looked at the castle up the hill. Thick walls ran around it and met up with the city wall on the backside. Two towers rose into the sky. The blue and gray flags of Feldor lined the top of the walls at regular intervals.

I'd like to live in a castle someday. Maybe I could be the baron's personal baker? I wonder what Father would think of me then?

As they waited, Raynor gave up sitting and began pacing the room, occasionally muttering to himself. Out of breath and face flushed, Elenor finally stepped into the room.

"It's about time. It's an honor to attend this, and you're going to make me late." Raynor said with an edge to his voice.

She fixed a stray hair falling from her elaborate bun. "I'm so sorry. I've been hurrying, but I wanted to look nice, and my hair wouldn't cooperate," she replied.

Brixton thought she looked perfect in her elegant dark blue gown.

"If we're late, you're going to be sorry," Raynor said, heading toward the door.

"Dear, you're being unreasonable. If you want me to look good, it takes time. I get ready as best as I can."

Raynor glared at her response and approached her with an ominous look. Without warning, he grabbed her arm and twisted it behind her back. She bent over in pain as he leaned in close to her ear. "You'll be ready when I tell you to be ready. Do you understand?" He pulled her arm farther back.

Brixton tensed. His mother's face contorted in pain, and a cry escaped her lips. He grimaced, knowing there was nothing he could do for her. "Y—Yes, I understand," Elenor said between clenched teeth. "I'm sorry!"

Raynor let go of her arm, and she held it gingerly in front of her as she stared at the ground. Brixton looked away from the scene, hoping the gesture would give his mother a bit of privacy.

"Good, now everyone into the carriage," Raynor said.

Brixton ground his teeth. *I hate it when he gets like this*, he thought.

It happened frequently. Usually, his mother received the abuse, but occasionally Mila or he was the target. Sometimes it happened after his father had been at the tavern drinking, but most times he didn't even have that excuse.

After collecting Mila, who was oblivious to the source of the tension that remained, they climbed into the carriage. Raynor insisted it was the only way for someone in his position to arrive. As they rode, Elenor rubbed her arm. It wouldn't be broken—his father was too careful to let that happen—but red marks were still visible from his grip. Raynor looked out the window, paying no attention to the rest of them. After only a few moments, their coachman opened the door, and the Fiero family walked out and up the castle's steps. Baron Edward Rycroft and his wife Eliana waited at the entrance to greet them.

Unlike the other three kingdoms in Terrenor, titles were not passed down from father to son in Feldor. The king in Felting selected the baron of each city, who in turn appointed his city's lords. Even the king himself was chosen by Feldor's high lords after the death of his predecessor. Baron Rycroft was selected five years ago by King Wesley when the previous baron died unexpectedly. Brixton's father never spoke with him on the topic, but he got the impression from the furtive glances and hushed conversations at the time that something sinister was behind the death.

The baron was a doughy sort of man who spent more time eating delicacies than dealing with city issues. His hair had receded, and wrinkles covered much of his body. He understood little about what it took to run a city and was the last person a soldier would want by their side in a battle—or possibly the first if they wanted to distract the enemy with an easy target. His position commanded respect, but nothing else about him did. According to Raynor, Rycroft only got the job because the king owed him a favor.

His wife was quite the opposite. Eliana put a great deal of effort into her appearance. Her hair was perfectly coiffed, her face was smooth, and her body was trim and tight. Even at the age of fifty-two, she barely looked a day over thirty.

"Welcome, my friends!" the baron said with open arms.

Brixton's father was all smiles, his sullen mood vanishing. "I thank you for your hospitality. Happy birthday to you, Eliana!" He bowed and kissed her hand. "You look particularly beautiful tonight." She blushed in response.

They made their way to the parlor where the other families had already gathered. It was an exquisite, hexagonal room that was sunken two steps down. Ornate windows looking out into the courtyard took up three walls. Velvety blue and gray fabric draped the other three, giving the illusion of secrecy as if something exciting were about to happen.

Thomas and Ethel Turnbill sat in a large cushioned seat. Thomas was the Lord of Justice—a position he had held for twenty years.

Seated next to them were Gareth Billings, his daughter Hailey, and Vivian—his most recent mistress. Years ago, Gareth was one of the greatest soldiers in Felting's army—the youngest ever to achieve the rank of captain. A battle injury left him unable to walk without assistance, but his respect earned him the title of Lord of Defense for Karad. His daughter, Hailey, was easy to spot with her bright red hair and was good friends with Brixton's sister, Mila.

Charles Marshall was the lord Brixton knew best because of the frequent dealings with his father. He and his wife, Josephine, were there with their two sons, Logan and Oliver, who were in their twenties and co-ran a local lending house.

Brixton's heart beat faster as his family entered the room. *I hope I make a good impression! Having a good relationship with these men and women could be valuable as I get older.*

"Now that we're all here, shall we enter the dining room?" the baron asked with a wave of his arm and a broad grin.

The four families followed their host into the large and brightly lit dining room. Brixton had eaten there a few times, and it never failed to impress. The ceiling stretched taller than his entire house. Flags stood on either side of an enormous stone fireplace at each end of the room. Hanging on the far wall were two sizable paintings—one of the city of Karad and the other of the Korob Mountains. A large table didn't even extend halfway into the room. The hall could seat well over a hundred people if needed. The most dramatic feature was the two large chandeliers hanging from the ceiling. Between their light and the fireplaces, the room was comfortably warm despite the cold weather outside. Brixton sat between his mother and sister, directly across the table from Hailey, who swapped silly faces with Mila until his mother put a stop to it.

"Elenor, did you hear about the Marlows' daughter in Felting?"

Eliana Rycroft asked while attendants served bread and cheese.

Brixton's mother angled her face to the host. "No, I'm afraid I didn't. Chelci, is it?"

"That's her. She was kidnapped!" Eliana selected some cheese from a platter offered to her.

"Oh my, that's awful!" Elenor said, touching her chest while her forehead wrinkled with concern.

"I know!" Eliana smiled with raised eyebrows, creating an image conflicting with the words she spoke. "They're offering fifteen gold sol for anyone who can return her."

Elenor's eyes were wide. "That's a big reward! I hope they get her back."

"That just goes to show the state our cities are in," Josephine Marshall chimed in from the opposite side of the table. "People used to be good—now, you can't trust anyone anymore."

"I'll send my sympathies to Darcius," Raynor said. He looked at Brixton as he sat up tall, puffing out his chest. "Brixton, Mila, you better not go and get yourselves kidnapped because I'm not paying a tid to any thieves that want to extort me." Raynor finished with a hearty laugh, which was joined by the other men around the table.

Brixton only blinked in response. *I wonder what Chelci Marlow would think if she knew what her parents were willing to pay to get her back safely? She'd probably feel loved.* The wistful thought made him jealous in an odd way.

During much of the meal, the lords took turns boasting about their accomplishments or discussing city issues.

"Charles, I hear you've recently acquired an iron mine?" Baron Rycroft asked.

"Ah, yes, I did. It's about halfway between here and Felting," Lord Marshall replied. "The previous owner lost money on it, and I was able to buy it for a steal. Rather than send the iron to Felting like before, I've decided to import it here to Karad."

Brixton's father and Lord Marshall exchanged a furtive glance, which caught Brixton's eye. *Wasn't iron what Father just fixed the price for?* he thought.

"Well, that sounds good," the baron said as he chewed around a large chunk of bread. "Thomas, did you find out who burned down the shops on Archibald Street yet?"

Lord Turnbill shook his head. "No luck yet, but the reports say it involved several men. A similar case just came up in the Docks as well. We'll find them soon, Lord Baron."

The baron nodded before turning to Billings. "Gareth, any word on Bale?" he asked.

Conversations hushed and a few utensils clinked as they were set down at the mention of the King of Norshewa. The heads around the table turned to the Lord of Defense, who dabbed the side of his mouth before answering.

"No news in several weeks, but last we heard, he remained camped at Bromhill. Waves of refugees seeking a safe haven continue to pass through the gap every few weeks. They are anticipating the worst for Rynor."

"Still no signs of Bale's army moving this way?" Rycroft asked.

"No, Lord Baron, but Karondir is ready if they do. Felting has extra battalions stationed there just in case."

While conversation during dinner was lackluster, the food itself was sumptuous. Duck soup followed a bread and cheese plate. Next was roasted garront, which was Brixton's favorite of the game birds. The most impressive course was the whole roasted boar brought out on a large board. Pears, tarrols, plums, and cherries with a sweet glaze completed the grand feast.

During the final course, the baron spoke to Brixton from the end of the table, a few seats down. "So, Brixton, I hear you've been learning about commerce from your father?"

Brixton lit up, eager to be included in the conversation. "Yes, sir!" He said, remembering to make eye contact. "Hopefully, I'll know as much as him one day."

"What do you intend to do next?" the baron asked.

Brixton opened his mouth to speak but froze. His father wanted him to show ambition and follow in his footsteps, but Brixton had his heart set on running a bakery. More than anything, he wanted his father to be proud of him, but he hadn't shared his bakery vision with anyone yet.

"Brixton will be going to King's Academy when the year starts," his father said before Brixton could speak.

Elenor hit her spoon against the bowl and froze, looking at her food. Brixton stared down the table at his father, his mouth hanging open. *What? When did we decide that?* He resisted the urge to say anything while he looked at the baron and forced himself to smile.

"Splendid! That's where I went to finish my education as well," Baron Rycroft said.

The conversation moved on, but Brixton couldn't think about anything else. King's was a four-year boarding school in Felting. *I don't want to go there. I don't want to learn a bunch of boring stuff I don't care about.*

The carriage ride home was silent and tense. Brixton waited for his parents to say something, but they never did. Upon entering the house, Brixton followed his father, who went straight to his study.

"Father? King's Academy?" Brixton said as he stepped into the room.

"Yes, what of it?" Raynor asked while pouring himself a glass of brandy. He sat down at his desk and grabbed a stack of papers.

Brixton clasped his hands in front of him and looked down at the floor. "That's a four-year school, and it's in Felting." He shifted his weight as he looked up. "I was wondering about possibly staying here . . . and living at home?"

Raynor stared at Brixton with narrow eyes. "Oh, you were wondering, were you? You think you've learned all you need to? How long do you plan to leech off me while running around like a little boy?"

Brixton tried to stand straighter as his heart pounded. "I don't think I need to continue school. I had been considering apprenticing with a local bakery, and then one day opening a store."

Raynor slammed the glass down on the table. "Bakery! You want to bake? Like a common servant?"

Brixton stayed silent as his father's fury rose.

Raynor stood and walked toward him. "Do you think I got where I am by accident? No! It's because I worked hard and learned everything I could. I worked as a grocer because I didn't have a choice, but you have opportunity and privilege. I will *not* sit by and allow you to waste your life and ruin our family's reputation!"

Brixton took a step away and looked back at the ground. "I'm not wasting my life, Father. I—"

"You *will* go to that school!" Raynor said, his face red as he shook his finger at Brixton. "I won't allow my son to end up a failure! Now, get out of my sight!"

Brixton left at the dismissive flick from his father's hand. He stormed through the house, holding back the emotion that had built. When he made it to his room, tears flowed freely, the large drops running down his cheeks.

A failure? That's all I am to him? I work so hard to get him to notice me, but all he sees is my mistakes. He doesn't even care about what I want.

A drop fell from his cheek onto his leather shoe, perfectly polished and free of scuffs. With an angry yell, Brixton took it off and flung it against the wall where it collided with a mirror, raining shards of glass onto the floor.

When he calmed down, the sound of his parents arguing in muffled voices bled through the wall.

"But we hadn't decided for sure that was what we were going to do!" Elenor said.

"I decided. That was enough," Raynor replied.

His mother said something else, but Brixton couldn't make it out.

"This is *my* family! If I want him to go to school, then he goes!"

His mother's cry followed a loud shattering sound. Their conversation grew quieter after that, but Brixton didn't need to hear any more.

He thinks my only hope of succeeding in life is through more education. Maybe he's right? Is baking a stupid idea? Would I be a failure if that was all I did? Brixton exhaled a long and slow breath. *I want to succeed, and I know I can do it. I will go to King's and show Father I'm capable of making something out of my life.*

9

Training Begins

A rtimus sat alone, eating his dinner. Veron had taken his supply of dried meat, so his meal consisted of vegetables from the garden. All day he struggled with his anger. *I did everything I could to help him. I offered to feed him, house him, and train him, but he rejected it. It's insulting,* he thought.

As he wrestled with his feelings, a knock sounded at the gate. Artimus went outside and opened it to find Veron on the other side with his head down. The boy held a sack in one hand and the missing sword in the other. Artimus' jaw clenched. His fist balled, but he fought to stop the anger.

After a moment of stilled silence, he motioned for Veron to enter. The boy shuffled his feet as he came through the gate. Inside the house, Artimus hung the sword back on the training room wall while Veron waited in the kitchen. When Artimus returned, Veron held out the bag of food.

"Are you hungry?" Artimus asked. Veron shook his head, looking at the floor. "Why'd you leave?"

Veron shrugged. "All that stuff—the trainin' and all—it sounded great . . . too great, I guess," he said as he kicked absently at the floor.

"I don't have a lotta faith in people to do what they say. I learned a long time ago to take care of myself. People look out for themselves, and if someone seems helpful, it's only a matter of time before they take advantage of you too."

Artimus pursed his lips and nodded. He took his dish from dinner and moved to put it away. "Sounds like a tough lesson to learn. Why'd you change your mind?"

Veron looked up. "I made a promise to a friend. I agreed to be more than a thief, but it's tough. If you'll take me back, I'd like to try again."

"I said I'd train you, and *you* agreed to it. Out of respect for you and your father, I aim to keep that promise," Artimus said.

Veron swallowed hard. "I've been a thief all of my life. I want to change, but I'm worried I'm just gonna steal again!"

The old man shook his head. "I knew you were a thief when I took you in, but that is who you *were*, not who you *are*." Artimus paused, holding his gaze, hoping the words would sink in. "You fall back on it because it's all you know, but as you stay here and learn, you'll find there are other ways."

Veron looked down to avoid his gaze, but Artimus pulled his chin up to look at him.

"You have worth, Veron. You may have been told otherwise all your life, but I believe you're in this world for a reason, and it's *not* for stealing bread and copper coins. You're destined for something great, and I'm going to help you find it."

* * *

Veron felt like he had just fallen asleep when the door opened.

"Time to get up," Artimus said. "Meet me downstairs." He left without waiting on a response.

Veron rubbed his eyes and looked out the window. It was still dark. *I figured I'd be able to get a full night's sleep, at least,* he thought, stumbling down the stairs to the training room.

"I was glad to find you here this morning," Artimus said, motioning as he went out the door toward the garden.

Veron hung his head as he followed. "Yeah . . . me too."

Artimus stopped at the garden shed—a small wooden structure with a dirt floor. The crowded walls displayed various garden tools, while clay pots and bricks piled on top of each other on the ground. Next to the bricks sat a stack of small rocks, each with either red or blue lines that looked freshly painted. Artimus bent over, grabbed one rock of each color, and handed them to Veron before they walked back to the training room.

"Do you know where Farrier Street meets the river?" Artimus asked.

"Yeah. Why?"

"Just before you get to the water, there's an abandoned building on the right side. I want you to take that rock and set it inside the doorway on the left." Artimus pointed to the stone with the red mark. "Next, do you know Dock Five?"

"Yeah, of course," Veron replied.

"I want you to take the other rock and set it at the base of the city wall just past that dock."

I don't get it. I must be missin' somethin', Veron thought.

Artimus walked to the hourglasses on the table and selected the larger one. He flipped it over and set it back on the table, the sand falling through. "And I want you to be back before the sand in this glass runs out."

Veron's eyes were wide as he looked at Artimus. "Those places are at opposite corners of the city! It'd take a while to walk to one of 'em and get back, much less both!"

Artimus' expression remained neutral. "I advise not walking then."
Veron blinked. *Is he serious?* Artimus' stoic face told him he was.
Veron turned and began to run.

After winding through the alleys of Upper Sherry, Veron eventually shot out onto Gate Street, heading north. No one else was out on the street early in the morning. It was strange running without someone chasing him—a foreign but welcome feeling.

Having no idea how long it would take the hourglass to run out, he pushed his legs to pump faster. Ignoring the stitch in his side, he passed Karad Square and turned left down Farrier Street. Sweat already began to mark his shirt as he fought to breathe. Although his body felt good before he began, his aches from the recent beating quickly returned.

At the end of the street, the river came into view as he found the abandoned building on the right. He ducked in the open doorway and looked on the left side. The floor was wooden with weeds growing between the rotten boards. He thought the instructions would make more sense when he arrived, but he was still confused. Veron set the red rock down on the floor and left the building, heading toward the Docks.

Between the two drop points, Veron tired quickly. *What's the purpose of this?* he thought, panting. *Maybe I should toss the rock here and head straight back? The old man'll never know.* He pictured himself arriving back at the house, acting as if he'd run the whole route. *No, I can't do that.* Grudgingly, he continued.

Out of breath, Veron arrived at the Docks, a large neighborhood encompassing several streets and hundreds of buildings. In the far corner of the area were five docks that jutted into the river where cargo and trade vessels unloaded. Boats carrying passengers usually moored farther upriver at the end of Archibald Street.

Just off the water was a series of large buildings that held goods before and after shipment. Workers labored sunrise to sundown, unloading boats and carrying supplies. Past the storage buildings were a scattering of residences and shops, catering to the myriad of workers. The neighborhood was dingy and not a pleasant place to live. A lingering smell of fish and garbage permeated most of the area. Although undesirable, it still contained many people because of the availability of employment the docks provided.

While Veron ran, a handful of workers milled about, casting funny looks in his direction. He arrived at the last dock and approached the wall beyond, finding nothing was there. He set the rock on the ground and headed back.

During the short run from the Docks back to Artimus' house, Veron labored to continue. Despite his exhaustion, he forced himself on through the debilitating cramp in his side. He navigated through the crowded streets and found his way back. Panting, he burst through the gate and stumbled into the training room to find Artimus sitting in a chair reading a book. Artimus looked at Veron then over at the hourglass, which had run out.

"How close . . . was I?" Veron asked between breaths.

"Run faster tomorrow, and maybe you'll figure it out," Artimus said.

Veron groaned. *I don't think I can run much faster.*

"Time to eat," Artimus said, clapping his hands together.

Veron followed into the kitchen. Breakfast was simple, some bread and cheese, which Veron scarfed down.

"How many people did you see while you were out?" Artimus asked.

"No idea," Veron said with his mouth full. "I guess there was a couple on Gate Street—"

"*Were* a couple," Artimus said, correcting him.

Veron sighed. "I guess there *were* a couple on Gate Street . . . one or two in the square . . . some around the docks . . . a lot more back in Upper Sherry—I don't know."

Artimus huffed and turned back to his food.

The question is pointless. Why's he upset?

After breakfast, Artimus led him into the sitting room and selected a book from the shelf. "Now, you start learning to read."

Veron's pulse quickened, a nervous smile spreading across his face. *I never imagined I'd learn to read. I always thought it was only for rich people. Maybe I'll be rich one day?*

Artimus scanned the book and pointed to individual letters, pronouncing the name and how it sounded. The sounds were familiar, but the process of naming and pairing them with a symbol was foreign to Veron as he attempted to repeat after Artimus.

After individual letters, Artimus introduced two and three-letter words. The jump from letters to words was challenging but exhilarating at the same time. Veron's mind soon felt like mush, and all the letters ran together. Thankfully, Artimus decided it was time for something different and led him outside.

The sun was high, and the air felt crisp but comfortable. Veron's fatigue from the morning run had all but faded. Artimus stopped outside the doorway, next to a pile of large rocks.

"Here are fifteen stones." He hit one on the top of the stack with his hand. "Do you know the alley next to the East Gate, just past the cartwright's shop?"

Veron leaned away as he eyed him. "Yeah?"

"Down that alley is a red door. Across from it is a short flight of steps leading to a small pit," Artimus walked back into the training room as he talked. "I want you to take all of these stones and place them in that pit"—he turned over the smaller hourglass—"and the time starts now."

Veron groaned. *Not this again!* He grabbed the first rock on top of the pile, the weight surprising him. At first, he tried to carry it with both arms in front of his body, but it forced him to walk like a duck. Grunting, he hoisted the stone up to his shoulder, so he could walk normally.

Veron took off at a slow jogging pace. His shoulder, right arm, and legs hurt by the time he made it to the pit. Unsure of how long it took—at least one or two minutes—he tossed the stone down, happy to be rid of the weight, and headed back to get another.

After returning from his fifth stone, the hourglass had already lost half its sand. He still had ten stones left—not a good sign. His legs ached more and more, and his pace slowed.

Before long, he started needing to drop the stone mid-way through the route to breathe and rest his legs. *I can't do this,* Veron thought, bent over with his hands on his knees as he heard Artimus' words in his head telling him to keep going. *But he's not here to tell me,* he thought with a smirk. Still, he picked up the stone and continued.

When Veron returned from the ninth trip, the last specks of sand fell through the hourglass. He exhaled with a loud sigh as he sat on the ground, exhausted.

Artimus walked up and stood over him. "What are you doing?" he asked.

"I only got nine of 'em," Veron told him.

"Nine of *them,*" Artimus said.

"Yeah, I got nine of *them.*"

Artimus looked at him, then at the remaining stones. "So . . . what are you doing?"

Veron's stomach dropped as he realized the hourglass running out would not save him from having to complete the task.

Forcing himself to stand, he grabbed the next stone. The last six stones seemed to take twice as long as the first nine. By the time he finished and returned to the house, he could barely walk.

That was the toughest thing I've ever done, Veron thought as he collapsed to the ground in the training room. Thankfully, Artimus allowed him to remain on the floor for a few minutes to rest.

Once he could get up, they went to the garden where Artimus worked and taught while Veron sat on the bench, grateful for the moment to relax. Artimus harvested ripe vegetables while he discussed the concept of wealth and where money came from. He talked about markets and how distribution worked. Soon, selling and distributing goods changed into a discussion on taxes.

"But that's not fair," Veron said. "The baron isn't doing nothin', and—"

"Isn't doing *anything*," Artimus said while picking weeds.

"The baron isn't doing *anything*, and people have to give him money just for ownin' land—"

"*Owning* land."

Veron shook his hands and let out a frustrated breath. "For *owning* land or"—he caught himself—"sell*ing* products?"

Artimus smiled. He wiped the sweat off his forehead, leaving a stain of dirt behind. "Many feel that way, but barons would argue that without taxes, a city would fall apart. No one would be there to keep the peace. No one would be ready to fight if the city were attacked. No one would light the streetlamps at night or keep the streets clean during the day. Also, no one would work to create laws to help the city be a better place to live."

"We don't need any of that," Veron said. "We can fight to protect the city and take care of the streets. We don't need their stupid laws!"

"Many agree with you, but a wise man keeps an open mind concerning issues with which he has little experience. Maybe one day, you'll change how you feel. Or maybe one day you'll help change the way things are done."

After his lessons finished, Artimus introduced Veron to a new experience. Bathing. Veron never noticed he was dirty and smelly, but Artimus did. His teacher insisted he bathe once per week. The public bathhouses were not expensive—only one pintid—but when Veron lived on the streets, even that was an extravagance. Artimus walked him through what to do. The fresh feeling after scrubbing layers of grime and dirt off combined with the warm water left Veron feeling like a new person.

Dinner was more of the soup Artimus had served before but included fresh cabbage and carrots from the garden. Veron had an even larger portion this time, the exercises leaving him hungrier than before.

"I'm sorry for not coming back to the orphanage after William died," Artimus said after swallowing a spoonful.

Veron paused with his spoon resting in his bowl, taken aback by the mention of his father. "That's all right. I wasn't your responsibility," he replied.

"I know, but after I fled Felting, I often thought of you—wondering what became of you. How did you end up in Karad?"

Veron looked down at his bowl. "The master at the orphanage wasn't a kind man. He hurt the kids and took our food, so my friend Fend and I decided to leave. Afraid of being caught and taken back, we hitched a ride on a cart and ended up in Karad. Here, we begged some, but that didn't bring in much. We had to resort to stealin'—food or coins, wherever we could find them. Fend was older and always knew what to do. I would've been dead without him."

Artimus sat up straight at the mention of stealing. "What happened to Fend?"

Veron took a deep breath and exhaled. "One day, some soldiers caught him after a job and killed him because of it." He was ready to fight off tears, but they didn't come.

Artimus' shoulders slumped, and his face drooped. "I had a son once."

Veron's head shot up. "I thought you weren't allowed to marry?"

"It was before I joined the Knights. I lived in Rynor, just south of the Gap of Thardor, with my wife, Cora, and our son, Archer. Our village was quiet, filled with farmers and shepherds."

"What happened to him?"

Artimus stared down at his bowl. "Archer was three when the Norshewan raiders came. They burned half of the village after taking whatever they wanted. Some of the people were able to flee, but most didn't survive." He stopped and was silent for a moment as he lowered his chin and swallowed. "I had been in the fields with the sheep and returned after I saw the smoke, but it was too late. I found Cora and Archer among the burned remains of our home." Artimus sniffed and cleared his throat. "That was many years ago. Not long after, I moved to Felting to join the Shadow Knights."

Veron sat quietly, unsure of what to say. "Archer . . . I like that name," he finally said, giving a weak smile. "I'm sorry about your family."

Artimus nodded.

"So, did people normally join the Knights when they were younger or older?"

"Most were young. We tried to find candidates around your age, but it could be at any time. The oldest recruit I found was forty-five. I was actually discovered by them when I was sixteen, but I didn't want the life of a fighter. Cora had already caught my eye, and I wanted a simple life in my peaceful village. Once my family was gone, my motivation changed. I wanted to be able to stop people like the raiders and make a difference, so I went back to the Knights."

Veron nodded and finished his soup as he pictured a forty-five-year-old man plodding down alleyways, carrying stones and racing hourglasses.

By the time they finished eating, the sun had set. Veron flopped down on a chair in the sitting room and laid his head back while Artimus put up their dishes. *I made it through my first day . . . just barely. I don't think I could've taken any more.*

"Time for your next lesson," Artimus said with a clap as he entered the room.

"What!" Veron's eyes widened.

Artimus motioned for Veron to follow, which he did with a sigh. The two left the house and went into the alley beyond the gate. Veron's legs were stiff as he shuffled along.

"What do you think the best weapon is that a warrior can use?" Artimus asked.

Veron shrugged. "A sword?"

"No."

"A knife?"

"No."

Veron racked his brain. "A bow?"

"No," Artimus said, shaking his head.

"I don't know. What?" Veron asked.

"Invisibility."

Veron stared blankly. *Is he jokin' with me?*

"If your opponent can't see you, they can't defeat you. If they don't know you're there, you have the element of surprise. If you're chased, they can't catch you. So, tell me, how is someone seen?"

"I guess by light shinin' on"—Veron corrected himself— "shin*ing* on them?"

"Yes! Light gives visibility to an object. But someone can also be discovered by sound or even smell. A guard will know you're coming if your sword clangs against a metal bar or if you haven't bathed in several weeks. Another way to be seen is by affecting your environment—a dog barking, curtains rustling, birds flying away. For someone to learn to become invisible, they need to master all of this. Tonight, we're going to walk the streets of Upper Sherry while invisible."

"How are we gonna—going to do that?"

"Do what I do," Artimus said as he walked down the alley, hugging the wall.

Most major streets in the city had lanterns illuminating the stone paths, but many of the smaller side alleys had nothing. Before getting to the next lamp ahead of them, Artimus turned left down a dark alley, and Veron followed. After only a few steps, Artimus stopped and pointed at the ground.

Small rocks were barely visible in the darkness. Artimus made an exaggerated effort of stepping to avoid them, and Veron did the same. As they rounded a corner, voices sounded ahead. Artimus ducked into a doorway alcove on the right and pulled Veron next to him, placing his finger over his lips. They flattened themselves as much as possible and held their breath. Two men walked by, giving off a musty odor barely an arm's length from where they hid. When the men had passed and were far enough away, Veron exhaled loudly, earning a scolding look from Artimus.

"Why do you think they didn't notice us?" Artimus whispered as he leaned in.

"'Cause they couldn't see us?" Veron replied.

Artimus shook his head. "Wrong. Even though it's dark, if they had turned, they would've seen us. They didn't see us because they weren't *looking* for us."

Artimus motioned for him to follow as he continued down the street, ducking in and out of shadows and stepping around puddles, broken pieces of clay, and loose rocks while Veron struggled to keep up. They didn't run into any more people as they made their way back to Artimus' house.

"Good job, Veron," Artimus said, clapping him on the back. "Day one of training is complete."

Veron sighed and slumped his shoulders with relief. He was done and needed some sleep.

10

Morgan

The next morning began like the previous. Artimus woke Veron up early and sent him on the same run. Sore and tired from the previous day, Veron grumbled as he navigated the streets. He briefly considered shortcutting the second rock but decided to push through and run the whole route. When he returned to Artimus' place, Veron found the hourglass empty again, which he expected. His side hurt, but slightly less than the previous day.

"How many people did you see while you were out running?" Artimus asked as Veron stumbled in.

Veron cursed in his head. "Uh . . . I passed three people between here and the first drop. Another five goin'—*going* to the second, six around the docks, and probably . . . fifteen more coming back here."

"Of the first three you saw, what were they wearing?"

"Um . . . I've no idea."

"It seems like you need to pay more attention to people."

Veron kicked at the floorboards as he followed the man into the kitchen for breakfast.

"Artimus, it's great to see you!" a man said as Veron and his teacher approached a grocery shop on Porter Way. The man smiled and shook Artimus' hands as they met in the street.

"You too, Morgan," Artimus said.

"Are you here to buy or sell today?" the man asked.

"Neither." Artimus placed his hand on Veron's shoulder. "I wanted to introduce you to my nephew, Veron."

Veron looked at Artimus, his forehead creased. *Why did he call me that?* he thought, turning his attention back to the shopkeeper who had extended his hand.

He seemed a friendly sort, average height and slightly overweight. The man wore a plain red tunic with brown pants, while a neatly trimmed beard framed his broad smile. Veron shook his hand and immediately felt he could trust the man even though they'd never met.

"Veron, it's great to meet you. I'm Morgan, and I have the pleasure of owning this fine grocery. You won't find better quality food anywhere in Upper Sherry," he said as he puffed out his chest and stood up straight.

"Except in my garden," Artimus said.

"True." Morgan laughed. "I buy a good portion of my vegetables from Artimus."

"Veron is my brother's son and will be staying with me for a while. I started teaching him about businesses and commerce in the city, and I was hoping you may be able to share a little of what you know?"

"I'd be happy to. I was about to go through some crates and restock my bins. Veron, would you mind helping while we talk?"

Veron looked to Artimus, who nodded. "Sure, sounds great." *The longer I stay here, the less torture Artimus can put me through back at the house.*

"Why don't I leave you here? Just come back when you're done," Artimus said to Veron before walking away.

Morgan motioned for Veron to follow into the shop. "So, you're learning how businesses work, huh?" he asked.

"I guess so. He only just started teachin', so I'm not sure what all I need to learn," Veron said.

The shop was a small but inviting space lit by the warm light coming through the windows. Two rows of wooden bins ran the length of the store, filled mostly with fruits and vegetables, but the back row held some bread, cheese, and herbs. The low ceiling might have caused a taller person to feel cramped, but Veron enjoyed the intimacy. On the left side, a small desk contained tidy stacks of paperwork.

Morgan led him to the back where a doorway led to another room. Crowded and smelling like fresh vegetables, the back room consisted of shelves stacked floor to ceiling with bags and crates of more food. A staircase led upstairs.

That must be where he lives, Veron thought.

"What we need to do is take this extra food, bring it out into the shop, and fill any bins that are low. We want all of them filled to the top. Sound good?" Morgan asked.

"Sure."

Morgan gave Veron a crate of beets while he took one of falend, a long stalk-like vegetable Veron didn't particularly enjoy. After finding the corresponding bins, Morgan instructed him on what to do.

"First, estimate how many you'll need, then move what's currently in the bin out of the way." Morgan demonstrated with the falend while Veron repeated with the beets. "Next, place the new items at the bottom of the bin and cover them up with the old ones."

When they finished, Veron admired the two full bins of produce.

"So, what do you know about how businesses work, Veron?" Morgan asked as they walked to the back to grab new crates.

"Um . . . I know you sell food, and I know people give you money. And if no one else around has cabbage, you can charge whatever you want for it." He paused. "And I know that 'stributors buy wool from sheep farmers outside of Karad and take it to Felting to sell for a lotta money."

Morgan laughed. "Yeah, I guess that's mostly true."

"Also, you have to pay taxes from everythin' you sell," Veron said.

"Correct, unfortunately."

"What if you don't pay the taxes?"

"Well, first, I'd probably get a warning. Then, if I still didn't pay, large men with clubs would show up to take it. Plus, I'd lose my license and have to close the shop."

"What if you sold things but didn't have a license?"

"Well, nothing for a while, but after the city found out . . . big men with clubs," Morgan said with a laugh.

They finished up their crates and went to the back for more.

"So, where do you get all the food you sell?" Veron asked. "Do you grow it?"

"No, I don't grow anything. I buy from other farmers, like Artimus. There are some others with gardens inside the city, but most of my supply comes from farms outside the walls. That's where I got started, actually."

"You went out and sold to farmers?"

"No, I was a farmer—my parents were at least. I grew up on a farm just out of the east gate. When I was around sixteen, I started bringing our crops into the city to sell, but they ran me out because I didn't have a license. So . . . I got one. At first, it was an awful shop, close to the gate, but that was enough to get me started. As soon as I had enough money, I was able to get this place here."

"Do you still get food from your parents?"

Morgan looked down as he shook his head. "They passed away a while ago, but I have a lot of other connections I work with now."

"What happens if food goes bad?" Veron asked.

"It gets thrown out, and I lose the money I paid. If it's not *too* bad, it'll end up on our family's dinner table. That's why I put so much effort into selling the older food first. Every carrot thrown out is less money for my family."

"What about . . . thieves?" Veron asked, trying to keep his tone casual. Inside, he had a lump in his throat.

"Thieves are the worst. Food going bad, I can control. Maybe I bought poor quality? Maybe I didn't rotate the supply well? Those are on me, but I can't control what other people do. The result is the same—less money to care for my family. I just have to trust in the goodness of others to do the right thing, I guess."

I wonder how many people I've stolen from have been like Morgan? Veron thought as guilt crept in.

"Do you know how coins work?" Morgan asked as he handed Veron a crate of apples to stock. Veron nodded. "How many pintid are in a copper tid?"

"Ten," Veron replied.

"How many tid are in a silver argen?"

"Ten."

"What about argen in a gold sol?"

"Ten," Veron said. He longed to stumble across a loose sol on the street sometime, but had yet to find one.

The two worked and talked for a couple of hours. Veron enjoyed the conversation and decided he liked Morgan.

"Well, I think that's about it for today," Morgan said. "You better head on home so Artimus doesn't wonder what happened to you. It was great talking with you, Veron. Tell Artimus I'll swing by tomorrow for a pick-up of whatever he has fresh."

Veron nodded as he left the shop and walked the streets back to the house.

Artimus read a book in the sitting room and looked up as he entered. "How was your time?" he asked.

"Good. Morgan seems like a nice guy," Veron told him. "He said he'd come by tomorrow to pick up some food."

Artimus nodded and returned to his book.

Veron felt awkward as he stood, shifting his weight between each leg. "Why'd you introduce me as your nephew?" he asked.

"It results in fewer questions. No one knows my past here, and I want to keep it that way. It's probably wise for you to do the same thing." Artimus paused before adding, "Also, being part of the Shadow Knights . . . in a way, William was my brother."

"So, what'd you do while I was there? Just read?" Veron craned his neck sideways, trying unsuccessfully to sound out the title of his book.

"I read for a bit. But first, I took a walk around the city to make sure there were two red rocks and two blue ones where they were supposed to be." He looked up from his book and locked eyes with Veron, raising his eyebrows. "I'm glad there were."

Veron swallowed hard. *I'm glad I didn't take that shortcut!*

* * *

In the afternoon of the third day of training, Artimus taught on the history of Terrenor in the sitting room. Veron listened while his teacher pulled a handful of books off the shelf and alternated between reading excerpts and adding his own commentary. During a discourse about the history of sea trade between the kingdoms of Tarphan and Rynor, Artimus' name sounded from outside of the gate. After marking his place in the book, he went out to answer it. Veron leaned over the chair and pressed his face against the window to see Morgan, the grocer, enter through the gate.

"Veron, it's good to see you again!" Morgan said with a wave as he entered the house with Artimus, glancing at the books scattered around the sitting room. "What are you up to there?"

"Just some trainin'—training," Veron replied.

"Training for what?" Morgan stepped into the room and took a closer look at the books.

"For life," Artimus said. "The boy has a lot to learn. Come on this way."

The two men walked into the kitchen, the wall to the stairs blocking Veron's view. Behind it, he heard Artimus list off his produce. "Nine carrots, six beets, three heads of lettuce, two of cabbage, and a pound of beans."

"Three tid eight pintid?" Morgan asked after a pause.

"Yes, three and eight."

Veron heard coins exchanging hands before both men came back into the room. "Veron, I'm sure I'll see you around," Morgan said, carrying a full crate of food. "Artimus, would you mind walking out with me?"

The two men walked outside. From where he sat, Veron saw them standing by the gate. They talked about something he couldn't hear, but his curiosity peaked when they began looking back at him.

Are they talkin' about me? he thought.

Before long, Artimus returned. "Where were we?" he asked as he took his seat and picked up the last book where he had left off.

Veron stifled a yawn. He didn't find historical trade routes interesting and struggled to stay awake. His mind moved from wondering what the men had talked about to thinking about his future. *What will all of this teachin' mean for me? Will I be able to be a warrior one day? Or will I be stealin' back on the street again? Only time will tell, I guess.*

Dinner that night was dried pork with vegetables. Artimus took a drink of water and wiped his mouth before speaking up. "Morgan said he likes you and that you did a good job working with him yesterday," he said.

Veron smiled at the compliment.

"He asked me if I thought you'd be interested in helping him in his shop."

Veron looked up from his food. "What do you mean by helping him?" he asked.

"His wife, Catherine, used to help at the store. They had a new baby a few weeks ago, and now she's not able to. It sounds like he could use another set of hands a few days each week."

"Yeah, sure. I guess I could help."

"He's offering to pay you too."

Veron's eyes sparkled. *Paid? I've never been paid for a job in my life! What would it be like to have money? How would I spend it?* His mouth suddenly turned down. "But what about all of our training? Will I still be able to learn how to fight?"

Artimus nodded. "Of course. We'd keep training when you're not with Morgan."

The smile returned. "Then, yeah. That'd be great!"

"Good. I thought you'd be excited. He wants you to come on Marketday, first thing in the morning,"—Artimus grabbed Veron's arm—"but listen to me well. If you steal a piece of food or even one pintid from him, neither he nor the Lord of Justice will be what you need to fear. You'll answer to *me*. Do you understand?"

Veron swallowed hard. "Yeah, I understand."

11

Grocery Work

Marketday morning, Artimus woke Veron up as usual. "Time to get up!" he said in a cheery voice.

Veron groaned and wrapped his pillow around his head. *He's way too happy this early in the mornin'*, he thought.

He wanted to protest, but Artimus was already gone. Shuffling downstairs, Veron found him in the training room, holding the hourglass with the two rocks set out. "Ready?" Artimus asked.

Veron tilted his head. "But I'm working at the grocery today."

Artimus made a show of looking outside at the blackness. "You think Morgan wants you there, now?"

"Well, not yet, but . . ."

"I figured not. Then you have time for a run."

"But I don't wanna be late for my first day!"

"You don't *want to* be late?" Artimus asked.

"No, I don't!" Veron gave a wry grin.

Artimus flipped the hourglass. "Then you had better run quickly."

Veron shook his head, grabbed the rocks, and took off.

After a week of running every day, the task had grown easier. He wasn't as out of breath, and his legs didn't tire as quickly. Not wanting to be late for work, he ran a little faster. When he eventually stumbled through the door, Artimus poked his head out from the kitchen. Veron checked the hourglass. Empty.

"Hmph," the old man muttered.

Veron grinned. *I had to have been close that time. I was definitely faster.*

"How many cats did you see today?" Artimus asked.

"Five," Veron said after thinking for a moment. "Two on Gate, one at Merchant's Row, and two more by the docks."

"How many carts of food did you run by that were already out in the streets?"

Argh, I didn't even think to check the carts. "Um . . . I'm not sure. Five or six, maybe?"

The dim pre-dawn light had given way to the glow of early morning. Veron grabbed some bread, fruit, and cheese for breakfast and left to head to Morgan's shop. The grocery didn't look open when he arrived, so he knocked quietly.

After a moment, the door opened, and Morgan greeted him with a smile. "Good morning! You're here bright and early. Come on in," he said.

The sunrise hadn't reached the shop's windows yet, and the dim room was lit by some candles in the corner. Veron's eyes had to adjust to the darkness as he followed Morgan inside.

"I told Artimus I needed an extra hand, and he suggested giving you a shot. What do you say? Are you up for doing some work?" Morgan asked.

"Yes, sir, I'm ready," Veron replied.

"Please, call me Morgan. I could use help three days a week—Marketday, Halfday, and Finday—in the mornings until noon. Postday and Prefinday are lighter, and I can manage on my own. And of course, we're closed on Weekterm. I can pay you one tid per week.

Does that sound okay?"

Veron's eyes grew wide. *One tid a week for working in the mornin' every other day?* "Yeah, that sounds great!"

"Okay, let's get to work then. The first thing I do each morning is set up the outdoor stand. Can you grab that end?"

Veron picked up one side of a heavy wooden structure with multiple shelves. The bottom dug into his hands as he struggled his way out the door, lumbering under its weight. He sighed with relief when he was able to set it down.

"When people walk down the street, I want their eyes drawn to the store. Some people will come here specifically to get something, but others will only come if something entices them to do so—that's where this stand comes in. It should catch the eye with the best-looking food—unique and exotic items that draw their interest."

Morgan went down the rows in the shop and selected items that looked colorful or interesting. Veron recognized most foods, but a few he'd never seen before.

"Paleno fruit!" Morgan said as he held one up with a flourish. "This comes from the south of Rynor. I bought them last Prefinday from a traveling merchant—the perfect thing to display. I bet a lot of people have never even seen one before."

Veron held one in his hand. It was about the size of a large apple but shaped like an oval. It was firm to the touch and had spines sticking out at each end.

"You have to be careful to hold it, but it's *deliciously* sweet to eat," Morgan said.

After grabbing a few more items, Morgan took the selected foods outside and arranged them on the stands.

"During the day, I want you to keep an eye on the display. When people select from the food there, make sure to restock it. We never want the display to run low. Also, keep an eye on the indoor bins, filling them when needed. I'll work with the customers and take their payment. When you don't have anything to do, I'd love for you to stand in the street, engaging with people to try to get them to come in. Also, keep an eye out for thieves. We don't want anyone nicking food from the stands. Does that sound okay?"

Veron swallowed the lump in his throat from the mention of thieves. "Sounds good," he said.

"Go ahead and prop the door open, and we'll get started."

Veron opened the front door and put a wedge at the base. He wandered into the street and looked around, not sure of what to do. A man pulling a cart of stone blocks dripped sweat as he labored past. A dog slunk out of a nearby alley, sticking its nose into corners, looking for scraps of food. Veron fiddled with the hem of his shirt as he waited.

"Hey, mornin!" he said while waving timidly to a gruff looking man. The man only glared at him in return as he passed.

A lady came by next. "How are you?" Veron asked.

"I'm good," she said with a polite look while she kept moving.

A group of three men and one woman came by next. "Hey, you wanna buy stuff?" Veron asked. One man made eye contact and shook his head. They all passed by.

Morgan came outside. "Not easy, is it?" he asked.

Veron lowered his gaze and pushed a rock around with his toe. "No, it's not."

"Here. Watch how I do it." Morgan turned to a man and woman who approached in the street. "Good morning, my friends! Would you like some fresh fruit to start your morning off?" They slowed their walk and looked at him. "We have plums just in from the hills of Tienn and even some delicious cherries from right here in the North Grove outside the city."

The couple looked at each other and paused. After a moment, they shook their heads and continued down the street. "No, but thank you," the woman said.

Morgan was not discouraged and engaged with the next woman who came by. "Good morning to you, my lady! What are you making for dinner this evening?"

"Meat pies," she said.

"I bet you could use some of the best peas, carrots, and onions in the city, couldn't you? I assure you you'll be able to tell the difference with our produce."

"Well . . . yes, I do need to get some."

She entered the shop while Morgan winked at Veron as he followed. The grocer showed her around and held her selections as she walked through the aisles. "I love a good meat pie," Morgan said as she shopped. "I bet your family does too."

"Yes. Their favorite meal is vegetable soup though, which I'm making tomorrow."

"Perfect!" Morgan said. "I'll tell you what, if you buy your vegetables for the soup while you're here today, I'll give you a special deal. They're all as fresh as can be and will still be just as good tomorrow."

"Yes, I guess I can do that."

The lady took another lap through the store, adding some beans, tomatoes, verquash, more carrots, and another onion to her pile.

"That'll be two tid three. Tell you what"—he quickly corrected himself—"make it two tid even."

"Thank you," the lady said as she handed over the coins.

Morgan helped her put all the produce in her bag and wished her a good day.

"You were great!" Veron said with wide eyes after she left. "Did you make that part up about givin' her a deal, or did you actually charge her less?"

Morgan looked at Veron. "Oh, I gave her a deal. Never cheat or mislead a customer. If you're dishonest, you'll lose them for life."

"But if she needed the ingredients for her soup tomorrow and would have paid the full price then, didn't you cost yourself some money?"

"It's possible, but that's assuming she was going to buy from me tomorrow. I didn't know her, which means she's not a regular customer. I'd rather sell her *discounted* food today than *no* food tomorrow."

A group of men came down the street, and Morgan was already moving to greet them. "Good morning, my good sirs! Can I interest you in some delicious fruit to take home as a treat for your wives? We have some perfectly ripe pears and even some rare paleno fruit from Rynor!"

One of the men stopped and looked at the paleno fruit. He ended up selecting two apples and handed over three pintid.

"Have a wonderful day, sir!" Morgan said as the men left. He turned back to Veron. "Few people come by intending to stop here. You have to figure out what you can say that'll draw their interest enough to get them to stop and see what we have."

"So, I need to think of things that can trick them into buyin' somethin'?" Veron asked.

"If you feed them stories, they'll be able to tell. The only way to genuinely reach someone is to be authentic with them. We *do* have the best produce in the city. I truly believe that because I put a lot of effort into making sure of it. I try to persuade them to buy from me because I believe it'll make their life better, not because I want to trick them into buying something they don't want. Why don't you give it a shot?" Morgan nodded toward a lady walking up.

"Good mornin'," Veron said. "We have some of the best produce in the city. Is there somethin' you need to be able to make dinner tonight?"

The lady paused for a moment then asked, "I'll need some potatoes. Do you have any?"

"Of course!" Veron said. "We have the finest potatoes in the city fresh from . . ." He paused and looked at Morgan. "Where they from?"

"Farmer Pellenor," Morgan said, "just outside the East Gate. I picked them up yesterday. Let me show you." Morgan exchanged a grin with Veron as the lady entered the shop.

The rest of the morning moved along similarly. Veron worked the street, and Morgan helped people inside and handled the money. From time to time, Veron refilled the outside displays and the bins inside. It amazed him to see Morgan's gift of talking to people. He appeared to genuinely care about everyone that came in, and each person left with a smile on their face.

Morgan's wife, Catherine, came downstairs with baby Will mid-morning to say hello. She used to handle the inside work while the two older children played but taking care of a baby was much more demanding. Their two older children—six-year-old Emma and four-year-old Jack—ran around at times throughout the day.

As noon approached, the crowd slowed. "Well, Veron, that was a great first day. You did an excellent job!" Morgan said. "The rest of the day is usually not as busy, so I can handle it myself. You're free to go."

Veron beamed at the compliment. "Okay, I'll see you in two days."

* * *

Veron tapped his fingers on the counter as he stared at the wall of the grocer's store. He barely even noticed when Morgan muttered under his breath after catching a finger between a crate and a display bin.

"Is something bothering you, Veron?" Morgan asked, grimacing and shaking out his hand.

The question brought Veron out of his haze, and he laughed to himself. "That's funny. I was about to ask you the same thing." He had been working with Morgan for two weeks, and they were beginning to learn each other's moods.

"I asked first," Morgan said.

Veron shrugged as he bit at the inside of his cheek and stared at the counter. "I've been trainin' with Artimus for three weeks now, and I don't feel like I'm gettin' anywhere. I'm doin' the same things over and over again, but I can't see much progress." He paused to take a deep breath and pick at his fingernails. "I know he's tryin' to help me be a better person, but I don't feel different. Sometimes I wonder if I should just give up and go back to my old life."

Morgan set down the crate he carried and came over to Veron. "I've known Artimus for years. He's a good man and has more wisdom than I ever will. If he has a plan and he's working on teaching you something, I suggest sticking with it. I'd bet he knows what he's doing."

Veron nodded. "Yeah, I know. It's tough to be patient though. So, what about you? What's botherin' you?"

Morgan exhaled loudly. "Taxes."

"What do you mean?" Veron asked.

"I just found out that the High Lord of Trade in Felting, Byron Hampton, issued a new five percent tax on imported goods."

"How does it affect us?" Veron asked.

"That means for all the food we sell in Karad that we buy from outside of the city—which is almost everything—we now have to pay five percent more to King Wesley. That may not sound like a lot, but it adds up."

Veron thought for a moment while he grabbed a crate from the back. "Can't you just raise the prices we sell by five percent? That way, you still make the same amount after the tax?"

"Yeah, we can, and we must, to stay in business, but are people willing to pay five percent more for their food? If we raise our prices, will sales drop? I don't know." Morgan shook his head with a sigh.

"When does the tax take effect?" Veron asked.

"The premweek of suether. It's due twice per year, at the beginning of each season," Morgan said.

"So . . . anything you buy during the rest of this wiether would be free of the extra tax, correct?"

"Yes . . . What are you getting at?"

"What if you contacted your suppliers and bought a thirty-week supply before the end of the season? That way, your food for the rest of suether would avoid the extra tax."

Morgan sighed and went back to stacking crates. "You can't do that with produce. The food will go bad after a couple of weeks."

"Yeah, but payin' for food doesn't mean you have to accept it yet, right?" Veron asked.

Morgan stopped and turned back to Veron, his head cocked.

Veron continued, pacing the room. "The tax is based on payments for goods startin' this suether. What if you contacted your sellers and asked them to bill you for thirty weeks of goods during the finweek of wiether? Then, as you receive food over the next half-year, you match it up against the credit owed. People who come to the shop to buy food will expect prices to be higher and will start payin' the new costs even though *you* didn't have to yet. You'll have to pay a lot upfront but will make an extra five percent for the next thirty weeks. If sales *do* drop some, the extra profit will hopefully make up for it."

Morgan looked like he wanted to shoot the idea down but closed his mouth as he thought. After several false starts, he finally spoke.

"I have enough money saved up to do that—just barely. The tax payment won't be due until *next* wiether, so that would give me plenty of time to recoup the investment. Veron, that could be an *excellent* idea!"

"And if you're committin' to such a large amount, I bet your suppliers would give you a discount from your normal costs. The tax doesn't affect them, and they should be happy to lock in the work," Veron said.

Morgan nodded along and laughed. "I bet you're right. Veron, you're quite the surprise. I love it! What's that old man teaching you over there?"

* * *

Veron awoke to the pitter-patter of rain outside of his window. After three weeks of routine, he rarely needed Artimus to get him up anymore. He wanted to hide in bed, but resistance was pointless. The rain didn't keep him from having to run, so Veron got up.

Although it was miserable to go out in the rain, Veron found his body's movement, combined with an increased heart rate, prevented him from noticing it. It felt refreshing after a couple of minutes. Taking the regular route, Veron flowed through the city. His legs were strong, and his breath was even. The medallion under his shirt bounced to the rhythm of his footsteps. He noticed everything and even waved at some of the regulars who he saw each day.

Returning to the training room, Veron glanced at the hourglass, curious to see its status. He was shocked to see a few grains of sand remaining. "Yes!" he said, throwing his arms up in the air. *I can't believe I made it!*

Artimus stepped into the training room and looked at him with a raised eyebrow. "How many people did you see while you were out?" he asked.

"Thirty-three," Veron replied. "Five before the first drop, eleven more before the second, mostly at the docks, and seventeen more on the way back."

"How many boats were anchored at the docks?"

"Three."

"How many shops on Gate Street had candles lit?"

"Only two on my way out, but as I crossed over it coming back, there were three more."

Artimus broke into a smile and nodded. "Nicely done."

Veron grinned as he rested his hands on his knees, panting. "So, when are you gonna teach me to fight?" he asked between breaths.

Artimus' smile disappeared, and his eyes narrowed. Silence rested heavily in the brief moment. "What do you think we've been doing all this time?" he said.

"Uh . . . movin' stupid rocks and talkin' 'bout things that don't matter."

"Interesting . . . I think you should come with me."

Veron's stomach dropped. *I should've kept my mouth shut.*

Veron followed Artimus to Karad Square then up High Street. Entering West Fairren, large buildings with ornate stone exteriors lined the wide and clean streets. The castle towered above them, looming ahead. Veron felt it staring at him disapprovingly.

"Do you know who lives there?" Artimus asked, pointing to a large house on the corner. Veron shook his head. "This is the home of Charles Marshall, Lord of Treasury for Karad. Do you know how he learned to fight?"

"No," Veron said.

"He learned to read and write. He learned about numbers and how to add, subtract, multiply, and divide. He practiced lending and learned how interest works. And he studied the political system and how the city and country operate. That's how he fights and how he got to be where he is."

I've never thought of fightin' in that way before.

They continued walking and turned down another street alongside the castle. "What about that house there? Do you know who lives there?" Artimus asked.

A stone wall with a wrought iron gate surrounded the property. Past the entrance sat a tall stone building with columns lining the front. "No, I don't," Veron replied.

"That's where Gareth Billings lives. He commands all the soldiers of Karad and is Lord of Defense for the city. How do you think he got to his position?"

"By bein' the best fighter?"

"Wrong. Billings is crippled." Veron jerked his head and looked at Artimus in surprise. "He was injured fighting Norshewan troops in the Gap of Thardor years ago and now walks with a cane," Artimus said. "While he was a great fighter when he was young, he's in his position now because he understands how to lead. He knows what needs to happen and motivates others to do it. His soldiers respect and follow him because they trust him."

They continued down the street and stopped in front of one more house, which Veron had walked past many times. It was the largest in the city next to the castle. The facade of the stone structure included carved wooden accents. A thick wall surrounded the building, and a large balcony extended out from the house on the second floor, revealing a wall of glass windows behind it. Two guards patrolled just inside the iron gate.

It's incredible. Twenty families could live in a building that size, Veron thought.

"This is the home of Raynor Fiero, Lord of Commerce. Do you

know how he learned to fight?" Artimus asked. Veron shook his head. "By working with a grocer when he was young."

"What?" Veron said, his mouth going slack.

"It's true. When he was young, he worked at a grocery. He continued his education as he grew and eventually operated a half-dozen shops on Karad Square." Artimus turned to face Veron fully. "Fighting isn't learning how to swing a sword, Veron. It's learning how to think and how to understand the way the city works. You need to learn how to make an opportunity when there is none. To be successful, you need to listen to people and understand how they work and what motivates them."

Veron hung his head as they walked back to the house. *The old man is probably right. I should be encouraged by it, but it just feels disappointin'. I may never get the chance to learn to use a sword.*

12

Bromhill

King Edmund Bale stood behind a small rise covered head to toe in heavy armor, and surveyed the city ahead through his spyglass, the sun having set long before. The wind whipped over the plain and tugged at the hem of his uniform. He didn't feel the chill. He was focused, looking for a sign. He saw nothing out of the ordinary in the city besides a couple of fires lit along the battlements at the top of the wall and the oblivious Rynorian soldiers. Ryker, commander of his army, stood by his side, dwarfed by Bale's towering frame and broad, muscular shoulders.

Bale lowered his spyglass and turned around. Behind him, an encampment of Norshewan soldiers stretched in each direction, surrounding the walled city of Bromhill. No one would be able to tell from high atop the walls, but in that sleepy-looking encampment, soldiers stood ready to attack. He turned back to the walls and lifted the spyglass again. His men waited on him to give the command.

The last few years had been brutal, gaining ground then losing it, taking one town then failing at the next in his quest to conquer all of Terrenor. Bale and his army had made their way to Bromhill, the capital of Rynor, where they stopped.

The city perched atop a hill, and a tall, thick wall surrounded it. Catapults were only minimally effective due to the height difference between the walls and the nearest flat ground. Bale was equally impressed and frustrated by the fortification that had successfully thwarted his plans thus far.

For the last two years, Bale's strategy had been to lay siege by setting up camp around the city, killing anyone who tried to leave or enter. Two years was a long time, and Bale and his army grew restless. Two weeks earlier, he and his advisors had a meeting to decide what to do.

"I'm telling you, they're getting food in somehow," Ryker said.

"How? Tell me how. There's no way! No one's coming or going. We have the city surrounded," Gatje—one of Bale's lead captains—said.

Ryker shook his head and clenched his fists. "I don't know. All I know is that they couldn't have stored up that much food. They're getting more, somehow. Otherwise, they would've surrendered or died by now."

"It's not possible," Gatje replied. "We searched. There are no tunnels or escape passages anywhere in the area. I'm telling you, they must be on the brink of giving up."

"We have to consider both options," Desmond, Bale's chief advisor, said, causing both men to stop their argument. "There may be a tunnel we have missed, which has allowed them to resupply. Or they may be on the verge of starvation and are about to surrender. There's no way for us to know, so we need to plan based on both options."

It was night. Candles lit the inside of the tent, revealing a small space with sparse furnishings. A table rested in the middle containing a large map of Bromhill, and the three men stood around it as they argued.

Bale sat in a chair to the side, deep in thought. He alternated between stroking his thick black beard and absently tracing the scar that ran down the left side of his face. "If King Petrous has already fled the city, then all of this is pointless. Gatje, are you positive there are no passages in the area? There's no way the king or his soldiers could have escaped?" he said, *his deep voice filling the tent, commanding attention.*

"No, Your Majesty," his commander said. *"I'm completely sure. The king must be in the city."*

Bale paused with his finger on his scar before jumping to his feet and causing his men to take a half-step back. The light from the candles flickered for a moment as a gust of wind found its way through the cracks of the tent. "I'm tired of waiting. We need to act."

"Very well, there are a couple of approaches we can take. We can attempt diplomacy." Desmond said, *looking around at the others. "We can flag them for a talk and deliver our terms."*

Ryker offered an upturned hand. "Which would be?"

"Surrender or be destroyed," Gatje said, *slamming his fist down on the table, his jaw clenched.*

"It won't work," Ryker said. *"If we were able to destroy them, we would've done it by now. Asking for their surrender at this point is a bluff, and they'll see through it."*

"If they're on the brink of starvation, they may take the deal out of desperation," Gatje said.

"Which they're not, because they're getting resupplied somehow," Ryker muttered.

"The other approach is assault," Desmond said. *"We've already discussed how that would work. Lots of ladders, attacking as quickly as we can, and hoping we can get over the walls fast enough."*

The men glanced at each other. "That's what they'll be expecting," Gatje said, *shifting on his feet. "They'll be ready for the ladders. They'll knock them down or kill our people before we can get up."*

"Not if we have enough at once, and we do it when they're not expecting," said Ryker. *"If we catch them by surprise, we can get soldiers up the ladders."*

"An assault may be possible, but it's far from guaranteed. The loss of life would be great," Desmond said.

"Men can be replaced," Bale said, his voice cutting through their discussion and silencing the men. "But we need to make sure we don't lose so many that the rest of our army cannot be effective. We have more battles to fight after Bromhill. Assault by ladders cannot be our only plan." *He walked to the map on the table and stared as the others waited. "We need to do something they're not expecting. We need to get our army inside the walls. Once we're in, only one thing matters—killing King Petrous."*

"Maybe they didn't make it," Ryker said, breaking the quiet as he and Bale watched the city.

A few hours before, five pairs of climbers had scaled the castle walls in its darkest corners. All teams appeared to make it over, so Bale focused his spyglass on the north side of the city as he waited.

Ever since Bale was young, he had an insatiable desire for authority. When he was little, he learned the power someone can have over another by how the other children in his village treated him. The impact of their ridicule and mockery was nothing compared to the effect his father's abuse had. Motivated by the need for control, he joined the army at the young age of fourteen and quickly gathered respect as he excelled. When given his first chance to lead as a battalion sub-captain, he never looked back, garnering victory after victory. The achievements he won and the subsequent titles he earned were never enough to quench his desire. Capturing Bromhill would be the next step in his quest.

A faint glow grew between the merlons of the sawtooth-shaped crenellation that ran along the battlement. In a few moments, the glow turned into flickers of flames as the corners of Bale's mouth lifted. The fire in the city had begun. He looked to Ryker. "Ready the men."

Ryker signaled with his sword to the waiting army, which was relayed to the companies and battalions around the city's exterior. Invisible in the darkness, the army was poised and ready to strike. After a few minutes, Bale nodded to Ryker, who signaled once again.

Silently, a ring of men surrounding the city sprinted to the walls. The slope was steep, but the wave of soldiers covered the hill like an army of ants over a piece of discarded food. Once at the base of the walls, long ladders appeared out of the darkness and lifted in place. Almost in unison, a roar sounded as men started to climb.

Lights along the top of the wall doubled, then tripled in number as Rynorian soldiers prepared for the invasion. Some ladders were knocked down before anyone even began to climb. Arrows picked off soldiers, sending them crashing to the ground. Through luck, determination, and sheer numbers, some Norshewan soldiers made it to the top where the Rynorian men waited behind the merlons.

While his men advanced up the ladders, Bale focused his spyglass on the drawbridge. So far, it hadn't moved, and he started to sweat. The fire in the city and the ladder attack on the walls were merely diversions to draw the enemy's attention. The actual plan was for their spies inside to take the gatehouse amid the chaos. In the shadows below the main gate, 5,000 Norshewan soldiers waited for their chance to rush through the gate.

Bale looked back at the walls. More men fell to their deaths. Broken ladders and fallen soldiers littered the ground at the base of the wall. *We can't keep this up for much longer,* he thought as he clenched his jaw.

Suddenly, he heard it, the faint clinking of a chain drawing out. The drawbridge moved slowly at first but soon sped up. When it was halfway down, the portcullis behind began to rise. The drawbridge hit the ground with a loud thud as thousands of soldiers swarmed it. They yelled and waved their swords as they stormed into the city.

Bale's heart skipped a beat as the portcullis stopped rising and began to lower. *The men inside the gatehouse must be dead.*

The Norshewan soldiers were ready though. A sizable wooden brace was jammed under the gate, preventing it from closing. By then, all remaining soldiers had abandoned their attempts on the ladders and headed for the entrance.

A grin crept over Bale's face. *I did it. I've won.*

Bale entered the city through the open gate with Ryker and a small force of men. Destruction was everywhere. Bodies littered the streets—Rynorian soldiers, Norshewan soldiers, men, women, and children. Mournful wailing echoed through the alleys, and the stench of death hovered like a fog. Unfortunately for the citizens of Bromhill, Bale's men had little restraint when it came to sacking a city.

A woman with matted hair and filthy rags for clothes ran toward the group. "Please . . . have mercy on us! They killed my son. Please!" she cried.

Soldiers intercepted the woman as she grabbed onto their armor, thrashing around with frantic eyes. Bale nodded at one of the men who seized the lady and took her back the way she came. As Bale continued down the street, the shriek of steel and the woman's scream faded into the background behind him.

The contingent made their way through the street to the castle where Gatje met them, fidgeting with his sword and glancing around nervously. Bale narrowed his eyes as he approached.

"The city is taken, Your Majesty," Gatje said, his armor untouched and shiny. "All remaining soldiers have surrendered their weapons."

"How was the resistance?" Bale asked.

"Surprisingly light. We expected they'd have at least 3,000 to 4,000 soldiers defending, but we estimate there were only 500 or so."

Bale's stomach twisted. *Something's wrong,* he thought.

"They don't appear to have been starving," Ryker said, looking at the bodies that littered the ground around them.

Gatje shifted his stance. "No, it seems they weren't. Their stores are uh . . . are still filled with food. Apparently, they *were* getting resupplied somehow."

"I told you," Ryker muttered from the side.

Bale's face reddened as he ground his teeth, putting together the pieces. He stood tall. "Resupplied? Using tunnels?" Bale asked, staring at the captain, but Gatje looked at the ground. "Gatje, where's Petrous?"

Gatje wiped his forehead as he fumbled his words. "We . . . um . . . We can't find him, Your Highness."

Bale had a quick temper, but he tried to stay composed around his men. Losing control was a weakness. "What do you mean you can't find him?" he said through clenched teeth.

"It—" Gatje swallowed hard, keeping his head bowed—"it's believed he's no longer in the city."

Bale's pulse quickened. As he stared down his captain, the rumblings of a laugh came up, unbidden. Unable to stop it, the chuckle grew in intensity as his men shifted their feet and glanced between each other. Bale drew a dagger as he sauntered toward Gatje, continuing to laugh. He rested his free arm casually on his captain's shoulder.

"The only thing that mattered was getting Petrous. You assured me there was no way he could escape," Bale said. His words were light, but the captain still shook.

"I—I'm sorry, Your Majesty. I don't think he's been here for a while. His quarters are barren as if they haven't been lived in for some time."

Bale's laughter ceased as he stabbed Gatje through the neck with his dagger. The smaller man uttered a short cry and fell to his knees as blood ran down his body. Bale narrowed his eyes and fixed his jaw. "Arrogant fool!"

None of Bale's men spoke or even dared move.

Bale turned to Ryker without a trace of laughter. "Any Rynorian soldier that will swear allegiance to me can fight for us. Anyone else must be put to death," he said.

"I'll see to it, Your Majesty," Ryker said, signaling four men to join him as they immediately left.

Bale stared at the city around him before unleashing a strained yell. *Two years. I waited two years for this moment, and now it's meaningless. Without the king, we captured nothing.*

13

Nasco

Chelci awoke, fighting her way out of darkness. *I'm alive!* she thought as her memory came back. Glancing around, she found herself lying on an unfamiliar bed in a foreign room made of roughly hewn wood. The furnishings were sparse. Light streamed in a window, and she heard the sound of chickens clucking. An unseen shuffling noise came through an open doorway to another room.

A white bandage wrapped her arm. When she moved it, pain radiated to her shoulder, reminding her where the injury came from. She wanted to get up, but as soon as she moved, a dizzy spell washed over her. With her good arm, she lifted the blanket on top of her before promptly covering back up. *Where did my clothes go?*

A dog trotted into the room with its tongue hanging out. It had white curly hair and a tail that stuck up like a flag, wagging frantically. The dog propped its front paws up on the bed and started licking her face. Chelci sputtered and pushed it away gently.

"Charlie! Stop that!" a woman said as she entered the room and shooed the dog away. It ran through the doorway but turned and sat, watching from the next room. "Sorry about that, dear. Charlie likes people, sometimes a little too much." She sat down on the edge of the bed. "Good morning."

Chelci tried to reply but only managed a rough croak.

"My name is Nevi Martin—well, Genevieve technically, but everyone calls me Nevi. I'm guessing you're hungry?" she asked.

Chelci nodded. Nevi left for a moment, and when she returned with a warm cup of broth, Chelci forced herself to sit up. Gritting through the discomfort, she used her good arm to push her upper body, but she hesitated as the blanket began to slip away, bringing a blush to her face.

Nevi smiled and set the cup down. "Here, let me help." She grabbed an extra blanket off the table beside her, unfolded it, and draped it over Chelci before helping her sit up straight. "I'm sorry about your clothes. I wanted to save them, but they were torn to pieces. I'll get some others for you to wear when I can." She grabbed the cup and held up the spoon. "Do you mind?"

Chelci shook her head, and the woman proceeded to spoon-feed her small portions of broth. It hurt to swallow, but the warm liquid coated her aching throat and felt good going down. Her stomach growled in celebration.

Nevi appeared to be younger than her own mother—probably by ten years or so. She was a little heavyset, in a robust sort of way, with curly auburn hair that bounced above her shoulders as she moved. What Chelci found most comforting was her eyes. A vivid blue color, they felt kind, and creased at the edges when she smiled.

Soon the cup of broth was empty, and Nevi set it down. "That's enough for now," she said. "You don't want to take in too much at once."

"What happened last night?" Chelci asked, questions filling her head. A scratch remained in her voice, but the broth had almost brought it back to normal.

"Last night, I sat by the fire and patched an old dress of mine while Russell, my husband, read a book. Two nights ago, however, Russell came across you, collapsed over the body of a dead wolf. You were freezing and about to bleed to death, so he brought you home. You've been tossing and turning, mumbling incoherently for the last day and a half. We cleaned you up as best we could and have been waiting for you to wake."

I can't remember anything since the wolves, Chelci thought.

"So, what's your story?" Nevi asked. "How does someone with a dress like yours end up in the middle of nowhere, starving, and fighting off a wolf to stay alive?"

I don't even know where to begin. This woman could probably help me get home now. I could have my servants back and my clothes . . . and my family. But do I want that? She glanced around the room as she thought. *No, I'm not ready to go back. If I tell her who I am, she'll probably end up taking me back to try and get a reward or something.*

"My name is . . . Elise . . . Elise Barton. My parents died last year, and I've been traveling from village to village ever since in search of a place I could settle," Chelci said. "The dress was a gift from someone I met. I was searching through the woods to find . . . wherever the next place was when I got lost and my food ran out. That's when I ran into the wolves. I was able to kill one of them before the others ran off. I guess I passed out after that."

"Well, I'm glad you're okay," Nevi said. "Once you're back to health, is there anything we can help you with? Any place you're trying to get to? Karad or Felting, maybe?"

"No!" Chelci said, a little too forcefully, making Nevi lean back. "I'm sorry. No, I don't have a particular destination. I'm looking for somewhere to live—a place where I can settle down and be who I want to be. I don't know . . . just make a life for myself, I guess."

Nevi looked down at the floor and was silent as she breathed slowly and deeply. After a bit, she broke into a smile which grew into a soft, warm laugh.

Chelci frowned. *What's so funny? I think I'm missing something.*

Nevi looked up and rested her hand on Chelci's good arm. "My husband Russell will be back later tonight," Nevi said. "Why don't you rest some more? I'll be back in a little while with some more broth and to change those bandages." She got up to leave and paused in the doorway. "Welcome to our home, Elise."

Nevi came back several times as the day progressed. Each time, she brought more broth, which grew easier to eat. During her visits, Nevi cleaned Chelci's wounds and changed the bandages. Her leg had received the worst of the injuries, while her back was covered in scratches.

After the sun went down, Nevi came in with a candle and a dress. "Oh no, I'm not wearing that," Chelci said, noticing the faded and dingy fabric, and imagining how many people had worn it before. "You can't repair the dress I was wearing? If not, I'd like something new."

"I'm sorry, but we don't have anything new, and your dress can't be fixed," Nevi replied.

"No!" Chelci said, her temper quickly rising. "I'm not going to wear that!"

Nevi paused for a moment, pursing her lips. She smoothed her own dress with her hands and breathed out. "It may not be as nice as what you *were* wearing, but it should do for now," she said. "The thing I like most about it is that wolves haven't shredded it. I got it from another family in town. Of course, you're free to walk around in your underclothes if that's what you prefer?"

Chelci huffed, unhappy with the options. Reluctantly, she accepted Nevi's help to get the dress on. She cringed at the coarse feeling of the plain linen. *I'd never wear this at home, but it's better than nothing, I guess.* At least the alternating blue and white pattern wasn't awful. "What town am I in?" Chelci asked.

"Nasco."

"Nasco? I've never heard of it."

"Just 'cause you ent heard of it . . . doesn't mean we're not here," a rough voice said with slurred words as a man staggered in from the room next door.

The man was of average height with short brown hair and an unkempt beard. Attached to his belt was a sword, and he held a bottle of clear liquid in his hand.

"Please be kind to our guest," Nevi said, taking the bottle from him. "Russell, this is Elise."

"I wasn't saying you weren't here—just that I hadn't heard of it," Chelci said, feeling defensive.

"Ahhh." Russell dismissed her apology with a wave of his hand. "You're lookin' better now than th'other night. I thought you's dead for sure."

Chelci blushed. "You must be Russell. Thank you for saving me."

"Don't thank me. I'sn't tryin' save you. I'st didn't want the wolves to find yer body and get a taste of meat. That'd only make 'em bolder," Russell said, almost losing his balance before he caught himself on the doorframe.

Nevi fidgeted as she watched her husband and cleared her throat before turning back to Chelci. "So, yes, Nasco is a little off the beaten path. We're a half day's ride by horse to Karad and about a day and a half to Felting, but we don't go to either often. We generally keep to ourselves."

"How do you survive out here?" Chelci asked.

"There's food in the forest and water in the stream." Nevi shrugged. "We make do. We have 514 people living here." She turned to Russell.

"I was about to let Elise get some rest. Why don't we let her be for a while?" Without saying goodbye, Russell turned and stumbled away.

"Sorry. He can be rough at times," Nevi said. "He's actually a lovely guy . . . usually."

"I'm sure he is."

"You get some sleep now, okay, Elise? I'll be back in the morning."

* * *

The next day, Chelci felt strong enough to move around. Longing to get outside, Nevi found her a sturdy walking stick, since both legs were still sore and her twisted knee wobbled from time to time.

Nevi had managed to patch Chelci's green cloak, the thick fabric easier to mend than the fine silk of her dress. Its appearance was a far cry from the quality it once was, but Chelci welcomed the familiar warmth. Wrapped in the cloak, they left the cozy house and stepped into the sunshine.

Opposite the house, the slope dropped off, leading to the woods beyond. To the right and the left, a crooked dirt path led to other homes, dozens of them. The buildings were smaller than any she'd seen in Felting. All were one story, and many had covered areas with chairs out front. While the design of each was different, they were all made of wood.

That's odd. I thought people built houses of stone, Chelci thought.

The dress itched as she moved, the cheap fabric nothing like her usual fine clothing. Chelci tried to ignore the stains on it. While mentally noting the flaws in her dress, she realized the one Nevi wore was in even worse shape. It was a simple, plain brown color, and the linen was coarse with ragged edges.

She doesn't seem to mind. I guess I shouldn't be too picky. Chelci's hair, which was now greasy and unkempt, bothered her too. *I wish I hadn't lost my comb. My parents probably wouldn't even recognize me if they saw me now.*

Leaning on her stick, Chelci hobbled along the path with Nevi, while Charlie the dog followed by her side. They passed men and women who nodded and waved. A woman around the same age as Nevi stopped and talked to her while Chelci waited and looked around. Children ran through the streets playing barefoot. Ahead, two girls waved goodbye to their mother and took off running into the woods.

How free they are here! They can run and explore and play. I bet no one makes them take lessons on proper formal dinner manners!

Charlie sat by Chelci's side with his tongue hanging out the side of his mouth and a grin on his face. She scratched under his chin as he lifted his head and leaned his body into her leg.

The other woman soon left, and the group continued along. "So, what's it like, living in a small village like this?" Chelci asked.

"I thought you came from other villages?" Nevi replied.

Chelci paused mid-step. "Uh . . . Yes, I did, but they were a lot larger. I like it here."

"I do too. I've been here all of my life. Russell and I lived next to each other growing up—just down the street there." Nevi pointed down another path as they passed.

Two men walked toward them with black uniforms and swords on their hips. The pleasant look on their faces and the fact that they waved as they passed helped soften their intimidating appearance.

They don't look like soldiers from Felting. I wonder who they are? Chelci thought. "Do you ever wish you lived in a big city . . . like Felting?"

Nevi shook her head. "I've been to Karad a few times. When we need supplies, we sometimes go into the city to get them, but it's not for me. Too crowded, too busy. The people I met were all mean and selfish. I feel sorry for the people who grow up there. They don't know any better and end up the same way. Life is more . . . peaceful here, I think."

I can't disagree with her, but that's all I've ever known.

Their walk brought them to the center of the village where shops surrounded a large, rectangular grassy area. People sat and chatted on benches while children played in the grass nearby. Charlie dashed off to join two other dogs rolling and chasing each other.

As they passed a few of the shops, Chelci peered at the displays of food and goods beneath covered awnings. *This must be their market square.*

A young man at a stand of baked goods greeted Nevi by name and said hello to Chelci. Charlie tried to sneak some food off the stand, but Nevi stopped him. They talked a moment, and the young man handed Chelci a slice of sweet bread as they left. It was still warm and tasted like honey and raspberries.

"Are you getting tired? Would you like to rest?" Nevi asked.

"Yes, that would be great," Chelci said before they sat down on an open bench. "This is amazing." She took another bite of the bread.

"Philip's bread? It sure is."

"No, I mean . . . Yes, the bread is great, but I meant this village. I love it! You're right. It just seems . . . peaceful. How do people know what to do?"

Nevi cocked her head. "What do you mean?"

"Like Philip back there. Were his parents bakers, so he had to be a baker?"

Nevi laughed. "Philip? No, his father's a builder. He actually helped build our house. Philip always loved baking, so he decided to open a stand. Most of the bread we eat comes from him."

Nevi looked around as if searching for something. "At the school over there"—she pointed to the corner—"Kyla was supposed to help her mother make clothes when she grew. As she finished up her schooling, she discovered she loved learning and had a gift for teaching. She always helped tutor other kids, so when Mrs. Fletcher passed away, Kyla took over as our teacher."

She turned and looked at Chelci. "In our village, we work hard to make sure everyone has a chance to be themselves. No one should be stuck doing something they don't like. Not everything is perfect though—no one *wants* to clean out privies, but it has to happen. People still die from illnesses. Villagers get in fights. But we encourage people to pursue their passions. As a result, people are *mostly* happy and work hard, doing what they love."

I want the freedom to choose my destiny and live how I want, too. This is what I've been looking for! As Chelci gazed around, she stopped. "What's that up there?" Her eyes were wide and sparkled with interest.

Up the hill from the square was a large building looking down on the village. It had a row of windows along the side and a large outdoor courtyard. The building itself wasn't what caught Chelci's eye. It was the men outside. Four pairs of them engaged in fierce sparring sessions with swords.

"Oh, the Academy—that's where Russell works. He's part of the village guard, and that's where they train potential candidates," Nevi said.

"Village guard? What's that?"

"Being separated from the rest of the kingdom has its benefits, but it also means we have no support. If raiders from a nearby village steal from us, we can't go anywhere for help. That's where the village guard comes in. Every two years, we have a dozen or so young men that go through the Academy. Practically every young boy in Nasco hopes to be in the guard, and nearly all of them attempt to make it. But because of the fierce competition, usually only one—two if they're lucky—are selected."

Chelci watched them fight. It reminded her of Jackson fighting with Barlan back in Felting. She couldn't stop the smile on her face. A passionate desire burned deep in her. She wanted to stay in Nasco. More than anything, she wanted to join the Academy.

14

The Martin House

Chelci stayed with Nevi and Russell Martin for several days while she continued to heal. Nevi was pleasant to be with, and Chelci loved their talks. The rude first impression she had of Russell wasn't dispelled, but she did start to see a kinder side as the days went on. He spoke more softly and was gentle with Nevi, even bringing her flowers once.

"Elise, are you feeling up to eating with us at the table," Nevi asked one evening.

"Yes, of course!" Chelci said enthusiastically, having smelled the roasted chicken and beans cooking.

She got up on her own and hobbled to the kitchen to sit with her two hosts. She eagerly dove into the prepared meal.

"Wow, this is good," Chelci said between mouthfuls. "I can't believe you cooked this yourself!"

"It's not difficult. Maybe I can teach you," Nevi said.

Chelci looked up from her plate and laughed. "I don't cook."

Nevi frowned. "So, what did you do for the last year?"

Chelci shrunk in her seat. "Uh . . . other people usually gave me food," she replied.

"Do you not *know* how, or do you not *want* to know how?"

"Well . . ." She wanted to say cooking was for servants, but if she was going to fit in, she'd best learn new things.

"Would you like to learn?" Nevi asked.

Charlie sat next to Chelci on the floor, whining with a sad look, hoping to get her to toss him a piece of chicken. She scratched his head.

"Yeah, I guess I could learn," Chelci said.

Nevi and Russell looked at each other. Nevi nodded at Russell as if nudging him to do something. "Elise, we . . . um," Russell said. "We know you lost your parents . . . so . . . you can stay with us if you want."

Nevi jumped in, adding, "We know you just got here and don't want to presume to tell you what to do, but if you're looking for a good village to settle down in, I don't think you'll find one better than Nasco. I know we can be rough at times"—she looked at Russell—"but if you're interested, we'd love for you to live here with us."

How could they be so quick to offer to take me in? They don't even know me! she thought, staring ahead in shock. She wasn't sure about Russell, but Nevi was great. *What about my family though? Can I leave Father forever? What if Mother were kinder? Should I really give up on them?* Charlie moved his head under her hand, forcing her to pet him. "Can I think about it?" she asked.

"Of course, dear. Of course," Nevi said. "We just want you to know you're welcome here."

After dinner, Russell left the table, and Nevi began cleaning up. Wanting some air, Chelci put on her cloak and made her way out to the porch. The sun had set a while ago, and the night was crisp. The crowded city of Felting had a rotten, damp feel, but Nasco smelled like trees and clean dirt. She sucked in a deep breath to savor it.

"How'd your parents die?" Russell asked from behind her.

Chelci jumped. She hadn't realized he sat in the chair in the corner of the porch. "Oh, I'm sorry I didn't know you were there. My parents . . . They uh . . . got sick," she replied.

"Of what?"

She scratched her head and glanced around. "I don't know. Some sort of fever."

"And they both died at the same time?"

"Yeah . . . well . . . a few days apart."

"Hmm." He didn't press any more, but Chelci felt unsettled under his piercing eyes. "I'm sorry for being rude when we first met," Russell said, leaning back in his chair.

Chelci narrowly prevented herself from gasping at the unfamiliar apology. "Oh, that's okay."

"I had too much to drink and wasn't myself." Silence hung in the air between them. Crickets chirped in the woods, and an owl hooted somewhere in the distance. "Have a seat if you like," Russell said, indicating to the chair next to him.

Chelci sat down, relieved to take the weight off her legs. She wasn't sure if Russell had more things to ask, so she waited, but he only gazed out at the trees across the path. Uncomfortable with the silence, she cleared her throat. "So, you don't have any kids?" she asked.

Russell remained quiet. She turned to look at him and was about to ask again when she stopped. Tears glistened in his eyes, and his lips quivered.

"I'm sorry! I didn't mean to—"

"It's okay," he said in a whisper, wiping his eyes. He cleared his throat before continuing. "Nevi and I have had two children. Thomas was our firstborn. We had him a year after we married."

Russell smiled. "His face and hair looked just like mine when he was born, but he had Nevi's eyes." He took a deep breath before continuing. "When he was a season old, he developed a breathing problem. The doctor couldn't figure out what was wrong, and he died one night in his sleep."

"I'm so sorry."

Again, they sat in silence.

Chelci pursed her lips as she waited. "You uh . . . You said you had two?"

Russell nodded his head. "Madeline . . . born three seasons after Thomas passed. She was strong and healthy, and we loved her more than anything. She always found cute ways to tell us she loved us too. Early in the morning, she'd get up and pick us wildflowers from the woods to leave by our bed for us to see when we woke. She loved making clothes and wanted to be a seamstress when she grew up. The dress you're wearing now, she made for a lady down the street." The joy on his face quickly changed to sorrow. "It was the last dress she made. She—" He cut himself off and was silent for a long moment. "I hope you choose to stay." Russell got up and walked inside.

Chelci paled. *I can't believe I turned my nose up at the dress. Maybe Russell has more of a heart than I thought?*

She continued to enjoy the air and listen to the crickets for a bit before going inside where Nevi still cleaned dishes from dinner.

"Elise, would you mind giving me a hand?" Nevi asked.

At home, she would never stoop so low as to wash dishes. But if she were going to stay there, she needed to stretch herself. "Um . . . sure," Chelci replied.

"Can you clean these while I take care of the food?"

Chelci looked at the basin of water and soap, filled with plates and forks and other cooking implements. "I'm not sure. I don't know what to do."

Nevi looked at her with a curious expression. "Have you never cleaned dishes before?"

"No, the—" She stopped herself from mentioning servants. "Other people always did them."

"Here, let me show you."

Nevi demonstrated how to scrub the dishes clean with soap and water, then dry them off with a towel before putting them up on the shelf. It was easy, and Chelci felt foolish for not knowing what to do.

Chelci grabbed the next plate to work on it. "So, Russell was telling me about Madeline," she said.

Nevi froze while placing a plate upon the high shelf. "What did he say?"

"He mentioned she was your daughter and made dresses, but that was about it. What happened to her?"

Nevi gazed toward the door as she exhaled a long, slow breath. After a moment, she resumed working. "Three years ago, a lady on the other side of the village was about to give birth, so I went to her place to help and asked Russell to be in charge of Madeline." She wiped the table with a cloth. "The night before, I heard a strange noise in the woods. I didn't want her going out there on her own, so I asked Russell to make sure she didn't leave the house without him. He thought I was foolish and imagining things.

"The next morning, I woke Russell when I returned. He had fallen asleep in his chair, but Madeline was gone. We asked her friends, but no one had any idea where she was." Nevi's face grew solemn, and she steadied herself against the table. "Russell found the first sign of her not far in the woods. A torn portion of her dress lay on the forest floor."

Chelci's eyes were wide. "What happened?"

Nevi paused for a moment and wiped at the corners of her eyes. "The entire village joined in the search. We spent two days scouring the woods in every direction. At the end of the second day, one of our neighbors found her body. It—" Nevi covered her mouth with her hand as she shook her head. Tears fell as she stood in silence.

"I'm so sorry." Chelci rested her hand on Nevi's shoulder. "Was it wolves?"

Nevi sniffed and collected herself. "It couldn't have been. Russell says I'm foolish, but I think it was a valcor."

Chelci's breath caught. Her eyes opened wide, and her blood froze. The valcor was the most feared animal in all of Terrenor, but she didn't think they actually existed. Parents told stories of valcor living in the woods, taking naughty children. According to legend, they were as large as a bear but lean and muscular. They were supposed to have long, sharp fangs and razor claws and only came out at night. Their shrill cries were so piercing they could turn anyone with unprotected ears to stone. Some said they could fly, and others said they shot fire from their mouths. No one had ever seen one and lived.

"I didn't think valcor were real," Chelci said. "Did anyone see it?"

Nevi shook her head.

Chelci narrowed her eyes. "So, if no one saw it, why do you think that's what it was?"

"I don't want to talk about it, and your ears are too young to hear such things." Nevi resumed stacking dishes. "During the evening I was gone, Russell was trying to read by the fire, but Madeline kept distracting him—pestering him to play. He got annoyed and yelled at her to go out and play with her friends." Nevi stared blankly out the open door. "Russell blames himself ever since that day. He buries his guilt with alcohol to dull the pain, but it never goes away. The night he found you in the woods was the same night she disappeared three years before."

Goosebumps ran along Chelci's arms. *What are the chances of that?* she thought.

"Every year on the anniversary of her death, Russell fights his guilt by patrolling the woods as if he's still looking for her. When he found you after being attacked, it was as if he found Madeline and had a second chance to make it right," Nevi said as she leaned against the counter and took a sip of water. "She would've been about your age."

"Russell said he wasn't even trying to save me—that he just didn't want wolves to eat my body," Chelci said.

Nevi laughed softly and shook her head. "Don't believe that. He has a tough time admitting how he feels. He wanted to save you more than anything. After he brought you back, he sat in your room, watching all night and all the next day. Finally, I took over and forced him to get some rest."

Mother never sat by my bed when I was sick. Father hasn't even done that before. They just sent attendants to take care of me, Chelci thought.

Russell came out of their bedroom and walked into the kitchen. Chelci looked at him with new eyes and an expression of admiration. "What?" he asked as both of them stared at him. "What is it?"

"Thank you for everything you've done for me," Chelci said, addressing both of them. "Assuming it's okay, I'd love to stay here and live with you."

She offered a hopeful smile that was immediately returned by a hug from Nevi. Both of them broke into tears, the drops running past their smiles. Russell kept his distance but rested his hand on Chelci's shoulder. Chelci felt warm inside. Love, acceptance, and hope felt foreign as the feelings flooded through her.

Breaking the embrace, Chelci spoke excitedly to Russell. "Once my leg is healed, can I join you at the Academy?"

Russell's head jerked in surprise. "Uh, I . . . No, you . . . Girls aren't allowed in the Academy, Elise."

Ugh. Just like back home, she thought with a frown. "Why not?"

"Well . . ." Russell looked to Nevi, but she just crossed her arms, raised her eyebrows, and stared back at him. He turned his attention back to Chelci. "Girls can't . . . They're just not able to do all that's needed."

"How do you know? I haven't even had a chance to go through the training yet. If I did, wouldn't you be able to have a better idea about whether I was able or not?"

Russell looked back at Nevi. "Girls have never been in the Academy before. It wouldn't work."

"Just because they've never been there before doesn't mean one wouldn't be able to," Chelci said.

Nevi raised her eyebrows again. "There is a first time for everything, Russell," she said.

"Yes, but . . . Okay, I'm not against girls, but you're too young," he told her.

"I'm thirteen and will be fourteen next season," Chelci said, hoping the extra year she exaggerated might be enough.

"Candidates must be seventeen before they're eligible to attend. We just started a class a bit ago, so even if it *were* allowed, you'd have to wait almost four years."

Chelci hung her head. *That's okay. I just need to be patient.* "Okay, I can wait. I'll join in four years."

"Wait, no that . . . That doesn't mean . . ." Russell struggled to speak.

"Isn't this village built on encouraging people to pursue what they're passionate about?" Chelci asked, looking back and forth between Russell and Nevi. "Don't you want people to enjoy what they do? What's the harm in giving me a chance?"

Russell sighed and threw up his hands. "Fine! In four years, you can attend," he said, causing Chelci to squeal with delight. "But the Academy is not easy!" he added. "It's dangerous and difficult. You'll go home every day tired, sore, and covered in bruises. You need to know there's virtually *no* chance of you even making it through the two years of training, much less getting selected for the village guard at the end. You understand?"

Chelci nodded. *All my life, I've wished to train the way the boys do. I'll have to wait a bit longer, but I'll get my chance.*

That night, Chelci lay in bed, her busy mind preventing her from sleeping. *Could these people be like a family? They seem kind and loving.* She frowned as she remembered the lies she told them. *Maybe I should tell them the truth? No, I don't want to be sent back home. I can't do that.*

Chelci thought back to her old life in Felting—the cruelty of her mother—the expectations placed on her.

I had no choice about what I became—what I did every day. Did I give up on my family too quickly? I'd love to see Father again. I wish I could talk to someone about all of this who understood. I miss Emma, and I wish I had Mr. Butters with me. The thought of her missing friends made her sad but couldn't dampen her excitement. *Still, I can't wait to see what comes in the future.*

15

Defending & Striking

Veron finished his run just before the sand ran out for the second time. When he entered the training room, it wasn't the hourglass that excited him—it was the two wooden swords leaning against the table.

"Are you ready?" Artimus asked.

"Yes!" Veron said, his heart skipping a beat. He couldn't stop grinning.

His teacher's face was stern as he spoke. "Learning to fight with a sword isn't about who swings his sword hardest or fastest. To be a good fighter, you need balance, quick thinking, and the ability to anticipate your enemy, moving your sword where he doesn't expect before he can react."

Veron listened with rapt attention, nodding as Artimus spoke.

"Whether on offense or defense, there are no new moves you can make. You must practice striking and defending against all possibilities. The more you rehearse, the readier you'll be when it matters."

He tossed one of the wooden swords to Veron, which was almost as long as his body. The grip was smooth, worn down from years of use. Veron stood tall with his shoulders back as he held the weapon in front of him. *It's lighter than I expected,* he thought.

"Before you swing a sword, you must learn how to stand. First, stand with your legs slightly bent and the left one in front." Artimus patted himself on his left knee to emphasize. "With your right hand near the guard and your left below it, hold your sword at head height with the tip pointed toward me."

Veron mirrored Artimus' movements. The stance felt awkward, bending his arms and legs in new ways.

"Good. This is dragon stance," Artimus said. "Next, drop your hands down by your hip and point the blade up, toward your opponent's face. This is horn." Artimus moved into shovel, then owl, then snake while Veron copied him. "You must learn each to where it feels as natural as walking. To practice, you will have a routine that reinforces each stance called the positura."

Artimus started in dragon and held it for a moment before moving into each of the other four stances. After he held snake a moment, he relaxed.

"The goal is to keep every muscle in your body alert while you hold each stance and move between them. What I just went through was one round. The positura goes through a round for every possible combination of stances."

"So, with five stances, there are five rounds?" Veron asked.

Artimus chuckled. "No, the first round was dragon-horn-shovel-owl-snake. Next is dragon-horn-shovel-*snake*-owl . . ."

Veron stared at him and paled. "That'll be a lot more than five."

"Yes, 120 rounds."

Veron's mouth dropped. *I don't think I can do that.*

"Let's begin!" Artimus said.

They stood side by side as they both moved. When Veron forgot a stance, he glanced over to double-check what Artimus did. He thought he would at least get a short break between rounds, but Artimus immediately called out the next sequence.

During the final rounds, Veron's arms were on fire. They shook with effort, trying to keep his sword up. He counted the seconds until he could finally drop them. Muscles he never knew he had in his back and legs ached. Even though his form faltered, Artimus, thankfully, did not correct him.

When they finished, Veron struggled to even hold on to his sword. Not only were his arms incapable of lifting it, but the sweat from his hands made gripping it difficult.

"Good work," Artimus said with barely a hint of sweat on his forehead.

After a break to focus on bookwork and allow his arms to rest, they returned to the training room in the afternoon. "Veron, what do you think the most important part of defense is?" Artimus asked.

"Um . . . blocking the other person's sword?" Veron told him.

"It's called parrying, and that's not correct. Why don't you try attacking me? Use any stance you like," Artimus said.

"You mean . . . just try and hit you?"

"Yes, try to hit me with your sword."

Veron held the sword with both hands in horn position and faced Artimus, heart pounding. He swung at the older man's shoulder, but Artimus parried it away. Veron tried the opposite side, going for his midsection, but again, Artimus parried.

Not even close, Veron thought, considering his options.

He tried an overhead swing, which was halted by the sword again, the solid block sending vibrations up his arm. Veron swung from different directions, moving quickly, but Artimus deflected easily. Not sure what else to try, he stopped to catch his breath.

"Now you defend while I attack," Artimus said.

Veron was nervous but ready. He parried away the first couple of swings, barely moving his sword in time. *I'm sure those were slow on purpose,* he thought. Fooled by Artimus switching directions, Veron found his sword on the wrong side of his body as a blow landed on the side of his chest. A dull thud sounded, and the impact jarred his body. Veron tried to ignore the pain and regroup, but the movements felt awkward, like he could never adjust his sword to the right place. Several more blows landed until the older man finally stopped.

"So, what did your defense accomplish?" Artimus asked.

"Um . . . I'm not sure," Veron said between heavy breaths, grabbing his stinging side. "I blocked some of 'em, but I got hit still."

"Yes, what else?"

Veron thought for a moment. "It tired me out."

"Yes, indeed. Why don't you try coming at me again?"

After catching his breath, Veron readied himself to attack. He swung toward Artimus' chest, trying to move before his teacher could react. Rather than simply deflect the sword, as Veron expected, Artimus stepped in and swung, colliding with Veron's sword above the hilt. The force knocked the weapon out of Veron's hand. He blinked to find Artimus holding a wooden blade to his neck.

"Again," Artimus said, picking up the sword and handing it back to Veron.

Veron hesitated before making a move. He pretended like he was swinging on the right but then switched to the left and aimed for Artimus' legs. Artimus again swung his sword simultaneously and connected with Veron's weapon about halfway down the dull edge. This time, Veron was ready and held onto the sword tightly, but the force from Artimus' blow pinned it against Veron's body, preventing him from attacking. While the blades engaged, Artimus stepped behind Veron with one leg and used his forearm to push against his shoulder. With nowhere to move his feet, Veron fell backward and dropped his weapon. He looked up and found Artimus standing over him with a sword held to his neck once more.

"Again," Artimus said.

What am I sposta do? Veron thought, feeling helpless.

Trying a new approach, Veron jabbed at Artimus' chest, but Artimus stepped to the side, pushing the sword out of the way with a light parry.

His back is undefended. Here's my chance!

Veron moved to strike at Artimus' back, but the older man was too fast for him. Their swords connected again. As Veron tried to think of how to get back into position, a punch landed in the side. The impact took his breath away as he dropped his sword and fell to the ground. Above him, the sword was held at his neck.

Artimus lowered his weapon and helped Veron to his feet. "Why do you think my defense worked better than yours?" he asked.

"Defense?" Veron said, struggling to catch his breath. "That wasn't defense. That was offense!"

Artimus cocked his head and raised an eyebrow. "Was it though?"

Veron's face was red. "Yeah, you attacked me!"

"In fighting, the most important part of defense is to prevent yourself from getting hit. There's no better way to keep from getting hit than by preventing your opponent from being able to attack in the first place."

"So, instead of defending, I should just attack the other person?" Veron asked.

"No, you must defend yourself first. But if your defense is simply parrying blows out of the way, your situation will never improve. Instead, if your opponent attempts to strike, you should counter their attack. This not only prevents them from hitting you but can also put you in a position where you may be able to strike back. A sword fight shouldn't be a long, grueling battle where opponents trade blows back and forth. Ideally, it should be two or three moves intended to disarm the other. Let's try again while you defend. I'm going to attack slowly, and I want you to stop me by countering my attack. Aim a bit above the hilt and then stop."

The moves began. Artimus swung at Veron, and Veron met the sword with his own, pushing Artimus' out of the way. Each repetition grew faster, but Veron kept up. Artimus varied the direction of his attacks, and Veron found his counter strikes left Artimus exposed each time. Soon, Artimus put sequences together in a row, growing to four or five moves at a time. Even though Veron was still hit often, the more they repeated the movements, the better he got.

"Good, now I want you to add something to it," Artimus said. "When fighting someone with a longer weapon—like a sword—the best way to prevent them from hitting you is to get in close, so they don't have room to swing. This will give you the chance to follow up with a shorter weapon like a dagger or a fist. Now, I want you to do what you have been, but step in as you swing."

Artimus began again, repeating the previous exercise while Veron focused on stepping as he swung.

"Yeah, I can see it!" Veron said, his eyes wide with excitement. "Not only are you open for me to attack, but you don't have room to come at me."

"Exactly."

Sweat dripped off Veron's body. His arms, legs, and sides ached from all the blows they had taken, and his mind was tired of continually anticipating sword movements. *It's more challenging than I thought it would be,* Veron thought with a grin on his face, looking forward to more.

* * *

After four days of practicing stances and defense, every muscle in Veron's body ached when he moved. Dark, purple-colored bruises covered him from the punishment of training. Despite the soreness, he woke up eager each day.

"Today, we work on striking," Artimus said as they gathered in the training room.

This is it! Veron thought. *It's what I've been waiting for!*

Veron picked up his sword. The wooden hilt no longer felt foreign in his hand. His painful blisters were beginning to harden, and his arms were slowly strengthening.

"But before we do so—the positura," Artimus said.

Veron's excitement diminished. Artimus completed the sequences with ease, but Veron struggled as always.

"Striking requires coordination, speed, and power. Any one of these missing will result in your death," Artimus said as he walked to the hanging log in the corner of the room, having given Veron only a brief moment to rest. "We're going to practice each angle of attack from each of the five stances you learned. This log will be your target. I'll demonstrate."

Artimus faced the log in dragon position and delivered strikes one after another. His form was perfect. Smooth, powerful swings punished the log as he showed off his taut muscles.

I have a long way to go if I want to be like that one day, Veron thought.

Artimus moved out of the way. "Your turn." Veron stepped up. His pulse quickened as his muscles flexed in anticipation. "Dragon stance," Artimus said, and Veron followed. "Diagonal right."

Veron stepped in and swung diagonally down from the right. As he connected with the log, its solid form reverberated up his arm, the blow leaving a small dent in the log.

"Again," Artimus said.

Veron swung again.

155

"Tapping your opponent with a sword will do nothing but get you killed. When you strike, use your body. Swing with power! Again!"

Veron attacked and put all his body into it. He grunted, and the dull thud of the log answered back.

"Other side. Go!"

Veron continued through all the moves, doing several strikes of each type.

"Great," Artimus said. "Now, do the same from horn."

Veron cycled through the strikes from each of the five stances. He finished tired and panting, but his heart beat strong.

In the afternoon, Veron groaned as he sank to his knees in the garden and began pulling weeds.

"Are you going to live?" Artimus said, glancing at Veron with a smirk.

"I'm fine. I just feel . . ." Veron rolled his arm around, testing how it felt. ". . . like I'm going to die."

The old man laughed as he crouched nimbly and worked on his own section.

A day filled with practicing striking had left Veron's body in shambles. His back screamed as he bent over, his upper legs were sore when he squatted, and his arms could barely pull weeds out of the ground. He longed to take a while to rest, but Artimus insisted he help in the garden.

"Did you enjoy being in the Shadow Knights?" Veron asked, trying to take his mind off of his soreness as he pruned the dead leaves of a verquash stalk. Artimus stopped his motion and looked over. "I know you said you wanted to live a quiet life and turned them down at first. Did you end up liking it?"

Artimus nodded. "I did." He returned to his weeds. "After I lost my family, they became my new one."

"Was the fighting fun?"

"No, fighting is never *fun*. But it was purposeful, and I enjoyed that. We saved lives, and we made a difference."

"What was your favorite part?"

Artimus allowed his knees to sink into the dirt as he stopped working and sat in thought, staring absently in the distance. "I enjoyed the teaching. Although I still mourned my son, Archer, I found the boys and girls we trained became like sons and daughters to me. I put everything I had into developing them and helping them learn—especially after becoming the Shadow Master. The desire for them to succeed drove me every day to wake up and work hard." He returned to the garden and focused on the weeds again. "I had been missing it."

"The teaching?" Veron asked. "Until I came along?"

His teacher held a clod of dirt attached to a bundle of clover. "Yes. Whenever I teach, I feel as if I'm passing along a part of myself to live on in someone else," Artimus said.

"Thank you," Veron said. "For taking me in. For not giving up on me."

"You're welcome."

"It's good too, the passing along of yourself, because . . . as old as you are, you probably won't even be able to walk down the stairs much longer." Veron pursed his lips together with a sideways grin.

Artimus' eyes widened as his mouth dropped open. Suddenly, an explosion of dirt hit Veron in the forehead, sending him reeling backward. After wiping the sediment from his face, he found Artimus bent over laughing.

"Oh no, you didn't!" Veron said, sputtering dirt from his mouth.

He jumped up and threw clumps of weeds at the older man, who deftly moved and dodged. Both teacher and student circled the garden, using the plants as shields as they took turns hurling weeds and clods of dirt at each other. Laughter bounced off the walls as Veron forgot about his soreness and reveled in the moment.

16

Offerdom

On a windy and overcast day, Veron was stocking the food display outside Morgan's grocery when he greeted two men entering the shop. They spent some time with Morgan and left shortly after, one man carrying all the food and walking behind the other.

"It's such a shame," Morgan said, shaking his head as Veron entered to join him.

"What is?" Veron asked.

"Slavery. It's awful and unfair."

Veron's forehead wrinkled. "Are you talkin' about that guy's servant?" Veron's eyes grew wide. "He was a slave?"

"Well, legally, he's a 'servant of justice,' but the title is misleading. Do you know the difference between a servant and a slave, Veron?"

"A servant is someone who gets paid, and a slave doesn't."

"That's part of it. A servant serves willingly. He's an employee who's paid for his work and can choose to stop at any time. It's tougher for the master to mistreat or abuse them because they could leave if he does. A slave serves similarly, but they're not there by choice. They don't earn money for their work, and they can't leave because they're owned. Masters often keep slaves in check through abuse and intimidation."

"Isn't slavery illegal in Feldor?" Veron asked.

"Yes, it is. It's criminal to take someone and force them into slavery, but did you notice the man's metal anklet?"

Veron shook his head.

"When people can't pay their debts or commit crimes, they're thrown into prison. The city often doesn't want to feed and take care of them indefinitely, so a common practice is to sell their labor rights. They become a 'servant,' but because it's against their will, in practice, they are slaves. These prisoners turned servants are identified by an anklet of metal on their left legs."

"Why don't they just run away?"

"The Department of Labor keeps track when they're sold. They register who they were sold to, where they're from, a list of collateral names, and brand them with a number. If a runaway is found anywhere in the kingdom, they're put to death."

Veron scratched his head. "What do you mean by collateral names?" he asked.

"A list of family . . . friends . . . anyone important to them. If someone runs away or rebels, anyone on their list can be killed. It's an awful thing to threaten, but it keeps them in line."

Veron's eyes grew wide. "Wow! Well, I guess they were prisoners to begin with, so isn't it their fault if they killed someone or something?"

"Technically, yes," Morgan said. "But how would you feel if you were hungry and got caught stealing a loaf of bread only to find yourself sold into slavery for the rest of your life?"

Veron swallowed hard. *I didn't think about that. As tough as I've had it, I still have a lot to be thankful for. At least I've always been free,* he thought.

Veron left Morgan in the shop and returned to the chilly air to continue stocking the display. While he focused on his work, footsteps approached behind him.

"Hey, street trash!" a voice said from the street.

Veron's stomach dropped. He knew the voice. He fought to stay calm as he turned around to see Slash, Coffin, and Bruiser. It had been several weeks since his run-in with them, but his side hurt as he remembered the beating he'd received.

"Whatcha doin' here?" Coffin asked. "You stealin' from this shop? You can't possibly be workin' here!"

Veron's body ached to run. His instinct told him to go inside and hide, but he forced his feet to stay planted where they were. He breathed in deeply, puffing out his chest as he stood. "Guys, I don't want any trouble. I'm just tryin' to work." He tried to look as solid as a stone while he fought to keep his legs from shaking.

"Looks like you've plenty of food to give us now!" Coffin said, eyeing the produce on display.

"Is there a problem here?" Morgan asked, stepping out of the doorway with the broom in hand.

The three thugs stared at the grocer and paused. None of them cowered back or started to leave, but they stopped advancing.

"No, no problem," Slash replied. "We're just saying hello to our old friend Veron here."

"Well, Veron is working now," Morgan said. "So, unless you guys are looking to make a purchase, I'm going to ask you to move along."

The three men moved slowly down the street, taking turns glancing back at Veron.

"Are you okay?" Morgan asked Veron when the others were out of earshot.

"Yeah, I'm fine. It's just some guys I've run into before." He grabbed his side absently.

"Why don't you work inside? I'll cover the street today."

I hoped I wouldn't see them anymore, Veron thought as he went inside the shop. Deep down, he knew running into them was inevitable, but seeing Morgan stand up for him was a welcome and unfamiliar feeling.

* * *

After being introduced to the basics of fighting, Veron settled into a new training routine incorporating sword work into his other familiar exercises. In sparring matches, Veron was no longer told what to do. He had to decide on his own when to strike and defend.

Artimus was unfailingly ready with a word of wisdom. "Always be moving! If you're standing still, you're dead." Veron moved his feet and delivered a weak swing. "Your strike should be difficult for your opponent to anticipate," Artimus said after blocking it and locking up their swords. "Don't hesitate to bind the opponent's sword." Veron freed himself only for Artimus to knee him in the gut and knock him to the ground. "I cannot emphasize enough the importance of grappling."

As the weeks ticked by, wiether gradually turned to suether. The weather improved, and so did Veron's skill with the sword. Before long, they set the wooden weapons aside and began to use steel. Even with dull blades, Veron worried he would hurt the old man, but he discovered quickly that he should be more concerned for himself. Artimus' skills were still far beyond his own. Every sparring match eventually ended either when Veron lost his weapon or when a sword rested against his neck.

While they kept up training with the sword, Artimus incorporated other weapons into the mix—bows and arrows, knives, staffs, shields, axes—working through the unique strategies of each of them.

Veron was ready for whatever Artimus threw at him. Eager to

take on any new challenge, he gave it his all every time.

* * *

"Have you ever been here before?" Artimus asked as they crested the hill, revealing the extent of the ruins.

Veron marveled as he stood with his mouth open. Breathing heavily from the ascent of the hill, he shook his head. The remains of a large circular stone structure stood before him. The floor was mostly intact but had lines of green where weeds filled the cracks. Around the perimeter were dozens of columns twice as tall as him. The pillars were smooth and flared outward with curving designs at both the tops and bottoms. Several had cracks in them, most had moss blanketing the north side, and some had chunks that had fallen out. A few columns looked to be missing entirely. The stone steps leading up to the structure had been reclaimed by nature many years before.

Back down the sloping hill to the east lay the road. On the west, the ground dropped off where the Benevorre River churned white through jagged rocks far below. North of the ruins stood the city of Karad with its tall walls and massive gates, and behind it, the Korob Mountains jutted out of the forested plains in the distance.

"What is this place?" Veron asked. "I've seen something up here from the city but never knew what it was."

"This was once an offerdom," Artimus replied. "A dome used to cover it, but it's long collapsed." Veron ran his hand along one of the columns, imagining how it used to hold up a stone roof. "When Norshand ruled Terrenor hundreds of years ago, they erected many across the land. People were required to come here to give an offering to the King of Norshand during the premweek of wiether each year."

"What sort of offering?"

"Livestock, grain, wool . . . whatever they had. The offering was supposed to be an expression of thanks to the king for his protection. If the proctors accepting the offerings felt someone gave too little, they were punished."

Veron raised his eyebrows.

"That's right," Artimus said. "Imprisonment, cutting off of hands, taking children, some were even killed—beheaded in front of everyone on that stone right there." Artimus pointed to a flat stone that looked like a seat, worn smooth from the winds of time.

Veron's stomach churned. *Taking children away for not giving a large enough offering?* "But how did they know what someone could afford to give?"

Artimus shook his head. "They couldn't. They'd judge a person by their look, but everyone dressed as a peasant to make themselves seem poor. As a result, the proctors randomly selected those with weak offerings and made examples of them."

Veron shuddered.

"It was a dark time for Terrenor. Norshandic rule was brutal and harsh. Cities collapsed. Disease ran rampant. The divide between nobles and commoners was greater than ever, but no one had the strength or organization to do anything about it."

"What happened to Norshand? Did people fight back eventually?" Veron asked.

Artimus removed his sword from the scabbard on his back and gazed at it while he faced north. The ruby in the hilt glinted as it caught the young light of the sun.

"Around three hundred years ago, the Shadow Knights were formed. United in their oppression, the original six knights made it their mission to free Terrenor. They first eliminated the five regents who held power through the land. Then, they took the fight directly to Daratill, where they killed King Vitrion."

"Just them?" Veron asked with a look of astonishment. "No army or anything?"

Artimus shifted his weight but didn't answer the question. "With the king dead, the lands were free to establish their own sovereign borders. Feldor, Rynor, and Tarphan formed independent kingdoms, and Norshand, who changed their name to Norshewa, was reduced to the land past the Korob Mountains."

"Wow, I never knew all of that," Veron said as he stared at the mountains. "Is that why we all speak Common Norshic?"

"That's right, all except Tarphan, who reverted to their native Tarphic language." A stiff wind picked up and rose over the hill to ruffle their clothes. "The mission of the Shadow Knights became maintaining the freedom of Terrenor and preventing oppression and injustice. This ruin serves as a reminder to me of what we fought for—why we existed."

Holding his sword, Artimus faced out and stared into the distance. Veron imagined people lined up to give an offering, afraid that what they gave may not be enough.

"I heard that Bale has taken Bromhill," Artimus said. Veron's hair stood on end. "Rynor's capital stood for hundreds of years. Now it's just one more thing to fall under Bale's control. If he conquers Feldor, these offerdoms will be the least of our worries."

Veron swallowed. "Do you need to . . . I don't know . . . go and kill him or something? To fulfill the prophecy?" The only response Veron received was the whistle of the wind. "When is it supposed to happen? Is he coming soon?"

Artimus continued to stare in silence. "I don't know," he said finally. "There was . . ." He stopped as he looked to the ground and fidgeted with his sword. "The woman who Dreamed the prophecy about Bale . . . there was something else she saw."

"What?" Veron stepped closer, wary of Artimus' tone.

"She said that after the shadow knight kills Bale, the knight will die of his wounds."

A shiver ran through Veron as he held his breath and pictured Artimus dying over Bale's body.

Suddenly, the old man turned and walked back to the center of the ruin. "While we're here, we'll train. First, the positura."

Shrugging off the words of doom, Veron nodded as he drew his sword from over his shoulder. He stood positioned next to Artimus as they began.

Artimus sat on his bed after wishing Veron goodnight and stretched his arms over his head. He bent to the side and groaned as the muscles over his ribs pulled. *The boy's doing well. There's something in him . . . a skill level not even his father had,* he thought.

He leaned over to blow out the candle but stopped as his gaze rested on the chest by his bed. His heart sped up as he stared. Artimus pushed himself off of the bed and knelt in front of the box. Running his hand over the thick wooden lid, he felt the intricate designs with each fingertip before reaching under his shirt. The small metal key felt heavy in his hand as he pulled it out. After inserting it into the keyhole, he hesitated. Seconds turned into minutes as he remained motionless, kneeling on the floor.

No. I can't do that to him, Artimus thought as he put the key back around his neck.

17

Higher Education

Three books lay open in front of Brixton as he sat at the long table in the library with his head in his hands. The first year of school at King's Academy drew to a close in a week, and he struggled. The classes were more challenging than he expected. Although he had been diligent with his studies, his grades hovered slightly above failing. The courses on history and writing were easy, but mathematics and economics gave him trouble.

Two important assignments loomed in economics. One was a project, assigned weeks before. The other was an examination grade—the culmination of everything learned during the year. Brixton hadn't finished the project yet, but he had worked out his ideas and gathered his data. What had consumed most of his time was preparing for the examination.

Brixton had difficulty remembering things. He wasn't a forgetful person who couldn't remember names or memories, but he had trouble recalling concepts. He managed to remember recent topics during the year, but in preparing for the year-end exam, he found he had forgotten much of what they'd covered.

Brixton flipped through pages and sighed. *I'm never going to remember all of this stuff,* he thought.

Although Brixton initially fought his father on the idea of coming to King's, his short-lived ambition of owning a bakery died as soon as he saw the other students from affluent families at the Academy. Baking bread and selling it at the market would never be able to pay for the prestige and power the families there held. Motivated by the desire to make a name for himself and represent his family, he wanted to succeed, both for his sake as well as his father's.

Brixton traded the book he read for a thick one titled *Tarphanic Economic Theory.* It had a sweet musky smell and was so old the binding was coming off. Needing a break, he massaged the back of his neck as he lifted his head from the table and stretched it to each side while he looked around.

Walls and rows of dusty, leather books surrounded the four long tables in the center of the library, and sunlight streamed in from the tall windows on each wall. Five other students were scattered around the tables looking in a similar state as Brixton with stacks of books and papers littered in front of them. At the other end of his table sat a boy from his class, Magnus Hampton. Magnus rubbed his chin as he pored over his reading. His father, Byron Hampton, was the High Lord of Trade, making the Hamptons one of the wealthiest families in Feldor. Magnus had a group of friends from Felting who he hung around with, and Brixton found his popularity intimidating.

I wonder what he's working on? He leaned in the boy's direction to see *Demands of the Trade Economy* as the title on one of the closed books. *He's studying for the same class! Maybe I should ask how he's doing?* Brixton slid his chair back as he stood to walk over. *Does he even know who I am though?*

"Hey, Magnus," Brixton said with a small wave as he stood in front of the boy, keeping his voice low.

Magnus glanced up with a questioning look on his face. Dressed identical to Brixton, he wore the King's uniform of a gray and blue tunic with brown wool pants. His hair was also short and blond. Someone could easily mistake the two boys for brothers.

"I'm Brixton. I'm in your mathematics and economics classes."

"Yes, I know who you are," Magnus said with a smile as he leaned back in his chair.

"What are you working on?" Brixton asked.

"Right now, studying for economics, but I need to stop so I can work on my project. How have you been doing? Are you ready for next week?" Magnus indicated to the chair opposite him with his hand.

Brixton eagerly took the seat. "Hardly. I don't get half of the math equations we're supposed to understand, and it seems I've forgotten all the topics we learned in economics over the year. I'll probably be studying straight for most of the next week."

"Yeah, the economics is pretty tough," Magnus said, bobbing his head as he spoke.

I doubt he finds it tough. He's the top student in the Academy. He's probably just saying that for my benefit, Brixton thought.

"What I'm worried about is the project," Magnus said. "I've thought some about it but keep putting it off. I have no idea what he's even looking for, much less what I'm going to do it on."

Brixton perked up. *I may be close to failing the class, but at least I have a great project topic.*

"Are you finished with yours? What did you do?" Magnus asked.

Brixton squirmed in his seat at the question. Professor Hartershire asked them not to work in groups on their projects. He wanted each student to have an independent idea that reflected their own work. *I don't want to violate any rules in a class where I'm already struggling.*

"Sorry, I didn't mean to make you uncomfortable. Don't worry about it," Magnus said. "I was just thinking of hearing yours as an example—something to get my brain thinking in the right direction. I have no clue what he wants."

I'm sure it's not a big deal. It could help him get started.

"You said you need help in mathematics, right?" Magnus asked. "I have a good grasp of that subject. If you like, we could get together to study?"

Brixton's eyes lit up. "Yeah, that would be great! Thanks!" *I can't believe Magnus is going to study with me!*

"Don't worry about it." Magnus began to collect his books. "I've gotta go for now . . . need to figure out a project topic. I hear some people have already started turning theirs in. Do you at least have an idea of what types of things Hartershire is looking for . . . to point me in the right direction? 'Research an economic trend and show how it impacts the kingdom of Feldor' is pretty general."

Brixton fidgeted again until his face brightened suddenly. "Okay, I don't know everything he's looking for, but I wanted to think of something that had a practical application. An idea the king, or whoever, could even potentially use," Brixton said, lowering his voice even more as he leaned in. "You know how sometimes kings and lords institute taxes to make money for the kingdom?"

Magnus rubbed his chin as he listened. "Yeah, my father just issued a tax on imported goods not long ago. I think it was to raise money for road improvements."

"Good example. So, I wondered . . . If you raise taxes, can you get to a point where it's so high that people change their habits to avoid it? And if their habits change, resulting in fewer taxes collected, can a tax end up bringing in less money than if it never existed?"

Magnus blinked and sat up straight. "Interesting. What'd you find?"

"I went to the Department of the Treasury and pulled financial records from the city for the last fifty years. Do you know what I found?" Brixton asked with a grin on his face.

"What?"

"For business taxes, there is a level of increase at which businesses start to close down, resulting in lower city income. Also, for sales taxes, there is a percentage at which people buy less, resulting in lower income for Felting."

"That's incredible!" Magnus said as his face lit up. "I bet that would be useful for the city lords to know."

"Yeah, I think so. I'm counting on it to bring my grade up because I'm not expecting good things from the exam," Brixton said as he sat back. "Anyway, I'm sure you'll come up with something. Your grade's probably so high that if you didn't turn anything in, you'd probably still pass anyway."

"I wish," Magnus said. "Well, thanks for sharing. That helps get me thinking." He finished stacking his books and stood up. "How about Marketday afternoon to study together? Will that work? I already have plans for Weekterm."

Brixton sat up straight and looked eagerly at the boy. "Sure, Marketday sounds great. I'll see you then."

This is great! With Magnus's help, I should be able to learn what I need. Plus, it will be nice to be friends with him. Who knows what kind of doors that might open down the road!

***

Brixton looked at the clock on the wall of the library. Marketday had arrived. Magnus was supposed to meet him four hours past noon, but the time had come and gone. His mathematics book was open, and he'd been staring at the gibberish for a while, waiting on Magnus to help him make sense of it. *I hope he hasn't forgotten. I really need his help with this,* he thought.

171

Brixton spent Weekterm studying economics and got about halfway through the write-up for his project, which was due the next day along with the math exam. Brixton picked at his fingernails while he waited. His leg bounced under the table. The pressure of the pending assignments left an ache in his chest that he was eager to be rid of.

After another few minutes, Brixton stacked his books in his bag and left the library, deciding to find Magnus. He followed the stone path in the direction of the dormitory. The warm afternoon sun shone at an angle, forcing Brixton to squint as he walked.

In the dormitory, Brixton knocked on the door to Magnus's room, but no one answered. *I wonder if he fell asleep.*

Footsteps sounded behind him, and Brixton turned, hopeful. Instead of Magnus, it was Vincent, one of Magnus' friends, walking down the hall. He was tall and built like a soldier with a permanent scowl on his face. Brixton usually tried to steer clear of him.

"Hey, Vincent, have you seen Magnus?" Brixton asked.

"No idea," the large boy grumbled.

Brixton hung his head, starting to get worried.

"Did you check at Fetzer's?" Vincent asked.

Fetzer's was the tavern across the way from the Academy—one of the popular hangout locations for students wanting to forget their troubles or avoid their work. *I sure hope he's not there right now,* Brixton thought. "No, we were supposed to study math together for tomorrow's exam," he replied.

Vincent exhaled a short laugh through his nose. "I doubt he's studying math. He's been good on that for a while."

A sinking feeling came to Brixton. *What if he never intended to study with me? Why would he say he would though? That makes no sense.* His heart pounded at the thought of studying alone. *I put it off until today. I'm going to be in trouble if I don't have someone to help me. I still need to finish the last part of my project tonight too!*

Brixton hurried out of the dormitory to head to the main class-room building. A few afternoon classes were wrapping up, and several students dotted the halls.

He passed Professor Hartershire's room and glanced inside. Magnus stood next to the professor, deep in conversation. *There he is!* Brixton breathed a sigh of relief and stepped into the room.

"Incredible!" the professor said. "I know several people who'll be interested to see this." He held a stack of papers in his hands as he spoke with Magnus.

That's great, Brixton thought. *He must have come up with a good project, after all.*

"How did you come up with the idea?" Hartershire asked.

Magnus stood tall as he spoke. "I've always been fascinated by our tax system, but sometimes I wonder the effect it has on the people of the city. Some taxes may simply be too much for people to bear. I've always said it to my father, but he never wants to listen to me."

As Brixton listened, his stomach churned. *What's he saying? What's his project?*

Professor Hartershire laughed. "Oh, I'm sure. Byron never likes taking advice from others. I know he never did from me."

Magnus continued, "If we tax people too high, is it possible they can't pay them? If that happens, do we end up losing money for the city when the intent of increasing taxes was to make more?"

Brixton felt dizzy. He rested his hand against the wall. *No, he didn't!*

"The data was easy to evaluate," Magnus said. "I pulled the financial records for the city and looked for trends. The results were interesting to see."

"This is incredible, Magnus," the professor said. "It's just the type of thing I was looking for in this project and is exactly what I'd expect a student of your caliber to come up with."

Brixton wanted to speak up, but his voice didn't work. He felt like he'd been punched in the gut. The only sound he managed to make was a gasp. Magnus and the professor turned.

"Ah, Brixton, it's good to see you," the professor said. "I hope you're ready for the exam tomorrow. I know you need a good result if you're going to get that grade up."

Brixton locked eyes with Magnus. His teeth clenched, and his fists balled. Inside he battled hurt and fear from the betrayal. Magnus tilted his head back and looked down his nose at Brixton as if daring him to speak up.

Hartershire continued to address Brixton, "I'll be interested to see your project too. You've had plenty of time to work on it, so hopefully, you've come up with a good idea."

He's not going to admit that it was my project. Very well . . . I'll have to do it. Brixton faced the professor and opened his mouth to speak, but his words caught. *But he specifically asked us not to share ideas. How am I supposed to explain how he stole my idea without admitting I told him?* The sick feeling returned as Brixton stood, wavering. *I'll say it was my idea first! But what if Magnus accuses me of stealing it from him?* Brixton's breath quickened as he realized his predicament. *Who's the professor more likely to believe came up with the idea?*

Magnus grinned smugly.

Brixton stood in silence with his mouth open. After a moment, he hung his head and muttered a few incomprehensible words as he left the room.

The hallway spun as Brixton fled. His breath came to him in heaving spurts. *It's not right! How could he do that? He was going to help me! Wasn't he? He's rising while I'm falling . . . Father was right. That's how people get ahead.*

He yelled a frustrated cry as he stormed out the front doors of the building. Magnus had won, and Brixton was in trouble. He had one day to go, and he needed to come up with a completely new project idea if he didn't want to fail out of school. Brixton swallowed hard as a fresh wave of fear flowed through him.

I'm going to fail, and Father's going to kill me.

18

Path to Medicine

Coming out of the woods, Chelci was able to view the city of Karad fully for the first time. The walls were shorter, and the size was smaller than Felting, but it was gigantic compared to Nasco, where she'd spent the previous year.

Now that the woods were behind them, the horses had more room to walk next to each other for the final stretch of countryside. Coming alongside Nevi, Chelci asked, "When's the last time you came here?"

Nevi glanced at her before looking back at the city. "Almost two years ago. I came with a friend who wanted to buy some fabric," she said.

"Why go all the way to the city? I thought you made your own in Nasco?"

"We do, but sometimes people want something new. What we make isn't as tightly woven as what we can buy in Karad."

"Do you think we'll be able to find the herbs we need?"

Nevi's mouth tightened. "I sure hope so . . . for Kyla's sake."

"What will you do if she doesn't recover?" Chelci asked.

"She will," Nevi said quickly. "If she doesn't . . . we'll have to find another teacher."

Usually, they had a healthy supply of herbs and minerals for healing on hand in the village, but some items were difficult to come by. When the village teacher, Kyla, took ill and didn't recover after weeks, Nevi decided they needed medicine Nasco didn't have. She volunteered to travel to Karad and, since school was temporarily on hold, she dragged Chelci along.

Over the last year, Chelci had been in school with Kyla, but whenever there was time, Russell had her doing all sorts of physical tasks to get in shape for the Academy, even though it was still three years away. She chopped wood, ran a trail through the forest, and helped him move heavy materials whenever he could find something that needed doing. She couldn't forget his motivational words: "If you're going to be there, I don't want you getting killed or—even worse—embarrassing me."

The training was hard but left her feeling invigorated. Still, she welcomed the break to rest and join Nevi on the trip. Early that morning, Chelci and Nevi saddled two horses and left before daylight. Finally, close to midday, they arrived at the city.

They entered Karad through a gate at the east end of the wall. Dismounting their horses and leading them by the reins as they walked the street, Chelci's senses tingled from being back in a city. The sounds and smells felt familiar yet oddly foreign.

Someone in the crowd caught her eye. *Is that Jackson?* Chelci thought.

The boy stood outside of a blacksmith shop. His hair and build reminded her of her brother, but it wasn't him. Her heart pounded as she laughed to herself.

He's not going to be here in Karad. The memory of her brother gave her a pang of regret, wishing she could be at home with him. *I wonder how Emma is? I wonder if Mother has softened any?* Chelci was enjoying her life in Nasco, but as she walked the city streets, she thought longingly of home.

Nevi scanned the shops as they walked, eventually turning left onto another broad street and stopping in front of a cart loaded down with dried herbs.

"What do you need?" the surly vendor asked.

"I'm looking for some herbs," Nevi said, pulling out a list. "Toad-grass, antispurn petals, baltam powder, turnfoil root, and barkleaf fungus."

The man dug through the baskets and drawers on his cart to collect what she needed. "No barkleaf," he said as he rummaged through a drawer. "Haven't seen any of that in a while. It's not grown around these parts."

Nevi frowned. "Do you know of anywhere I can find it?"

The man rubbed his chin as he looked down the street. "There's a shop a short way away that sometimes has rare items. You could check there?" He gave them instructions on how to get there.

Nevi handed the man a small nugget of copper, which he weighed on a scale, giving her a few small coins in return. "Is that it?" she asked as she inspected the coins. "I didn't think the herbs would be so much. Is there any way you could give us a deal?"

"I'm afraid not," the man said. "I already gave you the 'deal' pricing. Times are tight, and those items aren't easy to come by."

Nevi hung her head as she sighed. "Okay, thanks for your help." She tucked the herbs into a bag the horse carried. "Come on, Elise." They continued down the main street of the city, following the directions the man gave.

"What's barkleaf fungus," Chelci asked as they walked.

"It's a blue mushroom that grows at the base of barkleaf trees. You can't find them around here, but they're plentiful down south or over the mountains in Rynor."

"What do you use it for?"

"If you boil it in water and combine with honey and a few of the other herbs, it has powerful healing properties. I've seen someone in far worse shape than Kyla recover practically overnight after drinking a barkleaf elixir."

Chelci worried about her teacher. Even though she already knew many of the things taught at the school, she enjoyed the chance to make friends, and Kyla was kind—much nicer than her old teacher, Margaret.

After turning down a few streets, they approached the store they sought, where a man with a broad smile met them outside.

"Good day to you, young ladies! What beautiful horses you have. You look like you've been on quite a journey. Can I interest you in some fresh fruit or ripe vegetables?" he asked.

"No. Thank you, but we don't need that today. Are you Morgan?" Nevi asked.

"Indeed, I am! How can I help you?"

"We've traveled all day from Nasco, a village in the woods. We're looking for barkleaf fungus. Someone mentioned you might have some?"

Morgan's broad grin somehow grew even larger. "As chance would have it, I do! I purchased a bag from a Tarphan trader last month. I bet I'm the only shop in Karad that has any."

Nevi's eyes brightened. She and Chelci tied up their horses to a post and followed the friendly shopkeeper inside. Rows of food filled the cozy store. The aisles contained half-filled crates stacked askew as if Morgan had been organizing.

"Please excuse the mess. I have a boy who helps me in the shop, but he doesn't work here on Postday, so I'm a little behind in stocking. Wait here for just a moment." The man stepped into a back room and returned with a lumpy sack, which he set on a counter. "How many do you need?"

"At least three." Nevi looked over the bunches of mushrooms and selected three clusters that were a darker shade of blue than the others. After she was content with her choices, she turned to Morgan as she pulled the coins from her pocket. "How much?"

"Barkleaf fungus isn't cheap. That's gonna be one argen five tid."

Nevi paled and turned to Chelci as she breathed in quickly through her nose. "I—I don't have that. I didn't expect things to cost so much."

"I'm sorry," Morgan said. "That's barely above what I paid when I bought them.

"Can we do without it?" Chelci asked.

Nevi swallowed and shook her head. "I don't think Kyla will live without it. The other herbs help, but the barkleaf is what she needs most," she told her.

"Can we trade something?" Nevi looked down at her clothing, then at Chelci before walking outside to their horses. "The other herbs, maybe?" Chelci suggested as she followed.

Nevi shook her head as she searched through their bags. "We need them to work together. Plus, all of them together aren't worth that much."

"What about a horse?" Chelci said.

Nevi froze with her hand on her horse's back. "I've known Listle and Nora for most of my life." She took a deep breath as she gazed at the horses.

"Tell you what," Morgan interrupted as he joined them, carrying the blue fungus bunches, which he handed to Nevi. "Why don't we consider this a loan. If you make it back to Karad sometime, and if you have the coins, come and visit me."

Nevi's mouth opened to speak, but nothing came out. "I—I—Thank you!" she finally sputtered. She took the mushrooms and hugged the grocer. "It may be a while before I'm back, but I'll make sure to return."

"And if you don't, consider it a gift," the shopkeeper said.

Chelci and Nevi unleashed their horses and walked through the streets back toward the gate where they had entered the city. "Maybe people in the city aren't all mean and selfish?" Nevi said.

"Yeah, maybe not," Chelci replied.

As the street narrowed, Chelci led her horse in front so they could fit down the alley. At an intersection, a boy around her age carrying a large stone on his shoulder careened around the corner and almost collided into her.

"I'm so sorry!" the boy said. "I didn't know you were there. I should have slowed before coming around the corner. Are you okay?"

The boy breathed heavily but didn't seem phased by the weight of the rock or trying to talk while winded, despite the layer of sweat inching down his shirt. He was tall with bushy, brown hair and had a disarming smile.

"That's ok," she said, blushing. "I'm fine."

His eye twinkled as he gave an awkward half-wave before continuing down the alley. Chelci stood still, trying to steady her weak knees as she watched him go, enchanted by the brief encounter.

"Come on," Nevi said, shooing Chelci forward as she blocked the way. "It's gonna be dark by the time we get back as it is. We don't want to dawdle any longer here than we need to."

Chelci turned and proceeded along. They left the city and rode their horses along the path back to Nasco. The trip was long, taking the rest of the day and some of the night, but in all of that time, the only thing she could think about was the boy with the stone and the bushy hair.

19

Over the Years

Living and training with Artimus over the last four years had changed Veron. He could read and write with ease, and whenever he had free time, he pored through the books in Artimus' collection. After having read all of them multiple times, he used the money he earned to buy books he came across in the city. Eventually, he added dozens of new ones to Artimus' shelf.

No longer the small, thin boy who could barely hold up a sword, the years spent training had sculpted him into a young warrior. They had to replace the wooden striking log several times as his attacks grew stronger over time. When they traveled through the city at night, Veron was like a shadow, using darkness, distractions, and his ability to climb to move anywhere he wanted without being detected.

Despite his improvements in speed and strength, he still couldn't beat Artimus when they sparred. Veron consoled himself in the fact that the matches lasted longer, and after Artimus won, the old man was usually exhausted, which he never used to be.

Over time, Veron's salesmanship grew as well. He was engaging and warm to everyone who came by, and sales for the store grew so much that Morgan needed to find new food suppliers to keep up with the demand. After discovering the boy's skill with numbers, he raised Veron's pay from one to two tid per week and eventually up to three as he allowed Veron to handle more of the day-to-day business.

Life was good, but he still often wondered what his life would have been like if his father were still alive, or what Fend would have thought if he could see him now. Would he have learned to wield a sword if his father were alive to teach him? Would he have been able to stop the soldiers from killing Fend?

He sometimes thought of what it would be like to face Captain Mortinson in a duel. Imagining rows of people lined up, cheering him on, with Artimus shouting out pointers and his parents watching on with pride on their faces. At the end he'd disarm the captain and stand over him, the crowd roaring in applause behind him.

* * *

"Morgan could use more cabbage if you have any ready," Veron said as he arrived home on a chilly afternoon in the first week of wiether. "His other supplier has a beetle problem, so he needs all he can get."

"Sure, I have some that should be ready by next week, I think," Artimus said from his favorite chair in the sitting room where he read.

The last four years had not been kind to Artimus. His shoulders and skin sagged more than before, and his eyes looked heavy. Although he was prone to coughing fits and often groaned when he stood, Veron marveled at how the effects of his age seemed to disappear when he held a sword in his hand.

"Also," Veron said, his voice rising with excitement, "he wants to open a second store."

Artimus looked up from his book. "Really?"

"Yeah, he wants to open a new shop in East Fairren." Veron bounced on his feet as his arms swung by his side.

Artimus returned to his book. "That's a whole new type of customer. Good for him."

"Yeah, it is . . . and he asked me how I felt about running it."

His teacher looked up at him, cocking his head. "Really?" He stood. "What did you say?"

"I said yes! I know it's a big step, but I believe I can do it. He's applying to the Department of Commerce for a license this afternoon."

"That's exciting! When will it open?"

"In a couple of weeks, assuming everything goes as planned. He already has a place picked out."

Artimus beamed. His wrinkled face stretched taut as pride showed and a small tear formed in the corner of his eye. Veron had rarely seen him show emotion before. Artimus placed both hands on Veron's shoulders. "I'm proud of you, son," he said.

The word hit Veron like a hammer. Son. It felt like the words of a father. Through all the years of living and training with the older man, Veron had grown to see him as a father. He knew that as tough as Artimus was on him, he did love him like a son.

The last four years of training and learning had all led to this moment. *I can do it. I can run a store. I can live the life Fend told me to, and Artimus is the reason for it all. He saved me.*

Veron put his arms around Artimus, and they held in a tight embrace. Tears flowed from both of their eyes as Veron realized it was the first time he'd ever been hugged.

Lying in bed that night, Veron couldn't shut his mind off. *What doors will this new store open? Who knows where I can go from here! These last four years completely changed my life. Fend, I'm going to make you proud!* he thought, smiling.

Unable to sleep after lying in bed for hours, Veron decided to get up and go for a walk in the cool night air. He crept downstairs, trying not to disturb Artimus, but before he exited the front door, a sound from the training room drew his attention. A dim light shone in the room, so he inched through the kitchen to investigate. From the darkness of the doorway, Veron froze.

Artimus wore a hooded cloak Veron had never seen before. A candle filled the room with a dim light that flickered across the walls. Artimus held the ruby sword and performed some sort of training routine. At first, Veron thought it was the positura, just faster than usual, but he dismissed the idea after a moment. Artimus moved into a position and then attacked the air with a flurry of moves, one after the other. While executing the combination of positions and strikes, his feet were everywhere, stepping in and out, spinning around in a frantic pace.

A feeling of unease crept over Veron as the movements sped up. Artimus was already quick to begin with, but somehow, he moved even faster. Veron's heart raced, his breath quickening. *Something is wrong. This isn't possible,* he thought. He had never seen Artimus—or anyone—move that fast before. The sword moved like lightning.

After unleashing a seven-strike combination in the blink of an eye, Artimus leaped into the air. He flew higher than Veron thought humanly possible then fell to the ground with a final vertical strike where he stopped.

Veron's mouth hung open. *What was that?*

He ducked away, his heart beating wildly, afraid he saw something he was not supposed to. Panicking, he crept back to his room and lay in bed, unable to fall asleep.

20

Discovered

Raynor Fiero dodged between shoppers and horse-drawn carts on the crowded High Street. Annoyed by the commoners' presence, he grumbled as he walked, fighting the stress of all the things on his mind.

His son had been at King's Academy for the last four years and would arrive home in a week. When Brixton left, Raynor found him adequate at best, lacking drive, intuition, and the instincts it took to succeed. *I hope school whipped him into shape. I tried, unsuccessfully, to do so all his life. He needs to live up to the standard I built for our family rather than be an embarrassment,* he thought.

Another stress on his mind was his daughter, Mila, who would be of marrying age soon. She often spent time with Ashton, the son of a butcher on Karad Square. Ashton worked with his father, and Mila spent a lot of time at their shop. To prevent things from going too far with the lowly middle-class boy, one of Raynor's top priorities was finding a husband for her soon.

Oliver Marshall would have been a fine match, but he just married last year. One option was the Dearborn family. Jonathan Dearborn was a master mason and the guild leader for Karad. Their family was respectable, and he had a son around Mila's age.

If Raynor could choose anyone for Mila to marry, he wanted Magnus Hampton, the most eligible bachelor in all of Feldor. In one of the wealthiest families in the land, he was Brixton's age and currently at King's with him. He should be just old enough for marrying, but Raynor didn't have the pull he needed to influence a match like that.

Raynor entered the commerce office. A slightly overweight man with a grin on his face sat with Tucker as the clerk walked him through some paperwork. Their conversation indicated he was opening a new grocery. Raynor immediately disliked the man. *He smiles too much.*

He sat down in his office with the door closed and pulled out some ledgers—his personal finance records. Recently, his funds had fallen dangerously low, and he wanted to figure out what had caused it. As Lord of Commerce, he received a healthy income of one gold sol per week from the city, but he still kept his eyes open for ways to enhance his wealth.

For years, he had an arrangement with Lord Charles Marshall in the Treasury Department that served both of their interests. Marshall bought a failing iron ore mine several years back for next to nothing. To help him be profitable, Raynor fixed the price of iron, immediately increasing profits by over fifty percent. In return, Marshall skimmed some coins from the treasury to give to Raynor as payment.

Raynor also had arrangements with several shopkeepers who found themselves with unusually low license fees. The books stated the reasons for the low rates were "pre-existing agreements." The real reason was that they created an imbalance of favor he capitalized on. Raynor made sure the shopkeepers knew that if he failed to receive a substantial discount when he visited, they would find their fees increasing significantly.

When he checked his books, Raynor found that he hadn't received a payoff from Lord Marshall recently. *I'll need to pay him a visit soon.*

At dinner that night, Raynor and his family ate in silence. He looked around their large dining room, scowling at faded paint and chipped walls. They had the largest house in the city, but it took a lot of money to keep it up. The pressure to keep everything looking perfect weighed heavily on him. The considerable amount of money they had only went so far.

His wife and daughter sat across the table. Elenor was well attired, as always, in a fine silk dress, but recently, her face had begun to show more wrinkles, which the clothing did not fix. He scolded her to do something about it but had yet to see any changes.

"How was your day, dear?" Elenor asked their daughter.

"Oh, it was great!" Mila said, sitting up straight and smiling. "Ashton's father gave him the day off, and we went down to the river and skipped stones. The weather was beautiful, and we laughed the whole time!"

"I don't want you spending time with that boy," Raynor said before taking a drink.

Mila's mouth hung open. She looked back and forth between her mother and father. "What? Why not?"

Raynor slammed his goblet down on the table. "Because I said so!"

"Raynor," Elenor said in a soothing voice. "Is there a reason you feel this way about the boy? He seems to be very kind."

"Has he applied for a court permit?" Raynor asked, looking back and forth between his wife and daughter. He didn't need their lack of response to confirm what he already knew. "No, he hasn't. So, he shouldn't be spending time with you down by the river." Raynor grabbed the bread on the table and tore a chunk off of it. "He should be thrown into prison."

Feldor law dictated that anyone under the age of twenty wanting to spend time alone for the purpose of courting—outside of an arranged marriage—must have a court permit approved by the Department of City Affairs. Initiated by the upper class to prevent their children from falling in love with someone of a lesser station, the law was often ignored in practice, especially by the lower classes. Although seldom enforced, the penalty for courting without a permit was imprisonment.

"Father!" Mila said, pleading. "Please! You wouldn't! We're just friends."

"He's not good enough for you," Raynor told her. "He's not good enough for our family."

Mila's face turned red, and her arms were rigid by her side. She didn't speak or eat for the rest of the dinner.

As Raynor finished up eating, Renwick, their choreman, entered the dining room. "Sir, Lord Charles Marshall is here and has asked to meet with you."

Raynor drank the last of his wine and left his wife and daughter without saying a word. *Why would he be calling on me at home?* he thought.

Marshall waited by the front door, wearing a burgundy wool tunic and cape.

"Charles, this is a surprise," Raynor said.

"Yes, I apologize for showing up this late, but I have an issue that requires your attention. Would it be possible to speak somewhere out of the house?" Marshall asked, glancing around. "Your office, perhaps?"

"Of course." Raynor grabbed his cloak and followed him outside.

It was dark out, but lamps lit the stone paths that crisscrossed the wealthy neighborhood. Walking in silence, the two men pulled their collars up against the chilly air as thunder rumbled in the distance. Unfazed by the approaching storm, they arrived at Raynor's office a few minutes later. Once inside, Raynor lit two lamps and carried one with them into the back room.

"I hope this has something to do with my next bag of coins?" Raynor said as he shut the door and motioned for Marshall to sit. "I checked today, and it's been five weeks since my last receipt."

"No, this isn't about that." Marshall stopped and held a hand in front of him. "Well . . . yes, I do owe you a payment and will get it to you soon, but this is something new. I have an idea with which I could use your help. As you know, my department is in charge of replacing old and damaged coins with new ones. Some are melted down and recast into new coins, but we destroy them when we deem them in bad enough shape. I've been wondering if there's a . . ." Marshall paused and looked around before inclining his head toward Raynor, "*better* use for them."

"Go on. I'm intrigued," Raynor said, leaning back in his chair.

"We can't use the coins in Karad. It'd be suspicious if a large number of old coins started showing up. What if they were put back into circulation but spread out to the farthest corners of the kingdom?" Marshall asked.

Raynor looked down his nose at the man, refusing to give away his expression. "Where do I come in?"

"What better way to spread coins out than by using them to pay for imported goods?"

Ah, now it makes sense, he thought. In addition to his position at the commerce department, Raynor owned Fiero Imports, which bought supplies from nearby cities and sold them to local vendors. "So, you give me the coins, I put them into my business and spread them around the kingdom, and I pay you a percentage?" Raynor asked.

"You'd *pay* for the coins, five tid on the argen. That way, we split it," Marshall replied.

Raynor shook his head. "Three tid," he said. "I'm the one taking the risk by spending them."

"I'm the one taking the risk by failing to destroy them in the first place. We'd be linked in this venture. Five tid."

The clock on the wall ticked the seconds off as they stared at each other.

Raynor nodded. "Deal."

The two men shook hands as Marshall spoke. "You'll want to make sure to spread them out among different suppliers, and also mix them in with good coins to prevent any suspi—"

"Charles, don't insult my intelligence."

"Sorry, I just want to make sure."

"When do we start?" Raynor asked.

"I have a bag of coins ready to go at my office. We can start tomorrow."

They opened the back office door to head out and froze. A man stood inside the outer room with his hand on the front door, about to leave.

"I—I'm sorry," the man fumbled, his face looked stricken with horror. "I needed to follow up on something from earlier. I—I saw the light on and found the door unlocked. It's not important though."

The man hurried out the door and was gone. The two lords stood motionless, staring at the closed door. "I know that man," Raynor said. "He was here this morning applying for a grocery license."

Neither man spoke while they considered the situation.

"We need to silence him," Marshall said.

"What? No, we haven't done anything," Raynor told him. "All he heard was us talking. No matter what he says or does with that information, nothing could be pinned on us."

Marshall grew agitated. "Yes, but *I'm* the Lord of Treasury! If he speaks to someone, it'll result in a full investigation of my finances and our department!"

"But we don't even know if he heard anything!"

"I can't take that risk, and neither can you," Marshall said, pointing at Raynor's chest.

He's right. If it came to light, it would mean significant problems for me, Raynor thought. "I can take care of our grocer issue," Raynor said, breaking the tense silence. "But I'm going to need something in return. You're close with Byron Hampton in Felting, aren't you?"

"Yes, we go back many years."

"Do you have any . . . information you can hold over him?"

"Like blackmail?" Marshall asked.

"Yes . . . something that could force his hand?"

Charles Marshall raised an eyebrow as he broke into a broad grin. "I've got just the thing."

It started to rain as Raynor made his way down the alley, the wet accentuating the chill of the night. The light of the street lanterns cut through the darkness, illuminating the stone lane.

Raynor walked to a simple door and knocked. The overhang of the door shielded his face, but droplets continued to hit his head, rolling down the back of his cloak. He felt the dampness as moisture soaked his clothing.

Footsteps approached from the other side, and the knob turned. The familiar face of Captain Charles Mortinson with his strong jaw and trim beard looked back at him as the door swung open.

"Charles, I need your help again," Raynor said as he held out a small bag that jingled with coins.

Mortinson took the bag with a smirk and stood to the side. "Come in."

21

The Origine

Walking to the grocery, Veron tried to make sense of what he saw the night before in the training room. It seemed impossible, but he was afraid to ask Artimus about it. He hoped to figure out some rational explanation, but so far, he'd failed. To take his mind off it, he decided to focus on work.

"So, how'd it go?" Veron asked Morgan when he arrived at the store, eager to hear about his meeting regarding the new shop.

"Good, I uhh . . . I think," Morgan replied, shuffling some stacks of paper. "They said they'll review my application but didn't foresee any problems. I should hear back in a couple of days."

Something's off, Veron thought. *He's not his usual cheery self. He's not telling me something.*

"Can you go through our supplier list and see who can increase their shipments and by how much?" Morgan asked. "Then, once we see where we're at, we can figure out how many new sources we might need."

"Sure, no problem."

Veron sat behind the counter and pored through supplier papers. Morgan spent most of the day alternating between the street and helping customers inside, handling pretty much everything.

At one point, Veron glanced up to stretch his neck as someone came into the shop from the back storage room—a man he'd never seen before. "Excuse me. That's not part of the store," Veron told him.

"I'm sorry," the man said. "I was checking if you had any bolofruit. I didn't see any out here and thought I'd look in the back."

"No, we don't have any. I'm sorry. If you need to check anything in the back, let Morgan or me know, and we'll be happy to help."

"Sure thing," the man said as he walked out of the shop.

That was odd. Bolofruit? Veron shook his head and went back to the papers.

With no more work to distract him as he left Morgan's shop, Veron's thoughts returned to Artimus' mysterious night training. During dinner, Veron decided he couldn't take it anymore. He had to ask.

"I saw you last night," Veron said, picking at a potato on his plate. Artimus glanced at him, cocking his head. "In the training room."

Artimus' confused eyes widened. "Ah," he said as he looked down at the table and nodded. "Did I wake you?"

"No, I couldn't sleep. What was that? How could you do those things?"

Artimus took a deep breath in and slowly exhaled as he scratched his chin. After a moment, he lifted his eyes. "That's what makes a shadow knight."

Veron raised an eyebrow. "I thought the Shadow Knights defended the kingdom and were secretive and all that stuff?"

"Yes, that's true."

"So, what then? What are you not telling me?"

Artimus drummed his fingers on the table and spoke in a soft voice. "There's one aspect of being a shadow knight I didn't teach you. I didn't tell you about the origine."

"The origine?" Veron leaned in. "What's that?"

Artimus sat up straight. "When you walk, how does your body do it?"

"Um . . . I step with my legs?"

"Yes, but your mind tells them to move, and your muscles work together to allow it to happen. What about when you swing a sword?"

"I guess my mind tells my arms to swing, and my muscles do it?"

"Correct," Artimus said. "What about deciding how to defend a blow if someone attacks you?"

"I guess my mind sees what they're doing, then my body reacts."

"Yes, but do you have to think about it?"

"Not really. It all happens so fast, I just react."

"Yes!" Artimus said, his eyes lighting up. "All these physical and mental actions are the result of your mind and body working together. You think about what should happen, and your body's muscles, tendons, and bones make it happen. When you do this, it uses energy that your body has stored up. The Shadow Knights call this store of energy the origine. What sets shadow knights apart is the ability to tap into the origine and use as much as they like."

Veron leaned back in his chair, his head tilted. "I don't understand. What do you mean?"

"Through years of practice, we developed the ability to choose how much of it we use. By increasing our use of the origine, our bodies can function far beyond what the average person can do. By using the origine, we can swing a sword harder because our muscles contract more powerfully. We see what someone else does, and our mind can process it quicker. This gives us the ability to react faster than normal. We can run harder, jump higher, and even heal quicker."

"That's amazing! Why don't you use it all the time?" Veron asked, eyes widening.

"Ah, therein lies the catch," Artimus said, leaning back and wagging a finger in the air. "The origine isn't unlimited. We can't operate past what our bodies are capable of doing. All we can do is use up the energy more quickly. For short periods, this is great, but not for long. Once someone taps into the origine, even a small amount, their energy depletes quickly. In a fight, this leaves them vulnerable if it's used up."

Veron sat on the edge of his seat in rapt attention.

"For example, consider a well," Artimus said. "If you want a drink, you lower a bucket and bring up water, but you're limited to only drinking as much as that bucket can carry. Shadow knights can bring up as much water as they want all at one time. This is great if you're *very* thirsty, but there's only so much water in the well. If you use it all up at once, you're going to get really thirsty because it'll take a while for the well to fill up with water again."

"So last night—"

"Last night, I presume you didn't stay around after I finished. If you did, you would've seen me on the floor, unable to stand for several minutes as I regained my strength."

"So, why haven't you taught me yet?" Veron asked, raising his arms for emphasis, his face lit with excitement.

Artimus shook his head but didn't answer.

"Are you worried about the prophecy? That it might . . . be me?"

Artimus cleared his throat. "It doesn't matter. The ability to learn it has died out."

The muscles in Veron's face went slack. "What do you mean?" he asked.

"Not everyone can learn it—very few, in fact. When the Shadow Knights began hundreds of years ago, they developed a test to identify children who had the potential to learn. They traveled all of

Terrenor to find candidates with a combination of reflexes, strength, and focus. Only one child out of roughly three thousand passed. No one knows why, but around twenty years ago, we stopped finding new candidates. William, your father, was the last one discovered. We continued testing for another seven years until the knights were killed, but we found no more."

"Can you test me just in case?" Veron asked.

Artimus shook his head. "I tested you four years ago."

Veron's face fell, his fleeting hope quashed before it began. Still, he was curious to learn more. "You said it's hard to kill a shadow knight when you talked about surviving Bale's attack. What happened that night? How'd you live?"

Artimus looked away, staring off at a distant point. "When they attacked, I didn't have time to get out of bed before they stabbed me twice—once in the shoulder and once in the chest, piercing my heart. My body went into shock from the loss of blood. They left me for dead as they finished off the rest." Artimus winced as he spoke. "Normally, those wounds would kill a man in seconds, but I tapped into the origine right away, speeding up the healing process. My heart repaired itself, and my wounds closed up, but I lost a lot of blood and had used up all of the origine. I was healed but barely alive with no energy left. Had my wounds been any worse, I wouldn't have made it. I lay there for hours as my body regained strength, but the other knights weren't so lucky. They all could heal as I did, but their wounds were more serious. They didn't recover."

"Wait, so all these times we fought together . . . that you beat me?" Veron asked, tilting his head forward with eyebrows raised.

"You're asking if I used the origine to enhance my abilities so I could win?" Artimus said.

"Yes."

Artimus sat back in his chair but didn't respond.

"Did you?" Veron asked again, leaning in.

Artimus exhaled. "Not *all* the time."

"What? You've been cheating all this time!" Although he yelled, a smile covered Veron's face. *That means that I may be a better fighter than I thought.*

"It's not cheating, but . . . yes, I used the origine to increase my fighting ability." Artimus pointed at Veron. "Don't forget—I *am* almost fifty years older than you."

"That's cheating. If we fought straight up, who'd win?"

Artimus looked at him with a blank expression, tapping his chin. After a moment, he stood up and walked to the training room. Veron followed, his heart racing. Artimus selected a single-handed sword and a shield. "Choose," he said.

Veron looked at the wall and considered his options. His breath came quicker as if he were about to battle for his life, but a nervous grin covered his face. He selected the ruby-hilted sword off its holder and moved to the center of the room. The master and student stood across from each other in the ready position.

"No origine?" Veron asked, holding his sword in front of him.

"No origine."

The room was still as they stared each other down. Veron's pulse beat in his head. The grit of dirt on the wooden floor scraped as he adjusted his foot. Artimus remained motionless with his sword and shield raised.

Veron attacked first, his blade whooshing as it cut through the silence. Their swords clanged together, sending sparks into the air. The two traded blows as they whirled and danced in a fluid display of steel and sweat. Having a shorter sword, Artimus tried to get close, but Veron kept pushing back against his shield. The moment Artimus became off-balance, Veron attacked his side, but somehow the teacher parried it away.

I can do this. I'm faster than him, Veron thought.

Artimus moved next, alternating attacks with both his shield and sword. Veron fended off blow after blow as his feet shuffled backward. He braced his foot against the shield and pushed Artimus back again. A quick three-strike exchange of blades followed, giving neither a window of advantage.

"Don't fall back on your tricks, old man," Veron said, drawing a smirk from Artimus.

Veron's eyes widened as Artimus' sword came at him from above. Ducking to give himself more space, Veron held his sword up, the blades meeting just above his head.

Veron swallowed hard. *He doesn't have to kill me to prove a point.*

He stood as he threw Artimus' sword back off his own. The old man ran at Veron with his shield but stumbled forward as Veron spun to the right. Seeing his moment, Veron swung down hard on the outstretched weapon, just above the hilt, knocking it free. He scooped the sword up and held both blades to his teacher's neck. Veron panted as he stood, unmoving. His pulse beat wildly, and a huge grin covered his face.

Artimus' serious expression faded, and a smile replaced it. "Well done."

22

Closing Shop

At Morgan's shop the next day, Veron glowed. He couldn't stop thinking about the origine. *My father was able to do that! If I had those abilities, I could do incredible things!* he thought.

He pictured himself fighting Mortinson in Karad Square then single-handedly stopping Bale as he invaded Feldor. His smile faded as he remembered he wouldn't have the Shadow Knights' ability.

But look how far I've come! I beat Artimus. I've learned so much. Who knows what I'll be able to do in the future?

"You sure are in a good mood today," Morgan said. "Did you meet a girl or something?"

"Haha, no. I'm just happy," Veron replied.

"Well, if you're so happy, maybe you can use that joy to sweep the floor. It's a mess."

Veron glared at him as he grabbed the broom with a huff and made his way through the aisles. While he swept, three soldiers walked in the front door of the shop. Veron froze when he recognized the large one in the front. Captain Mortinson. Dark memories flooded Veron—sprinting through the streets, Mortinson stepping on Fend's leg, the soldier running his friend through. He started to shake with anger but also fought the fear of being recognized.

Should I duck behind the bins? Should I try to run out the door? he thought.

"Where's Morgan Fenster?" the captain asked, looking at Veron with a blank stare.

He must not recognize me. Of course not. That was a long time ago.

"I'm Morgan. Is there a problem?" the grocer said with hesitation, stepping out from the back room. He glanced at Veron, his forehead pinched with confusion.

Mortinson motioned to the other two soldiers, and all three of them spread out. "We need to search your shop," he said as the soldiers overturned bins of food and threw baskets off of shelves.

"Hey, what's this about? Stop that! This is *my* store! If you're looking for something, I'm sure I can help you find it!" Morgan shouted, raising his hands.

"Captain!" one of the soldiers yelled from the back room. He returned, carrying a small leather book.

Captain Mortinson looked through it for a moment then closed it. He nodded to his soldiers. "Fenster, you'll come with us."

Two soldiers stood behind Morgan as Catherine and her three kids appeared at the bottom of the stairs with concern on their faces. "Morgan, what's going on?" Catherine asked.

"Daddy, are you okay?" Emma said, her blond hair pressed against her mother as Catherine held her close.

"I don't understand. What's this about? I haven't done anything!" Morgan said. He turned to his family. "It's okay. I'll get this straightened out."

The soldiers said nothing as they left the shop with Morgan, and Veron stared after them. *Why would they take him? What did he do? Did that guy from yesterday put something back there?*

201

Veron worked the shop for the rest of the day, cleaning up as best as possible from the soldiers' mess. He waited on Morgan to return, but the grocer never showed. When Veron left at the end of the day, he tried to console Catherine, assuring her that things would be fine, even though he had no idea if it were true or not.

* * *

The next morning, Veron returned to the shop as soon as he could. Instead of finding Morgan preparing to open, a sign rested on the front of the door: "Shop closed by decree of the Department of Commerce."

Veron didn't see anyone inside, so he knocked loudly and waited. After a bit, Morgan approached behind the glass window. The shopkeeper's clothes were disheveled, and his face was heavy with grief as he let Veron in.

"Morgan, are you okay? What happened? The store is closed?" Veron asked, hearing shuffling and activity overhead.

"Honestly, I don't know what happened," Morgan said, scratching his head. His eyes were bloodshot, and his hair was a mess. "They claim I've underreported my earnings and evaded taxes. They say I owe two sol one argen to clear it and avoid going to prison."

"What!"

"Thankfully, we had just enough stashed away to cover it, but we're broke now." Morgan hung his head. "Additionally, they denied my application for a store permit in East Fairren and canceled my license to operate here."

"What? They can't do that!" Veron exclaimed.

"They can. And now I'm prohibited from owning any businesses within the kingdom of Feldor."

"What's their proof? What was that book they found?"

"They claim it is a ledger of sales showing unreported income, but it's not mine. I think . . ." Morgan stopped as he shook his head. "No. It doesn't matter. It's better that you don't know anything."

"What? What is it?"

"Forget about it. There's nothing we can do about it now."

"Morgan, there was a guy." The shopkeeper's eyebrows raised as Veron spoke. "There was a guy here two days ago who I'd never seen before. While you were outside and I was at the desk, he came out of the storage room, claiming he was looking for some bolofruit. The whole thing seemed odd. I bet he planted the ledger."

Morgan held his chin as he nodded. "I imagine you're right."

"Why would he do that? What are we going to do about it?" Veron asked, his heart rate increasing as he thought through plans.

"Nothing." Morgan set his hand firmly on Veron's shoulder, settling the energy bubbling in him with his firm grip and sincere eyes. "We're going to do nothing. Do you understand?"

Veron exhaled then shook his head. "Do you know what you're going to do?"

"We can't stay here anymore because we don't own this building. We have to be out today. I've already lined up work down at the docks, and Catherine plans to take up cleaning laundry. It may not be glamorous, but we'll get by."

It's just not fair, Veron thought.

"Take as much food as you and Artimus can eat when you leave. We can't sell it anymore, and it'll go bad before we can eat it all."

Veron smiled weakly, wanting to thank him but thinking it didn't seem to fit the moment. He looked at the piles of food around the store. *It's such a shame.*

"Also, can you take a crate of food up to Old Lady Withers? She's having trouble getting by and could use it. I gathered some stuff up over there." He pointed to a container on the counter. "You know where she lives, right? Down the alley at the end of Porter, by the wall?"

Veron nodded. "Sure, no problem."

He walked out into the street, carrying the crate piled high with various vegetables and fruit. *I can't believe it. How can this happen to Morgan? Things were going so well, and now it's all gone.*

He got to the end of Porter Way and turned up the alley. The walls were narrow in the forgotten corner of the city. The gutters stunk, and garbage littered the ground. While he walked, something shuffled behind him, accompanied by raspy laughter. He glanced back as he rounded a bend, and his heart sank. Veron hadn't seen Slash, Coffin, and Bruiser in years, but they looked as vile and cruel as ever.

Veron set the crate down. He braced to run but stopped himself. His fists clenched. The unfairness of everything made him feel bold. *I've run from them long enough,* he thought as he turned and stood as tall as he could between the food and the three men, staring them down.

"Whoa, looks like street trash wants to play!" Coffin said.

"Why don't you leave the food where it is and walk along? We won't hurt you, and everyone will be happy," Slash said.

Veron didn't move. "No."

"Mmm, that's the wrong decision," Slash told him as he pulled out a dagger.

Bruiser took a club out of his belt, and Coffin had a knife of his own. The three men stared at Veron with smirks on their faces.

Bruiser approached first. Cocking his arm back, the large man swung the club at Veron's head, the bludgeon whistling through the air. At the last moment, Veron ducked under the weapon and jammed his knee into the large man's gut. Bruiser groaned as he doubled over, clutching his stomach. Veron slammed both hands on

Bruiser's arm, knocking the club to the ground. Just as Slash lunged with his dagger, Veron dodged to the side and snatched up the fallen club in the same movement.

Freshly armed, Veron used the club to block Slash's next attack before spinning to hit Bruiser in the head. The large man went down with a crash, moaning on the ground while he held his head. Turning back to Slash, Veron went on the offensive, striking three quick blows. Slash tried to block the third one with his dagger, but the impact knocked his weapon away. The thug yelled and backed off several steps down the alley, grabbing his hand.

Veron turned to Coffin, who had been blocked by the other bodies in the narrow alley. The tall man held his knife out but appeared hesitant to use it. Veron lunged forward, feigning an attack, causing Coffin to turn and run. Slash held his injured hand as he followed Coffin, leaving Bruiser crawling after them.

Alone again, Veron tossed the club down in disgust, picked the crate of food back up, and continued on to Old Lady Withers. A smile covered his face as he walked away. He had faced one of his oldest fears and emerged victorious.

"Artimus!" Veron called, entering the house.

"What is it?" a voice replied from the kitchen.

Veron set a large crate of food down on the table where Artimus ground something in a bowl just before the man reeled into a fit of coughing. Veron frowned. "Are you okay?" he asked.

Artimus held his chest as his cough settled. "Yeah, I'm fine. It's just my cough acting up," he said and nodded at the crate. "What's all that?"

"Food from Morgan."

Artimus cleared his throat. "He's back? What happened?"

Veron related the rest of the story that he pieced together, leaving out the part about his run-in with Slash and his gang. Artimus shook his head in disbelief.

"He's hiding something that he won't tell me. Someone set him up," Veron said. "Can't he, or maybe we, go to someone and help clear it up?"

"I don't know. Someone must have had a reason to want to ruin Morgan, which would explain the ledger, but it would be nearly impossible to prove anything. He's probably holding something back to protect you." Another round of coughing racked Artimus' body before he returned to grinding in the bowl. "Let me give it some thought tonight."

Veron indicated to the bowl. "What's that?" he asked.

"Some herbs I'm grinding up. It should reduce the coughing and help me sleep well tonight," Artimus told him.

"Okay. Let me know if you need anything."

Before going to sleep, Veron took out a box from under his bed. Over the last four years, most of the money he earned from working at the grocery went into the box. He opened it and counted twenty-four silver argen and seventy copper tid. The coins totaled up to just over three sol. The money represented freedom for him—to maybe get his own place to live one day or start his own business. He wasn't sure what all he could buy with it, but he knew it had power.

As much as Veron was excited to think about what he'd be able to do with that money one day, he didn't need it right then. Morgan did. Tomorrow, he planned to go to the Department of Commerce and see what sort of influence he could exert on Morgan's behalf.

As he drifted off to sleep, he imagined the look on Morgan's face when he told him he could have his shop back.

Veron woke with a feeling of unease. The hairs on the back of his neck prickled, but his mind still felt sluggish. A faint shuffle drew his attention until a sound sent a chill through his body.

"Hello, street trash," said a harsh, raspy voice.

His eyes jolted open. The moonlight through the window illuminated his worst nightmare—Bruiser and Coffin holding knives to his throat, and Slash standing next to the bed.

"Well, what do we have here?" Slash said, inspecting the box sitting on the table next to his bed.

Veron's breath caught. Slash had discovered the box filled with four years of hard work—his three sol. He wanted to scream but didn't dare make a sound.

"Boys, our friend Veron has been collecting money for us. Isn't that kind of him?" Slash said, shaking the box and smirking at the clinking sound it made.

An evil laugh came from Bruiser and Coffin. Veron felt nauseated.

"I didn't appreciate what you did earlier today," Slash said. "You broke my hand, and Bruiser is still in a lot of pain. You owe us. I think this box might make up for that though. What do you think, boys?"

Again, they laughed in response. Veron considered fighting back, but most likely they would cut his throat before he got anywhere. *Maybe if I yell, Artimus will hear?* he thought.

"We appreciate your generous gift to us," Slash said, carrying the box toward the door as the two men with knives backed off.

His crooked smile evaporated as Slash looked to Bruiser and spoke in a low voice, "We can't have him following us." The two men stared at each other for a moment until Bruiser nodded and looked to Veron.

"Your turn to see how this feels," Bruiser said as he pulled the club from his belt.

Veron paled and tried to scramble backward, but he wasn't able to dodge as the club hit him solidly on the head.

When he woke again, Veron's head pounded. Touching his temple, his fingertips came away wet with a red smear in the dim light. Something acrid reached his nose, and he sneezed, setting off a sharp pain in his head and causing him to hold it.

What's that smell? he thought.

Something at the back of his mind tingled. He knew what it was, but his brain wouldn't focus on the thought. A memory of him and Fend sitting around a small fire for warmth surfaced and he jolted up.

Something is burning.

Veron jumped up, ignoring the throbbing in his head, and ran to the door. Tendrils of smoke curled around his feet as it seeped in from the crack underneath his door and a strange orange glow flickered across the floorboards. Focusing on the distant roaring noise, he turned the metal door handle and discovered an inferno waiting on the other side. His hand jerked back as the pain from the scalding handle registered in his mind. The force from the heat through the doorway pushed him back like an invisible hand.

Flames covered the door across the landing and most of the wall going down the stairs. The immense heat was unbearable. Veron tried to shield his face with his arm, but it did little good.

"Artimus! Artimus!" he yelled but could barely hear his own voice over the roar of the fire. His eyes burned, and he coughed.

Veron looked around frantically for something to help, but there was nothing. Steeling his nerve, he held his arms in front of his face as he lunged at the opposite door and kicked, putting all his weight into it. The frame splintered as the door flew open, and Veron dove through. His throat hurt. His body felt singed. Once in Artimus' room, he slammed the broken, partially burned door shut. It blocked most of the heat but wouldn't last long.

The room was dark and hazy. Light from the cracks in the broken door revealed a thick smoke filling the space like a blanket. Artimus lay in his bed.

"Artimus!" Veron yelled, but the man didn't move. His chest constricted as he hurried to the old man's side and kneeled to find a wet, sticky pool. The orange glow of the fire illuminated a steady drip of blood falling from the edge of the bed.

Veron's heart leaped into his throat, and with a shaking hand, he pulled the covers down. Artimus' throat had been slit.

"No!" Veron cried, choking on a sob.

The pain in his head was nothing compared to the ache that filled his heart. It was as if his very soul had been ripped away as he stared at the horror in front of him. Tears blurred his vision as he leaned over to clutch the man to his chest, but when he moved the body, Artimus coughed.

"You're alive!" Veron shouted. His heart fluttered with hope. *He probably used the origine to heal, which will leave him too weak to walk. I can't carry him down the stairs because they're covered in fire,* he thought, looking around. *The window!*

Veron stood up, grabbed the small table by the bed, and flung it through the glass. Cold air entered the room and fought against the blazing furnace on the other side of the wall as the pane shattered. After clearing the frame of shards, Veron cradled Artimus against his chest. The pain in his head returned as he struggled with the weight, but Veron ignored it as he stumbled to the open window and set the old man down on the slanted roof outside.

"The chest," Artimus managed to say through labored breaths as he motioned with his eyes to the chest next to the bed.

Veron grabbed the wooden box and slid it out onto the roof before crawling out himself.

Out on the roof, Veron dragged Artimus to the edge. Flames had consumed the front portion of the house already. *The rest will be gone soon*, he thought.

He pushed the chest off the roof first, resulting in a solid thump as it hit the ground below. Carefully and as fast as he could, he grabbed Artimus by the hands and lowered him as far as he was able. The old man groaned from the movement before Veron dropped him the last few feet.

With the heat of the fire growing closer, Veron jumped, and the ground rushed to meet him. The hard landing knocked him over and stung his legs, but he shook it off and scrambled to his feet. Veron picked up Artimus once again and carried him out to the garden. He laid him down on the bench, far enough from the flames of the house, before returning to do the same with the chest.

"Artimus! Stay with me! What can I do?" Veron's eyes were wide as he set the chest down and knelt by his side.

The old man's breaths were ragged. Even away from the smoke, he struggled to breathe as his eyes remained closed.

Veron's thoughts flashed back to Fend lying on the ground, bleeding after being stabbed by the soldiers. He remembered seeing life leave his eyes as he watched helplessly. *I won't let that happen again.*

Artimus' eyes opened again, and he looked at Veron, wincing in pain as he struggled to breathe. "There's nothing you can do," he said in a weak voice, managing a slight shake of his head. Artimus indicated with a nod toward the training room. "Get the sword."

"What?"

"Can you get the sword?"

Veron knew which one he meant. Flames engulfed most of the house, but the training room had not been consumed yet. He ran back to the house and opened the door to the training room. Smoke filled the space, making it hard to see and breathe. Flames leaped through the doorway to the kitchen, but the wall of weapons hadn't been touched. Veron grabbed the sword with the ruby hilt.

Once he was back in the garden, a loud crash sounded behind him. The upper story of the house collapsed in on itself, sending a wave of heat that surrounded him like a blanket. He shielded his face with his arm until the scorching blaze subsided.

Veron turned to Artimus. Blood soaked his shirt and dripped steadily on the ground under the bench. The wound to Artimus' neck appeared to be partially healed but still bled.

Veron knelt beside him and offered the sword to him, but Artimus shook his head. "No . . . for you," he rasped.

Why do I need it? Veron thought, setting it down on the ground. "You can heal yourself, right? You can get better?" he asked in a panicked voice.

Artimus shook his head as he sputtered a weak cough. "I've done all I can. My origine is spent, and it wasn't enough."

Veron shook his head. "No, you can do it! Just rest for a moment, then you can heal the rest of the way!"

Artimus peered back with a calm that scared Veron. "Son, I'm dying."

Tears spilled down Veron's cheeks. "But you can't! You're the last shadow knight. Remember the prophecy. You have to defeat Bale!"

Artimus struggled to take a breath in and slowly shook his head. "No." He coughed again and swallowed. "You passed," Artimus whispered before he broke into a fit of coughing.

Veron wiped his tears. "What? What do you mean?" he asked.

Artimus managed a weak smile. "The test—you passed." Veron's eyes grew wide. "I'm sorry I lied. I wanted to protect you. I didn't want it to have to be you."

Artimus struggled to raise his right hand as he dug underneath his shirt and pulled out a necklace with a key. Placing the key in Veron's palm, he folded the boy's fingers around the metal object and covered Veron's fist with his own hand. He nodded to the chest on the ground.

"Learn from the book," he whispered. "The prophecy is for you. You must be the one to defeat Bale."

The roar of the fire disappeared as time seemed to slow. The hard metal of the key rested in Veron's hand, but everything was strange, as if he escaped reality and looked at himself from outside his own body. The color drained his face. *I can't defeat Bale! That would mean . . .* He swallowed hard. *Artimus can't die. This can't be happening.*

"Veron, your father would be proud of you," Artimus said, smiling at him.

The words brought Veron back to reality. His chest ached at the thought of his father. "Artimus . . . thank you." It was all he could get out as tears rolled down his face.

Artimus nodded and squeezed his hand. The smile on the man's face belied the chaos that surrounded them. Amid the flames and the noise, despite the blood and the pain, Artimus was at peace. The pressure from Artimus' hand loosened, and soon his arm went slack as his head fell back.

Grief flooded into Veron like a river unleashed from a dam. He sobbed as he held Artimus in his arms. The man who was his teacher, friend, and father, was dead.

Veron was completely alone, once again.

II

Discovery

23

The Academy

Chelci's breath fogged in the cool air. The sun had risen, but thick clouds held it back, leaving a chill that persisted. It was the second week of wiether, and the temperature would be getting colder each day. She had lived in the small village of Nasco for the last four years while she waited to enter the Academy's training center. According to Russell, she would be the first girl to be admitted, which made her both proud and a little scared.

Approaching the training building, she was dressed for whatever awaited her. Her loose-fitting brown linen pants were light and airy and allowed her legs to move freely. Her cream-colored shirt had loose sleeves down to her hands, and she wore a brown wool vest over the top. Her leather boots fit snugly. *Mother would probably collapse in shock at the sight of me,* she thought with a laugh.

Over her time in Nasco, Chelci had stopped wearing dresses, which was all she had known in Felting. While most women in the village still wore them, it was not uncommon for some to wear pants, which Chelci readily adopted. She found them more suitable for all the physical work she had been doing.

After four years, she was taller, stronger, and more confident. In

Felting, she spent a lot of time primping her hair and face and cared about having the best clothes, but those things no longer mattered. She usually just kept her straight brown hair tied back. With only a few changes of clothes, she often wore the same thing several days in a row since she was the one who had to wash them.

Butterflies flitted in her stomach as she entered the building. Russell was already there, having left early to get things prepared. She showed up a bit later and was the last to arrive. Standing next to Russell was a man about his same age who had brown hair down to his chin and wore a coiled rope that ran across his chest and over a shoulder—another instructor, she assumed. The rest in the crowd were all boys. All eleven of them looked much older and bigger than her. They stood huddled in groups, talking, but as she walked through the door, all conversations stopped as the boys stared at her. Several snickered and pointed in her direction.

Red splotches crept up her neck. *I'm the first girl ever to do this. I wonder if I'm in way over my head?*

Chelci recognized all the boys. Aleks and Finley were her friends from school and were the most welcome faces. They were both at school when she started but graduated in her first year. Both had always been kind to her and gave a small wave as she came in. She knew Reece and Landon from around the village. They occasionally hung out and played in the square together. The rest she only knew from names or faces.

Inside the training building, most of the far wall contained windows, which looked over a courtyard beyond. Rough wooden boards made up the other walls and high ceiling. The large open space they stood in was divided into different sections. One area had ropes hanging from the ceiling, and another had an assortment of weapons displayed on racks and shelves. Part of the floor was padded with some sort of matting, leaving most of the area open. To

Chelci's left, a doorway led to another room with desks.

As she looked around, Aleks and Finley moved over to stand by her. "I'm glad you made it," Aleks said. "Too many guys here already. I was worried you chickened out."

Before she could respond, Russell spoke up. "Now that we're all here, we can get started."

All the boys quickly quieted down and turned to look at him.

"My name is Russell," he said. "I'll be your head instructor for the next two years, and this is Bensen, my assistant." The other man gave a quick wave. "Welcome to the Academy. Our job is to find the best of you. A guardsman should be strong and fast. He should be able to defend himself and attack when needed. He must be a quick thinker who needs to listen and obey. He must put his own needs aside for the good of the village. A guardsman's job is to protect and defend, and we take that seriously."

Russell looked around the class of twelve as the words soaked in.

"At any time during training, if Bensen and I feel one of you isn't capable, you'll be cut. After two years, we'll decide if any of you are good enough to be selected for the village guard. In the meantime, we'll beat you into shape as best as we can." Several of the boys muttered between each other. "This won't be easy or fun. If any of you realize it isn't for you, you are free to quit at any time," Russell said to the group but stared at Chelci. "Now, go around and introduce yourselves."

The boys took turns giving their names. When she introduced herself as Elise, it didn't even sound strange after four years of using the name.

Royce, one of the larger boys she didn't know well, raised his hand to speak. "Sir, I thought only boys were allowed in the Academy?"

Chelci flushed while everyone turned to her again. "Elise is joining us in this class," Russell said to everyone. "If she can do what's required, she can stay, but she will receive *no* special treatment. She'll have to do the same work required of the rest of you. Is that clear?"

"Yes, sir," mumbled a few of the boys.

"Is that clear?"

"Yes, sir!" all the boys replied in unison.

"Good." Russell looked to Bensen and nodded.

"Everyone grab a bag from the corner and follow me outside," Bensen said in a booming voice as he threw a bag over his shoulder.

Chelci followed the other boys to the bags. A large boy named Gael bumped into her hard, and she fell into the wall, drawing a laugh from him, Royce, and another boy named Tate. Chelci gritted her teeth and jumped up. She grabbed the last bag and slung it over her shoulders, surprised by the weight. It was easy enough to get on her shoulders, but she worried about what they would have to do with it.

As she made her way to the door, Russell caught her arm. "I stuck out my neck to get you here. You live with us, so I can't show even a hint of favoritism," he told her. "If Bensen decides you're out, there's nothing I can do about it. Understand?"

She nodded.

"Good. Now don't fall behind."

Chelci ran outside, where the rest of the boys waited.

"These bags are going to be your new best friends," Bensen said. "When we run, keep them on your shoulders. If you can't carry the bag anymore, you might as well go home. If you finish longer than two minutes after I do, you'll be going home. Let's go!"

Bensen took off running along a trail in the woods. Chelci knew the path around the village well after running over it for the last four years. When she was on her own, she enjoyed it because she could go at whatever speed she wanted, plus she had Charlie running alongside to keep her company. All she could think about then was keeping up with the group, and the pace Bensen set was punishingly fast.

For the first part of the run, the heavy bag made it challenging, but Chelci managed. As soon as they started the first long uphill section, a hopeless feeling of dread washed over her. *I don't know if I can keep up!* she thought. Her legs burned as she trudged up the hill, her run quickly devolving into a walk. She focused her gaze in front of her feet and kept moving.

Over the next rise, Chelci breathed a sigh of relief as they enjoyed a moment of flat trail. The group had thinned out during the uphill portion. About half the boys were still with Bensen in the front, while five of them lagged. She was at the back of the pack but soon passed Lionel, who was significantly overweight, and then Landon, who was thin and out of shape, not long after.

The trail continued to alternate between uphill and downhill. At one point, they passed Nevi and Russell's house. Nevi stood on the porch with a broom, and the older woman smiled and waved. The small gesture gave Chelci a boost of optimism as she continued.

Soon, she found herself just behind Finley, who glanced back.

"I guess . . . I need . . . pick up the pace . . . if I don't want . . . beat by a girl, huh?" Finley managed to say through heavy breaths as he struggled to keep going. His face was flushed and sweaty.

Chelci didn't have the energy to answer him, so she just weakly smiled back.

Bensen had a pocket watch out when she and Finley stumbled across the finish line. "Eighty-two seconds," Bensen announced. Landon arrived shortly after. "112 seconds—cutting it close, bean pole. It's good for you that I went slowly today."

Another minute after that, Lionel struggled over the last hill, walking as fast as he could go. He came to a stop in front of the group, panting with his hands on his knees.

"Lionel!" Russell said from the doorway to the building. "Time to go."

Lionel hung his head in defeat. He went inside to drop off his bag then waved goodbye to the others as he walked back to the village. *He looks so disappointed. Poor guy. At least I wasn't the last—or even second to last!* Chelci thought.

Aleks didn't even look like he had broken a sweat as he walked over to where Chelci and Finley stood. "Nice job, you two," he said.

Chelci wanted to scowl at him as she struggled to catch her breath, assuming the comment was a jab at how slow they were, but one look at his plaintive face revealed he was genuine. "Thanks," she replied.

Following the group back into the building, Chelci received a wooden training sword. It was well worn on the pommel and dented along the edge from years of sparring. Her heart raced. *I'm going to learn how to sword fight!* She looked around at the other boys. *I hope they don't beat up on me. What if I get paired off against Gael?*

The freshly armed group followed Russell through the back door, where they spread out into the courtyard overlooking the village. To Chelci's relief, all they did was practice basic stances and strikes on their own. Most of the boys knew what they were doing already and joked about how easy it was. She would spar with them soon and wanted to learn as much as she could before that happened.

It was a difficult first lesson. *Everyone else seems to be doing this so easily, Chelci* thought as she stumbled through a movement. *Why won't my body move how it's supposed to?*

Her arms and legs were exhausted from repeating the movements. Even though the sword wasn't real, it was still heavy. The years of chopping wood for Russell helped, but her arm strength was still nowhere near that of the rest of the boys.

"Now hold," Russell said as the candidates fully extended in a lunge. After a moment, Chelci's arm began to drop, unable to maintain the position. Gael motioned to Royce and Tate, pointing at her and snickering. Her face flushed with anger and embarrassment. As much as she enjoyed learning about sword fighting, she sighed with relief when the training session finished.

They moved from activity to activity all day, and everything they did exhausted her in new ways. Her favorite exercise was climbing the ropes. It reminded her of climbing trees as a child. Two ropes hung from the rafters down to the mat below. The larger boys, who breezed through the sword motions, struggled—several didn't even make it to the top. Aleks and Finley were both successful. Tall and skinny Landon, who barely made it back on the run, climbed the rope with ease. Once they had all attempted it, Chelci took her turn. Her body was light, and her grip was firm. She pulled her way up and touched the top within a matter of seconds.

"Whoa!" a couple of voices exclaimed.

Chelci grinned as she received a high five and a smile from both Aleks and Finley. Her hand felt slightly raw from the rope, but she barely noticed. Gael, Royce, and Tate avoided eye contact.

They stayed at the ropes for a while, giving each person a chance to take several turns. After a time, Gael couldn't make it more than a couple of pulls. Chelci went after him and flew to the top once more.

Rope climbing led into classroom time, where they talked about village defense strategies and scenarios they could encounter in the guard. Chelci welcomed the break to be able to sit.

The last activity of the day was archery. They took bows and arrows to a range in the woods while everyone practiced their marksmanship. Chelci had never used a bow before and could barely draw the weapon. Her aim was wild, hitting the target next to hers twice, which caused the other boys to snicker.

After an embarrassing time at the archery range, the day was finally over, and everyone was dismissed. Chelci was beat. She had never worked so hard in her life. As she stumbled her way down the hill to the village, Aleks and Finley walked past her.

"Nice job today, Elise," Aleks said, his long brown hair covering the side of his face. He was tall and well built—a feature he inherited from his father, the village blacksmith.

She blushed at the compliment, but her spirit soared. "Thanks!" Not only did she not die, but she had done all right. Apparently, other people thought so too.

24

The Course

The next morning, Chelci groaned as she rolled out of bed. Her arms and legs weren't working the way they were supposed to. Every muscle in her body hurt, and she wasn't sure she'd be able to do anything, much less even walk to the training hall.

"Russell, I think you're going to need to carry me," Chelci said, half-joking as she dragged herself around the house to get ready. His only response was a scowl.

At the Academy, they passed out the wooden swords as they arrived. Chelci's stomach dropped as Russell began matching them into pairs.

I hope I get someone small like Landon or Reece or someone kind like Aleks or Finley. All I really care about is not being paired with Gael, Royce, or Tate, Chelci thought.

"Elise, you work on your own," Russell said after he announced the other five pairs, some staying in the building, and some going outside.

Whew! Thank you, Russell! Her smile of relief quickly changed to a frown. *But if I don't pair up with someone, I'm not going to learn.*

While she practiced on her own, she watched the other boys sparring. Their movements were messy and ugly as they learned to defend and attack.

They're learning, and I'm not. This isn't fair. He's singling me out. He said he wasn't going to take it easy on me. Chelci figured that after a while, the pairs would shuffle around, but it didn't happen.

"This is called the course," Bensen said with the rope draped across his chest as they stood outside, uphill from the training hall.

Chelci could see most of it from where she stood. Platforms, logs, walls, and a couple of high structures dotted the woods.

"To have a chance of being selected, you should be able to run it in around eight minutes or less by the end of your two years. But don't worry, it will take you some time to get there, so don't stress about the time today. We'll run it as a group first to learn the obstacles, but later, it'll be on your own. The course is a series of obstacles, and Russell and I will always be watching. If any of you even *think* about skipping or cheating an obstacle, we'll send you home." He beckoned with a wave of his hand. "Follow me."

Everyone took off at a slow pace, following their instructor.

The first obstacle loomed ahead, a tall spider web of ropes. They had to climb up one side, over a log at the top, then back down the other side. Chelci stayed in the back and waited as the large boys struggled their way up. Once she began, she found it easy—just like climbing a tree. While she ascended, Royce stepped on her hand as he came down the other side. He apologized but then laughed right after. Her hand stung, but she continued moving.

Six successive walls as high as Chelci's midsection came next. The taller boys planted their hands on the top and easily flung their legs over, but Chelci and Reece struggled. Being the shortest, their height slowed them down.

Just around the corner loomed a "ladder" of sorts that consisted of individual wooden beams spaced apart as far as she was tall and held together by ropes. Navigating between the beams was awkward and a little unnerving due to the height.

After making it to the top, they dropped down a series of gradually lowered platforms on the other side. The next challenge was the hardest one for Chelci. Three wooden walls of increasing height stood before her. The first she clambered up without too much difficulty. She had to stretch to grab the top of the second then work her way over. The last seemed impossible. She jumped for the top, but her hands wouldn't reach. She tried to get a running start, but it was no use.

"I'm too short," Chelci muttered with an exasperated look, breathing heavily.

"You and me both," Reece said next to her. They were the only two who hadn't made it yet.

Chelci tried again. She ran at the wall and jumped. Her body slammed hard into the surface, her face jarring from the impact. Her hand stretched as far as it could go. No good. She fell back to the dirt. Reece tried next with the same result.

I can't make it. I can't go around it though. If they see, they'll kick me out. She pictured herself walking to the finish with her head hung low in defeat before being sent home.

Reece ran at the wall again, this time successfully grabbing the top and pulling himself up.

Chelci's stomach dropped. *Now, I'm the only one left!*

"Grab my hand," Reece said as he held his hand over from the top.

I need to be able to do it on my own. But I can't stay here . . . Maybe just for today, she thought.

Reluctantly, she nodded. She jumped and seized his hand. Reece pulled her up enough for her to grab the top and climb over. Chelci's shoulders slumped as the two of them ran to catch up with the group. Catching up turned out to be easy because a line of boys backed up at the next obstacle.

The obstacle ahead was to cross a narrow board over a shallow pit. If anyone fell, they had to go back to the start. Most boys required a couple of tries before making it across. Chelci went last but made it on her first try.

The final obstacle was a series of bars to swing underneath, followed by five ropes to pass between without touching the ground. The obstacle was easy with a strong grip, but a couple of the boys had to wait and shake their arms out between attempts.

A short jog later, they all arrived back at the beginning, barely winded. The course itself was short, so running it alone would take no more than a few minutes. It was the obstacles that took time.

I wonder how long that took us? I'm sure it was well past eight minutes. I need to figure out how to get over that wall. Hopefully, it'll be a while before they time us.

"Now that you know what the course is like, you get to do it timed." Chelci's heart sank as Bensen shattered her hopes. She groaned as he continued. "Line up behind Arturo there. You'll start every two minutes. I'll mark your start, and Russell will give you your time when you finish. Any questions?"

No one said anything as they shuffled into a line.

"Good. Arturo . . . Go!"

The boy took off down the path.

Chelci's hands felt clammy, and her stomach was nauseous. *What am I going to do about that wall?* From a distance, she saw Arturo navigate through the course. Two minutes passed.

"Aleks . . . Go!" Another two minutes. "Kohen . . . Go!"

Landon went next, then Reece, then Gael and Finley. She tried to watch them on the course, but eventually, they all blended together.

Just after Finley left, Arturo returned.

"12:20," Russell said as Arturo collapsed to the ground.

Not far behind was Aleks.

"10:45."

"Nice, Aleks!" Chelci said. She smiled as she gave him a high five before he bent over and grabbed his knees to breathe.

David started next, followed by Kohen coming in at 11:04. Royce took off, then Tate.

"12:50," Russell said for Landon as he crossed the line.

I hope I can get better than 12:50, Chelci thought. *I hope I can even finish! If I can't clear the wall, will they kick me out?*

Chelci was the last to start. Watching the others on the course, she thought the next arrival should be Reece, but Gael ran down the final stretch instead.

She frowned. *I guess Reece got passed. I hope he's not stuck on the wall.*

"9:30 for Gael."

Chelci counted down the seconds in her head. Bensen said there wasn't anything riding on this first attempt, but she needed to prove herself. She needed to complete it. When Bensen signaled her, she took off like a dart.

She heard her breathing as she ran. Each step reverberated through her body as she moved as fast as she could. The rope tower was easy—she breezed up and down it with no issue. The short walls slowed her down considerably though as she struggled over each. The tall log ladder wasn't bad, although she battled with a couple of the rungs.

Chelci's legs started to feel heavy as she bounded down the platforms from the tower. Her breath labored. *I didn't expect it to be this tough!*

Chelci paled as she approached the three tall walls. The first two posed minimal issue, as they had the first time. After pausing to catch her breath, she ran toward the last barrier and jumped as high as she could. Defeat. She walked back and tried again with an even farther running start. Nothing. Several more tries yielded the same result. Her shoulder hurt from where she slammed into the wooden boards repeatedly. She held it gingerly as she rested for a moment, feeling the seconds tick by.

I've got to do this. I can't fail. Chelci looked at the barrier. It stared back at her, mocking her weakness and lack of ability. "You will *not* get the best of me!" Chelci shouted, pointing at the wall.

Her face was red, and her eyebrows narrowed in a crease. She yelled as she ran at it. When she jumped, rather than stretch with her arm, she kicked her foot on the wall. The push lifted her higher in the air. Her heart soared as her fingers nicked the top, just missing being able to hold on.

That's it! she thought as she walked away from the wall, preparing for another attempt. She ran. The kick felt more natural that time. At the apex of her leap, her fingers got a firm grasp of the top. She yelled with excitement as she pulled her body over. *I can do it!* She grinned, unconcerned with how out of breath she was.

The balance obstacle gave her little trouble, as did the bars and ropes after. Chelci saw the finish line ahead. All the boys had finished, and several appeared bored as they waited.

"14:03," Russell said.

Chelci was heartbroken. She panted as she leaned over and held her knees. *I have to cut that down to eight minutes?* she thought.

Finley walked over to her. "Don't worry, Elise. It's only the first time."

The words weren't helpful. She didn't even look up. "What did you get?" she asked.

"11:20," Finley said.

"Nice job." She bit the side of her lip as she stared at the ground in thought. *I'll never make it if I can't do a lot better. If I can get that wall on my first try, that will cut off a lot of time.* The thought made her hopeful. *Still, I have a long way to go.*

"Okay, everyone, follow me," Russell said, leading the way through the woods.

The path they took went downhill for about ten minutes. The group trudged along, dodging trees and navigating over boulders. The canopy was thick, blocking out much of the sun, which was high in the sky.

Chelci felt better as her heart rate slowed. She enjoyed the casual walk.

"Where do you think we're going?" Chelci asked Aleks as he walked beside her.

"The swamps are ahead, but I don't know what we'd be doing there. I'm just glad we're not running," Aleks said.

"Yeah, really. What do you think his rope is for?" Chelci nodded toward Bensen, who walked at the front of the line.

"I have no idea. Maybe in case any of us need to be tied up?" He smirked.

Before long, the ground flattened out, and a foul odor filled in the air.

"Ugh, what's that smell?" Royce asked.

"Tate's mom farted," Gael said, earning him a bunch of laughs and a punch on the shoulder from Tate.

"Cut it out!" Russell said. "We're here."

Russell stopped in front of a brackish pool of muddy water with a green and orange film across the surface. Bugs flew through the air, and many rested on the thick water itself. Tendrils of plants snaked through the fetid liquid like long, narrow fingers waiting to grab onto anything it contacted. The smell was awful, as if an animal—or many—had died and had been dumped into the pool.

The candidates all lined up along the edge and stared into the filthy bog as Russell addressed them. "David."

"Yes, sir," the boy replied.

"Why are you at the Academy?" Russell asked.

"Because I want to be in the village guard, sir,"

Russell nodded. "Royce, why do we practice fighting with swords?"

"So, we can improve our skill and be able to defend the village when it's needed, sir," Royce said.

"Aleks, why do we train to run with heavy objects?"

"Well, you never know what you may need to do—chasing someone, running from someone. You might be carrying heavy weapons or armor. If you're trained for it, then you'll be able to do whatever is needed. And it could mean your life—or someone else's," Aleks replied.

Russell stopped and stared at all of the candidates. "Yes, everything we do has a purpose. In this bog, we have lost a golden dragon egg." Several boys snickered. "The village is in danger, and we need this egg to protect it with its magical powers. I want you all to jump in there and find it. You have thirty seconds . . . starting now."

Several boys started talking at once, but Chelci ignored them. She knew there wasn't an *actual* dragon's egg, but there must be something they needed to find, and after her dismal performance on the course, she needed to be the one to find it. Bracing herself for the cold, she jumped, sinking into the chilly, grimy water to her chest.

Her feet were buried in some sort of sludge-like bed of mud and decay. She couldn't see into the depths, and her arms weren't long enough to reach down, so she took a deep breath and dunked her head. The temperature of the water threatened to expel the breath from her lungs. She kept her eyes closed, feeling through the plants and mud, trying not to think about what was in there. Pulling herself through on the muddy bottom, she was unable to find anything.

When she couldn't hold her breath any longer, she came up for air, well past thirty seconds. She kept her eyes closed as she wiped the mud and muck off her face. The rancid smell was all around her, and she had to fight back her gag reflex. She blinked her eyes open and looked to see if anyone else found the egg. Her heart stopped.

All the other boys, as well as Russell and Bensen, stood on the shore, completely dry. Most of the boys were bent over laughing—Royce, Gael, and Tate, worst of all. At least Aleks and Finley were polite enough not to laugh.

"What an idiot!" Tate said. "Hey, dummy! There's no such thing as a dragon egg."

What made her most upset was Russell, smirking and shaking his head. Chelci felt a hot flush creep up her face as her shoulders slumped.

There never was anything there, she thought as she stumbled her way out of the muck, hitting the water in frustration as the boys continued to laugh. Everyone made a show of giving her a wide berth and fanning their noses.

"We've included this in training for the last ten years, and this is the first time anyone has jumped in," Russell said to the group while continuing to shake his head.

The laughter seemed like it would never end. Chelci wanted to dive back under to get away from the ridicule.

For a moment, Russell didn't speak. He watched with his head cocked as Chelci squeezed the wet muck out of her clothes. When the laughter settled, he spoke up. "Gael, what do you think the purpose of that exercise was?" he asked.

"To see who's an idiot and who's not?" Gael said before he, Tate, and Royce devolved into another round of laughter.

"I said everything we do has a purpose." He turned to Chelci. "Elise, what do you think the purpose would be of telling you to look for a dragon egg to protect the village?"

Chelci shrugged, refusing to look at him.

"The purpose was to see who would do it," Russell said.

Chelci was on the verge of tears. "Well, congratulations then. You found the first idiot in ten years, stupid enough to fail your test!"

"Elise," he said with a kind voice. "The purpose was to see who'd follow a command when your desire told you to do otherwise. We wanted to see who would put their own comfort aside to pursue something that could protect the village. I found the first person to *pass* the test . . . ever."

All residual laughter from the boys ceased as they stared at Russell. Chelci's eyes were wide as she looked at him. Her mouth hung open. She laughed, short at first, but then she broke into a big grin and laughed fully.

I may not be the best at everything. But I'm top of the class in at least one area. A funny expression showed on Russell's face she had not seen before. Her cheeks glowed with warmth as she realized what the expression meant.

He was proud of her.

Chelci tiptoed through the house, avoiding the creaky floorboards and trying not to wake Russell or Nevi. The front door opened, and she stepped into the cold night air, moving to stay warm.

The village guard patrolled the edge of the town each night, so Chelci kept to the interior. She walked through the dark, dodging houses and keeping an eye out for guards. At the edge of the town, the training center stood in front of her. Seeing no guards around, Chelci slunk past it into the woods.

The lantern she brought sparked as she lit it, and the light roared through the darkness. Glancing back to the village, she couldn't even see the training center. *The hill should keep anyone else from seeing the light.*

She walked to the center of the course and set the lamp down, giving a small amount of light to most of the obstacles.

If I'm going to be good enough at this, I need practice—a lot of it. But I can't let everyone else know that I have to put in so much effort. Doing this at night is the only way.

Chelci returned to the beginning of the course and looked through the woods. In the dim illumination, she could faintly make out the various obstacles. Ignoring the butterflies in her stomach, she began to run.

25

Returning Home

Brixton Fiero arrived in Karad by carriage. In the last four years, he had come back a handful of times, but this time, it was for good. Trunks filled with clothes and all his belongings from school loaded up the top of the carriage.

The vehicle rolled to a stop outside of his family's house in West Fairren. Seeing the tall stone structure with its large balcony and ornate windows made him feel at home. Two servants came out to take care of the luggage while Brixton walked inside.

In the end, King's Academy had been a good experience for him. During the first year, he was in danger of failing out. Brixton blamed it on Magnus Hampton for stealing his project, but his grades had been in jeopardy even before that. Thanks to a well-placed bribe—financed by his father—he made it to his second year. From then on, things got easier. He never excelled but was able to pass all of his classes.

"Brixton!" his mother exclaimed as she jumped up and greeted him with a hug. "Oh, you've grown so much!" She smiled and looked him up and down.

Elenor Fiero had aged in his absence. Her face looked worn with creases at the corners of her eyes and mouth. Her blond hair had a few gray streaks and had begun to thin, but it was barely noticeable.

"Hello, Mother," he said, smiling back before shifting his gaze to his father, who remained seated. "Father." Raynor's mouth set in a frown, which seemed fixed on his face after years of discontent. *Not much looks to have changed with him,* Brixton thought.

Raynor nodded. "Brixton. Welcome back. Were you able to learn anything from the four years of school I paid for?" he asked.

"Raynor!" his wife chided in a light-hearted tone. "He graduated, so of course he learned something."

I wonder how long he's going to hold paying for school over my head? Or for bailing me out my first year.

Elenor turned to Brixton. "Your sister's around here somewhere. I know she'd love to see you."

After assuring his mother that he was well and that his trip was uneventful, Brixton followed the servants as they carried his luggage down the hall. Ahead, Mila and a friend turned a corner, walking toward him.

Mila cried out and ran to him with a big hug. "Brix, you're back!" she said, giving him a big hug.

Mila? She had grown, both in height as well as the maturity of her body. *She's not a child anymore. She must be as tall as Mother now!*

At first, Brixton didn't notice her friend, but he couldn't stop looking once he did. Hailey Billings was no longer the giggly red-headed girl he once knew. She was now tall, self-possessed, and beautiful. Her bright red hair had darkened into a deep crimson hue. She wore a rich blue dress that hugged the form of her body, and her glittering necklace matched the sparkle in her eyes.

"Hailey? Hello. Um, it's uh . . . good to see you again," he said.

"Hello, Brixton," Hailey said. "I hope the Academy was educational and enjoyable."

"Yes, it was, but it's good to be home."

The two girls made their way down the hall as Brixton watched Hailey walk away. Coming home, his main goal was to find a job, but now another desire filled his mind . . . one made up of long, red hair.

The Fiero family had a special dinner feast to celebrate Brixton's return. It consisted of beet and potato soup, grilled herring, and roasted pheasant with assorted vegetables. Nearly everyone at King's came from well-to-do families, so he had excellent meals during his time there—still, it was special eating at home.

"Brixton," his father said. "Now that you've completed your education and are back in Karad, have you given thought as to what career you might pursue?"

Brixton was ready for this question as it seemed to be the only thing his father cared about. *What will you do with your life? Will you be successful and honor the Fiero name?*

Brixton had battled with his answer for the previous year. His father was very successful and could open a lot of doors and provide opportunities. Unfortunately, he hated the idea of working with the man. Brixton imagined the pressure and intimidation he would feel. Ideally, he wanted to find a similar job without having to work with his father.

He sat up tall and looked his father in the eye as he gave his well-rehearsed response. "Yes, Father, I have. I'd like to follow in your footsteps by working in finance, commerce, or lending. I'm considering applying to one of the lending houses in the city. Another idea I had was working with the Department of the Treasury, or possibly even as a clerk in your office to get started. I hoped to visit some of the businesses around and see if they have any openings, but if you know of an opportunity, I'd appreciate any leads."

Brixton leaned back, smiling from how well he'd articulated himself. Ultimately, he wanted to avoid working with his father, but wording his response that way would show deference and respect, which his father would appreciate. *I hope he'll be impressed at how I've thought through the different options,* Brixton thought.

"Very good, it's decided then," Raynor said. "You'll work as a clerk in the Department of Commerce. I finally fired Roland a few weeks ago and have been holding off selecting a replacement. You'll start next week."

Brixton's jaw fell slack. Fighting to keep his face from revealing the disappointment he felt, he was tempted to say no to the job just to spite him. *It should open up great opportunities. The pain should be worth it,* he told himself as he groaned inside.

"I look forward to it, Father," Brixton said without giving voice to any of his concerns. "Thank you."

The family ate in silence. Brixton waited on someone to ask more about school, but it didn't appear they were interested.

"Mother, Father, did you hear about the King's Academy Blademaster Championship?" he asked.

"Blademaster Championship?" his father repeated.

"It's an annual sword fighting competition at the Academy."

Raynor scoffed. "It sounds like a bunch of kids got together and made up a fancy name to make themselves feel important."

Brixton cleared his throat and fidgeted in his seat. "I . . . some of the other students and I started it last year."

"Ha! I knew it," Raynor's deep laugh grated on Brixton's nerves.

Brixton didn't know what to say. He had looked forward to sharing this with his parents for a long time, but his father was putting it down before he even began.

"What about it, dear? Tell us about this championship," his mother said.

Brixton leaned forward. "It's actually a huge deal. We started it last year to give students a chance to exhibit their swordsmanship and compete against each other. Most of the students and professors—even a couple of the high lords in Felting—came to watch. I wrote to you about it last year. Do you not remember the letter?"

His parents exchanged a look. "It must have gotten lost in the mail," his father said.

I'm not sure I believe that, Brixton thought. "Well, it was such a hit that we held it again this year, and guess who won?" He looked to his parents in eager expectation. His raised eyebrows accented his bright eyes, but his parents stared dumbly back. "Me! I won!"

"Congratulations, dear. That's great!" Elenor said with a smile. They both turned to his father, who tore into the pheasant. "Raynor?" He looked up with eyebrows raised. "Don't you want to say something to your son about his sword . . . thing?"

"It's the Blademaster Championship," Brixton told her.

His father looked at him then threw the bones of the bird down on his plate. "No, I don't want to say anything!"

Brixton flinched, startled by the harsh reaction.

Raynor continued, "I grew up poor. My father was a wheelwright and didn't make enough money to put food on the table most nights. I worked hard when I was young. Every time I scraped something together to sell, to get money for our family, I didn't get a 'congratulations'—I got to *eat.* So, if Brixton beats a couple of his school friends with a sword, I'm not going to congratulate him on it because it doesn't matter."

"It wasn't a couple of friends, Father. Thirty-eight people competed," Brixton said, picking at his vegetables with his fork.

"If you want to get recognition, go out there and do something worth bragging about!"

Why does he have to be such a jerk? Well, I'm proud of myself, Brixton thought.

Mila leaned over to Brixton and said quietly, "I think it's great, Brix."

The family resumed eating dinner in silence. When they were about finished, Raynor caught Elenor's eye, causing her to shake her head. Raynor waited for a moment, then cleared his throat. "On this great evening of Brixton returning home, I have even more exciting news," he said.

His mother breathed in sharply and stiffened in her chair. *This may not be as exciting as I'm supposed to believe*, Brixton thought.

"Byron Hampton and I have come to an agreement that'll be great for us all, especially for Mila."

Mila turned to her mother with a worried look on her face, but Elenor wouldn't meet her gaze.

"Byron's son Magnus and our daughter Mila are to be married!" Raynor said as he raised his glass.

Brixton froze.

"What!" Mila shouted. She looked at her father then back to her mother. Her eyes were wide, and her jaw hung open. "No! I don't want to marry *Magnus*! I love Ashton!"

"I said you weren't to spend time with him anymore," Raynor said as he lowered his glass. "Magnus will be an excellent match for you, and he comes from a great family."

"But I don't want to marry him!"

"I don't care if you want to. It's been decided."

Mila yelled as she stood up and stormed out of the room.

Brixton ached to yell and stomp off just like his sister, but he managed to restrain himself from an outburst. *I don't want Magnus marrying into our family!*

"Raynor, I told you she wouldn't want to do it," Elenor said.

"It doesn't matter what she wants. It's good for her *and* good for us."

Elenor shook her head but didn't say any more. After a moment, she set her napkin on her plate and left the room, following after her daughter. Brixton and his father finished their meals in silence.

I spend four years at school, learning and growing, but when I come home, nothing has changed, Brixton thought.

* * *

Brixton's first day of work arrived on Marketday. He walked with his father down High Street, having accepted his fate to work with him—at least for a while. *Maybe it will be better than I'm expecting? Perhaps he'll see I can do something well?* he thought.

The Department of Commerce building loomed ahead. Brixton had been there countless times, but walking to it that morning caused his stomach to turn. Nervousness and excitement battled inside of him. As he walked through the door, the familiar office felt foreign to him, like he was experiencing it for the first time. Tucker and Heath stood to welcome him, and his nerves faded.

"Tucker, would you show Brixton the ropes?" his father asked without breaking stride while heading to his office.

"Of course, Lord Fiero," Tucker replied.

"I'd like to put him in charge of business licenses," Raynor said, pausing in the doorway.

Tucker scrunched up his forehead. "But, sir, I handle the licenses. I worked here for years before I was ready to be able to take that on. Are you sure—"

"Yes, I'm sure. Show him what he needs to know."

Tucker paused for a moment. "Yes, my lord." The words met an already closed door. He turned to Brixton. "Busy man. Of course, I don't have to tell you." Tucker led him to the desk in the corner.

"This one is yours. I guess you'll be in charge of licenses then."

"I'm sorry about that," Brixton said.

Tucker waved the comment away. "No, it's fine. I don't mind. Here, let me get a few things for you."

The clerk returned to his desk, gathered up some papers and files, and brought them to Brixton. Tucker's face looked pained as he handed the stack over.

Tucker showed Brixton the forms he needed to use and how to fill them out. He explained the filing system he'd created and where to put papers. Dealing with so many records, their department relied a great deal on accessing historical information, so finding something when needed was important. Tucker was very organized, so if Brixton could stick to the processes, it should be easy to keep everything straight.

I just need to avoid mistakes, he thought, glancing at the closed door to his father's office.

Later that morning, Brixton's first customer arrived. The front door opened, and an older man walked in, who Tucker greeted warmly. "I was hoping to discuss a reduction of my seasonal license rate," the man said. "Who can I speak to about that?"

Tucker looked over. "It's all you, Brix."

For a moment, Brixton froze, thinking through what to do. "Um . . . yes. Come over and have a—take a . . . um . . . and sit down," Brixton said, already sweating. "So, who are you?"

"My name's Sutton Fielding. I run an apothecary shop on the east side of the Bottoms where I've been for twenty-one years."

"Ok. Mr. Fielding . . . apothecary." He wrote down notes as he listened. "And you want a rate reduction?"

"Yes, that's right. When I first started, my seasonal rent was three argen, but a few years ago, it increased to six. My business struggled from the increased amount, and in these last couple of years, the neighborhood around it has gone downhill. My customers aren't able to pay what they used to, and as a result, I've been losing money every week for the last year." Brixton nodded as Sutton continued. "I was hoping I'd be allowed a rate reduction. Possibly to go back to the three argen I had for so long?"

Brixton wasn't sure what to say. He stared dumbly at the man who leaned forward with eager eyes.

The silence caused the man to continue. "Four or even five argen would, of course, be helpful too."

That sounds reasonable, Brixton thought. *If he can't make money, his business will close down. A reduction in the rate would lower the city's income, but it would be much better than a closed business, which brings in nothing. But is that the right call?* He looked to Tucker for help, but the clerk had his back turned, appearing to be working on something else. *He's ignoring me.*

"Um . . . Tucker?" Brixton asked.

The clerk turned. "Yes?" Brixton held his hands up as a sign of needing help. Tucker sighed and came over. "First, pull the business records," he said.

Brixton walked to the cabinet, thumbed through the papers, and pulled out the file in question.

Back at the desk, Tucker helped talk him through it. "So, here's the neighborhood data, here's the building details and history, and here are the sales and tax records."

"Okay, so what do I do?" Brixton asked.

"It's your call." Tucker lifted his palms. "You're in charge of business licenses."

I think he's enjoying this. Brixton wiped the sweat off his forehead. "Right. Okay." *Whatever I decide will be wrong, and Father will yell at me about it.* "Maybe I should get my father's opinion?"

"You could do that," Tucker said, shrugging.

Brixton hesitated for a moment before walking to the office door. As he was about to knock, Tucker stopped him. "Wait, no. Don't bother him about this." The head clerk sighed and turned to address the man. "Mr. Fielding, we appreciate your concern over the business rent. I'm sure the increased rate has made things more difficult, but based on your sales history and the values in the area, the six argen rent is fair. It should be feasible for a business such as yours to be able to pay. Perhaps you need to take a look at your expense base or supply cost? Maybe you can increase your margins? I believe if you put some effort into that, you'll find the seasonal rent will be negligible."

The man hung his head. "I know you're right. I just wish I could see where to tighten things up. When I was younger, my mind worked better with things like that." He stood and shuffled his way toward the door.

Brixton tried to make eye contact to thank Tucker, but the head clerk watched Mr. Fielding as the apothecary left with a sad expression on his face.

"Mr. Fielding!" Tucker called after him. "I've spent a lot of time looking through expense reports and analyzing businesses. If you like, after I'm off work today, I could come to your shop. If you can get all your papers together, I could help look things over and maybe make some suggestions to help you be more profitable?"

The man's face lit up. "Oh, sir, that would be wonderful! Thank you so much!"

Tucker sat down as Mr. Fielding left. "Thanks for your help, Tucker," Brixton said, relieved.

"It was nothing." After a pause, Tucker turned his chair to face him. "I'm sorry for how I was at first."

Brixton froze. *I can't remember anyone ever apologizing to me,* he thought.

"I was hurt that you were taking the license work away because I put a lot into building that process," Tucker said. "I didn't want to be helpful because I wanted to see you struggle, but that was wrong. I don't want you to fail. I didn't want you to ask your father because I knew how he'd respond, and I wanted to save you from that."

Brixton chuckled. "Yeah, I guess I can picture it too. Thanks, Tucker." Brixton settled back at his desk, thankful to have his first customer behind him. *I'm glad Tucker is here. I guess I have a lot to learn, and it's good to have someone on my side.*

26

Resolve

Veron had stayed with Artimus' body while the building burned, deteriorating to nothing. At one point, the flames found their way to the garden, but Veron was too much in shock to try to save any of the food.

When daybreak came, the rain started and turned the coals into wet ash and charred timber. Nearby, townspeople gathered to gawk, but they kept their distance when they saw Veron with Artimus' body.

After hours without moving, Veron finally got up, grabbed a shovel from the shed—which had survived the flames—and dug in the freshly charred garden. When he had a hole deep enough, he pulled Artimus' body into it as gently as he was able. Seeing his teacher lying at the bottom of the grave unleashed a whole new wave of grief. Veron fell to his knees and cried once more.

Once composed, he filled the grave back in and leaned on his shovel, standing in the dirt. The rain continued to fall, but he'd long since noticed. Grief filled him deep within his soul.

How did this happen? Artimus was like a father, and now he's gone. I was about to run my own store. I had money, food, and shelter. I did what

Fend wanted, and now it's all gone. The hopeful future that was finally within reach had disappeared.

His teeth clenched as Slash and his gang came to his mind. *They took this from me, and now they're out there with my money,* Veron thought, his jaw tightening and arm shaking. *And Mortinson took it all from Morgan. And Bale took it all from my father.* He swam in the rage for a moment until he realized there was nothing he could do about it. He released a loud sigh that grew to a yell and dropped the shovel in the dirt.

Veron considered the possibility of trying to find Morgan. His family moved somewhere in the Docks the day before. He was sure they would help if he asked, but they were going through a hardship of their own.

I don't want to burden them. I'm in this alone.

Having nothing left for him at Artimus' house, Veron carried the chest and the sword and left, returning to the old abandoned house he had shared with Fend many years earlier. To his relief, it was still there, and it was still empty. The broken chair and remains of two straw beds were as he remembered, but the stench of decay and rotten wood pervaded the space. Veron hoped the familiarity would be comforting, but it only reminded him of his life as a thief. All the progress he made over the years seemed for nothing. Once again, Veron was hungry and alone, and life seemed hopeless.

* * *

Veron sat alone for days, wrestling with his thoughts. Inertia had become his enemy, preventing him from doing anything despite the chill of early wiether, but hunger finally prompted him to get up and move. Four years before, he walked the city with purpose, determined to try to find a way to escape his life. Now, Veron wandered with no goal and no plan.

The streets were the same as always, but they felt different and foreign to him. A girl ahead in the lane sat on a wooden step. She couldn't be older than ten and reminded him of his past life. She had a smile on her face and held a small portion of bread, which she ate happily.

How can she be happy? Life is miserable. How dare she smile? Veron's lips curled at the corner as his hands clenched.

He paused in front of her, causing the girl to stop eating and stare up at him. Veron reached and took the bread from her hands. The girl yelled and jumped up, punching his arm, but he didn't even feel it. Before he could stop himself, he pushed. The girl fell to the ground in the mud and started crying before scrambling to her feet and running away.

Veron took her seat as he ate the bread. He waited for a smile to come over his face as it had for the girl, but it didn't happen. What came instead were tears.

What have I done? What have I become? he thought.

He curled up on the step, hoping that if he balled himself up tightly enough, he could protect himself from the world. It didn't help. The world remained.

* * *

At the abandoned house, Veron wavered between grief and anger. He held onto the emotions because he was afraid of the solitude that waited past them. Eventually, they did recede, and he was surprised at what he found. He knew what hardship was like and how it felt to lose hope. He had been there and survived. After the grief and anger faded, it wasn't fear that remained. It was resolve.

Although he was physically in the same place he'd been many times

247

in life, he now had knowledge and skills. He knew how businesses worked. He knew how to read and write, which in itself was more than the majority of the people south of Split were able to do. He also could fight.

I've been training to be a shadow knight. I know much of what they did, and now I'm the only one left. Veron's pulse raced. His stomach felt queasy as he tried to steady his breathing and considered what that meant. *No. I'm no warrior. I don't even know how to . . .*

His attention turned to the ornate chest sitting in the middle of his room, which he'd avoided since Artimus died.

Maybe my answers are in there?

Veron took the key he'd been wearing around his neck. Inserting it into the lock, it clicked when he turned it. The wood creaked as he lifted the lid. Inside, staring back at him, rested a large, thick book with a dark cover and gilded edges. *Chronology of the Shadow Knights* was written across the front.

Veron's eyes grew. *Can I learn how to use the origine from this book?*

He lifted it out of the chest and found two other things underneath. One was a back scabbard for a sword. The other item was a black, hooded cloak made of high-quality fabric—the one he saw Artimus wearing that night in the training room. On the cloak, over where the heart would be, was the Shadow Knights' symbol—just like his medallion. He touched his shirt where the metal object hung, feeling comforted by its presence.

Putting the cloak and scabbard back, he set the book in his lap and opened it up. "Code of the Shadow Knights" was printed in large flowery script across the top of the first section. Underneath, it listed eight points:

1. *Serve the kingdom above self and others.*
2. *Consider the needs of anyone less fortunate than you.*

3. *Never use your position as a knight to elevate your status in life.*
4. *Do not be jealous of another knight's victory. Their success is a cause for celebration.*
5. *No matter how skilled or wise you are, there is always someone better, so have the attitude of a learner.*
6. *Never hurt another person except as necessary to uphold the code.*
7. *Killing is always a last resort.*
8. *Never allow your abilities to be known.*

This is how my father lived. I bet he would be proud if I followed in his footsteps. It was comforting to consider but conflicting as well. *I don't live up to this code. I never have. Maybe I'm not able to follow this path? Surely there's someone else out there who can stop Bale?*

After the code was a section that discussed the history of the group. The Shadow Knights were founded in the 213th year of the Era of Justice by a man named Talon Shadow.

According to the book, Talon developed the skill to tap into the origine after visiting an ancient spring hidden high in the Straith Mountains where spirits passed on the knowledge and ability to him. He then traveled the kingdom to recruit others who could learn. Once they had six in their group, the Shadow Knights formed. Talon's sword, named Farrathan, recognizable by the ruby embedded into the hilt, became the symbol of the Knights.

Veron looked at his sword, which lay on the ground, and stared at the ruby. *Whoa! That's my sword! Farrathan!*

After the history section was the part of the book Veron was most interested in. It was titled "The Origine."

Artimus said I passed the test. I'm not sure what it takes to pass or even what the test was, but I must have something in me. If I have the ability to learn how to use the origine, I want to develop it.

He thought back to Artimus in the training room that night—how fast he moved. His mind turned to the offerdom up on the hill outside the city. He imagined lines of people waiting to find out if their offering would be enough. He saw the horror on their faces when someone chopped off a father's head . . . or a child's. He envisioned the Shadow Knights being attacked in the night by thirty of Bale's men. He pictured his father fighting bravely as he was pierced by arrow after arrow.

Veron ground his teeth. *Bale can't win. If I'm the only one left, I'll learn to be a shadow knight, and I'll stop him.* He took a deep breath until a brief laugh escaped. *Maybe I don't have to die. If I know the origine, I can heal myself! Right?*

He smiled as he turned back to the book and read through the passages. There were pages and pages of descriptions about what the origine was, but as he read, his excitement waned. None of it made sense.

The origine is not something you can learn to control. Instead, it must be felt . . . When you reach inside and touch the origine, you are in control of your power . . . The depth of your energy is limited, but can be tapped into when desired . . . Channeling the origine is like reaching inside to sustain you . . . Like a metal ring circulates the transfer of energy, your body must exhale its power . . .

It went on, saying similar things over and over. Veron felt he understood less about it after reading. Nothing in the passages said what he should do. No instructions told him how to start or how to use it. It didn't discuss what it felt like or how to know if it's right. He thumbed through the book, but the end was just an archive, listing all the past members of the Knights. He closed it in frustration.

Veron wanted to try but wasn't sure what to do. He waved his arm in the air and tried to make it go really fast, but nothing happened. He thought hard and flexed the muscles of his stomach but didn't feel anything was different.

I wish Artimus were here. I don't know what to do, Veron thought. *I'm not going to learn any more about the origine from this. I need to get up and do something.*

He left the house and decided to go for a run to clear his mind. He didn't follow his usual path but meandered through the streets and alleys. He crossed over to Upper Sherry before heading north into East Fairren. His clothes began to dot with sweat. His heart rate increased, the familiar sensation bringing him comfort, reminding him of his time training with Artimus.

As he emerged from an alley into Karad Square, he slowed to a walk. *I can't just train to fight Bale though. Maybe one day I'll be ready, but I have a long way to go. For now, I need food, and I need a way to live . . . and I can't go back to being a thief again.*

Veron sat on a bench awhile and watched the shopkeepers. He understood so much about how things worked compared to when he was young. Back when he lived on the streets, all they were to him were potential targets to steal from. Now, Veron knew how they operated and what made a store successful or not.

He walked into one of the grocery stores on the square and meandered through the rows of food. The shop was well organized. It was clean, and the aisles were wide. The food was more expensive than Morgan's shop, which was understandable given its location. Veron wasn't looking to steal anything, but the owner still kept a sharp eye on him.

"You need to rotate your apples better," Veron said to the shop-keeper.

The man looked at him in surprise. "I'm sorry?"

"Your apples. There are ones close to going bad at the bottom of the bin. If you don't sell them soon, you'll have to throw them out. So, you may want to put them on the top."

The grocer looked at him oddly, and Veron was suddenly aware of his appearance. Mud and blood still stained his white shirt, and he was sure his face was a mess.

"Oh, I didn't notice. Thanks," the grocer said. He went over to check out the apple bin while Veron left through the front door.

Veron walked farther into the city, wandering down the streets and alleys of Prinvestor, the affluent area north of Karad Square. Just below the North Gate, down a small street, something caught his eye—a large old wooden door he'd never noticed before. The door was on a rail and made to slide open, but a rusted-over chain secured the handle to the opposite wall. It didn't look like it had opened in a long time.

Some of the door's wooden slats were missing or rotted away, allowing him to see through. Behind the door was a large dirt courtyard open to the sky above it. *Looks like a stable from a long time ago*, he thought.

Several open-air stalls made a "U" shape around the edge of the courtyard. Above each stall was a second floor. Half of the second floor was an open-air loft, but the other half contained rooms. On the ground level on the left side was a separate enclosed building.

Veron remembered there being a Royal Stables that opened in West Fairren many years back. It was a big deal and was supposed to be the nicest and largest around. Most people living in the wealthy area would be quick to leave a run-down old stable if something nicer and newer came along.

This place probably went under around that time and has been empty ever since. It's such a shame. All of this space is wasted when it could be put to good use by someone. An idea hit him suddenly. *I could do something good with this! I'm no longer a street kid who picks pockets and steals loaves of bread anymore. I'm experienced and educated, and I know how to do something great with this space.*

His eyes lit up with excitement. All his life, Veron wished for what would never be. He lamented the opportunities he would never have, but that reality was no longer true. He had the tools he needed. If he failed to take action, it would be because he chose not to, not because he couldn't.

His exuberance came crashing down for a moment as he considered the things he needed to turn his idea into reality. He needed permits, lots of people, plenty of goods, and above all, a lot of money. These were no longer barriers anymore. They were only challenges. Challenges he could get around, and Veron knew just where to start.

27

Getting Started

Veron walked along the river toward the docks, surrounded by the typical midmorning bustle of activity. Three large boats had recently docked, and haggard-looking men bowed by a life of hard labor unloaded goods. Some operated heavy hooks to pick up larger items, but most boarded the boats and carried what they could out of the cargo hold and off the deck. They either set the goods on the street or took them directly into warehouses across the way.

After scanning the crowd for several minutes, Veron finally saw his friend walking down the plank from a small boat at Dock Two. His arms were filled with two crates of live chickens that flapped their wings in protest as he carried them to shore. It had barely been a week since leaving the grocery, but Morgan had already lost weight. His beard and hair were unkempt, and the ever-present smile was nowhere to be found.

Veron made his way over. "Nice chickens!" he said as Morgan set them down.

Morgan turned in surprise and immediately broke into a grin which settled into a look of relief. "Veron!" He grabbed him up in a big hug. "It's so good to see you!"

Morgan's enthusiasm and joy were infectious. Veron couldn't help but smile back. He had been trapped by grief for days, so the feeling was welcome. "Do you have a minute to talk?" Veron asked.

"Sure! It's about my break time anyway. Hold on a moment."

Morgan hurried to an older man with a ledger taking notes then returned shortly. "Okay, I've got fifteen minutes," he said.

They walked over to an empty Dock Three and sat at the end with their feet dangling over the flowing water below. Birds cawed as they flew overhead, and the refreshing smell of the river filled the air. For a brief moment, Veron forgot all the awful things that had recently happened.

"I'm so glad you're okay," Morgan said. "When I heard about Artimus' place, I got there as soon as I could, but no one was there." He hesitated for a moment. "I saw the grave. I assume that was . . ."

Veron nodded.

"What happened?" Morgan asked.

Veron hung his head and related the events that happened since they'd last been together. He told him about Slash and the gang, the stolen money, Artimus dying, and the house burning. Morgan wiped tears away as he listened.

"I'm so sorry, Veron. I know how much he meant to you. I insist that you come and stay with Catherine and me. You need a place to stay and food. We'd be happy to take you in," Morgan told him.

"No. Thanks for the offer, but it's not necessary. I have a place," Veron said. "It's not very nice, but it keeps me dry. And I'm about to get into business, so I should be making good money soon too."

Morgan tilted his head. "Oh? What are you going to do?"

"How would you like to operate a grocery again?" Veron asked.

Morgan gave a short laugh. "That sounds great, but I can't. I'm prohibited."

"From *owning* a business, right? That doesn't mean you can't *work* at one. Correct?"

Morgan tossed his head back and scratched his chin. "Yeah, I guess so."

"I plan on opening a business—a market of sorts. I need someone to operate the day-to-day activities for the grocery, and I can think of no one better than you, Morgan. I'll be the owner, and you'll work for me. There's no prohibition against that. Under that arrangement, you can continue to buy and sell groceries the way you always have but without the attention of the city to get you in trouble."

Morgan's eyes were wide. "I . . . um . . . I don't know what to say. Of course, I'd love to do that!" he said while gesticulating with his hands. "But how's that possible? How are you opening a business? You said you lost all your money."

"Let me worry about the money. All I need to know is, are you on board?"

"Yes! Count me in!" Morgan said, beaming with a broad smile and a look of relief. "So, what do I need to do? When do we start?"

Veron rubbed his hands together, feeling eager. "I have some details to work out first, so keep doing what you're doing for now. Once we're officially ready, I'll let you know. In the meantime, I want you to think about any other people you know who may be interested in joining up, especially ones that may be down on their luck and are looking for a fresh start."

Morgan raised an eyebrow. "Other grocers?"

"No, other types of merchants. Butcher, cobbler, baker, tailor, anything like that."

"Gotcha." He looked up and rubbed his chin again. "Yeah, I know a few that I think may be interested."

Veron's voice dropped, and a crease formed between his eyebrows. "Okay, so you're the expert. How much will this cost?"

"How much will *what* cost, exactly?"

"Starting up a grocery from scratch. How much money would we need to outfit you with a healthy starting inventory of food and supplies?"

Morgan whistled and thought for a moment. He furrowed his brow deep in thought. "To get started, you'd need—not counting whatever license fee you'd need for the business—one, maybe two sol. But keep in mind, if you're going to have four or five different vendors, you're probably going to need one to two sol for *each* business."

Veron swallowed hard. *This is going to be tough. No! Challenges, not barriers.* "Okay, good to know."

Morgan needed to get back to work, so they said goodbye. As he walked away, Veron turned abruptly back to Morgan. "Oh, I forgot," he said. "Do you have a nice outfit I could borrow by chance? Something that would help me look more respectable?"

Morgan thought for a second. "Yes! I do! One of my best outfits was from my younger days, and it doesn't fit me anymore. I've been holding onto it in case I lose some weight." He hit his stomach and laughed. "If I keep working at these docks much longer, I may be able to wear it again soon! If you can wait around a few hours, I'll take you by my new place when I'm off work."

Veron wandered the area while he waited and soon found himself by Dock Five, where a small pile of blue striped rocks next to the wall caught his eye. He picked up one and rolled it in his hand while memories of Artimus flashed in his head. Waking up early in the morning. Sword fighting. Learning to read. Working in the garden. The hug Artimus gave him. The way he looked as he lay in the grave.

Veron wiped a tear away. *I won't forget, Artimus. I'll keep training. If I'm the only remaining shadow knight, I'll be the best one I can,* he thought.

He made his way back to the main docks and found a wooden crate to perch on. Veron observed the workers laboring and sweating, moving the never-ending piles of cargo. None of them looked happy. *If my market plan doesn't work out, there's a real possibility I may end up working here soon.* Veron shuddered at the thought. His plan was bold. He was taking a considerable risk, but he didn't have anything to lose. *I'm so glad to have Morgan on board,* he thought, feeling less alone knowing his friend was with him.

* * *

The next morning, Veron got up and made his way to the community water trough in Kulling Square. He got there early because he didn't want anyone to see him trying to bathe himself in their drinking water. Having been spoiled by the convenience of the bathhouse, he now needed to find more creative ways to clean himself. Veron stripped down to his underclothes and splashed water over his body, scrubbing his face and hair. The cold of the morning left him shivering as he rushed to finish.

After using his dirty clothes to dry off, he hurried back, practically naked, to his place. He was freezing but mostly dry by the time he returned. The tightly woven fabric of Morgan's suit was fancier than anything Veron had worn before. It fit him surprisingly well. Ornate buttons trimmed the maroon outer jacket on each side of the open front and at the end of the long sleeves. The collar stood up to cover the sides and back of his neck. The jacket fabric matched the leggings, which extended to just below the knees, and a lighter colored vest served as an accent to the dark jacket.

Thankfully, Morgan also thought to loan him a white shirt, a pair of stockings, and his nice pair of black shoes. The shoes were a little large, but Veron didn't complain.

I wish I had a mirror. I'd love to see how I look.

Veron the street kid entered the ramshackle house, and Veron the businessman walked out minutes later, heading into the city. He felt out of place in the fashionable clothes, but his excitement outweighed the discomfort.

Veron knew a fair amount about operating a business but little about starting one. He needed help to learn what paperwork and costs were involved. Funds would be difficult, but he had some ideas for that. First, he wanted to find out how much would be needed. Because of Morgan's recent trouble, he decided it would be best to keep him as far away from the process as possible, so he was on his own.

Veron wasn't sure exactly where the Department of Commerce was but knew it was somewhere near Karad Square. The square was packed with people when he arrived—horses and carts, men and women, shopkeepers and customers.

Who do I ask?

A young, well-dressed man, not much older than him, walked confidently in his direction.

He'll probably know where to go. Veron waved his hand and tried to make eye contact. "Excuse me!" he called.

The young man stopped and looked back with an odd look on his face, like he wasn't accustomed to strangers stopping him in the street to ask questions.

"I'm sorry to bother you, but I've just arrived yesterday from Felting and am new to town. I'm trying to find the Department of Commerce. Do you know where it'd be?" Veron asked.

"Yes, I do. In fact, I happen to work there—just started this week," the young man replied, holding out his hand. "Brixton Fiero, at your service."

"Brixton, great to meet you. I'm Veron. Veron Stormbridge."

28

Department of Commerce

"Well, it seems my luck is starting to turn. I guess I picked the right person to ask," Veron said.

Brixton had a casual smile and friendly-looking eyes. Veron immediately felt at ease. "So, why are you looking for the Department of Commerce?" Brixton asked.

"I need to apply for a business license."

"Well, believe it or not, I am the one who processes license applications. Why don't you follow me? I was heading to the office now."

Veron followed as Brixton led the way.

"So, you came from Felting?" Brixton asked as they walked up the street.

"Yes, I ran a market there. My father started it years ago, and I've been working there since I was eight. He passed away four years ago, and I've been running it on my own since," Veron told him.

"What was the market you ran? I wonder if I know it. I just graduated from King's Academy."

Veron tried to keep his face calm, but inside he panicked. *I have no idea what any street or place names are there, or even where the school is located in the city.* "It was down a small street kind of out of the way . . . off River Street?" Veron said. He didn't mean for the last part to sound like a question, but it was too late now. He figured with most of Felting surrounded by rivers, there was a good chance a River Street existed somewhere.

"Yeah, I know River Street, but I don't remember any markets there," Brixton said, causing Veron's breath to catch in his throat. "But I mostly just stayed at the school and the taverns near it, so I wouldn't know either way."

Veron breathed a sigh of relief.

"So, why the move here to Karad?" Brixton asked.

"I turned the market over to my brother. He's two years younger and has been learning the business as I did. Now that I feel comfortable with him operating on his own, I'm ready to expand." Veron dodged a horse pulling a cart as he continued his story. "I'm happy with the business my father left me, but I want to prove myself. I want to build my own market empire, not simply be handed down what my father made for himself. If he were still alive, I'd want him to be impressed at what I can do on my own."

Brixton listened eagerly and nodded his head. "You said earlier that your luck is starting to turn. Is everything okay?"

Feigning reluctance to share, Veron paused for a moment. "I'll be fine, but thieves attacked me on the road from Felting."

"Are you okay?" Brixton asked.

"Yeah, I wasn't hurt, but they took my money pouch with ten gold sol." Brixton whistled. "That's what I was going to use to get the market up and running," Veron said.

"That's awful. Well, if you need a temporary loan to get going, I can recommend a few lending houses that should be able to help."

"I would appreciate it. Thank you." *So far, so good,* Veron thought. They arrived at the office, and Brixton opened the door. "Come on back with me," Brixton said as he led him to his desk, indicating to a chair to sit in. "Tucker, Heath, good morning." The other two clerks returned the greeting as Brixton took some forms out from his desk.

The office smelled pleasantly like dry paper. It reminded Veron of Artimus' sitting room where he kept all the books. The memory stole his mind for a moment as a pang of regret hit him.

"So, tell me about this market you want to open," Brixton said, jolting him back to the present.

Veron quickly collected his thoughts. "Do you know the abandoned stable near your North Gate? I believe the area it's in is called . . . Prinvestor?" he said.

Brixton tilted his head for a moment as he stared at the ceiling. "Yes, I think so. It hasn't run for years, I believe. Let me see what I can find on it." Brixton walked to a large filing drawer against the wall and thumbed through it. "Here we go!" He brought over a folder of papers. "North Karad Stables closed down eight years ago. It has a large open space and a small number of enclosed rooms. It looks like in the years following their closing, several other local shops closed as well. It sure would be nice to get that neighborhood going again," he said as he looked at Veron. "So, what specifically do you plan to do with it?"

Veron leaned forward. "I want to have a place where people can go to get all of their needs in one stop. It will have a section for fruits and vegetables, then another for meat and cheese, then another for bread. And a place with a tailor to fit people for clothes and a cobbler and a haberdasher, and who knows what else!" He flung his hands in emphasis as he spoke. "People will choose everything they need and pay when they're done. I already have a few local people ready to work. I just need a license to get started and a loan to make some repairs and get inventory in."

"That sounds great. I can't wait to see how it turns out. With your experience, it shouldn't be an issue approving the application."

Veron gave a small smile, but inside he was jumping with joy. *I'm going to be able to make this happen!*

"Based on the size of the building and yard, empty for eight years . . . Your fee will be . . ." Brixton wrote numbers on a piece of paper to calculate, "one sol and eight per season."

Veron's joy quickly dissipated as he fought to keep his smile from fading. He knew to expect it, but hearing the amount was still shocking.

Brixton wrote on another sheet of paper. "If you want to advertise around the city, the permit fee for that is another four argen per season, and if you want a loan to get things going, here are three lending houses I recommend. Tell them the Fiero family sent you, and you should have no trouble getting approved." He handed the paper to Veron.

"Great. Thank you! I'll visit them." *This is just what I needed. Why am I so nervous?*

"Do you have any connections here in town yet?" Brixton asked. "Where are you staying?"

Veron fidgeted with the hem of his suit. "Oh, um . . . at an inn just down the street. No, I don't really know anyone yet."

Brixton leaned back in his chair and tapped his desk with the pen. "Tell you what . . . since you're new in town, I insist you be our guest at dinner. Will you join us? I'd introduce you to my father now, but he's not in yet."

Veron raised his eyebrow. "Your father?"

"Yes, I'm sorry, I forgot to mention. My father is Raynor Fiero, the Lord of Commerce for Karad," Brixton said.

Veron's eyes opened wide, and his mouth dropped. *Fiero. I knew that name sounded familiar,* he thought as he remembered the large house near the castle Artimus pointed out to him years before. *Should I be scared or excited? I don't know. I don't have a good reason to turn him down, I guess.* "Yes, I'd love to join you," he said.

"Great! Our house is the large one on Ventnor Way. You head down that way," Brixton indicated by pointing up the street, "then turn left. We're a couple of minutes' walk down Ventnor on the left. Number 48. You can't miss it."

The two shook hands, and Brixton escorted him to the door.

"So, come back whenever you have the starting funds for the license," Brixton said. "And of course, we'll need your tax history for your market in Felting as a business reference, but then you'll be all set!"

Veron's heart skipped a beat. "Tax history?" He tried not to panic.

"Yeah, just your standard papers on the business. You know, showing the history and everything. Nothing fancy. I look forward to seeing you tonight!"

How can I get around this? Veron walked away, running his hand through his shaggy hair. *It has to be approved. Trying to fake tax documents would be too risky. If they wanted to verify them, I'd easily be caught and thrown in prison. I'm going to have to try to do this without the paperwork. I need Brixton, or possibly his father, to want to approve my license even if I don't have all the paperwork.* The chance to have dinner with them took on all new importance. His future depended on it.

Veron spent all day thinking of how he could make an impact at dinner. He came up with a variety of outlandish scenarios, ranging from standing on the table and juggling dishes, to challenging Lord Fiero to a fight, to skipping dinner and breaking into the office to write his own license. Unfortunately, he didn't feel any of them would work.

He paced the length of his dusty room, being careful not to soil his outfit with the grime around him. Ideally, he would have preferred to change for the evening, but since they were his only presentable clothes, they would have to do. His plan was ready, but he wasn't sure if it would be enough. Everything depended on how they responded to his story. If any one of several points unraveled, all would be lost.

Veron arrived just before the sun set. Seeing the house reminded him of how small and insignificant he was. He remembered when Artimus brought him there several years before and recalled that Lord Fiero used to work at a grocery when growing up—information that could be helpful.

After knocking on the door and waiting only a brief time, a servant opened the door. *What do I say? Do I need to prove I'm allowed to be here? What if he turns me away?* Veron thought.

"Hello, I'm Veron Stormbridge, and I've been invited to dinner."

"Welcome, young sir," the servant said. "Please follow me."

Wow, that was easy! He wasn't used to looking like he belonged anywhere important.

The foyer of the house was impressive. A sizable hanging chandelier looked as if twenty lamps were all melted together into one curving and elaborate display of wealth. The paintings, rugs, and lighting along the hall were exquisite.

At the end of the hall, the servant stopped at the entrance to a sitting room and announced in a clear voice, "Master Veron Stormbridge."

Brixton jumped up from his seat and hurried over. "Veron, I'm so glad you could make it!" he said, shaking his hand with a smile.

"Me too. Your house is . . . nice," Veron replied, looking around the room. He carefully tried to flatter and not gawk at the extravagance, which was unlike anything he'd experienced before.

"Thank you. The city's been good to us. Let me introduce you to my mother." He indicated to a woman as she stood from her chair by the window.

Her long blue dress was made of rich fabric and accentuated by straight blond hair that fell past her shoulders. "Elenor Fiero. It's great to meet you, Veron," she said. "I hear you're new in town. I'm glad Brixton invited you over. It's *so* difficult to establish yourself in a new place without connections."

"And this is my younger sister, Mila, and her friend, Hailey," Brixton said as he gestured to the girls sitting together on a cushioned seat.

Veron gave a small wave to the girls. They appeared slightly younger than he was and wore similarly styled dresses, Mila in yellow and Hailey in green. The girls both smiled politely and waved back. Both were distractingly pretty, but he forced himself not to pay attention. *I have more important things to focus on,* Veron thought.

"And my father should be . . . Ah, yes! Here he is now," Brixton said.

Raynor Fiero walked into the room, distracted by papers and mumbling with a stern frown on his face. Looking up briefly, he nodded toward Veron while continuing into the dining room. "Am I going to eat alone, or are you all coming?" he said without turning around.

The rest of his family exchanged glances and followed. *It may be more challenging to make a good impression on him than I anticipated,* Veron thought.

Brixton motioned for Veron to sit next to him at the table. As Veron sat, an overwhelming feeling hit him. Two knives, three forks, and two spoons set at his place. He had no idea what to do with them and worried he would give away his charade by lack of etiquette.

Two servers came in right away with drinks and bread. Veron's stomach growled at the sight of food, and he cleared his throat in an attempt to cover the sound. He couldn't remember the last time he ate but didn't want anyone here to know that.

Not wanting to do something foolish, he decided to watch others. Mila was the first to move. She took the smaller knife and used it to spread some smooth red creamy substance on her bread, which she ate. Veron decided it was safe to repeat what she did. He wasn't sure what the red stuff was but found it delicious.

"So, Veron, I hear you've just moved here from Felting?" Elenor asked.

Veron finished his mouthful of bread. "Yes, my lady, I arrived yesterday," he replied.

"Please, call me Elenor," she said before taking a drink of wine.

Veron nodded. "I've found your city to be quite lovely so far. Your son was kind to help me out this morning as well as invite me to join you all tonight, for which I'm most appreciative."

Raynor Fiero continued to read as if no one else were there.

"All I did was direct him to the office and help with his paperwork," Brixton said. "He's applying for a new business license, and it's going to be amazing!"

His father briefly looked up at Veron for a moment before returning to his reading.

"That's right. I'll be opening up a market near the North Gate as soon as I can get everything straightened out," Veron said.

"It's going to be an enormous market!" Brixton exclaimed. "Unlike anything we've seen here before!"

Raynor set down his papers and looked up. "Is that so?" he asked. "What makes it different?"

Veron sat up straight and tried to speak clearly. "Well, my lord, I plan to take what would normally be several different types of stores and combine them into a single, larger business. Customers will shop as if it's one large market and will pay once for everything they need."

"Interesting," the Lord of Commerce mused, leaning back.

I have his attention. Now I need to keep it. "Yes, I'm excited to bring this idea to your city. I think it'll help build up the area around it. From what I understand, several businesses failed after the North Karad Stables closed. This new market should help revitalize the area and bring in other businesses too. It should result in *a lot* of new tax income for your city."

Raynor leaned forward, but his eyes remained narrowed. "Opening a large market may be successful, but the customers you'll attract will simply be diverted from other established businesses. How would moving their patronage to your shop create any new tax income?"

Veron had anticipated the question. He knew the lord's excitement about his venture would all depend on how he responded to what he said next. "Indeed, some customers would simply come from other shops, but you'll find that the novel concept will draw new people from outside the city walls to venture into the city to shop. Often, they buy and trade with each other directly from farm to farm or in small stands in the countryside. The ability to buy all they need in one place will be exciting enough for them to come into the city. Those are the people you want to attract because, currently, their money's not part of your tax system. This is an untapped revenue stream for the city."

Veron smiled as he finished and awaited Raynor's response.

Raynor drummed his fingers on the table. The rest of those at the table watched him for a response. "I think that could be an excellent idea . . . *if* it works."

Veron sighed inwardly with relief. "Yes, my lord, it will. In Felting, I wondered the same thing. When my father started our market years ago, it was just a grocery. After he passed away, I had to do everything myself, and I decided to try growing it. I knocked down the walls to the adjacent shops and added other vendors. First was a baker who contributed bread and pastries. Next was a butcher who had some of the best meat in the city. After that, we added a clothing section where a tailor and milliner set up shop."

Raynor nodded his head as Veron spoke.

Veron continued, "We found that someone looking to buy a hat often got their hat but also went home with some bread and vegetables. As soon as we expanded, we found our customer base grew significantly. We saw countless people from outside Felting come into the city just to shop at our market. We were located in the middle of the city there, and we still drew them in. Here, in Karad, our shop will be placed close to the North Gate, which should make it even more accessible."

"Excellent!" Raynor said, playfully hitting the table. His eyes were bright with excitement. "I ran a half dozen shops back in the day. I can't believe I never had the idea of combining them like that. I'm interested to see how this goes."

Servants came out and served bowls of soup to each person. The soup smelled incredible, like a mixture of lemon and sage, but Veron had more important things to focus on at the moment. He had them interested. Now it was time to see how strong that interest was.

"I can't wait to get started," Veron said. "I'd love to get it going tomorrow if it were possible, but unfortunately, it seems I'll have to delay for a while."

"What do you mean?" Brixton asked.

He took the bait! "Well, I received a letter from my brother today. He must have sent it as soon as I left," Veron said.

"Is everything okay?" Elenor asked.

"Oh yes, nothing to worry about. We have a second home in Tienn up close to the mountains. Our market runs so smoothly on its own, so we like to get away from time to time to relax. Apparently, their commerce department heard we were looking to expand and are desperate for us to open our new market there. They're supposedly planning to give us a low seasonal rate to be there."

Brixton and his father exchanged a look. Veron couldn't tell what it meant, but it was probably good.

Veron continued, "Personally, I'm tired of Tienn. Karad is a much more impressive city, and I'd prefer to open our new market here." Raynor's face relaxed a bit. "However, since I have to go back to Felting to get my tax history anyway, I might as well continue to Tienn to see what they're offering. If it truly is that much better of a deal, it might make more sense to open there instead."

"Tax history? What do you mean?" Raynor asked.

Veron acted surprised by the question. "Oh, well . . . Brixton insisted I have the tax history for my market in Felting before he approves my license here. I don't have it with me, so I'll need to travel back to get the paperwork. If I didn't have to go get them, I'd just as soon stay here and get started on the new market in Karad." *There it is. The dice are thrown, and I've done all I can. The only question now is how badly they want me.*

Father and son looked at each other. Brixton lifted his shoulders as he held out his hands and spoke up. "Well, yes, I asked him to bring his history as a business reference," Brixton said.

"If you're ready to get things going, I'm sure we can skip the tax records to get your license processed," Raynor said.

It worked! Veron thought, keeping his face impassive while celebrating on the inside. "Oh, well, that is generous. It sure will save me a lot of effort, and I appreciate it . . . But, with Tienn offering a great deal on my license rate, it might end up being more profitable for me to go there instead. I may need to think about it a bit anyway," he told them.

"What rate did you set?" Raynor asked Brixton.

"One sol eight argen," Brixton said as his face reddened. "Because the space is so large! Honestly, I thought it was a good deal based on the size."

Raynor turned to Veron. "I'm sure Tienn would be a good city as well, but if it'd help make your decision, we can set your seasonal rate at one sol and two."

I can't believe it! This couldn't have played out better in my wildest imagination! Veron had to restrain himself to avoid yelling with excitement, so he took a spoonful of soup as he pretended to consider the offer. "Yes, I think that sounds agreeable," Veron said after he swallowed. "I appreciate your generous offer and would be happy to establish my market in your city."

The rest of the dinner was excellent—cod, vegetables, and finishing with some sweet fruit. While they ate, Veron noticed Mila and Hailey frequently talking in hushed tones. Anytime he looked their way across the table, they glanced at him around the centerpiece and then whispered to themselves.

After the meal, everyone stood, and Veron sensed it was time for him to leave. "Thank you for welcoming me into your home and for sharing this wonderful meal. I truly hope to see you all again soon," he said.

Raynor shook his hand. "We'll see you tomorrow at the office to sign the papers, right?"

Brixton spoke up quickly. "He had his money stolen, Father. He needs to get a loan first."

"Well, surely, he has some left. How would he be living in the meantime?" Raynor turned to Veron. "You have enough to get started, right?"

Veron stared with wide eyes, unsure of how to respond. He opened his mouth to say he needed some time, but to his horror, the opposite came out. "Of course. I have enough for that. I'll see you tomorrow." He offered a weak smile as his insides churned.

Veron left the Fiero house, walking into the chill night. Inside, he battled between the excitement of getting approved and the alarm of needing to find the money in one night. He required two sol two argen to cover the license and the remaining portion of wiether's fee. It should be easy for a person of his supposed station to get but was next to impossible for someone living on the streets. Luckily, he happened to know someone who *did* have that sort of money. And being rightfully Veron's, he would have no qualms about stealing it back.

29

The Heist

I t was a couple of hours before midnight when Veron arrived on the roof of the building. He perched atop an old warehouse, just down from Morgan's old grocery. Most people in the city were back in their houses already, but Veron was pretty sure Slash, Bruiser, and Coffin were at a tavern somewhere. He didn't know where they lived or where they drank, but every time he ran into them had been around Upper Sherry.

Maybe I'll get lucky and spot them walking home, Veron thought.

No lights reached him, so he didn't worry about being noticed. He could see clearly down either direction of Porter Way. If they walked by, he would spot them for sure.

The breeze blew, and the temperature dropped. After dinner, he had the sense to change out of his nice suit. If he ruined it by climbing on roofs, he wouldn't be able to forgive himself. When he changed, he grabbed the Shadow Knights cloak from the chest, throwing it on over his regular clothes. The black fabric, combined with the hood to hide his face, rendered him practically invisible. His trusty pry bar weighed down the cloak pocket.

If I can track them down, and if they still have most of the money they took, I could get around three sol from them, which is just what I need.

Veron sat hiding for what must have been a couple of hours. During the time, a handful of people walked down the street. He rubbed his hands together to keep them from freezing and couldn't feel his nose after a bit. Finally, his ears perked at the sound of a bottle breaking. His head snapped to the left, and he watched.

Out of a small alley feeding onto Porter Way emerged three men. Veron was a long way away, but he knew it was them. Bruiser and Coffin looked more than a little inebriated, barely able to walk a straight line. Slash turned back and yelled down the alley they came from, sending all three into a fit of laughter.

Veron's heart raced and stomach turned at the same time. He made his way down the side of the building to the alley beside it. Once he reached the bottom, he crept toward the street, staying against the wall in the shadows.

Footsteps grew louder, and Veron held his breath as they appeared directly in front of him. Luckily, they kept walking down the street, oblivious to his presence. Veron remembered his lesson from Artimus years ago.

"They didn't see us because they weren't looking for us."

When they were out of sight around the building, Veron peered around the wall. He kept an eye on them until they arrived at another alley where they turned. He moved to keep up.

Visibility was poor due to the serpentine path of the alley, but Veron could hear their loud footsteps. He hurried along the lane with light steps and his hood drawn up, darting from shadow to shadow and checking around each bend of the narrow street. He found them again, stopped at a rusted metal door, one of several along the side of a decrepit building. Bruiser dropped his keys as he tried to unlock the door. Eventually, it opened, and they went inside, closing the door behind them. The light reappeared in a second-floor window soon after.

This is where they live. And this is where my money is!

The building was a dirty two-story structure stained with soot and mildew on the outer walls. A narrow alley ran between it and an identical building on the left. Veron approached the adjacent building. Finding a drainpipe on the far side, he used it to climb to the roof and sneak across to the opposite end.

Across the alley, through a window, a lamp lit on a table showed Slash walking around. Soon he lay down on his bed and extinguished the flame of his lamp. *From how drunk they looked, the others are probably passed out already.*

After giving Slash long enough to fall asleep, he decided it was time. Veron leaned over the edge and peered at the street far below while flashbacks to the fateful roof jump that cost Fend his life came to his mind. He could hear the sound of slate tiles shifting and feel the sensation of Fend's arm slipping through his bloody grip. His heart sped up from the memory.

No, I won't let fear control my life, he thought.

Veron got a running start and leaped across the space, landing on the roof as quietly as he could. It was solid, and his feet held firm. On the backside of the building, a small balcony projected from the wall just below the roofline. Veron lowered himself down from the roof and discovered the door to the balcony unlocked. He smirked as it opened without a sound.

As he entered the room, loud snoring greeted Veron from beds on both sides of the dark space. *This must be Bruiser and Coffin's room.*

A second door presumably led to the rest of the floor. He kept the one to the balcony partly open both for light and in case he needed a quick escape. Hoping for some warmth, he was disappointed to find the room just as cold as outside. Veron quietly searched. A bookshelf was empty. A small table contained nothing but a half-burned candle.

A chest sat next to each bed, but when he opened them, he frowned. Both held nothing but old clothes.

As he moved to leave the room, one of the snoring sounds stopped as a body jostled. Veron froze. He paled as the bed creaked from the sound of a body rising. Without hesitating, Veron retreated to the wall and hid between the chest and the bed on the opposite end of the room. He ducked his head as low as he could, hoping the black cloak and hood would hide him.

They're not looking for me. They won't see me, Veron thought.

"Bruiser. Hey, Bruiser." The bed next to him shook.

A bleary voice answered back. "What? What is it?"

"Where's the blanket?" Coffin asked.

"What?"

"The other blanket. Where is it? I'm freezin'."

"I don't . . ." Bruiser mumbled something incoherent. "In the chest, by my bed."

Veron's heart raced as his arm rested on the chest. Before he could even think, he moved. Keeping low and moving on the balls of his feet, he slunk silently across the room before Coffin could get around the bed to where he was. Veron hid behind the angled door to the balcony. Shrinking against the wall, he heard the chest open moments later.

"Where's the stupid—there it is." After some rustling, the chest closed with a loud bang.

An agitated Bruiser spoke up. "Can you keep it down?" A body rolled in the bed. "You idiot, you left the door to the balcony open. No wonder you're freezin'."

Veron's stomach felt ill with his body tucked into the darkness behind the angled door. He crouched and moved again, hoping the darkness was enough to conceal him. He crossed the room and ducked behind Coffin's bed as he heard the balcony door close behind him with a slam.

Veron's heart pounded. Blood raced in his ears. After a moment, a body settled onto the bed next to him, but he didn't dare move. He remained still for several long minutes until the sound of snoring resumed again and his heart rate slowed. Exhaling a sigh of relief, he stood. *I've got more to search.*

Exiting their bedroom, Veron discovered a short hall leading to three more doors. The first one was locked. Judging from its placement, he figured it led down a flight of stairs to the street. The nonstop sound of snoring behind him helped muffle the creaks of the wooden boards as he tiptoed down the hall. He passed the next closed door—Slash's bedroom—and entered the last room.

The space could have once been used as a kitchen but was bare. A rotten smell of decay assaulted him as he entered the sparse room. Broken glass littered the floor, which he deftly avoided. A shelf next to the window leaned against the back wall, empty. In the middle of the room stood an old table, leaning heavily to one side and riddled with gouges on the surface.

Nothing of value here. That leaves only one place to check, Veron thought.

Back in the hall, Veron cautiously pushed the door open to Slash's room. Just enough light came through the window to reveal a simple room with a bed, a small table, and a bookshelf. Soft, rhythmic breathing that came from the bed was barely audible over the snoring from down the hall.

The bookshelf contained nothing of interest. He checked the small drawer in the table—nothing. His heart beat a little faster when he saw two chests under the bed. He slowly pulled out one, making sure the scraping on the wooden floor wasn't louder than the breathing. Once it was clear of the bed, he lifted the lid—nothing but clothes. After he pulled out the second chest, his pulse increased. It was locked.

Locked! This must be it!

He couldn't break the lock in the room, so he slowly stood and lifted the chest. It was heavy and bulky, but he managed to shuffle his way out the door and into the hall without making a sound.

After carefully closing the door to both bedrooms, he pulled out his pry bar. He leaned on the end of the tool as he tried to control the amount of pressure he put on the chest. With a soft crack, the lock broke. Veron's heart pounded as he opened the lid.

A faint moldy smell wafted out of the chest as he rummaged through more clothes until his hand hit something hard. Three daggers rested next to the clothes. He took one of them and put it in his pocket.

Lifting the pile of clothes, his heart skipped a beat as he held his breath. At the bottom of the chest, barely visible in the dim light, rested his box . . . the one they took . . . the one where he kept his money. *I found it!*

He lifted it out of the chest, and his hands trembled as he opened the lid. Veron's heart instantly sank, and nausea returned. Three silver argen. *Three! What happened to the twenty-four and the seventy tid? That was only a couple of weeks ago! How will I be able to get the money I need now?* He was heartbroken and furious. His body hurt as panic set in. Putting the three argen in his pocket, he closed the lid of the chest.

Veron stood for a moment and listened to the muffled snoring through the door. *How did they spend that much money in such a short time? It obviously wasn't spent on things for their place here. There's no way they ate and drank that much. Maybe they're keeping it elsewhere?* The thought fixed in his mind, and he couldn't shake it. *I can't give up. I have to find that money.*

Veron crept back into Slash's room. The rhythmic breathing still confirmed his safety. *If he wanted to keep money safe, what would he do?*

Putting it in a locked chest was the obvious place. To truly keep something safe, it would have to be well hidden. He crouched and felt the floorboards, looking for a loose one. He slid his hands carefully over the wood, even crawled under the bed and felt there with no luck. He sat on the floor next to the bed, unsure of what to check.

Every moment I stay here puts me at risk. I need to hurry.

Suddenly, the room was quiet, and Veron froze. The breathing had stopped. He slowly turned to look at Slash. The man's eyes were still closed, and in a moment, the breathing began again. Veron exhaled. He didn't realize he was holding his breath, too.

Veron pulled back open the drawer in the table for a closer inspection. All that was in there was a used rag and a few old buttons, but faint scratch marks showed in the corner. *What's that?* he thought.

Using one of the buttons, he poked at the edge of the drawer base. Once it wedged, he gently lifted, and the drawer bottom raised along with his hopes. Carefully, he removed the false bottom, and the faint glint of moonlight shone off coins—a beautiful pile of them, copper and silver. His heart beat so loud and fast that he thought it would wake everyone in the house.

Veron had found his stolen money.

He looked over at Slash, anticipating his eyes to be open and looking straight at him. The face was no more than an arm's length away, but his eyes were still closed. Veron took the coins out a few at a time. He had to move slowly to prevent them from jangling together in his pockets. Every second he took to pick up a coin felt like an eternity.

He worked until every last one was gone, not even bothering to push the drawer back in before he left. The coins rustled as he moved, tiptoeing across the floor. He tried to keep the floor from creaking and the coins from jingling. It was the longest walk of his life.

In the hallway, the muffled, steady snoring continued, and Veron sighed with relief as he closed Slash's door again. *Thank you, Artimus, for all that training. I'm now the master of invisibility!*

A floorboard groaned under Veron's foot as he turned, and a startled sound came from Bruiser and Coffin's room. The snoring stopped. Veron froze and listened, but the noise didn't resume. Veron heard his own breath. Sweat formed quickly across his brow. *I need to get out of here.*

The next moments seemed to happen in slow-motion as he raced down the hall to the balcony. Veron's feet caught on the chest he forgot was there, and he fell toward the floor, the wooden boards rushing to meet him. The chest echoed as he kicked it, and the scraping sound as it slid across the floor sounded like an alarm bell. Dozens of coins spilled from his pockets and rang like instruments as they collided with each other on the hallway floor.

Everything was going wrong. Veron wanted to jump up and run, but he was upside down on the floor, fighting to get control of his body again. A commotion sounded all around him. Feet hit the ground ahead from Bruiser's room. His balcony escape was ruined. Finally, back on his feet, Veron frantically scooped up as many of the coins as he could.

"Hey!" he heard in front of him.

Bruiser stood in the doorway of his room with Coffin just behind, blocking the path to the balcony. Veron left the rest of the coins and backpedaled to the only empty space as the men barreled toward him, yelling.

When he got to the kitchen, he closed the door behind him just as the roaring thugs arrived, but he had no way to lock it. He wanted to get the table to jam under the doorknob, but if he moved to get it, they would open the door.

Why did I have to trip? I was so close!

Veron held the knob and leaned with all his weight into the door. His feet crunched on glass as they slid on the gritty floor, unable to find traction. His legs ached from the strain. Unfortunately, the men were much stronger and heavier than him. After only a few hits with their bodies, the door flew open, knocking Veron against the table.

He scurried to the other side of the table, but there was no escape. Bruiser and Coffin were in the room, and Slash stood in the doorway.

"Veron. I thought we already took care of you," Slash sneered. "You made a mistake in coming here."

"It's *my* money!" Veron said, breathing heavily.

"It *was* your money. Now it's ours," Slash said as he pulled out a knife. "I think it's time we get rid of this trash once and for all. Grab him."

Coffin reached Veron first and tried to grab him by the shoulders. Before he could get a hold, Veron dropped down and slammed his knee into the side of Coffin's leg. The man screamed in pain as the leg bent, and he fell onto the table.

Before Veron could do anything else, Bruiser pinned his arms behind his back and lifted him to a standing position again as Slash approached with his knife. The thug's eyes narrowed as he readied to attack. Held tightly from behind, Veron jumped and kicked out with both feet, pushing Slash back.

The dagger! With his arms pinned behind his back, he could just barely reach it. Veron took the knife out of his pocket and plunged it as deeply as he could into Bruiser's leg, who screamed as he let go of Veron and fell to the ground.

Freed and with a weapon in hand, Veron felt better about his odds. Slash's eyes burned with hatred. He lunged at Veron, jabbing at his chest with the knife, but Veron stepped to the side. He parried the strike with his own dagger and followed it up with an elbow to the face, bloodying Slash's nose.

With Slash doubled over, Veron saw an opening for the door. Before he could make a run for it, Coffin's good leg kicked out the back of his knees. The shock and loss of balance knocked him on his back. Slash, with a raging and bloody face, leaped through the air at him. His knife aimed at Veron's heart, but Veron caught him in the chest with his feet.

Using the momentum of the man's body, Veron kicked up and sent him flying upside down over the table. Slash flailed in desperation, trying to cut him, but what his knife found instead was Coffin.

Finally free, Veron got up and ran as quickly as he could. Before leaving, he glanced back at the scene from the doorway. Slash lay crumpled against the wall, blood dripping down his face. Bruiser sat on the ground, groaning and clutching his upper thigh where an enormous amount of blood covered his pants and the floor. Coffin lay spread out on the table. His leg was bent unnaturally, and Slash's knife rested motionless, embedded deep into his chest.

Veron's chest heaved at the sight, but he fought the urge to throw up. He turned and ran, scooping up the rest of his money on the floor of the hallway. A key over the doorframe opened the locked door, and Veron scurried down the stairs where he unlocked the door at the bottom. Unharmed and with heavy pockets, Veron took off into the cold night.

30

Building a Market

When Veron woke, a broad smile covered his face. The events from the previous night's dinner and his midnight raid at Slash's place seemed too unbelievable to be real. The jingling of coins in his pockets convinced him it was. *Fifty-six tid and nineteen argen! That's two and a half sol,* he thought.

He despised the three thugs but still felt sorry for them. Coffin couldn't have survived that stab wound to the chest. Veron had never been responsible for someone's death before, and it was tough to bear even though he didn't feel he was the one at fault.

I need to keep my eyes open around the city though. Now more than ever, I don't want to meet them on the street.

Veron's priority for the day was to close out the paperwork on the license and move forward with the preparations that needed to happen to make his market a reality. He changed into Morgan's outfit and set off into the city.

Veron opened the door to the Department of Commerce to a warm greeting, and Brixton waved him over to his desk. "Good morning! Are you ready to pay?"

"Yes, two sol and two, correct? One sol two argen for the fee plus one more sol for the season?" Veron asked. *I'll have to pay for the advertising permit after I get a loan.*

Veron handed over the coins, and Brixton pulled out papers. A formal-looking sheet said "City License" in gold lettering across the top in bold print. After a moment of writing below the title, the details listed Veron Stormbridge as the holder, the lot number of the location, and the date it was effective, which was that day. Brixton stood up and motioned for him to follow as they walked into the back office.

"Veron! It's good to see you again," Raynor Fiero said, looking up from the papers at his desk. "I hope you enjoyed last night?"

Veron laughed on the inside, knowing that Raynor would never know the full truth of how much he enjoyed it. "Yes, my lord. It was an amazing night," he said, flashing a relaxed smile.

Raynor signed the paper Brixton handed him. "How long do you think it'll take to get things up and running?" he asked.

"Hopefully, not long. It depends on how long it takes to find the right workers and get the inventory and supplies we need. First, I'll need to get a loan though."

Raynor looked at his son as if he were about to ask him a question, but Brixton spoke first. "I gave him names, Father."

He nodded. "Good, good. If you have any trouble with those lending houses, you come and let me know."

"Yes, my lord. I absolutely will," Veron said. He'd never had someone offer to vouch for him before. It felt good.

Raynor spoke again. "I have to say, it's quite impressive seeing a young man with such bright ideas taking the initiative. I hope your intelligence and business acumen will rub off onto my son here." He smiled, seemingly oblivious to the hurt look on Brixton's face. "I look forward to seeing how this market comes along. Good luck to you!"

"Thank you, sir."

The two young men left the back office. Brixton appeared to shake off his father's comment and spoke as if nothing bothered him. "So, the main thing you need to keep in mind now is tracking your sales. Heath is our auditor and regularly visits businesses to make sure their sales are being accounted for accurately, so you'll see him from time to time. Your next seasonal license fee is due the finweek of wiether. And the ten percent tax of sales is due the premweek of suether. Our office here is open Marketday through Finday and closed on Weekterm."

"Thank you so much. I'm sure I'll be leaning on your knowledge and experience many times in the future. You seem to know a lot more about all of this than I do," Veron said, hoping the encouragement would take away the sting of his father's rebuke.

Veron shook hands with the clerks and bid them a good day. With his mission accomplished, he left the Department of Commerce. His pockets were significantly lighter, but he held an official City License in his hand and beamed with pride.

I wish Artimus could see me now. I wish my father could see me now, he thought. Since he couldn't see either of them, there was only one other person he wanted to share the moment with.

Morgan was loading material onto a boat when Veron found him. He waved, catching Morgan's eye as he walked down the plank.

"Nice outfit," Morgan said as he approached. Morgan's own shirt looked more tattered and even looser on his body than it did the other day. Even though he smiled, Veron was concerned about the gaunt look of the man's face.

"This thing? Ha! It's just some old used piece I got handed down to me," Veron said, causing both to laugh.

"So, how are your 'details' working out?" Morgan asked.

"Perfectly!" Veron unrolled the license to show to him.

Morgan's eyes widened, and his mouth hung open. "How'd you get that? Where'd you get the money? Or references?"

"I told you. It was just some details to work out."

Morgan was speechless, then broke into a laugh. "Veron, you'll never cease to amaze me."

"So, you wanna come and check out the space I got?"

"Absolutely, but I have a few hours still left to go here."

"Come on, Morgan. This is a new job! You don't need to load boats anymore!"

"Yeah, and I'm excited about that, but I agreed to work. I'm not about to back out of my commitment just because something better comes along," Morgan said, inclining his head forward and raising his eyebrows.

Veron felt foolish. *I still have a lot to learn.* "I'm sorry. You're right."

"I only work a half-shift today, which ends at the afternoon bell," Morgan said, indicating toward a clock hanging on the side of the warehouse. "Meet me here, then."

Veron was hungry. Having a pocket of his own hard-earned money, he realized he could buy food with it. He walked up Dock Street and milled about Kulling Square. A butcher shop sat on the corner that sold grilled meat on a stick in addition to raw meat. Beef, lamb, and chicken skewers were displayed out in front of the store. Anytime Veron walked past the shop, he always smelled them and longed for one.

"Can I have one of each, please?" Veron asked.

The butcher grunted at him and handed over three skewers of meat. "Nine pintid."

Veron handed him one copper tid. "You can keep the change."

The meat skewers were some of the most delicious things he'd ever eaten. For most of his life, he ate scraps of thrown away food or whatever people would give him, and while Artimus was a great man, he was not a great cook.

I can't believe I've been missing this all of my life, he thought.

Veron sat on a bench while he ate, wanting to take his time to enjoy the food. While he sat, he observed life in the square. A dull roar filled the space around him as dozens of people talked at once. Children played chase with each other. Men and women stood with their carts of goods to sell, trying to get the attention of those passing by. Birds cawed overhead as they flew and looked for food that had fallen on the ground. Builders hammered nearby.

I need people, supplies, building repairs, then, eventually, customers, Veron thought, becoming overwhelmed by the list. *But first step, repairs.*

Veron turned around, looking for the source of the hammering. At the north end of the square, a man stood, hammering a doorframe into place. Veron walked over. The man was sweating from exertion while a boy a few years younger than Veron held the frame.

"Hello there!" Veron said, waving to get his attention.

The man stopped mid-swing and turned with a crease between his eyes. "Hello," the man replied.

"I'm sorry to interrupt you, but I was curious about what you were working on."

The puzzled look went away as the man talked about his work. "The doorway to Mr. Herrington's place was falling apart. The door wouldn't even close anymore. He kept trying to shimmy it straight, which helped for a bit, but the problem wasn't the door—it was the frame. So, my son and I are building him a new frame, and we're almost done." He smacked the new wooden frame with the palm of his hand for emphasis.

"Yeah, that looks great. I'm Veron, by the way." Veron extended his hand.

"Jacob. Nice to meet you," the man said as he shook his hand. "This is Brock, my son."

Jacob was a strong man in his mid-thirties with short, dark hair and a messy beard. He looked as if he spent most of his life doing hard, physical work. His son, who couldn't be more than fourteen or fifteen years old, was almost as tall as his father. The rest of his body didn't look like it had caught up with his height yet, so as a result, he was lean and wiry.

"Do you do a lot of carpentry work?" Veron asked.

"I used to. I had a shop on Dock Street, where I kept all my tools and gear," Jacob said as he set a nail in place and hammered it in after a few blows. "I had people stop by all the time needing a variety of jobs—mostly repair work. Doors, windows, floors, walls, ceilings."

Brock continued to hold the frame while Jacob drove in another nail.

"My favorite job was a barn I built outside the city," Jacob said. "The Kensington Farm. You might have seen it out the South Gate, thirty minutes' walk from here on the left side?"

"Yeah, I've seen that," Veron said. "Their barn is amazing! You built that?"

"Brock and I did. I was quite proud of that."

Veron tilted his head. "You said you used to do a lot of work. What happened?"

Jacob was preparing another nail but stopped. His face turned dark. "A year ago, I took a job for Thomas Turnbill, the Lord of Justice."

"Wow!"

"My thoughts at the time too. I had no idea why he wanted to use me, some carpenter from the Bottoms." He sniffed and wiped his nose with the end of his sleeve. "He lives in an enormous house in East Fairren and wanted me to re-do all the wood trim inside. It was in oak—as if that wasn't nice enough—but he wanted it done in parthe wood."

Veron raised an eyebrow. "Parthe?"

"It's rare . . . from the mountains in the south of Tarphan. It's a hard, dark, rich colored wood that costs a fortune to transport. In reality, it looks about the same as walnut—which is one-tenth the cost—but he didn't care as much about the look as he did the name. I estimated it'd take thirty weeks to complete the job, and they offered to pay four sol plus materials for it."

Veron's eyes widened. *That's a lot, even for thirty weeks of work.*

"It sounded too good to be true, and it turns out that it was," Jacob said as he shook his head. "Brock and I worked hard and finished in twenty-seven weeks. Some of the best work I've ever done, and it looked beautiful. When Ethel Turnbill 'inspected' the work, she insisted it was rubbish. She refused to pay me, insisting they'd need to hire another carpenter to re-do all my work, but I know they never did that. The job was perfect."

Jacob looked down at his hammer as he spun it absently in his hand. "I went to the constable's office to file a complaint, but they laughed and sent me away as soon as they heard the name Turnbill." His voice grew softer. "Twenty-seven weeks with no pay is devastating. We used all the money we had for materials, even took out loans against the shop. Without their payment, we lost the shop, the license—everything. Now, my wife, son, and I sleep down that alley over there. I work odd jobs that I can find, like this door, but not having a shop makes it difficult to get much work."

"That's awful. I'm so sorry," Veron said.

"It's okay," Jacob said. "We may have lost a lot, but we still have each other. I trust that things will work out in time."

How can that happen? Are all the city leaders like that? Jacob might be just the kind of guy I need, Veron thought. "Well, today might be your lucky day," Veron said with a twinkle in his eye. "I have a job for you—one that should keep you working for a while—and it even comes with a place to sleep if you're interested."

Jacob leaned his head back and stared.

Veron continued, "I understand if you're hesitant and get that you're probably wary of things that seem too good to be true, but there's no catch."

Jacob looked at his son, who shrugged his shoulders. "What do we have to lose?" He turned back to Veron. "Sure, we'll check it out."

Veron nodded, pleased. "How much longer will this job take, do you think?"

"Maybe an hour or so."

"Great, when you finish, why don't you come by? Do you know where the old North Karad Stables used to be years ago, up in Prinvestor on Elderberry Street?" Jacob nodded. "Great! That's where the job is. I'll see you there."

Veron walked back to the docks in high spirits. He arrived just after the bell and found Morgan ready. The two made their way through the city. It was a long walk from the Docks to Prinvestor, but Veron was thankful for the distance because it meant less chance to run into Slash around Upper Sherry.

Morgan stepped cautiously as they approached, not appearing to trust the old wooden sliding door. Veron pulled out a key he received from the Department of Commerce and used it to unlock the chains. After unwinding the links that held the door in place, it took both of them pulling to slide the door open.

"All of this is yours?" Morgan asked as they walked into the courtyard. His neck craned forward, and his mouth hung open.

Veron nodded while he looked around, a grin forming on his face. He could barely believe it himself. *Before, it was just an idea. Now, it's real. It's even bigger and better than it initially appeared through the slats!* he thought.

The entire area sat in a bowl shape. Two-story buildings surrounded the space on each of the sides, creating a protective barrier. The stables, nine in total, were uniform in size with wooden walls and dirt floors. The lone enclosed building on the ground level seemed in good shape. Its walls and ceiling were intact, and it had plenty of room to be an office or possibly to keep materials.

At the corner of the yard, steps led to the second story. Morgan and Veron ascended them to a walkway circling the complex. The left side of the second floor was a series of six small rooms. They were all empty, but each could easily hold a bed as well as a table and chairs.

Probably meant to be rooms for stable hands or possibly even for rent to travelers.

On the right side of the second story, an open loft ran the length of the space on top of the stables below. Above the loft, a short, rickety wooden roof meant to keep the rain off.

Standing in the loft, Morgan looked at Veron. "This is amazing! I can picture it now—a market like this city has never seen. How much did you have to pay for this?" he asked.

"The license fee is one sol and two," Veron replied.

Morgan stopped and stared. "Per . . . week?"

"No, per season."

Morgan opened his mouth, looking incredulous, but no sound came out. "What?" he finally said after a sputtering start. "That's less than I paid for my tiny grocery. How'd you accomplish that?"

Veron smiled and shrugged his shoulders. "I persuaded them they needed to let me have it for a good price."

Morgan burst into a fit of laughter.

"Hello?" a voice said from the open gate.

Morgan and Veron turned toward the source. Down in the middle of the courtyard stood the carpenter, Jacob, with his son, Brock.

Veron lifted his arms in the air in celebration and came down the stairs to meet them. "You made it!" he said. "Jacob, Brock, this is Morgan, the greatest grocer in the city."

"That's a little overselling me, I'm afraid," Morgan replied as he shook their hands.

"Someone once taught me only to speak of things I believed. Otherwise, people would know if I wasn't genuine," Veron said, winking at his friend. "Jacob here is one of the best carpenters in the city."

"You don't know that. You haven't seen my work," Jacob said with a wry smile.

"I saw your door, which was fantastic, and I've seen your barn. Do you disagree with me?"

"No, I agree," the carpenter said, chuckling.

Veron smiled. "Well, there you go! So, here's the job I promised," he said, motioning with his arm to show the entire area.

"You want me to renovate a stable?" Jacob asked. "Sorry, but you don't strike me as a stable operator."

"No, I want you to build me a market."

Jacob paused and looked around. "As in, selling food and stuff?"

"Fruits, vegetables, bread, meat, grains, clothes, shoes, hats, armor, weapons. Everything someone might want to buy in this city, I want to sell in this market."

Jacob wandered through the space, pointing out the areas that needed work. "We'll need to replace most of those boards. The front walls of the stalls will need to come down, but we can salvage most of the wood and use it in other areas. Maybe we can build tables that jut out into the courtyard from each stall? That'll give you more display space for goods."

Nice, Veron thought. *I think he's going to work out great.* He looked to Morgan, who raised an eyebrow, appearing impressed as well.

"I'll need to rebuild the steps, so no one falls through," Jacob went on as he made his way upstairs.

"I want to make these rooms livable for the workers of the market," Veron said.

"They're in surprisingly good shape but will need a few structural repairs," Jacob said. "And before you fill them up, we'll need to add to or replace at least some of the support beams below. Otherwise, this whole second floor is going to collapse. What do you want to do over there? More display space?" He pointed at the open loft area.

"How difficult would it be to finish off some more rooms?" Veron asked.

"Not hard at all. We'd need some wood and time, but the task would be easy," Jacob replied.

"So, this is the job," Veron said. "I need you to get this place in shape so we can turn it into a market, and hopefully, to help us continue to renovate as time goes on. You can use one of the small stalls to store all your tools. What rate do you require?"

Jacob thought for a moment, stroking his chin. "Well, this would be a big job that would take a while. I'd need a decent rate to pay for a place for my family to live. Could you handle six tid per week, plus materials?"

Veron smirked. "You and your family can take one of the rooms upstairs to sleep in, and I'll pay you one argen per week, plus materials."

Jacob's eyes grew large. He grabbed Veron in a bear hug. "Thank you! You don't know how much this means!"

Veron hugged the man back. "It's okay. I think I know."

31

Loan Acquisition

J acob started the next day with Brock along to help. Veron
decided the priority was fixing the sliding door and converting
the stalls into shopping areas, so that was where they began.
From the connections he made during his short time at the docks,
Morgan already found three potential shopkeepers to add to their
team—a baker, a tailor, and a chandler. Veron talked with the new
people in the courtyard as they arrived.

Henry Mallour showed up first with his wife, Greta. Mostly bald
and walking with a shuffle, Henry was every bit of fifty-three years
old. He started as a tailor thirty years before and spent most of the
time operating a shop in Karondir. He did the selling and measuring
while Greta sewed. They lost both their sons to illness and their
shop to a fire a couple of years back. They moved to Karad to get a
fresh start, but unable to get the money to start a shop, Henry found
himself working at the docks to save up. Two years later, he was still
there.

Danyel Barton was a little younger than Henry. He had a full head
of dark brown hair and a large beard, which was more of a reddish
hue with streaks of gray in it. He worked at the docks and drove

carriages filled with goods to and from the warehouses, making deliveries to other areas in the city and the surrounding countryside. Moving goods earned his money, but baking was what excited him. After his wife died from the blue fever, Danyel learned to bake a variety of bread as well as pastries and other sweets. He took his baked goods with him to work and sold them to dock workers. Morgan was one of his patrons, and Danyel was the first person he approached to ask to come and check out the new venture.

While Veron talked with Danyel in the middle of the courtyard, a young woman entered through the gate. "Hello, can I help you?" Veron asked.

"Yes, I'm looking for Veron Stormbridge," she said before noticing Morgan and waving at him across the courtyard.

"Ahh, well, you found me, and I guess that makes you Washburn? You sell candles?" he asked her.

"Chloe Washburn. Yes, nice to meet you," she said as she shook his hand.

Morgan mentioned he had a chandler coming. I assumed it was a man—quite a pleasant surprise.

She didn't look like she belonged with the rest of the crew. When she first walked in, Veron thought she was the daughter of one of the wealthy neighbors who lived in the area. Her long blond hair was stunning, and her sharp jawline gave her an elegant appearance. Upon closer inspection, Veron noticed her dress was ratty and her face smudged with a faint shade of dirt. It didn't take away from her beauty but did identify her as someone who likely came from south of Split.

"I'm glad you made it, Chloe," Veron said. "Can you tell me about yourself?"

"Sure. I'm twenty-two. I used to be married until my husband Patrick died earlier this year in an accident at the docks. Karad

Shipping Company paid me two argen as a recompense from the accident, but that money has long since run out."

"I'm so sorry," Veron said. *She's so young to have lost a husband already.*

"I learned to make candles from my mother when I was young, and after losing Patrick, I began selling them. I can't afford to get a shop, so I peddle them up and down the docks."

"How many do you sell?"

"On a good day . . . ten to fifteen candles, but at two candles per pintid, the money barely covers the cost of the wax and wicks to make them. If I can sell here, I'm sure the new market would be a more profitable place to sell from."

Veron did some math in his head and chewed the side of his lips. *That's not going to add much profit to the market. I can't turn her away though. Maybe she's right? Maybe selling here will be more profitable? But perhaps her beauty is clouding my judgment?* He laughed to himself as he shook his head.

Since everyone had arrived, Veron decided to address the group. He stood on an old crate next to one of the stables. "Thank you for coming, and welcome to North Karad Market!" he said to them, lifting both arms as he indicated to the space around him.

Everyone was quiet as they looked around the courtyard.

"I know it's not much to look at yet, but it will be. In no time, this market will be the grandest and most unique in all of Karad. We'll be the talk of the city! Each of you will have your own section. You'll choose what to sell, where to source material from, and how to price and market your items. But you won't be competing with each other. You'll all be working together in one market."

Veron paused to let the idea sink in.

"For pay, each of you will receive one silver argen per week."

Half the group nodded, and the other half beamed with delight.

Veron didn't want to pay too much, but he felt it was better to pay well than have a team of underpaid people who grumbled and complained.

"In addition, you will each share in the profits of the market," Veron said, noting looks of surprise and confusion. "Each season, after we pay our taxes to the city, fifty percent of the profits will be paid back as a bonus, which I will divide up based on your individual contributions to our team. Right now, that split consists of you five who are here. Eventually, I hope to have ten or so people in the group. Yes, that means the sharing percentage will drop, but with a larger market, the profits should be bigger as well. So, that's the plan! If each of you are with us, I want you to start planning. Think about what supplies you require and what inventory you need to start. I want us to open in two weeks."

Veron looked over at Jacob, who he caught by surprise with the timetable. "Can you do it? Can our stalls be ready by then?"

Jacob looked at his son while he considered the question. "Um . . . Yes, we'll be ready," he said.

"So, I need a total from each of you. How much money do you need to get started?" Veron asked the shopkeepers.

While each of them considered the question, Jacob came over to Veron. "I appreciate you including me in the profit-sharing thing. I promise you our work will be the best quality for as long as we're here," he said.

Veron jumped down from the crate. "And I hope that'll be a long time. It'd be helpful to have someone around full-time for upkeep. Plus, once your work here in the market slows down, I thought perhaps you could set up shop in one of the stalls where you keep your tools." Veron hit his hand on the wall of the stall behind him. "If people see your work and know you're a carpenter for hire, that could help get future business as well."

Jacob paused as he fought back tears. "That sounds great. Thank you, Veron."

"North Karad Market, huh?" Morgan asked as he approached.

"Yeah, you like it?" Veron said.

"I do. Have you given thought as to how we can get the word out about the market? People won't just magically start showing up. We'll need to have some sort of plan," Morgan said.

"Not yet, but I'll think about it. We've got time." Veron gathered totals from each person, including Jacob, who needed raw wood supplies. *Altogether, I'll need around eight sol. Plus, I need to be able to pay the workers weekly. I think a loan of ten sol would do it,* he thought, marveling at the number. *It would take me six years to earn that sort of money at my old pay rate.*

The amount made him sweat. The idea that someone would give him the money seemed far-fetched, but Veron couldn't think of any other sources to get it from. He needed to get a loan.

* * *

The next day, dressed in Morgan's maroon outfit, Veron made his way down Farrier Street. He had three names of recommended lenders, and he desperately hoped one of them would work out. The day felt unseasonably warm for early wiether. The sun was high in the air, and sweat formed under his layers of fancy clothing.

Veron opened a door with the sign of 'Karad Lenders' above it. The office was small, and a damp, musty smell filled the air. The compact windows at the front of the building didn't let in a lot of light, so the whole office felt dim. Two desks faced each other from either side of the room, and a man sat at the one on the right, engaged in writing. He looked to be around thirty years old with sharply combed brown hair and glasses.

"Yes?" the man asked, glancing up with a frown on his face.

"I'm here to apply for a loan," Veron said.

"Indeed." He looked Veron up and down. "Oliver!" he yelled before returning to his writing.

Another man emerged from the back room who looked nearly identical to the first—the hair, the suit, his height—but was a few years younger and had a beard.

"Welcome. I'm Oliver Marshall," he said, shaking Veron's hand. "You'll have to excuse my brother, Logan. He's grumpy all the time. It's not just you." He spoke the last words in a feigned whisper.

Veron liked him much more than the first brother.

"Please, come sit!" Oliver said, ushering Veron to a seat in front of the desk on the left. "So, you're here for a loan?"

"Yes, sir. My name is Veron Stormbridge. Raynor and Brixton Fiero said I should come to see you—that you were the best."

Oliver smiled at the compliment. "Really? Raynor is a great man. Any friend of his is a friend of ours. What sort of loan do you need?"

"I'm opening a market in the place of the old North Karad Stables. I need a loan to get it fixed up and collect inventory. Raynor was so excited about it that he even cut my license fee in half to help get it going quicker."

Oliver nodded as he jotted notes down on a sheet of paper. "Sounds impressive. The standard rate set by the Treasury Department is twenty percent annually. We typically look to give two-year loans that are divided into equal payments every six weeks." He looked up from his paper with a sparkle in his eye. "However, for a friend of Raynor, I'd be willing to go with sixteen percent." Oliver returned to his notes. "How much will you need?"

Veron's heart beat fast, his throat dry in anticipation. "Ten sol," he said, holding his head high, trying to appear confident.

Oliver stopped writing mid-word and looked up with one eyebrow raised. He whistled, indicating the significance of the request. "Ten sol?"

"That's right," Veron said. "It'll set us up with the supplies we need to open in two weeks. We should turn a profit almost immediately and should have no trouble paying the loan back on schedule each period."

Oliver returned to his writing. "All right, ten sol. I assume you have collateral of some sort?"

Collateral? What does he mean? What do I say? Veron said nothing as his mind raced.

Oliver looked up. "A land deed, a business license . . . something?"

"I have the license for the market?" Veron's voice was no longer confident.

"Not for *this* business, but something else you own—tax records, proof of value for something in your name. Anything?"

I have no idea. I don't have anything like that. His mind jumped to his sword. "I have a sword. It has a ruby in the hilt."

"Sorry, but no sword is worth even close to ten sol."

Veron leaned in, speaking softer, "Raynor said that if you gave me any trouble that I should let him know." *I'm not sure if I'm threatening him or only vouching for my credentials.*

"Yes, the word of Raynor Fiero means a great deal, but we can't simply lend someone ten gold sol without proof that they can run a viable business or collateral to weigh against it. I need assurance of something of value you can put on the line—something at least *close* to ten sol. Otherwise, who's to say you don't take our money and hit the road? I don't mean this as an offense to you, but it's simple business pragmatism."

Veron knew it was a lost cause, so he tried to find a way to save face. "Oh, yes, of course. I understand. I have plenty of collateral, but proof of it is all back in Felting. Once I'm able to travel back and collect the necessary documents, I'll return." He stood to his feet, ready to be out of there.

"We look forward to your return, Mr. Stormbridge."

Veron shook Oliver's hand and left the office.

Not long after that meeting, Veron had a nearly identical one at the Feinstein Lending House, the next name on the list. The same pitch with the same result. They wanted collateral. Veron walked with his head lowered, down the street to where Morgan waited on a bench.

"How did it go?" Morgan asked, his shoulders raised, and face lit up with eagerness.

Veron shook his head as he sat down. "Awful. Not even close. I mentioned the Fiero name and their recommendation, but all they wanted was collateral—just like the first one."

Morgan's shoulders dropped. "Unfortunately, that's the way these lenders are," he said. "They don't like risk. If they're going to put themselves out there, they need some sort of assurance in case you don't pay them back. Didn't Fiero say to let him know if they gave you trouble?"

"Yeah, but that's the *last* thing I want to do. It'd raise more questions about my background, which I can't have anyone unraveling because that's what sold the license agreement." Veron felt sick. "Everything depended on this. I have no idea of any other way to get the money we need."

"Well, there's still one more place on the list, right?"

Veron shook his head. "It won't do any good. They won't be any different. I need . . . I don't know . . . a new approach or something." Veron leaned back as he thought. "What do these lenders want?"

"They want someone they're confident will pay them back. They want—"

"They want money . . . ultimately," Veron said, feeling dejected.

Morgan stood quickly and began pacing. "They want someone to *borrow* their money and return it to them with interest. So, why would they approve someone for a loan?"

Morgan seemed excited, but Veron simply shrugged. *What's he getting at?* he thought.

Morgan answered his own question. "If they believe the individual will be able to pay it back . . . or . . . if they're worried about losing a good customer." The grocer had a grin on his face. "Come on, Veron. I have an idea."

An hour later, on Market Street, just four buildings down from the Tax Assessor's shop Veron blundered into years earlier, Veron entered Holden Merevail's office as a bell announced his presence. The wood-carved sign out front simply said "LENDING" in faded letters. The office was empty except for an old man who poked his head out from around a bookshelf.

"Yes, can I help you?" the man asked.

"You must be Mr. Merevail? I'm Veron Stormbridge. It's great to meet you!" Veron replied.

"It's good to meet you too," Mr. Merevail said as he came over to Veron and shook his hand, motioning for him to sit in front of the desk. "And please call me Holden. How can I help you today?"

"I've been working with Raynor Fiero on a new business venture, which I plan to open in a couple of weeks. It's going to be a fantastic market in Prinvestor up near the North Gate. I paid for the license and have enough to cover the labor and most of the supplies, but Raynor suggested I come to you to get a loan for the rest of the start-up money."

"Well, you've come to the right place then. I should be able to help you with that," Holden said.

"I told Raynor I didn't need a loan for it. I have a good bit of capital and should have no trouble funding the business from what I already have, but he insisted that I'll be freed up to do it right by getting a loan. He argued that I could invest in the best materials to set us up for success, which will help us be even more profitable in the long run. Personally, I prefer not to have to pay interest to someone else when I can keep it for myself, but who am I to argue with the Lord of Commerce, right?"

"Indeed, he is a persuasive man," Holden said with a knowing smile.

"I funded my last market in Felting myself, and it wasn't a problem. It took fifteen sol to get it off the ground, and it was great. We doubled it back within a year, but I can see his point. I don't want to tie up all my money in the business."

"So, how much of a loan are you looking for?" Holden asked.

"Only ten sol. That should be plenty to get things going." Veron tried to act calm but felt the opposite on the inside.

Holden nodded as he considered the amount. "Ten sol . . . very well, that should be doable."

Before he had a chance to be talked into a corner, Veron decided to go on the offensive. "Now, I assume you'll want some sort of collateral or proof of business ownership, obviously. Unfortunately, I don't have it here, as all of my business ventures are based in Felting, but I'll be traveling back there in a few days. When I return, I'll bring the paperwork, and we should be able to finish up the agreement, if that works for you?"

"Yes, of course, that sounds great. I'll have the paperwork ready for you when you get back."

"It's just that . . ." Veron paused as if weighing options in his head, "I don't know. Ten sol on a two-year loan at the standard twenty percent rate . . . That's going to be a lot of interest." Veron shook his head. "I don't know if I want to pay that." Veron took another pause

as he appeared to think. "I guess I'll have to give it some thought."
Just then, the bell rang, and Morgan came into the office.

"Morgan?" Veron said, frowning and leaning back.

"I'm so sorry! I didn't want to interrupt, but I thought you might want to know before you signed anything," Morgan said and passed a letter to Veron. "Oliver came by to give this to you."

Veron unfolded the blank piece of paper and pretended to read it to himself while Holden and Morgan waited. "Wow!" he said, looking at Morgan. "He'll go with sixteen percent, and he doesn't need the paperwork?"

"He wants to close it now, I guess," Morgan said.

"Wow, okay . . . I guess we'll go with that then." Veron turned back to Holden. "I apologize, Holden. I um . . . I think we're all good for today. I appreciate you taking the time to meet with me."

Veron stood as if to leave while a crease formed between Holden's eyebrows. "Wait . . . Oliver? Was that Oliver Marshall?" the lender asked.

Veron paused before saying, "Yes, he and I met earlier."

"Hold on! You don't need to go to him. If you're willing to sign now, I can approve your loan!"

I can't believe it! It worked! Veron looked at Morgan as if weighing his options. Inside, he was jumping with joy.

"I can take you down to . . . fifteen percent," Holden said. "And you don't need your proof of collateral."

Holden sat back, looking pleased with himself. Veron beamed inside but tried hard not to show it as he acted as if he considered the offer. When he had waited as long as he dared, he nodded. "Okay, that sounds good to me." He sat back down. "Where do I sign?"

"Splendid!" the lender exclaimed as he pulled some papers out of his desk. Veron snuck a smile in Morgan's direction while Holden went on. "Since you don't have collateral, I'll just need you to sign a personal guarantee instead."

Veron's breath caught. "A personal guarantee?"

"Oh, it's just a formality," Holden said as he filled out a couple of blanks on a form. "It means that *you* are guaranteeing to pay the loan back, which is pretty much the same thing you're doing anyway. With your background and connections, that shouldn't be a problem."

Holden smiled at Veron as he slid the form across the desk and handed a pen to him. The smile was supposed to put him at ease, but it wasn't successful.

Veron stared at the pen. He knew he shouldn't hesitate, but something about it gave him pause. *I need to sign now, or it will ruin the illusion I've created. I wish I could discuss this with Morgan, but that would make me look weak.* Tension radiated as silence hung in the air. He tried to keep his arm from shaking as he took the pen.

Morgan whispered over his shoulder, "Veron, maybe we should—"

"It's okay, Morgan," Veron said, cutting him off. "I don't mind guaranteeing the loan." Veron took the paper and signed his name as the beat of his pulse echoed in his ears.

The two men closed the door to Holden's office and began walking back to the market. Veron wanted to feel triumphant, but something seemed foreboding.

"Do you know what you just signed?" Morgan asked.

Veron cringed at the question, assuming there was something he was missing. "I agreed to pay back the loan?" he replied.

Morgan exhaled. "When someone takes out a loan for a business, the lender wants collateral, which is a license or title to something of value. That means, if they stop making payments, the lender can legally take the other item from them."

"Yeah, I get that."

"A personal guarantee means the collateral is *you*," Morgan said. "If you're unable to pay the loan back, Holden can take whatever value he's missing from you directly."

"But I don't have anything, so there'd be nothing to take," Veron said, hopeful that he'd found a silver lining.

Morgan stopped walking and shook his head. "If he can't take anything of value *from* you, then he's allowed to take *you*."

A queasy feeling developed in Veron's stomach.

"If you miss *one* payment, Holden will start to look more closely at Veron Stormbridge, and he'll discover that your story doesn't check out. As soon as he believes you can't pay back the loan, he can *legally* take you. You'd be his slave, or he could sell you to someone else."

Veron's legs felt weak, and his stomach turned. *What have I done?* "I had no idea."

Morgan put his hand on Veron's shoulder. "It's okay though. It doesn't have to come to that. You just need to make sure you're able to make your payments."

Veron nodded as they continued. The heavy coins from Holden jingled in his pocket as he walked. *That sound should feel exciting, not ominous. I have the money though, and now I can build the market. There's no turning back.*

32

North Karad Market

Veron marveled at how quickly things moved once he had the loan. Jacob and Brock made quick work of their woodworking priorities—building tables, fixing the gate, and replacing steps. Each of the workers and their families soon moved into the upstairs rooms, but Veron was content to sleep in the loft until they finished more. Morgan reconnected with his grocery suppliers, and the Mallours got to work right away making clothing.

"How can you make clothes already? How do you know what size people will be?" Veron asked as Henry was hard at work cutting fabric and Greta sewed.

"These—" Henry held up a stack of shirts they had already finished "—are for display. That way, people can choose a style and color they like from the examples, and we custom make a new one for them.

"Makes sense. This looks great, Henry."

Chloe set up her shop at the far right of the courtyard. *Why am I nervous?* Veron thought as he walked up to her. *She's attractive, that's for sure, but I'm usually fine talking with anyone.*

He picked up one of her finished candles absently and did a double-take. It was intricately designed like a carved work of art. Each candle had two colors that revealed themselves in layers.

"Wow, this is amazing!" Veron said, holding it to his nose. "And they smell great!"

Chloe looked up from where she dipped candles. "Thank you," she replied.

"You've been selling two of these for a pintid?" Veron asked.

"Oh no, those were just basic candles. Since we're selling in Prinvestor, I think we can get away with something nicer." Her eyes lit up as she picked up another of the finished candles. "These are colored and scented with oils, and I think they can sell two for a tid."

Veron nodded. "Yeah, I think that's better."

She pointed to different piles, naming them. "Evergreen, willow, borrell, sage, and cinnamon."

"How'd you get these different colors?" Veron asked.

"It's easy. I dip it in one color, then in the water, and then I dip it in another color, then back in the water, and repeat. Once it's thick enough, I use a knife to carve designs in them, showing off the colors."

"You have a real talent. They're beautiful."

Chloe blushed.

Veron couldn't think of anything else to say, so he started walking away. "I'll see you later!" he said as he waved and turned to leave. *"I'll see you later?" That sounded so stupid. Why did I wave?*

Veron stepped over a pile of lumber and took in the scene. The main structural repairs to the market were close but not done yet. A low buzz rumbled through the courtyard as the workers kept busy with preparations. Overall, he felt good about their progress, but the bakery was stressing him out. They hadn't built an oven yet, which was going to take a couple of days.

Where is Danyel with the material? Are we going to be ready in time?

Veron thought.

As he glanced around, Morgan approached. "So, did you have a plan for how to get the word out about the market yet?" the grocer asked.

Veron cursed internally. He'd been so stressed and distracted by other things that it had slipped his mind even though Morgan kept pestering him about it.

Before he could answer, Danyel led a horse pulling a cart of bricks and mortar into the courtyard. "Veron, are you ready to build an oven?" he called across the space.

Veron turned to Morgan to address his question. "Yes, yes, it's all taken care of," he lied. "Will you stop bugging me about it?" He left the grocer and walked to the cart full of bricks. "Ok, Danyel, I'm ready to help, but I'm going to need you to direct me. I've never done this before."

The two men unloaded the supplies from the cart by the area where they intended to build the oven. Veron breathed a sigh of relief as they began to work. It was the last major piece needed, and they were going to get it done.

* * *

Veron woke up on Marketday earlier than usual, anticipating the opening day. Numbers ran through his head as he considered upcoming expenses that would be due. *I wonder how many customers are going to show up?*

Veron lay in the loft on a simple bed of hay with the chest and his sword tucked behind a stack of empty crates. The short covering above him kept him dry, and the stacked boxes blocked the wind.

He admitted defeat on trying to sleep and got up. The sky hadn't even started to lighten, and the air held a chill. He lit a lantern and dressed in a new outfit he had paid the Mallours to make for him.

Arriving at the top of the steps, he startled himself and almost tripped on his own feet. Chloe stood on the balcony. "Oh, hi," Veron said, not expecting to see her there. "Couldn't sleep either?"

Chloe shook her head. "No." She continued to look forward out over the railing.

Her wool dress was green and white and covered to her feet. The way it looked on her in the flickering light of the lantern made his legs feel weak.

"It's a really good thing you're doing here," she said.

"Um . . . Thanks? What makes you say that?"

Chloe turned to look at him. "You're taking a risk with this place and the loan you took out. A market is a big deal, and you're putting a lot on the line. Every one of the people here needed hope in their lives, and you're giving it to them." She tilted her head as her eyes narrowed slightly. "You know, you don't strike me as the son of a rich merchant."

Veron swallowed hard. *Does she suspect me? No one but Morgan knows who I am, and even he doesn't know the full story.* "What do you mean?"

"You care too much about others. Everyone I've seen who grew up wealthy only cared about themselves. You're different though," Chloe said.

Veron felt like sunlight filled him up from the inside as a grin grew on his face.

"You care about people in need," she said. "As if you've been there before."

Veron's grin faltered. He turned to look out to the courtyard. He drummed his fingers on the railing as the silence waited patiently. "I *have* been there before. I didn't grow up the son of a wealthy merchant. My father died when I was young, and I've never met my mother. I lived on the streets for much of my life, so I know what it's like to be hungry and afraid, not knowing where my next meal would come from. I've been embarrassed about the clothes I wore and how I smelled. I know the feeling of not having a safe place to sleep. I . . ." A tear rolled slowly down his cheek. "I . . ."

Chloe put her hand on his back. "It's okay. I've been there too. I'd be there right now if it weren't for you. You're a good man, Veron Stormbridge," she said.

Her sweet smile and words comforted him. He sniffed and wiped his cheek. "Thanks."

The two stood for a while, staring into the courtyard. Rooftops of the buildings around them dotted the sky, and the city wall towered in the distance. The cool morning air swirled around them. Soon, the sky started to lighten, and other people began stirring in the surrounding rooms.

Veron cleared his throat. "Well, I guess it's time." He smiled at Chloe and tapped the railing before proceeding down the steps for opening day.

The energy was electric in the air once everyone was downstairs. Morgan's food was displayed. The Mallour's clothes were out. The smell of warm bread filled the courtyard with a welcoming presence as Danyel baked fresh rolls and pastries. Chloe's candles—sorted by scent and color—looked beautiful and smelled incredible.

With his heart racing and body tense in anticipation, Veron opened the sliding gate. The rebuilt wooden door glided effortlessly along its rail with "North Karad Market" freshly painted on the outside. He blinked at the empty sight. Nothing. No one was in the street as far as he could see in either direction. His shoulders slumped.

I knew people wouldn't be lined up, climbing over each other to get in, but I hoped there would be at least someone, Veron thought. *That's all right. They'll come soon.*

After a few minutes, the first potential customers appeared, and Veron watched eagerly to see if they would come in. They glanced in as they walked by, more out of curiosity than interest, before continuing down the street.

More people walked by as time went on, but no one entered the courtyard. Veron tried standing in the street to steer people in. "Come check out our new market! Today is the first day of North Karad Market. Come and see what we're offering!" *Why are they not coming in? We need to sell. If not, we won't be open for long, and I'll be in serious trouble with Holden.*

Finally, after around an hour, a lady walking by stopped, looked, and came through the gate.

"Welcome to North Karad Market!" Veron said with enthusiasm. "Feel free to browse all of our offerings. When you have everything you need, let me know."

The lady looked over the candles and clothing. She stopped for a moment at the bread before continuing. She eventually selected a head of cabbage and left after giving Veron two pintid. Veron looked around and saw the downturned faces of everyone.

"That's okay! It's our first sale, and we should be excited! It doesn't have to be the biggest," he said as he attempted to be cheerful. He didn't feel cheerful though.

The day didn't improve. Of the few people who entered the market, most merely looked around, and only a few bought anything. Veron was glad for the customers they had, but it wasn't nearly what he expected.

After the sun went down and they closed the door, everyone gathered around in the courtyard, looking dejected. Veron didn't have it in him to motivate the group.

Morgan easily sold ten times as much food back at his old shop in a day! Are we doing something wrong? he thought. *This wasn't what I expected—what we need. Maybe I should just forget all of this and focus on training to be a shadow knight?*

Everyone stared at Veron, waiting on him to say something. *I don't know what to say.* Veron hung his head.

Morgan spoke up. "It's okay, everyone. This was just the first day. Business will grow." He clapped Veron on the shoulder before heading up the steps.

Veron's mind drifted to imagining himself leading an army and fighting Bale in the middle of a windswept plain. *But I need to earn a living while I train.* He remembered the loan. *And if I can't pay the loan back, then I'm really going to be in trouble!*

* * *

Morgan was right. Business did grow, but not by much, and not quickly. By the end of the week, they were still a far cry from the sales they needed. Everyone was dispirited, and the atmosphere was grim. Food was already going bad and being thrown out.

Veron thought ahead to the loan payments and the wages he owed his workers. The remainder of his funds weren't going to last long unless something changed soon. The personal guarantee he signed loomed over his head like an ax waiting to fall. His stress was only exacerbated by the grumbling that grew among his workers.

Veron stood in the loft, leaning on the railing, looking over the courtyard as the workers closed up below. His face was sour. His head and shoulders hung as if defeated.

"Keep your head up, Veron," Morgan said as he walked up to join him. "Once we get traction, it'll get better."

"But what if we're broke by the time that happens?" Veron asked.

Morgan gazed across the space and lowered his voice. "I need to ask you something."

Veron's stomach turned at the vocal change. *Oh no. Something's wrong.*

"I've been giving you space on it, at your request, but I can't ignore the thought that your plan to promote the market never actually existed," Morgan said.

Veron felt like his breath was knocked out of him. *I totally forgot about it!* His mind raced to come up with an excuse, but there was none. *It's entirely my fault.* "I'm sorry, Morgan. I got so distracted by everything else that I forgot about it. You kept trying to help, and I snapped at you." Veron drooped his head and shook it. "You're right. I never came up with a plan."

Morgan nodded. "It's okay. You've had a lot on your mind. Do you want some help now?"

Veron looked up at his friend and pleaded with his eyes. "Yes, please! What would you do?"

Morgan clapped him on the shoulder before heading down the steps to the courtyard below. "Brock?"

The carpenter's son looked up. "Yes, sir?"

Arriving in the courtyard, Morgan took a few coins from his pocket and handed them to the boy. "Run to the printing press on Gate Street. They should still be open. Get . . ." Morgan stopped to think for a moment, ". . . fifty sheets of paper."

Brock nodded and took off running.

"Does anyone have any paint or brushes?" Morgan asked the rest of the group.

"I do," Jacob said. "Two brushes and some black paint."

"Perfect! We'll need those. Do you think you can make some wooden stakes too? Around this long"—Morgan gestured with his arms—"that you can stab in the dirt?"

Jacob shrugged. "Yeah, sure. No problem," he said before setting off.

Morgan turned to Veron. "You did pay for the advertising permit, didn't you?"

Veron's stomach turned again. "No, I didn't. I meant to, but . . . I didn't have the money at the time."

Morgan hung his head and sighed. "Can you talk with your friend at the Department of Commerce? We need it now."

"Veron! How's the market coming along?" Brixton asked, appearing to be the only one in the Department of Commerce when Veron entered.

"Eh, not great. This was our first week, but we're struggling to get customers in," Veron said, glancing around the empty office before sitting by Brixton's desk. "Running solo today, huh?"

"Yeah, they all left a bit ago. The new guy has to stay late to close. It's okay though." Brixton waved his hand to dismiss the issue. "Is there something I can help you with?"

"Yeah, I forgot to pay for the advertising permit when I got the license, so I was hoping to do so now. Four argen, right?"

Brixton's look soured. "You have to pay that when you sign for the license or at the beginning of a season. You can't just add it on whenever you want."

"What?" Veron's heart beat faster as he imagined waiting until the end of the season to get the permit. "No, we need to be able to advertise. We can't wait."

"I'm sorry, but that's the rule. Father was very clear about it."

Veron ran his hands through his hair and groaned. *Morgan's gonna kill me. We can't wait until next season,* he thought. *We may not sell enough to stay open that long.*

Brixton stood and walked to the front door, where he glanced out the window. "Tell you what," he said as he returned. "If you can part with . . . two argen, we can consider things good."

A cry of surprise escaped Veron's lips. *I can't believe it. I expected to pay four!* A huge grin covered his face. "Thank you, Brixton. Oh, that's great! Tell your father I'm thankful for you stretching the rules." Veron handed over the two argen.

"Whoa, whoa! He doesn't need to know about this." Brixton slid the coins into his own pocket as he inclined his head forward. His voice dropped in volume as he said, "Trust me. I'll make sure you don't run into any trouble. But no one else needs to know."

Veron froze and wrinkled his forehead. *He's keeping the money for himself.* "But aren't you—"

"Veron," Brixton said with a smile. "Don't worry about it. Go and advertise. You're all set."

Getting permission was a relief, but the way it happened didn't sit easy with Veron. As he left the office, he tried to shake off the feeling by turning his mind back on the market. *Okay, now let's see what Morgan has planned.*

* * *

Veron rolled open the door on Marketday to start their second week of business. Thankfully, he now had a better expectation for what awaited behind the door, which was nothing. Like the week before, all the workers were excited. The early morning started slowly, but by midmorning, traffic had increased. Veron couldn't help but grin as he noticed the change. The afternoon grew even busier. The workers no longer stood around but moved from customer to customer, tempting them with their goods. Veron was often backed up with people ready to pay.

"Well, you sure didn't waste any time," a voice behind Veron said.

Veron gave a lady her change and turned around. "Brixton!"

316

Brixton stood in the middle of the courtyard in a sharp gray tunic, looking around and taking in the scene. "Struggling to get customers in, huh?" he said.

Veron beamed with pride and stood tall.

"Walking through Karad Square, I saw a sign on the corner, 'Grand Opening - North Karad Market - on Elderberry Street'. Then, I saw another sign. Then, I saw five more. I guess I just had to come to see it for myself."

"And if you wandered outside of the city, you'd have seen twenty more posted at each crossroad in the surrounding vicinity," Veron said.

Brixton raised an eyebrow and nodded. "Nice touch. I wouldn't have thought of that."

"Well, to be honest, I didn't. Morgan, our grocer"—Veron nodded in his direction as he helped a lady with some food—"was the one who came up with the idea."

Brixton looked around the courtyard again. "This looks good, Veron."

"Thanks. I hope to add more to the market soon. We have a lot of space still, and I think a better variety of products will only help the traffic."

"And look at you, rubbing elbows with these sorts," Brixton said, glancing around at the other workers. "Impressive dedication. You're going to do great."

Veron fought to keep his face from showing the offense he felt. *I know we come from two very different places in life, but I'm proud of these people and thankful to have them in my life.*

After Brixton left, they stayed open another hour or so and continued to see many people. Cheers erupted as they slid the door closed at the end of the day. In total, their sales were almost ten times their next best day.

Mary, Jacob's wife, cooked up a large pot of stew in the oven with some scraps she got from Morgan and Danyel. Everyone sat together, eating food, talking about life, and toasting in celebration of a successful day. Veron found himself sitting next to Chloe, which made the moment even better.

When the sun had set, Morgan dragged a large metal bowl into the courtyard and started a fire. Danyel got out a lute and played music. Mary joined him on the flute, and Brock banged on a box like a drum. The lively music lifted their spirits even more, and Henry and Greta stood up to dance.

Veron went from enjoying the happy celebration to sheer terror in the brief moment it took Chloe to stand and pull him to his feet to dance with her. *I have no idea how to dance!* he thought.

He was relieved to notice Henry didn't appear to either. The tailor just bounced around while holding Greta's hands and laughing. Veron's hands felt clammy, but he took Chloe's in his, her warm smile helping him feel at ease.

"I don't know what to do!" Veron said over the music.

"It's okay. Just follow me!" Chloe replied.

Chloe began moving her feet to the rhythm of the music, and Veron copied her. They spun together and bounced to the beat. Bathed in firelight while she twirled and laughed, Veron found Chloe to be more beautiful than ever. He didn't want the song to end.

After the song finished and he sat down, Veron's mind raced. *What did that mean? Does she like me?* His heart pounded as he continued to sneak looks at her. *She's older and used to be married, but that's all right.*

As Veron was lost in his thoughts, a new song started, and Chloe went to Danyel and took his hand to dance. Jealousy, pain, and a sense of betrayal filled Veron—feelings he never expected—but after a moment, he laughed at how silly it was.

Chloe's not mine. Maybe one day that could change though. He sat and watched the two dance with a whisper of envy.

33

Steel Advantage

Chelci, Russell, and Nevi sat around the table. Chelci only poked at her food while the others ate.

"Is something wrong, Elise?" Nevi asked. Charlie had been sleeping in the corner and poked his head up at the question.

Something *was* wrong. During her first few weeks at the Academy, Russell kept pairing the boys together anytime they sparred and left Chelci to practice alone. Having an odd number of candidates, she thought they would take turns at first, but it continued every time. What began as a mild frustration had grown into anger.

Chelci sat silently for a moment, tightening her grip on her fork, debating whether to say something or not. "I know we're not supposed to question anything," she said, staring at her food, "but *how* am I supposed to learn to fight if you won't let me spar with anyone?" She looked up at Russell as her voice rose. "If you're trying to keep me from getting hurt, it's not helping! I'm going to have to start fighting at some point, and all you're doing is allowing them to get better and better while I fall farther behind!"

Russell's eyes were wide as he leaned back. Chelci's cheeks flushed, and she dropped her gaze back to her food as the silence settled around the table. Neither Russell nor Nevi said anything for a while, but Chelci noticed Nevi fix a stern glare at her husband.

"I don't want you to get hurt," Russell said, "but you make a good point. It probably won't help." He slowly nodded before returning to his food.

What does that mean? Does that mean he's going to change? I believe it does, Chelci thought as she snuck a look at Nevi, and they both grinned at each other.

* * *

"Code Blue?" Aleks asked.

"Medical emergency," Chelci replied.

"Code Orange?"

"Attack from . . . an individual or small group of outsiders," she said, pausing to think.

"Red?"

"Attack from a *large* group of outsiders."

"Yellow?"

Chelci had to think for a moment. She and Aleks walked up the hill to the training hall, quizzing each other on the names of the village alert codes. The brittle leaves crunched under her feet as she walked by his side.

She was dressed in her usual training outfit—brown pants and vest with a loose shirt underneath. She found it was easier to wear the same thing every day since it was just going to get sweaty and dirty over and over again. Most of the boys did the same thing. Aleks wore his predictable plain black wool pants with a red shirt.

"Missing person?" Chelci said as Aleks grimaced. "Wait, no! Disturbance among the villagers! Purple is missing person—child or adult."

"Yes. Green?" Aleks asked.

"Natural disaster."

"Brown?"

"Animal bite or sting."

"Nice, I think you got them," Aleks said, nodding.

"Don't forget Code Black, monster attack!" Chelci raised her hands, pretending to be a monster, and growled, making both of them laugh. Finley invented Code Black when they learned the village code alerts, and it had been their favorite ever since.

Five weeks had passed at the Academy in Nasco, and Chelci finally wasn't waking up sore all over. She had gotten used to the constant running, fighting, and climbing. The training was brutally hard, just as Russell told her it would be, but she loved it. When "Bean-pole" Landon dropped out by choice, their class dropped down to ten. After Russell had finally included Chelci in the sword fighting pairs during sparring time, her skill had improved some, but progress was agonizingly slow.

While her initial reception was cold from many of the candidates, most warmed up to her. Aleks and Finley were her closest friends. The only boys she could tell still did not want her there were Gael, Royce, and Tate. The three of them always stuck together and refused to say a word to her. Aleks, Finley, and she called them the Furies because they always seemed mad about something.

When Chelci and Aleks arrived at the training facility, Bensen addressed everyone. "First up today, you'll be running the course again. We'll see if any of you are getting close to eight minutes yet."

Chelci's heart leaped. They had practiced it a few times but had not been timed since that first attempt weeks before. She was eager to prove herself.

Over the last few weeks, Chelci had snuck off to the course almost every night to practice. She worked individual obstacles as well as ran the whole thing until her legs felt like they wouldn't work anymore.

Her first timed run was abysmal and embarrassing. She needed to improve if she were going to have a chance to make it through training.

I hope I can get my fourteen-minute run down to at least twelve or eleven minutes, she thought.

The boys lined up outside as they had previously, with Chelci hanging at the back. She barely even paid attention as they each took off.

Bring up my feet, swing my leg over, land in the center, kick hard and push up. She was lost in thought as she envisioned what she needed to do for each area of the course.

"Kohen, 10:05," Russell said. "Landon, 11:17. Arturo, 10:46."

Chelci ignored the rest as she focused. When Bensen gave her sign, the rest of the world faded away. She ran, every footstep feeling right as she turned the corners around the trees. Her body was light as she climbed. Her feet were confident as she jumped. Coming down the platforms from the high ladder, she passed Reece. She didn't even glance to see his expression. The high walls felt like old friends as she mounted each of them, her hands and feet placed in the perfect positions.

The only moment that threw her out of rhythm was when she approached the balance obstacle. She nearly stumbled as she saw Tate fall off of it just ahead of her. Judging from his frustrated expression and the way he pounded on the ground, she guessed it wasn't his first time falling. She smirked as she deftly moved across the board and passed him.

Come on. You can do this! she thought, willing her body forward.

The last obstacle was quick and easy. Her heart pumped wildly. Her legs ached. Her lungs struggled to keep the air her body required.

After rounding a large tree, the finish line loomed ahead.

Russell's head popped up. Finley hit Aleks on the arm to get his attention before pointing at her. She smiled as she crossed the finish.

"8:04!" Russell said with a yell.

"Yeah!" Aleks said with a grin as most of the boys clapped for her. *I don't believe it!*

She smiled broadly and gave a weak wave to the others. Her excitement quickly waned as exhaustion caught up and she fell to the ground. She tried to breathe, but no matter what she did, it hurt. She writhed on the ground, trying to find a position that brought relief.

"12:20," Russell said as Tate arrived moments later.

"She cheated, obviously!" Gael yelled to Russell.

Chelci vaguely heard the accusation but was too tired to pay attention. *I think I might pass out,* she thought.

After a few minutes of lying down, she got to her feet with Finley's help. Her legs wobbled, but their strength was returning. Off to the side, Gael, Tate, and Royce argued with Russell and Bensen. She couldn't tell what they said, but their faces were red.

After a moment, Russell walked to Chelci. "Elise, there's a concern that you didn't run the course completely," he said.

"What!" Chelci said, craning her neck forward. "No! I ran all of it."

"People feel it's possible you took short-cuts on obstacles to improve your time. Did you?" he asked.

"No, I didn't." *I can't believe he would accuse me of that.* She glared back at him.

Russell nodded his head solemnly. He looked to Bensen and shrugged.

"Time me again," Chelci said.

Russell cocked his head. "You'd run it again? Now? Aren't you tired?" he asked.

"Yes, of course I'm tired. But I don't want any of you thinking I cheated. Time me. Have people stand out in the course to watch." Chelci folded her arms over her chest and stood tall. Her face was firm.

Russell looked back at Bensen and nodded.

After another few minutes to slow her heart rate, Chelci walked back to the starting line. Her breath was back to normal, but her legs felt wobbly still. *Everyone is watching. You have to make this count,* she told herself.

When Bensen motioned for her to start, she gave it everything she had. She pumped her legs, ignoring their protests. Her body pleaded with her to stop and breathe. The boys watched her at every turn, waiting to judge her a success or a failure. Seven minutes and fifty-seven seconds later, she crossed the finish line to thunderous applause.

Chelci grinned from ear to ear as most of the boys congratulated her on her performance—all except the Furies. They didn't even apologize for accusing her of cheating. *I needed that win,* Chelci thought. Most of her performance at the Academy had been less than stellar, so she was thrilled to have something to help her stand out. *Maybe these boys will respect me more now.*

Her high from the morning was reversed by the last activity of the day. Sword fighting. Out of all the things they worked on, sword fighting was the one thing Chelci struggled with the most, and unfortunately, she knew it was probably the one thing that mattered more than anything else.

"Today, we're going to trade in your wooden swords for steel," Russell said.

Cheers arose from most of the group—all but Chelci. *I knew it would come eventually, but I'm not ready!* she thought.

While she had improved over time, she was far from where she needed to be. Chelci was proud of the improvement she'd made at archery after weeks of practice but grew more and more frustrated at her lack of progress with the sword. She understood the concepts, but her body wouldn't do what she wanted.

Bensen passed out swords to each of them. "You'll carry these with you when you leave," Russell said. "Have it with you everywhere you walk and even when you eat. You can take it off to sleep." A few of the boys chuckled.

Chelci received her sword and a scabbard to affix it to her waist. The blade was blunted, which was a relief, but the tip could do some damage. As she held it, her heart sank. *This is even heavier than the clunky wooden one I can barely wield!*

"Today, we'll work on forms and moves only with the new weapons," Russell said. "Tomorrow, we'll resume sparring."

Chelci let out a breath she was holding. *At least I have one day of reprieve.*

Going through the forms, she found the new sword unmanageable. Her arms tired quickly. She was on the verge of tears as she stumbled around with the heavy weapon. As soon as Russell dismissed them for the day, she hurried out the door as quickly as possible.

Chelci wiped her eyes as she walked back to the village. *What was I thinking? I'm never going to be able to do this. It had seemed so fun to see Jackson doing it, but maybe I should have left that ambition alone? Running the course was exciting, but I have no shot of making it if I can't hold a sword. I should probably quit now. What will I do if I quit? What will I do if I don't quit but can't make it?*

The memory of Jackson reminded her of home—Emma, her father, food, clothes, servants. She had grown content not being rich over the years, but she still had plenty of fond memories of her childhood. A force pulled at her heart, stirring emotions long dormant. She wanted to feel the warm hug of her father and hear him tell her that he loved her once more. She longed to run and play with Emma again. A smile grew on her face as she considered what it would look like if she were back at home.

"Hey, Elise," Aleks called as he ran up from behind. "Are you ok? You ran out of there pretty quickly."

She sniffed and wiped her nose to eliminate the last vestiges of her tears. She looked down at her feet as she continued walking. "It wasn't the best day, I guess," she said.

Aleks shook his head and blinked. "What do you mean? You were amazing on the course today!"

"Yeah, that was good, but . . . I can't sword fight. I'm not getting better, and now with these heavier swords, I feel like I'm taking steps backward."

"Just keep at it. Your strength and skill will improve with time."

Chelci shook her head. "I'm thinking about quitting."

"What? No! You can't!" Aleks told her.

"What good will it do to continue?" Chelci argued. "I understand what needs to happen, but my body won't do it."

"Why don't you come over and practice with me . . . tonight, after dinner?"

Chelci stopped and looked at him. His eyes were welcoming. *He really does want me to stay.* A warm feeling brushed over her body as she took in his broad shoulders and sharp jawline. *Does he like me? Do I like him? No, he's a good friend, but I don't see him that way.*

An image of the boy with the stone in Karad flashed into her mind, but she quickly pushed it away as she came back to the present.

"Thanks . . . sure. Practice would be great."

After dinner, with her clunky sword attached to her hip, Chelci went to Aleks's house. His father was the village's blacksmith and had a workshop just off the square with plenty of space to move around and practice in.

"Okay, let's see what you have. Come at me," Aleks said.

Chelci attacked with a few strikes, but he easily parried them away. The clang of metal on metal was in sharp contrast to the dull thud of the wooden swords. She tried feinting by moving her sword to the other side just before a swing, but the weapon was so heavy and slow that it didn't fool him. She kept trying but wasn't getting anywhere close.

"It's impossible," she said, releasing a cry of frustration. "I can't move quickly enough." Some loose hairs fell in front of her face, which she tucked back out of the way.

"Why don't you try defending now?" Aleks said.

Chelci took a deep breath and readied herself. Once her sword was in position, Aleks attacked her with slow, obvious strikes. She blocked the first two but couldn't move her sword around for the third and was hit on the side.

"Ow!" she yelled.

"I'm sorry!" he said, lowering his sword and holding his hand up. "I'll stop."

"No, it's okay. I have to learn. It's part of the process."

"Do you know what the problem is?"

"Yeah, my lack of strength, speed, and general sword fighting ability."

Aleks laughed. "No, it's that your sword is too heavy for you."

Chelci narrowed her eyes. "Really? You think?" she said, dripping with sarcasm.

"No, I mean it. You *are* strong for your size and—" he paused mid-sentence "—being a girl." Chelci shot daggers at him. "No, it's just that . . . I think you're very strong. This sword is just too much. Come here."

Aleks led the way to the other side of the workshop, where a pile of swords leaned against the wall. He rummaged through the stack, clanking the blades together. "My father crafts a lot of swords. He made the ones we're using right now for the Academy years ago. He loves making some for kids to play with. Most use wooden ones, but for the ones that want it, he makes blunted steel swords that are short and light. Aha! Here!"

Aleks pulled a sword from the stack and held it out to Chelci. She set the heavy one down and took the new blade. It was similar to the other but shorter by a hand and a bit thinner. Leather wrapped the hilt, which made a tight grip in her hand. She lifted it and swung it through the air.

"Wow! This is much lighter than even the wooden ones we used! This is amazing! I wish I could use this instead of the other one."

"Take it," Aleks said.

Chelci looked at him in shock. "No, I can't possibly take it."

"I insist! My father made that for me eight years ago, and I haven't even touched it in the last four."

Chelci's face lit up. "Thank you. I love it!" she said before frowning again. "But it won't do me any good to learn on this because I still won't be able to move with the heavy ones."

"Who says you have to use the heavy sword? Just use that one!" he said, indicating the one she held.

She shook her head. "There's no way Russell will let me use this when everyone else has heavy ones. That would give me an advantage, which isn't fair."

"Wrong. This sword will give you a *disadvantage*. Hold it out, pointed at me."

They both pointed their swords at each other. Aleks' sword came to her chest, but the tip of her blade stopped well short of him.

"See. Disadvantage," Aleks said. "Also, if we're fighting and our swords meet, the extra weight on mine will give me an edge every time. It'll take a lot more effort for someone to win with a short and light sword like the one you have. However, you'll be able to move and react quicker with this lighter sword, which you can't do with the heavy one. I think that'll far outweigh the disadvantages for you. Basically, it's your only hope of being able to keep up with the others."

"Do you think they'd let me use it at the Academy?"

"Absolutely! Kohen said he planned to bring his own sword from home. When it comes to sword fighting, all they care about for the village guard is if you're able to defend yourself and attack when needed. They won't care which weapon you use."

She looked the sword up and down in admiration. *Maybe this will work*, Chelci thought. *Perhaps I can have a chance after all.* "Okay," she turned to face Aleks with an eager expression. "Let's fight."

* * *

"Royce, you're with Elise, outside," Russell said as he went down the list.

Chelci anticipated it, but it still made her cringe to hear it. They'd settled into a rotation of sparring partners so that everyone got a chance to practice with all the other candidates. It was their first day using actual steel, and she would have loved someone a little easier to match up against. Royce was probably the second-best fighter in the class behind Aleks. He was easily six years older and almost twice her weight. Of the three Furies, he was Chelci's least favorite.

"What's this?" Russell asked her, touching the hilt of her smaller sword as she walked outside.

"It's a sword Aleks gave me. It's smaller and lighter, so I can maneuver it better," she said as he stared at her with a funny look. "The goal is for us to learn how to fight, correct? You want the guard to be able to defend themselves and attack when needed, so it shouldn't matter what weapon they use as long as they're able to do what's required, right?"

Russell nodded but didn't say anything. After a moment, he motioned for her to go. She tried, unsuccessfully, to hide a smile as she hurried outside.

Royce waited for her in the courtyard with a grin on his face. "This'll be fun," he sneered at her. "Let's see how many times I can beat you today."

Royce lunged at her with a strike to her shoulder, but she parried it out of the way. The clash of steel resonated through her hand and up her arm. He tried again on the other side, but she was ready. He tried several more strikes at various places on her body, but each time she maneuvered the light sword where it needed to be. His face grew darker each time she blocked him. Each swing of his sword seemed to be harder than the one before.

Not only was she able to move her sword quickly where she needed, but its lighter weight helped her to be able to move her feet easier too. She dodged and moved, running circles around Royce as he repeatedly and unsuccessfully tried to hit her. Sweat flew off of his arm and dripped from his nose. He grunted as he swung, unable to pin her down. Finally, he paused, trying to catch his breath.

While he rested, Chelci was ready. She struck, fast and accurate. Royce yelled in surprise. Had he not held his sword pointed in the right direction, he wouldn't have blocked it. His mouth hung open, but Chelci didn't pause. Before he had a chance to move, she spun and struck him hard in the side. He fell to the ground, dropping his sword and groaning.

Cheers exploded around her. She was so focused on their fight that she didn't realize the whole place had stopped to watch them. In the windows of the building, faces of candidates pressed against the glass with mouths agape. Russell and Bensen both stood by the doorway with grins on their faces.

"It's not fair," Royce said. "How's it okay for her to use a fancy sword, but we have to use these clunky ones? I thought you said she wouldn't get any special treatment?"

Everyone quieted down and looked to Russell. Rather than speak, he walked over to the pair and held out his hand to take Chelci's sword. He lifted it, inspected the blade, and spun it in his hand. Then, he turned to Royce and extended it to him.

"What do you think?" Russell asked. "Do you *want* a sword like this? Because if you do, I'll gladly provide one."

Royce took the sword by the grip and raised it. The sour look of distaste on his face gave him away. It was clearly too light and short for his liking, but he didn't appear to know what to say. The boy was silent.

"Royce? Which do you prefer?"

Royce looked down and kicked at the ground. "I prefer the heavier one," he mumbled.

Russell leaned in and spoke in a loud whisper that all could hear. "Then don't complain about it being unfair." He took the sword out of Royce's hand and gave it back to Chelci before addressing the whole group. "If anyone else would like a smaller sword, instead of your current one, I'll be happy to get one for you. Now, back to work!"

Royce glared at Chelci and grabbed his sword off the ground. They continued sparring until it was time to move on to another activity. After the initial fight, Royce's cocky attitude was gone. He attacked less and defended more, but Chelci's quickness was too much for him. By the time they finished sparring, he was able to get two hits on her and knock her sword away once. She bested him thirteen times.

Chelci sat in the tree with her legs dangling below. Birds chirped around her, and leaves rustled in the wind. She craved the daily free times because it gave her body a chance to rest, and her favorite place to do so was in the tree down the hill from the Academy. It was a molopyr tree, known for growing impressively tall and containing a maze of limbs, which grew plentiful and close together.

Maybe I can do this? she thought. After entertaining the idea of quitting, she had begun to be excited about the prospect of returning home. She wanted them to see who she had become—her strength and confidence. But now that she felt better about sword fighting, she might actually have a chance of making it in the guard. *But is that still what I want?*

As she sat in thought, Bensen strolled along the path toward her. "Hey, Elise," he said as he leaned against a branch. "That was some impressive work with the sword today."

Chelci sat around his head height, so she looked down at him as she replied while blushing. "Thanks. I was happy for the lighter sword. It made a big difference," she replied.

Bensen looked at the ground and fumbled with the hem of his tunic. "I . . . uh . . . also wanted to apologize about the obstacle course yesterday. I believed the boys when they insisted you had cheated. I didn't think you were able to do that—to improve so much."

"That's okay."

Bensen looked up to meet Chelci's eyes as he spoke, "No, it's not okay. I shouldn't have doubted you, and I'm sorry. You have a lot more in you than I gave you credit for."

Chelci's face lit up from the compliment. She had worked hard to be able to be where she was, and she didn't take that for granted. *I'm just glad he's noticed it,* she thought. "What's the rope for?" Chelci asked.

Bensen looked down at the coiled rope crossing his chest, which he always wore. "Have you ever not had a rope with you when you needed one?"

Chelci scrunched her face. "No. I don't think so."

"Me neither." He patted the rope. "You never know when one might come in handy."

Chelci gave a short laugh. "How long have you been doing this with Russell?"

"Training at the Academy?" Bensen looked back up the hill at the facility as he rubbed his chin. "Eight or nine years."

"Wow! That's a long time."

"Yeah, this is my fifth Academy class."

"So, you worked with Russell when he lost his daughter?" Chelci asked, curious to know more about Russell. "What was that like?"

Bensen took a deep breath in as he raised his eyebrows. His exhale was long and slow. "That was a rough time—not just on Russell and Nevi—on the whole village. We'd never experienced a loss like that before."

"So, what do you think happened? Nevi says it was a valcor."

Bensen stared at the ground for a long moment, and Chelci wondered if he forgot the question. "I was the one who found the body," he finally said.

Chelci's eyes widened as she leaned forward as far as possible on the tree limb. "Really?"

Bensen nodded. "I don't know what it was. The claw marks. The destruction. It was terrible." He shook his head.

"It wasn't wolves?"

He shook his head. "I shouldn't say any more."

"Come on. No one will tell me! Everyone else around here must know!"

Bensen stared at her with a serious expression. "Before I settled in Nasco, I traveled a lot. I'd seen a lot, but I'd never seen anything like that. The body was torn in half, severed at the midsection. And the two halves were found high up in the air . . . in two separate trees."

Chelci's stomach lurched at the image. She had to grab the branch to keep from losing her balance. She tried to force the image out of her head. *Why did I have to push to know? Still, I don't think that proves it was a valcor. What could do that?* "Thanks for telling me," she said in a shaky voice.

Up the hill, Russell stepped out of the building and yelled to anyone in the area. "Time to go!"

Several boys shuffled out of the training center with bags on their shoulders.

That must have been awful for Russell and Nevi. No wonder he started drinking so much. But actually . . . I don't think I've seen him drink since my first night here. She jumped down from the branch. "Well, Russell is lucky to have someone like you with him, Bensen. And so are we." She nodded toward the center. "I guess it's time to run."

34

Change of Plans

King Edmund Bale threw on a heavy fur robe over his underclothes and left the bedroom. It was dark outside the palace, but he wasn't ready to sleep yet. The room next to his was a grand but intimate meeting room. A fire burned at the end in an attempt to fight off the ever-present cold of the northern kingdom, filling the room with light as well as a smoky smell. Dark wood covered the walls, most of which were ringed by bookshelves containing massive leather-bound tomes. Several comfortable lounging chairs were in the room, as well as tables strewn with various maps of Norshewa and the whole of Terrenor. At the side of the fireplace, two large double doors led out to a grand stone balcony overlooking the Noravorre River as it wound its way beside the Norshewan capital city of Daratill.

"Good evening, Your Majesty," Desmond said, standing from his chair and giving a slight bow in his red and black robe. "Is there anything I can do for you?"

"Tell my wife to get dressed and leave," Bale said, taking a seat in a chair in front of the largest table.

"Of course. Which one is it?" Desmond asked as he made his way toward the bedroom door.

"Juliette. Wait, no . . . Camille."

Bale's chief advisor disappeared through the doorway to the bedroom. Bale currently had five wives, but the number generally fluctuated somewhere between four and eight. As he conquered towns, he often added one or two to his list, depending on who caught his eye. They reminded him of the control he had over his kingdom. Before marrying him, they always received a choice, but it was usually along the lines of, "Marry me or watch me kill your parents and everyone you know." So far, he had never been turned down. From time to time, one of them would displease him and find themselves guilty of some crime against the kingdom soon after. Their swift execution kept the other wives in line and created an open spot for the next woman.

Desmond entered the room again, followed closely by Camille. Compared to the king's hulking frame and many scars, Bale's youngest wife was quite the opposite. Short and beautiful, her long, dark hair and pear-shaped eyes identified her as being from the coast of Rynor. Her skin was smooth and tight, and the clothing Bale provided her covered little of it. She kept her eyes fixed on the ground and shivered as she walked through the door leading to the women's quarters.

"Are there any more complaints from Nortris?" Bale asked his advisor as he grabbed a piece of bread off a platter.

"No, Your Majesty," Desmond said, standing next to the table.

"Good. The last thing we need is other cities getting ideas."

"I agree, but it doesn't appear we need to worry about that. It seems even the most belligerent can be tamed."

"Fools all of them," Bale said with disgust as he threw a tough portion of bread back onto the plate. "Do they think funding an army is cheap? Or that there's no cost to build a palace our nation can be proud of? These accomplishments are ones our people should take pride in, not complain about!"

He grabbed a leg of chicken and began to eat while grease dripped down his beard and coated his fingers.

"Threatening to kill the children of anyone withholding taxes is bound to get them to pay," Desmond said.

"Maybe we should make an example out of a few of them, just to make sure," Bale's eyes were wide as he stared at his food with an evil grin.

Desmond shifted on his feet. "We *could,* if that's what Your Highness prefers . . . but it may be wise not to provoke them since they are cooperating now."

"Fine," Bale said as he exhaled deeply. For several moments, he sat in silence, lost in thought. The ticking of the clock was the only sound that could be heard over the low simmering crackle of the fire.

"The harvest this year appears to be plentiful," Desmond said.

"I'm tired of being cooped up here. I want to be out there fighting!" Bale said, ignoring Desmond and allowing his passion to show in the strain of his words. Usually, he was cautious to keep his emotions in check, but Desmond was his oldest and most trusted friend. When alone with him, he felt free to be himself.

Desmond leaned back at the sudden change in the subject. "I know you do, Your Majesty. But remember, you have a country to run. People need you here to make decisions and keep them in line. When you were off at the war front, things fell apart here in Daratill. You need to leave the fighting to Commander Ryker and your army."

"But they're not getting anything done! Our last major victory was four years ago when we took Bromhill! And *I* was the one who made that happen!" Bale said, raising his hands in exasperation.

"You did take Kandis after that as well," Desmond pointed out.

"Since I came home, it's been nothing but defeat and setback."

"I understand, Your Majesty. However, I don't think that has to do with you being here. No one could have predicted how King Petrous and his men would pick at your army in bits and pieces for years, hiding in the hills around Palenting. There's simply no way to attack or defend against them."

"And now we're not even defending Kandis anymore. All our men are back at Bromhill to defend them because it's the only place we know they can't get us. So, now we're not even doing anything, and we still haven't gotten Petrous!" Both men rested in silence. "We need a new approach. What we're doing is not working."

Desmond took a step closer to the table. "I hate even to suggest it, but I wonder if it might be a good idea to leave Rynor and focus our attention on Feldor instead?"

"Absolutely, not!" Bale shouted, standing up and pacing the room. "I've spent over a decade fighting them to take that stupid country. I won't give up just because it's hard! Terrenor *will* be reunited under Norshewan rule. Once we control Rynor, *then* we'll turn our attention to Feldor."

"Of course, Your Majesty," Desmond said, bowing his head. "I'm only saying that you shouldn't be afraid to change a plan when it—"

"Afraid!" Bale yelled as he slammed his fist on the wood. He shook his finger in Desmond's face. "Don't ever call me afraid again."

Desmond shrunk back. "I'm sorry, Your Majesty. It won't happen again."

"I've never been afraid in my life," Bale said as he turned to face the fire. *A ruler cannot be weak. I must never show fear.*

Fear. The word brought memories to his mind unbidden. Bale remembered how unnerved he was when the woman from that town predicted he would be killed. He had gripped the pommel of his sword to keep his hand from visibly shaking in front of her. The prophecy was only made worse by the proclamation that it would be a shadow knight who did it. He had always written off the legend of the Shadow Knights, believing them to be nothing more than a fairy tale.

No one can do all the things they're supposed to be able to do, he had thought. *Still . . .*

Bale remembered cowering at his castle in Daratill as his men scoured Terrenor for the group. He told them he needed to stay there to deal with Norshewan issues, but that wasn't why. They couldn't know he was afraid of a prophecy. He gave the same excuse when they found the Shadow Knights and went to eliminate them all. What frightened him the most was hearing the report from his men when they returned—the five who lived to return.

Bale's men outnumbered them three to one, and they struck while the knights slept. It should have been a total victory. Instead, twenty-five of his best men lost their lives. The reports sounded impossible, as if his men hallucinated. *Moved like lightning, kept fighting when they should have been dead, stronger than ten men.*

Bale wasn't able to sleep for weeks, even though the knights were all killed. He often pictured himself facing one of them, looking into the knight's eyes and cowering before turning to run. He always ran.

How was it a prophecy if it never happened? Was it wrong to begin with? Bale thought. Not knowing left an unease that had remained with him ever since. He fought it by trying to appear confident and brave. *They can never see my fear.*

The roaring of the fire sounded especially loud and rescued him from his memories. Soon, another noise caught his attention—someone approaching quickly in the hallway. Chainmail jingled with the steps. The door to the room burst open, and Ryker entered. Dried blood decorated his uniform, and his face was pale.

"Ryker, what are you doing here? I thought you were in Bromhill?"

Bale asked, staring intently.

"I—I was, Your Majesty," Ryker said.

"Your letter, two days ago, said all was good, and you were sending raiding parties out from the city to search the hills?"

Ryker's fingers tapped at his side. He glanced at Desmond before turning back to Bale. "Yes, that was the plan, but we never got the chance. They attacked us. Petrous and his men."

Bale leaned his head back and stared blankly. "And you came running back to tell me this?" After a moment of silence, his stomach began to feel upset. "Ryker, where is our army?" he asked.

Ryker's mouth opened, but nothing came out.

Bale's face reddened. He fought to keep his voice measured. "It took us two years of siege and a full assault to take that city. Don't tell me Petrous did it in a few days?"

The clock offered several more ticks. "They did it in one night. What's left of our army is camped just south of Molvaigh. We fled the city when it was apparent that it was lost," Ryker replied.

Bale stared at him with his jaw set. *We spent years in Rynor. Now, the few accomplishments I've had are lost,* Bale thought, lowering his head as he closed his eyes. He rubbed his temples in a futile attempt to make the pain lessen. "What happened?" His voice was calm and tense.

Ryker swallowed hard. "Around the first change of the watch, some of our men on the wall saw soldiers running through the castle grounds. They went to get a better look and discovered a stone wall was moved to the side in the far edge of the castle garden with a continuous stream of dark shapes coming through it."

"The passageway?"

Ryker nodded. "Before the men had a chance to do anything, yells began in the city, and an alarm bell rang, but it was too late. Their surprise and knowledge of the city left us wholly unprepared." Ryker looked to the ground as if he were afraid to speak the words. "A third of our army was slaughtered before we even knew what was happening. We fought them"—his voice wavered—"but it was no use. Those who survived made it out the gate and fled to the hills. I—I didn't know what to do. I accept full responsibility for this, and I accept whatever punishment you deem fitting."

Ryker knelt on the ground with his head bowed.

No one moved or said a word as the fire crackled. Bale stared at the top of Ryker's head as a soft laugh rumbled in him. Ryker's body stiffened at the sound. While still disgusted over the failure, Bale was intrigued by the irony of the timing.

Maybe it's a sign? Perhaps we shouldn't be in Rynor, after all? he thought. "Stand up," Bale said.

Ryker lifted his head hesitantly then stood.

"If you abandon a post again, I *will* kill you," Bale said, pointing at him while Ryker nodded emphatically. "You'll make it up to me when we take Feldor."

* * *

"I still say Karondir is the most logical approach," Ryker said.

"I don't think we can do it," Desmond replied. "You say our army is down to around 5,000 now? Karondir is built to survive an attack. If anyone from Norshewa or Rynor is ever going to invade Feldor, they're going to do it through Karondir, and they know this. That's why the walls are thick and their soldiers are plentiful. We'd lose every one of our men before we took the city."

"Then we get more soldiers. We haven't conscripted for the army in five years. We can easily add a few thousand more." Ryker looked back and forth between Desmond and Bale but found no positive support. "Karondir is the gateway to Feldor. We'd cripple their army as well as their trade routes into Rynor. It's a key, strategic piece that's necessary for conquering the land."

After deciding to turn his attention to Feldor, Bale had wasted no time planning. Along with Desmond and Ryker, he stood around the sizable dimensional map of Terrenor in the Hall of Dignitaries where they had debated for hours. The impressive hall was where foreign visitors were usually met. Ten sets of red and black marble columns ran the length of the room. Gold-trimmed chairs sat around the edge, but the most impressive feature was the glass Norshewan emblem of a bear and crossed swords embedded in the wall at the end of the room. The blue tint of the glass gave it the appearance of ice, which was reinforced by the chill of the room.

"I disagree," Bale said, his booming voice echoing off the marble. "Karondir *is* a strategic piece, but it's not necessary to start there. If we conquer *Felting* first, the lack of leadership and support will leave Karondir alienated."

Ryker inclined his head toward Bale. "Respectfully, Your Majesty, how do we get there? Surely we can't march down the road while Karondir shoots arrows at us as we pass?"

Bale shook his head and pointed to the city of Karad. "We'll come from here. Once Karad's army is neutralized, taking Felting from the north should be easy. And once those two are in our control, Karondir will have nothing left to fight for."

Desmond and Ryker stared at the inaccessible city on the map until Desmond spoke up. "So, how do you propose we get there? Surely not bringing our army through the Kyrd Forest? We'd get lost in there and *all* end up dead."

"No, through here," Bale said as he pointed at the mountains to the north.

"Over the Korob Mountains? You must be mad!" Ryker said. Bale glared at him, and Ryker immediately shrank back. "I'm sorry, Your

Highness. I spoke out of turn." Ryker's shoulders slumped as he fixed his gaze at the floor.

"Mad?" Bale repeated. "Madness would be giving up a heavily fortified walled city at the first sign of the enemy coming through the back door. We *can* go over the mountains. Karad does have a decent army, but they would never expect an attack from the north. It'd give us an incredible advantage and keep us well clear of Karondir."

"Forgive me for questioning, Your Majesty," Desmond said, "but how will we bring our supplies over the mountains? And how would we keep our soldiers from freezing on the journey?"

"Norsh bears," Bale said.

His advisor nodded his head. "I know they've experimented in Bryveld with taming them to use in hauling quarry rocks. They're strong. If they can be kept in line, that may work."

"Their thick hides protect them from the elements," Bale went on. "We can muzzle them, blindfold them, and string them in a row to keep them tractable. They can easily carry four times their own weight."

"So, what about the soldiers. How can our men survive the cold?" asked Ryker, still facing the floor but inching up with his eyes.

"Wallum skin," Bale replied.

The wallum was a cold-water animal with a thick skin that hunters of Nortris went into the North Sea to catch. Their hides were generally used to insulate buildings, and the meat was a delicacy.

Ryker looked up. "A cloak from one *could* keep a soldier warm enough to make the trek, but wouldn't we need several thousand of them? If we started now, that would take . . . probably four years to make enough, right?"

"Not as long as that," Bale said. "I started on it a season ago, and we already have 2,000 made."

Desmond snapped his head to Bale with his eyebrows raised. "Very well. The Korob Mountains it is then," Ryker said. Desmond nodded. "Yes. Then, we attack Karad."

35

Forward and Backward

Brixton jingled the coins in his pocket without thinking as he walked to the Karad Lenders office. The Fiero family was wealthy, but growing up, his father hardly ever gave him any money of his own. When Veron had paid him the two argen for the permit, he felt alive, like he had the power to do something for himself. The money was almost as much as he'd earned from his regular wages over the last six weeks at the Department of Commerce. He was thankful to have a job but coming in on the ground floor under his father's thumb was difficult. The pay was abysmal, and his prospects to distinguish himself and be promoted were extremely limited.

He opened the door to the lending office, causing Oliver Marshall to lift his head and nod in friendly recognition. They had known each other since Brixton was young. His brother Logan and another clerk sat in the office, but Brixton wanted to speak with Oliver alone.

"Do you have a moment to talk?" Brixton asked.

"Sure, Brixton, what can I do for you?" Oliver replied.

"Is there somewhere private we could go?" Brixton said while shifting his eyes around the room.

Oliver looked at the other two men engrossed in their work before indicating with his head for Brixton to follow him. They exited through a back door to an alley between their building and the furrier's shop next door.

"I wanted to talk to you to see if there might be an opportunity for me," Brixton said. "The Department of Commerce doesn't pay much, and the prospects for advancement are poor. My father sort of forced me into the job, but my true interest is in finance. I don't want to say anything to my father, but I was wondering if you had any positions here that I might be able to fill?"

The ends of Oliver's mouth curled as if Brixton were telling him a joke. "Oh, you want a job? Of course, I'll do what I can for someone from the Fiero family." He scratched the stubble on his neck. "We don't need anyone right *now*, but we will be looking for a new accountant by the end of the season. I'm sure the pay would be *significantly* better than what you're making now, but it's not an entry-level role. You took financial classes at King's, right?"

Brixton's eyes grew wide. "Yes, many! I have a great deal of knowledge already. I know I could do the job!"

Oliver nodded as he spoke. "That's great. I think we could probably arrange something. Tell you what, if you had something to sweeten the pot, I'm sure I could make sure you moved to the top of the interview list—when it's time."

Brixton's heart sank. *I know what he wants—the same thing I got from Veron. I can't say no.* Reluctantly, he pulled the three argen two tid he had out of his pocket and handed it over.

"Great!" Oliver said with a smug grin as he put the coins in his own pocket. "I'll be excited to get to work with you. Don't worry. I won't say anything to your father."

"Yeah, thanks," Brixton said, less enthusiastically. *Whatever it takes to start making a name for myself, and get out from under my father, will be worth it.*

* * *

At the end of their busy second week of sales at North Karad Market, Weekterm brought with it a well-earned and much-enjoyed break. After the long hours they put in and the emotional ups and downs they faced, they all needed a day off—Veron most of all.

With the market finally running smoother, Veron decided it was time to get back to his Shadow Knights training, and the free day was the best time to start. Early in the morning, well before the sun rose, he strapped on his sword and left the market.

The wind picked up as he ascended the hill, and Veron pulled the black Shadow Knights cloak tighter against his body to ward off the chill. As he approached the ruins, the sun started to peek over the Straith Mountains to the east, illuminating the tops of the stone columns of the offerdom in a reddish-orange hue. It seemed like ages since Veron had been there with Artimus.

Where would I be without him? He gave me a chance and taught me so much. Now, it's all on me. I'm the last hope of the Shadow Knights. It's up to me to prevent Bale from conquering Terrenor and turning places like this back into sites of oppression and fear. A wave of nausea hit him as he imagined himself dying from his wounds after killing Bale. *No, that doesn't have to happen. I can learn to heal.*

Veron shook the thought off as he removed Farrathan from its scabbard. He stood at the edge of the offerdom, staring toward Norshewa as Artimus once had. The imposing Korob Mountains created a significant barrier between Feldor and Norshewa, which helped him feel safe, but unease still tugged at him.

What if Bale is coming through the Gap of Thardor at this moment?

How could I possibly stop him? Veron shook his head at the thought. *The only thing I can do is keep training.*

Veron moved to the center of the ruins and began. It had been several weeks since he had used a sword, but he flowed through the positura as if he'd been doing it all of his life. Once finished, he practiced strikes. Veron swung the sword fluidly. His feet danced, and his body spun as the cloak swirled around him. Sweat dripped off his face and the tips of his hair, but Veron didn't stop. He was strong and one with the sword.

When his body was no longer willing to continue, Veron sat on the top step of the ruins and retrieved the Shadow Knights book from the bag he brought. The first time he read through it, he expected to find the instruction easy to follow. He was looking for a secret or something that explained the steps he needed to take, but it made no sense. He decided to try it again.

Veron opened the book to reveal the Shadow Knights' member archive, which he didn't review last time. The first name on the list was the founder, Talon Shadow. Veron scanned through the hundreds listed and found Artimus Raleon near the end. He paused as he looked at the last line—William Stormbridge.

If I can figure this stuff out, maybe I can write my name in the book, right after my father's? He pictured what it would look like—Veron Stormbridge, written in black ink on the line below William. *I'd be the last one.*

His heart sped up as he remembered the prophecy. *Everyone on this sheet is dead. It has to be me to stop him. How's that supposed to happen though? Is he supposed to just show up at the market one day and challenge me to a fight?* He scoffed aloud. *I guess I need to learn how to use the origine if I'm going to be ready.*

Looking for help, he flipped through the book, reading the old pages over again and trying to see with new eyes. He discovered one passage he must have skimmed over the last time that seemed to be more helpful:

To access the depth of the origine, you must clear your mind of what you expect your body to be able to give. Once your mind is no longer limiting your body's actions, then you will be able to ask what you need of it.

In asking, your body must be willing to give. If you ask beyond what it is capable of, you will lose the connection and risk losing the body. When it is willing and able to respond, the ability of your body is no longer limited by typical physical requirements. Achieving a pure connection renders the mind and body with nearly unlimited capacity.

Veron still wasn't sure what it all meant. *How do I clear my mind? If I do it, how do I ask my body to give? If I can do that, how do I control it?* Sitting on the step, he closed his eyes and focused. *Clear my mind. Clear my mind.*

He tried to think of nothing, but all that did was make him think of something. The market came to his mind and how they needed people to keep showing up. Before he knew it, he pictured Artimus' house and the room he used to sleep in. Then he forced that from his mind and ended up thinking about Chloe and how she looked in the dress she was wearing the day before.

"Argh!" he yelled in frustration. *This is pointless,* Veron thought.

Veron shook his arms out and tried again. He closed his eyes and tried to focus on nothing, sitting completely still. When his mind was as blank as it could be, he flexed his muscles and punched his arms at the air as fast as he could. Nothing was different. He waved his arms in the air trying to make them move quickly, but nothing happened.

Veron exhaled heavily. *I just need to keep working on it.* He placed the book back in the bag and sheathed the sword on his back before he trudged down the hill back toward the city.

* * *

Determined to succeed, Veron committed fully to his training—running, sword work, strength training, and reading through the book. He woke up early and practiced every day. With Artimus gone, he had an expectation to live up to. It was as if Bale could show up any time, and the names in the book all looked to him to fulfill their purpose.

At the market, the weeks flew by as the heart of wiether came and went. Sales continued to be steady, and everyone's spirits were high despite the harsh chill of the weather.

Bundled in a new cloak, Veron walked the courtyard, making sure everything was going well. As he made his rounds, a man of average height with a round face and deeply set eyes came up to him.

He looks familiar, but I'm not sure where I know him from, Veron thought.

"Excuse me. Are you Veron?" the man asked.

"Yes, I am. How can I help you?" Veron replied.

"My name's Robert Brighton. I run a butcher shop in Upper Sherry."

That's where I know him from. Artimus sometimes got meat from his shop.

"I noticed you didn't have a butcher in your market here and wondered if you might be interested in one."

Veron's heart leaped. *Adding a butcher should bring in a lot of new customers.* "I am. But if you already have a shop, why would you want to come here?" Veron asked, realizing he shouldn't just take anyone who walked in off the street.

"My shop's struggling and has been for a while. The meat is good, and my cuts are good. It's a rough area to run a butcher shop from though. The people in the area can't afford luxuries like meat. However, if my shop were here, things would be a lot different. If you're willing, I'd love to have a shot on your team," Robert said.

"How can I be sure you'll do a good job?" Veron asked.

"That's fair. If it helps you feel better, I'd be willing to start risk-free to you. For the first two weeks, I'll take no pay. After two weeks, if you don't feel I'm a good fit, we part ways at no cost to you with no hard feelings. If you decide to hire me, you pay me for the two weeks I worked and keep me on the team going forward. I guarantee that you'll want to keep me around though."

Veron raised his eyebrows. "Okay, that sounds fair. Do you need a room? Do you have a family?"

"No. No family. It's just me, but I'd appreciate a room."

"Jacob, our carpenter, just finished building a new room up in the loft," Veron said, pointing it out. "You're welcome to make yourself at home in that one. What do you need to get started?"

"I have all I need for now. I can bring my knives, cutting boards, and other supplies up from my current shop."

"Great. Welcome to North Karad Market."

* * *

When suether arrived, Veron sat in the office, poring over the books. His first season had just ended, and he was hard at work calculating the taxes owed as well as bonus payouts to the team. Things started rough with slow sales and hefty expenses, but sales grew. Robert turned out to be as good a butcher as he had sold himself to be, bringing in many new customers since meat was in high demand in Prinvestor. Overall, it was a promising beginning.

352

Perspiration beaded on his forehead as he leaned over the desk. Warm weather was finally returning, but it wasn't the temperature in the office that had him sweating. *Something is wrong,* Veron thought as he scratched through numbers on the page and started again.

He jumped as the door opened suddenly and Morgan entered. "Sorry, Veron, I didn't mean to scare you," Morgan said.

"No, it's fine. I was just focused, I guess," Veron told him.

"Is everything okay? You look worried."

Veron took a deep breath before he said, "Close the door."

Morgan did. The chair scraped the floor as he sat.

"The numbers aren't adding up," Veron said.

"What do you mean?" Morgan asked.

"The season was good. After our slow start, sales were consistently high almost every day, and our total sales were close to thirty sol," Veron said.

"Wow, that's amazing!"

"Yeah, but after the labor, taxes, loan payments, and the seasonal license fee, we only made a profit of nine argen."

The enthusiasm on Morgan's face disappeared. "That's it?"

"Yeah, our sales are high, but our expenses are too. We're paying really high wages, which means we're barely clearing a profit."

"Okay, that's disappointing, but still, a profit's a profit."

Veron shook his head. "I haven't gotten to the bad news yet. We're *supposed* to have a profit of nine argen, but we don't have it. *Physically,* we've actually lost twenty-one argen."

Morgan leaned forward. "What?"

"Somehow, we're missing three sol."

Veron's words filled the small space as Morgan stared back, blinking several times.

"Maybe you did the math wrong?" Morgan said.

Veron shook his head. "I checked it three times," he replied.

Both of them looked out the window at the other workers in the market. "Do you think someone took it?" Morgan asked as he stood and walked closer to the window.

"It has to be. You and Catherine are the only ones I totally trust, but any one of the others could have had access to the money."

Neither spoke for a moment. Veron felt like his stomach was in knots.

"We need to find that money soon, or we're done," Veron said.

"What do you mean?"

"It took a lot to build all we have here, and we're barely making a profit to dig us back from it. Once you add in the missing three sol, we only have enough money left for half of suether's expenses before I can't pay Holden for the loan."

Morgan shook his head. "I didn't realize it was that bad. I don't get it though. They're all making good money. Why would any of them risk it by stealing?"

I know precisely why people steal. Veron exhaled loudly. "I don't think I can do this, Morgan. I jumped in blindly, not knowing what I was doing, and now I feel like I'm in a boat that's sinking of my own doing." Veron dropped his head and ran his hands through his hair. "I don't know enough about running a business to make this work. Even *without* the theft, in perfect conditions, we're barely staying alive. I've not only endangered my life but all of yours as well."

"Hey, look at me," Morgan said as he sat in the chair next to him and leaned in close. "I worked at the docks, barely earning enough to feed my family. Jacob and his family lived on the streets. Chloe, Danyel, Henry, Greta, Robert—you gave *all* these people something to live for. What you have done here has given us all hope. You didn't build this market for you. You did it for *us*. You didn't have to pay one argen a week, but you wanted to because you care. You're running a business that serves the community and cares for its people. You *are* making a profit. We just need to figure out this theft issue. Don't you for a *second* think you can't do this though, because I know you can."

"Thanks, Morgan. That means a lot." Veron rubbed his chin as he considered what to do next. "I can't tell everyone someone is stealing. We need to start locking up the money. And we need to have a profitable second season."

* * *

The next day, Veron took the taxes he owed to the Department of Commerce. Brixton jumped up from his desk when he entered. "So, how'd you do?" he asked.

"Sales were good—twenty-nine sol two argen," Veron replied.

"Nice! How was the profit?"

"Eh . . . not great. I was disappointed by it, to be honest." Veron left out the part about the missing money.

Brixton playfully hit him in the chest for emphasis. "Hey, something is better than nothing. And in only your first season. I knew the market was going to be a hit."

Veron paid the tax owed to Tucker, and Brixton walked with him back to the door. "You realize this earns you bronze-star status, right?" Brixton said.

Veron hadn't thought about it. Most merchants in Karad had no status awarded. When they had sales over twenty sol in a season, they achieved bronze-star status. Silver-star status was given when merchants reached over thirty-five. At the height of his market, Morgan barely made it to bronze.

Brixton stared at Veron expectantly with his hands out. "Bronze-star status?" he repeated.

Why does that matter? What's he getting at? Veron thought.

"The festival? This Weekterm? You can come now." Brixton said.
"What festival?"

Brixton hit himself lightly on the side of his head. "What festival?
Where have you been?"

He led Veron outside and pointed to a poster against the side of
the building. Veron noticed the same sign was on several other
properties.

Karad Festival of Lords
Weekterm the Premweek of Suether
Location: Karad Castle
All families of lords, officers, title holders, bronze & silver-star merchants
are welcome
Food, music, games, dancing, and quarter-staff contest

"It's this Weekterm. You *have* to be there!" Brixton said, looking at
Veron for an answer.

*I don't want to spend time talking with a bunch of snooty rich people.
But I don't know of a good excuse not to be there.* "Of course. I wouldn't
miss it," Veron said.

"Excellent!"

"What does it mean by lords and title holders and such?"

"Oh, that just keeps out the peasants. You must have a title or be a
distinguished merchant, which you are! It makes for a much more
enjoyable time. Otherwise, most of the important people wouldn't
want to be there."

*How unfair. The poor people in this city could use a festival more than
the lords and wealthy merchants,* Veron thought.

"Well, I need to get back to work. I'll see you this Weekterm!"
Brixton said as he went back into the office, leaving Veron on the
street to ponder their city's inequality.

36

Festival of Lords

Weekterm arrived, and Veron felt terrible about leaving everyone from the market behind. They teased him, wishing him to have a good time with his "rich and famous friends" at the festival. Wearing a new blue and white outfit from Henry and Greta, he walked up High Street and approached the castle gates. Veron had never been inside the castle before, and the prospect was intimidating but exhilarating at the same time. Soldiers stationed at the gatehouse stepped aside after finding his name on their list.

Veron knew he needed to keep up his story as a wealthy merchant used to nice things, but he couldn't help but gawk at the grandeur around him. The walls looked higher and even more impressive from inside than they did from the outside, and they were as thick as two men laying end-to-end.

Continuing along the path, Veron found another smaller gateway that led to a large inner courtyard where the festival attendees gathered. Easily two hundred people filled the courtyard, but it didn't even feel crowded. Tables everywhere were loaded with food and drink, and musicians played a lively song under one of the archways.

Veron had never seen anything like it before in his life. The green grass was perfectly trimmed, and a maze of bushes and flowers decorated the space. Around the grassy area ran a walkway rimmed with intricately carved stone arches displaying blue and gray banners. At the far end of the garden, a large fountain in the shape of a tree shot water from each of its branches. Each direction he looked had passageways leading to other parts of the castle. Above him, three stories of windows peeked out over the verdant scene below.

"Never been in the castle before, huh?" a voice said.

Veron jumped. He didn't even notice Brixton walk up to him in his crisp black tunic and light gray pants. "Sorry, no—yes, this is my first time here. It's . . . big," Veron said, nodding his head and looking around, trying to downplay how impressed he was.

"It's nothing compared to the one in Felting. You should see it!" Brixton said.

A beautiful and familiar-looking girl with crimson hair and a green velvet dress came up and put her arm through Brixton's. "Veron, right?" she asked.

"Yes," Veron said, unable to place where he knew her from. *She sure appears familiar with Brixton.*

"You remember Hailey, I'm sure?" Brixton said. "She was at our house when you came for dinner."

"Yes, of course! It's good to see you again, Hailey."

"I hear you've done some great things with that new market of yours," Hailey said.

The compliment brought a smile to Veron's face. "Oh, thank you. Yeah, things have been going well. I'm fortunate to have some great people working there. They've really done all the work."

"Well, I hope you enjoy the festival," Brixton said. "Have you signed up for the quarter-staff contest yet?"

"Um, no, I hadn't. What's that?" Veron asked.

Brixton's eyes widened. "Oh, you *have* to sign up. Everyone does it! I actually have some skills with the staff," he said, puffing out his chest as he glanced at Hailey. "But you don't have to be good. Most people aren't, and it's still fun. I think it's supposed to start in a few minutes."

Veron had no intention of signing up for the contest. He didn't want to fight with spoiled rich snobs for sport, but he followed Brixton to the table anyway where a woman sat taking names on a sheet of paper.

"I've got one more name for you," Brixton said to the woman.

Veron held up his hand to stop him. "Brixton, I don't know if I—"

He froze mid-sentence. The sheet in front of the woman held roughly fifty names, and one near the top caught his eye and made his blood turn to ice. Charles Mortinson.

Captain Mortinson is competing? Would I have a chance to fight him? Am I good enough to fight him? Veron thought.

"What's your name, lad?" the woman asked Veron.

Veron pulled himself out of a daze and looked at her. "Veron Stormbridge . . . Yes, I'd like to fight." *I'm not about to miss this opportunity.*

Veron turned and scanned the crowd. Near the fountain, he found who he searched for—a tall, strong man with a trimmed beard talking with a group of soldiers. Captain Mortinson.

I sure hope we get a chance to fight.

In a matter of minutes, a trumpet sounded, indicating the start of the competition, and the contestants gathered together. A large board holding their names indicated who they were to battle. A well-muscled man with dark hair stood up, leaning heavily on a cane—Gareth Billings, the Lord of Defense. The cane made him easy to pick out.

"Attention all quarter-staff contestants! We now begin the competition! You'll take turns battling one opponent at a time," Gareth said. "To win, you must either knock your opponent down or disarm him. The padded helmets are to protect your heads. Winners will advance until the last man remains. As a reward, in addition to being declared the quarter-staff champion and receiving one gold sol, the winner will receive a kiss from my daughter, Hailey."

He gestured toward Hailey, who stood to the side. She smiled and waved at everyone as the crowd whistled and cheered. *Whoa! A gold sol could be helpful right now!* Veron thought. He glanced at Brixton, who didn't look pleased. *I wonder how Brixton feels about the winner kissing Hailey? They seem to be close.*

Forty-nine names were displayed on the board, and it appeared Veron could have as many as six rounds if he won them all. His first was against someone named Worm. He wasn't sure if that was a real name or a made-up one, but they were scheduled to be the fourth fight.

Veron watched the first three battles, which were all pretty short. The first one ended when a skinny man, who didn't even know how to hold the staff correctly, had it knocked away. He laughed about it and shook hands with the man who defeated him. The next two fights ended when men fell on the ground. A hard blow to the chest knocked one down, and the other tripped on his own feet and fell over before a hit even landed.

Maybe I can do well at this? If everyone is like these guys, fighting shouldn't be too difficult, Veron thought.

Veron put his helmet on and took his staff, which was sturdy and felt like the one he used with Artimus. As he walked into the circle, his face dropped. His opponent didn't look at all like a worm. He was short and stout and had a fierce look on his face. A light breeze danced through the courtyard bringing the murmur of voices with it as he faced his rival.

Worm came at him, swinging with a yell. Veron deftly sidestepped while the other man's staff crashed to the ground where he stood a moment before. Veron hit him in the back, but it wasn't enough to knock him over. Worm recovered and faced him again, swinging left then right, but Veron moved to block both blows. As he stopped the second swing, Veron stepped in with his body. He put his right foot behind Worm's leg and shoved him with his shoulder. The short man fell with a solid thud onto the grass.

I won!

The crowd cheered for Veron as Worm got up, threw down his staff and helmet, and stomped off. Veron grinned. He had never fought in front of a crowd before, and the experience was exhilarating.

Due to the odd number, some men didn't have to fight in the first round—Brixton being one of them. When he eventually fought, he won against a tall, older man who moved rather well for his age. Still, Brixton was able to disarm him by knocking his staff away. Both Brixton and Veron won their next two fights easily.

"I see that skill you were talking about. You're doing great," Veron said to Brixton, his wavy brown hair matted and sweaty from the helmet.

"Thanks," Brixton replied. "I wish my father would realize that."

Veron followed Brixton's eyes to see Raynor watching the event from the other side of the crowd. "Does he put a lot of pressure on you?"

"Haha! That's putting it mildly." Brixton looked down and kicked at the grass below him. His shoulders sagged. "He won't stand for a son who's not the best. I never even wanted to be a soldier, but he made me practice fighting all of my childhood. I won the junior sword fighting cup three years in a row. I thought it was what he wanted, but he never seemed to care. He didn't even show up to watch."

I wonder how my father would have treated me had he lived?

"You're doing well, too. How were you trained?" Brixton asked.

Veron thought quickly. "In Felting. My brother and I practiced together."

Brixton nodded, staring absently ahead. "I really want to win today," he said after a moment.

Veron assumed he referred to impressing his father but noticed Brixton looking at Hailey, who still stood next to her father. She saw them both and waved.

I think Brixton's goal is to get to kiss Hailey, or maybe to prevent anyone else from doing so, he thought.

As the rounds went on, Veron kept his eye on Captain Mortinson. Whenever the man fought, Veron watched how he moved and the way he attacked. His opponents never had a chance.

He's cunning with his moves and brutally efficient.

Veron barely survived the fourth round. The man he fought was much stronger, and he almost lost his hold on the staff from the punishing hits. Thankfully, due to some quick movement, he dodged a couple of blows and knocked the man over when his balance was compromised. Soon, only four competitors remained—Veron, Brixton, a man named Brody, and Mortinson.

"Get ready to be knocked on your butt!" Brixton said as the two squared off.

"I'm ready," Veron told him.

Veron wanted to win, but if he did, he'd feel bad for Brixton. He considered letting Brixton knock him down but decided he wasn't about to miss his chance to fight the captain. Veron lunged, hitting Brixton square in the chest and knocking him back.

"Ooph, that's gonna hurt," Brixton said as he rubbed his chest.

Without warning, Brixton stepped in and attacked, but Veron

knocked the staff away. Brixton tried the other side, but Veron blocked it again and took his own futile swing at Brixton's head. The other boy was quick. Brixton kicked with his right foot and pushed Veron away. Back in the ready position, they circled.

Brixton moved with a two-handed swing. Veron stepped in to stop the blow out of instinct, glancing Brixton's staff out of the way. Veron brought his weapon back and caught Brixton in the padding on the side of his head. Brixton staggered but remained upright. Veron finished with a decisive blow to his back that sent Brixton to the ground.

The crowd cheered as Veron extended his hand to his opponent with a smile. Brixton accepted the hand to help him up, but his face was downcast.

"Sorry, Brix," Veron said.

"Nice job," Brixton replied, grimacing and holding his back where he was hit.

The next match was a brutal fight where each man took turns beating the other. Mortinson was strong and fast. His age hadn't diminished his skill. Although Brody was a strong opponent, in the end, only one kept his feet and was declared the winner—Mortinson.

Veron's face was unreadable, but inside, his heart leaped with excitement. He harbored a deeply rooted revulsion for the man and wanted more than anything to be able to beat him up with a staff.

A brief moment of dread came to Veron as his stomach jumped. *What if he recognizes me?* He quickly shook it off. *He didn't recognize me in Morgan's shop. It's been many years since we've crossed paths before that.*

"Ladies and gentlemen, this is the final round of our quarter-staff competition. Captain Charles Mortinson versus Veron Storm-bridge," Lord Billings announced.

The fighters donned their helmets and took up their staffs.

Mortinson waved to the crowd with a smile, but Veron didn't take his eyes off the soldier. Both men stood facing each other while slowly moving their feet in a circle, waiting for the other to make the first move.

The smell of trampled grass and sweat permeated the air. The rumble of the crowd filled the courtyard. Some chanted for the captain and some for Veron, although he didn't even know who they were.

Clear the mind. Clear the mind. Veron tried to tap into the origine. *Focus. You can do this.*

Momentarily distracted, he almost missed the attack. Veron ducked underneath Mortinson's swing to his head. Anticipating the reverse jab to follow, Veron blocked it with his own weapon.

He's much stronger than me! Veron swallowed.

Even though he blocked the blow, it almost sent his staff flying from his hands. With their weapons connected, Mortinson pushed, trying to knock him over. Veron spun away and moved to create space. The wind had stopped, and the air was heavy. The chanting grew louder as Veron took in quick breaths while they circled.

Mortinson advanced. He tried several quick blows on alternating sides, which Veron swiftly blocked. What Veron wasn't ready for was the fifth hit. Instead of swinging at his body, Mortinson brought the staff up between Veron's legs with a crooked grin. Veron jumped, using his staff for leverage. Mortinson's grin changed to fear as his weapon found nothing but air and Veron's feet collided into the captain's face.

The crowd gave a collective gasp as Mortinson staggered back, checking his face with his hand to make sure he wasn't bleeding. His good-natured attitude was gone. Veron stood in a ready stance with two feet on the ground and his staff held prepared to strike.

"Come on!" Veron yelled.

The sun was high by this point, and both fighters dripped with sweat. Veron wiped his forehead to keep his sight clear while the captain seethed through gritted teeth. Mortinson lunged with a yell and swung hard at Veron's head, but Veron ducked again.

While ducked, Veron struck at the captain, the staff connecting with his left side and then the right. Mortinson groaned as he brought his staff back and aimed at Veron's side. Veron used his own to block and redirect the captain's down to the ground. As soon as they touched the ground, Veron pivoted the backside of his staff and struck the unguarded side of Mortinson's head as hard as he could. The staff shook as it connected with the soldier, and Veron felt the reverberation up his arm. Mortinson lost his grip on his weapon as he spun around and fell to the ground with a resounding thud. Veron had won.

The crowd went wild, cheering and chanting his name. Veron looked around, realizing the impossibility of the moment. The wealthiest people of the city, the lords and ladies and merchants he had been oppressed by all his life, were all cheering his name in celebration as he stood over his defeated foe. He beamed, taking in the moment.

This was for Fend. This was for Morgan. This was for me! Veron thought.

He wanted to spit on the fallen captain or maybe hit him a few more times while he was down but looking at him on the ground changed his mind. The arrogant pride in Mortinson's face had been replaced with a downturned look of disappointment. He had been beaten by a boy in front of all his peers and was probably in pain. Veron walked to where Mortinson lay and gritted his teeth as he held out his hand. Mortinson narrowed his eyes and swatted the hand away as he got up on his own. Veron smirked as the captain walked off.

Gareth Billings motioned for Veron to come. "Congratulations, Veron! You are our quarter-staff contest winner!" he said as he handed him a solid gold sol and took a bronze-colored medal with a ribbon and placed it around Veron's neck. He motioned to his daughter with a smile. "Your final prize!"

The crowd cheered again.

Veron had forgotten about the promised kiss. He had been so focused on Mortinson that it slipped his mind.

Hailey came up to him with a mischievous look on her face. Holding his arms, she leaned in and whispered in his ear, "I was hoping it'd be you."

With somewhere between confusion and a look of triumph on his face, he turned his cheek to her. His eyes widened when her lips met his in a brief but electric kiss. She winked at him before turning away. The crowd cheered again, and Veron looked back out at the faces, unable to do anything but grin after the kiss. He found Brixton's face, which was unreadable as he clapped along with the others.

In the excitement of the kiss and the cheer of the crowd, Veron's thoughts turned to Chloe. *I wish she had been here to see my victory. I wish the kiss had been with her.*

Veron hung around the festival for a while. He wanted to sample more of the food, but he also enjoyed getting congratulated by people everywhere he went. As he stood by the fountain, talking with an older woman who insisted Veron looked just like her son, Raynor Fiero and Baron Rycroft approached. The woman quickly took her leave. Veron had never met the baron but knew who he was by sight. He felt butterflies in his stomach.

"Impressive fighting, Veron," Raynor said, nodding his head. "Where did you learn the quarter-staff?"

"A friend taught me," Veron said.

Raynor took a drink from a goblet he carried. "Most unusual for a merchant. Have you met Baron Edward Rycroft yet?"

"No, I've not," Veron said as he extended his hand to the baron. "It's an honor to meet you, Lord Baron."

"And you too, Veron. You were excellent with the staff today. Beating Captain Mortinson is no small feat," Rycroft said.

"Thank you, sir."

"Maybe we could use him against Bale? What do you think?" the baron said to Raynor with a grin.

Veron jerked his head at the name. "What?" he said as his pulse quickened.

"Oh, not really," Rycroft said. "We were just talking about how Edmund Bale was run out of Bromhill in Rynor, and I was wondering if he'll try to attack Feldor now."

"As I said, Karad is too far away," Raynor said. "If anything, Karondir would be his first target, but they're well prepared for such an attack."

"Enough of that. Today is a festival," the baron said, waving the topic away with his hand. "Veron, I hear you've been creating quite a commotion with that new market of yours. I might have to come by and see it for myself!"

Veron's shoulders relaxed. He smiled at the thought of the baron coming by their market, exchanging coins for candles, and being measured by the Mallours for a new outfit sewn on the dirt floor of an abandoned stable. "You're welcome anytime, Lord Baron," he replied.

"I have to say, Veron. I'm quite impressed with what you've done with that market in such a short time," Raynor said.

"Thank you, Lord Fiero. That means a great deal."

The men took their leave, and Veron's thoughts turned to Bale.

Will he attack Feldor? Would he make it all the way to Karad?

Having enough excitement for the day, Veron felt it was time to head home. He wanted to say goodbye to Brixton and found him along the courtyard wall, engaged in conversation with Hailey. As he caught their eyes with a wave, Veron noticed Hailey gesticulating sharply as she spoke while Brixton's face was red.

I wonder what that's about? he thought.

As he approached, they were all smiles. "Leaving so soon?" Brixton asked.

"Yes, it's time to go."

"I saw my father cornering you earlier. Looks like he's taken quite a liking to you. I'm sure he wishes he had a son more like you." Brixton said it with a playful voice, carrying a hint of jealousy.

Veron wasn't sure how to respond. "I'm sure he's proud of you."

"Well, you were great with the staff today. If I couldn't win, I'm glad it was you," Brixton said.

"It was just a lucky day, I guess. Hailey, it was great seeing you again," Veron said. She smiled back and waved her fingers as Veron headed back into the city.

Having failed to impress at the competition, Brixton quickly grew tired of the festival. He stayed because of the obligation he felt to mingle with the elite of the city. Every day at the Department of Commerce felt more and more frustrating. His chances of doing anything important were slim, and his prospects never changed. It seemed ages since he first spoke with Oliver Marshall about the accountant position at Karad Lenders. Brixton went by to check in regularly, but the answer was always that they weren't quite ready to hire yet.

I wish I'd held onto my money. So far, it's done nothing.

Across the courtyard, he noticed someone he did not expect

to see—Byron Hampton, the High Lord of Trade in Felting. His position was one of the most respected in the kingdom. Although his son Magnus and Brixton's sister Mila were to be married soon, Brixton hadn't had a chance to meet the man.

Brixton had disliked Magnus ever since his first year at the Academy when the other boy had stolen his project. Brixton almost failed out of school because of it and had to be bailed out by his father, which he deeply resented. Although he detested Magnus, they were about to be related, and it wouldn't hurt to try to be friendly to his father.

Who knows what doors he could open?

Hailey had wandered off, so he decided to go over and introduce himself to the high lord, straightening his shirt and fixing his hair on the way.

"High Lord Hampton? Hello, I'm Brixton Fiero. I graduated from King's with your son last year. I'm Mila's brother."

The high lord was not particularly striking, but he did hold his body with an air of confidence, which projected both power and sophistication. He was only slightly taller than Brixton and was clean-shaven with neat, light-brown hair.

"Brixton Fiero . . . Yes, Magnus mentioned you were there—Raynor's son," Byron said. Brixton thought he heard a tinge of anger as he spoke his father's name. "It's good to meet you. What have you been doing since school?"

"I'm working as a clerk in the Department of Commerce." He immediately felt ashamed and wished he had something more distinguished to say. "For now—while I build up some experience. Soon, I hope to get a job in finance."

Byron looked down his nose at him. Brixton felt even more ashamed as the high lord stared at him. "So, your father got you a job, did he? If you get a finance job, you may soon be working with

369

my son, Magnus. He decided to settle here with Mila and is moving to Karad next week."

Brixton's toes curled at the revelation. *Great. The last thing I want is to have Magnus around Karad.*

"He's going to be an accountant at one of the lending houses here," Byron added.

Brixton's stomach turned, afraid of what that meant. His voice wavered, heart pounding as he asked, "Which lending house is that?"

"Karad Lenders. He'll be working with the Marshall brothers."

Brixton's jaw clenched as he seethed.

Brixton found Oliver Marshall near the fountain, speaking with his father, Raynor. He walked up and interrupted their conversation, not even caring that his father stood there. "I hear that Magnus Hampton is moving here and taking an accountant position at Karad Lenders," Brixton said with a stern look.

By this point in the festival, Raynor was so drunk that he barely appeared to notice the interruption.

"Brixton!" Oliver replied with a smile. "Hello. Yes, Magnus is going to be an accountant with us. He comes highly recommended. Did you know him at school? He should have been in your class, I believe."

"Yes, I know him," Brixton said. "But . . . the accountant job . . ." Brixton inclined his head to emphasize his point.

Oliver wrinkled his forehead as if he didn't understand. He glanced at Raynor before turning back to Brixton. "Yes, he should be well qualified for the job. I'm excited to have him," he said, looking at Brixton with a blank stare.

I can't believe it. He's going to act like nothing happened between us. "Don't you think a job like that would be good for someone . . . here in Karad, maybe?" he asked.

Oliver exhaled with a sharp laugh through his nose. "If the right person were here, then yes, but there's nothing wrong with hiring someone from another city—especially one who's as well-connected and *wealthy* as the Hampton family."

Brixton's heart sank. *I bribed Oliver with what little I could afford, but the Hampton family paid more. So that's how it's done.* He slowly nodded his head. "So, what about my um . . ." Brixton trailed off. *He should give me that money back, at least.*

"What are you talking about, Brixton?" his father asked, waving his arm haphazardly. His words slurred.

"Yes, what are you talking about?" Oliver said with a haughty look on his face that dared Brixton to say more.

Brixton's face was red, and his breath came quickly. *I can't say it. If Father knew I was trying to leave the job, he would be furious.* "Nothing . . . Nevermind." He walked off, defeated.

Brixton kicked the grass as he shuffled away with his head down, but he wallowed in pity for only a moment. He promptly lifted his shoulders and straightened his back.

This isn't going to stop me. I'll just have to find my own way to advance, he thought as he left the courtyard.

37

Moving Up

Watching the pink sky of the remains of the sunset, Brixton sat moping on the balcony of his family's house, kept company by a bottle of wine, as Hailey approached.

"Do you mind if I join you?" she asked. Brixton shrugged as she sat and cuddled up against him.

A week into suether, the days warmed quickly, but the evenings remained crisp and cool. Brixton typically found sitting on the balcony to be peaceful. The castle rested just up the hill, and the rest of the houses of West Fairren surrounded them, but neither the view, the wine, nor the company brought Brixton joy.

"What's wrong, Brix?" Hailey asked.

"What do you mean? Nothing's wrong," Brixton snapped at her.

She glared at him, then proceeded to smooth out her green dress. "You've been in a bad mood all day, ever since the festival."

"I said I'm fine."

He wasn't even sure why he was in a bad mood, and Hailey asking him about it made it even more frustrating. He was still angry and disappointed about the accountant position, but he didn't think that was completely it.

Recently, Hailey and Brixton had started hanging out more together. She had grown into a beautiful young woman, and as soon as she started paying attention to him, his desire toward her had grown as well. A week before the festival, having grudgingly received the approval from both sets of parents, he received a court permit, allowing them to meet freely. To his dismay, as soon as his intentions toward her became official, the excitement began to fade. He still liked her but no longer felt the intense craving to be with her. Instead, it felt like an obligation. Her family connections were important, and he didn't want the embarrassment of backing out, so he simply continued forward.

Why am I upset? Brixton wondered. He thought back through the day at the festival. *Was it losing the accountant job? Father's attention to Veron? Losing the competition? Hailey kissing Veron?*

"Do you like Veron?" Brixton asked with a tone that sounded harsher than he intended.

Hailey's arm was around him, and she tensed at the question. "Veron, your friend? Sure, he seems nice," she said.

He turned to look at her. "No, I mean, do you *like* him?"

Hailey leaned away for a moment then playfully hit him on the chest. "What? No! Not like that. I've only *met* him twice, silly. I like *you*," Hailey hugged him tighter then met his lips with a kiss. "I had to kiss him because of the contest, but I would rather it had been you. Is that what's been bothering you?"

He looked back out at the city and took a long drink from the bottle. *Why do I have to talk about what's bothering me? Why can't she leave me alone?* He breathed in deeply and let out a loud sigh. "I'm not making anything of myself." He hated admitting she was right about something being wrong.

"What do you mean?"

Brixton sloughed off her arms and leaned forward in his chair. "I've grown up with tutors all my life. Between them and my father, practically every moment was a learning opportunity. I even graduated from King's, and here I am, an entry-level clerk."

"There's nothing wrong with that, Brix."

Brixton looked at Hailey and pointed for emphasis. "Your father was a distinguished fighter at my age. My father already ran multiple businesses. I feel like I'm so far behind." Brixton stood and walked to the railing.

"Behind what? You're not competing against anyone."

I know she's right, but it doesn't feel right. I wish I'd been able to get that accountant position. I feel like I'm competing against everyone, and right now, Magnus Hampton is winning.

"What do you want to make of yourself?" Hailey asked.

Brixton took a long drink and looked longingly out at the city. "I want to be important. I want to own something big"—he turned excitedly to face her—"like Veron does with his market. Maybe have a great title like my father or yours. Maybe even be baron one day!" he said.

Still seated, Hailey unsuccessfully tried to stifle a laugh, and Brixton was taken aback.

"What? You think that's funny?" he asked.

"I'm sorry," she said, letting the laugh escape. "Do you think someone will choose you to be a lord or a baron one day?"

Brixton stared at her with a fierce look. "You don't think I can—that I don't have what it takes?" *How dare she mock me.* He tightened his grip on the bottle as he gritted his teeth.

"I don't know. Sure, you could do it. I just have a tough time picturing it, that's all."

Brixton threw the nearly empty bottle against the stone wall. It shattered, sending shards of glass and red wine across the balcony.

"I could do it! You have no idea!" he shouted. Hailey recoiled as her eyes grew wide. Brixton stepped away and looked back out onto the city. "I'll be something one day. You wait and see." The wind died just before he spoke, and his words hung ominously in the air. *This city is not going to hold me back.*

"You can let yourself out," he said without looking in Hailey's direction. The scrape of a chair and shuffling of feet mixed with the muffled sounds of Hailey fighting tears. *Why is she crying?* Brixton gripped the railing of the balcony tightly until he released his hands and sighed. *I shouldn't have thrown that bottle. I shouldn't have yelled at her.* He kicked himself and turned around to say something, but she was gone. His remorse was too late.

Brixton sat back down, feeling even worse than before. He continued to look out into the city and think of what he could do with his life. The castle beckoned to him. The houses around challenged him to be successful. More than anything, he didn't want to be another nobody, living in the city in insignificance. As he thought of his situation, he remembered something his father told him years before.

"Elevating yourself requires someone else to fall."

Brixton shook his head as he pondered the words. *I thought I could do it all, but I can't. I wanted to be kind to others and also be successful, but Father was right. I'm tired of being looked over. It's time to take action, and I intend to do just that.*

With a clear idea of what he needed to do, he made his way down through the house and out the front door into the waiting night.

* * *

The commerce department was busy on Marketday. Taxes were due during the premweek of suether, which meant they usually flooded in on Finday and often the following week, and Tucker was hard at work processing the collections. It was his job to balance businesses' sales with taxes paid and make sure they matched. Heath sat at his desk, updating paperwork on sales history, and Brixton had three new license applications to work through.

Brixton glanced up from his work, his palms sweating in anticipation. He stared at the closed door to his father's office for a long time as he picked absently at his fingers. He looked at Tucker.

It's time, he thought as he stood up and walked past the other desks to his father's office.

"I like that shirt today, Brixton. You look good. Is it new?" Tucker said as he passed.

The comment caught him by surprise as he was about to knock on the door. "Um . . . Thanks. Yeah, it's pretty new." *Tucker! You're not making this any easier!*

"Are you okay? It looks like you're sweating a bit," Tucker said, pointing at his forehead.

"Oh, yeah. I'm fine. It's just a little warm in here." Brixton knocked on his father's door.

"Come in!" a muffled voice said.

Brixton opened the door as his father quickly covered up a letter he had been writing. *That's odd. I wonder what he's writing about?*

"Yes, what is it?" Raynor asked.

Brixton closed the door and sat across from his father. "I'm hesitant to bring this up, but I noticed something that concerned me, and I figured you'd want to know." His father sat back in his chair, listening. "I was glancing over the tax reports on Finday, at the end of the day, and it looked to me like some of the totals were off."

"What do you mean 'off'?" Raynor asked.

"Well, I saw a sales report sheet on Tucker's desk after he left. It was for Dane, the locksmith—I know he's a friend of Tucker's—and I was curious to see how his business was doing," Brixton said. "One of the columns caught my eye when something didn't look right. The numbers didn't add up. The total at the bottom should have been the addition of the sales numbers above it, but it was slightly less. I figured maybe he made an arithmetic error, but I looked at a couple of other sheets and found similar issues. Now, I'm not accusing Tucker of anything, but it seems to me that either he's making some simple errors or he's underreporting business earnings. But I have no idea why he'd do something like that."

His father stared at him with a stony expression. "If he were misstating the earnings, it'd be easy for him to skim off the tax money that had been paid."

Brixton softly gasped as if he'd never considered the idea.

"Tucker's been a good worker for years. I have a difficult time believing he would either make mistakes like that or steal," his father said.

Brixton held up his hands. "I'm not saying he's doing either. I just figured you'd want to know."

"How much were the sales under-reported by?" Raynor asked.

"That was one of the things that seemed most odd. Each one was off by exactly one sol."

"Which would be one argen in taxes we could be short." Raynor sat for a moment in thought. "Thank you for bringing this to my attention." He nodded, letting Brixton know he was dismissed.

Brixton went back to his desk and stared at his papers. He hoped no one noticed how much sweat covered him as his heart pounded.

"Tucker," his father said, standing in the doorway to his office.

"Yes?" Tucker replied.

"Can you come here? Bring your tax papers."

Without hesitating, Tucker jumped up. He had a smile on his face as he collected his papers and entered the office. The door closed behind him.

Brixton felt sick. His stomach churned, and he had to fight to keep from running outside to vomit. He felt the same way the night after the festival when he came into the office and altered the numbers on Tucker's reports. Brixton needed a promotion, and unfortunately for Tucker, he was in the way.

Brixton tried to act like he was working, but he couldn't stand the wait. He kept glancing at the door. He had to clench his fists to keep his fingers from tapping. *What's happening in there?*

At first, he couldn't hear anything, but eventually, muffled sounds came through the door—pounding on a desk, some shouting. He recognized the timbre of his father's voice even though he couldn't distinguish what was said. They went on for ten minutes or so, and eventually, his father burst through the door, flushed in the face. Tucker followed behind.

"I swear they were right! I always double-check my numbers, and there is no way I missed all of those," Tucker said. Usually, he was calm and collected, but he looked like a cornered wild animal.

"I agree," Raynor replied as he shuffled through papers on Tucker's desk. "I don't think it's possible you just happened to miss all of them either."

Brixton blanched. *Oh no! Surely, he won't suspect me, will he?*

Raynor opened Tucker's desk drawers one at a time.

Come on, find it! Brixton thought.

From the back of the bottom drawer, Raynor pulled out a small stack of coins and held them up to Tucker. Brixton's shoulders relaxed, and he slowly exhaled the breath he'd been holding.

"What's this?" Raynor asked.

"I—I have no idea. I didn't even know that was there!" Tucker shook. His eyes were wide and shifted around.

"Four silver argen?" Raynor said with a cold, hard tone. "Is it *chance* that there are four underreported accounts?"

There would have been more if I could have scraped together more coins, Brixton thought.

"I —I don't know what to say. I didn't do this!" Tucker said.

A lump began to form in Brixton's throat. *This isn't good. He doesn't deserve this. Should I say something? Should I stop this?*

Raynor punched Tucker in the stomach and pushed him down to the ground, where the head clerk coughed and sputtered. "Heath, notify the constable."

Heath ran out of the door. Raynor stood over Tucker, who muttered incoherently between tears, clutching his stomach.

"You're finished here, Tucker. Tax manipulation is stealing against the city. You'll go to prison for this."

Brixton was sick inside. *I should say something. It wasn't him! It was me!* His thoughts felt like a yell, but the cry didn't escape. Brixton had known Tucker almost all of his life, and the man had always been good to him. *I didn't mean for it to go this far. I didn't think about what would happen to him. If I had, I wouldn't have done it.* Brixton knew the truth of the matter though. *If I am going to rise, then someone else has to fall. I'm sorry, Tucker.*

Heath returned with a city constable and a soldier who took Tucker. "No, please! I didn't do anything. What about my wife? My kids?" the clerk pleaded as they dragged him away. "Raynor, you know I wouldn't do this!" The door closed behind him, silencing his appeals.

Brixton's stomach settled, and his heart rate slowed. Raynor returned to his office, and Heath went back to his desk. Brixton was about to go back to work but needed to seize the opportunity. He entered his father's office.

"Wow, that's crazy. Who would've thought Tucker would do something like that?" Brixton said.

"Never underestimate what people are capable of," Raynor replied, buried back in his papers as if nothing had even happened.

"You know, Father, if you like, I don't mind going over all of Tucker's reports and double-checking things. We probably need to make sure they're right. I know it's busy right now, but we need to get them finished soon. I'll stay late to finish up my work on the license applications too."

"Sure. That's fine."

Brixton fought back a smirk as he returned to his desk. *So far, so good.*

* * *

The next day Brixton went straight to work on Tucker's everyday responsibilities, not giving Heath or his father a chance to worry about them. After a week of working double duty, Raynor officially promoted Brixton to head clerk. Heath, who had worked there longer, sulked about it and didn't speak to Brixton for days after.

After years of trying to impress his father or simply get him to recognize any ability, something finally went Brixton's way. He felt terrible for Tucker but decided he wouldn't let things like that stop him anymore. No one would give things to him in life, so it was up to him to make it happen.

38

Misfortune at the Market

The missing money at the end of their first season was only the beginning of Veron's concerns. Over the first half of suether, new problems developed regularly. One day, Morgan's produce supply had an infestation of bugs that seemed to come from nowhere. They had to throw out almost the whole inventory of food.

A week later, they found several rolls of the Mallours' fabric riddled with claw marks from some sort of animal. Morgan jokingly accused Henry of keeping a pet valcor in their stall at night. Normally, Veron would have found the reference to the mythical creature amusing, but the financial impact that resulted killed any humor for him.

The biggest scare was when Chloe left one of her candles lit by mistake one night. The wind knocked it over while they slept, and it set fire to one of the display tables. It would have quickly spread, burning up the steps and then the entire market, but thankfully Morgan's son, Jack, heard the crackling of a fire and woke everyone. They used a rain barrel to put out the fire just in time.

Two weeks after that, thieves snuck in and stole a lot of their inventory. Veron was the one to hear the intruders first. Yelling from the balcony sent them scurrying, but not before they had loaded up and made off with several crates of clothing, fabric, candles, bread, and produce. The lock to the gate lay broken in the street.

Veron stared out the window of the office in a daze. The stress was taking a toll on him. He hadn't been sleeping well, and his stomach hurt constantly. Instead of making up their profit deficit, they were in an even worse hole now. The rest of his money had been paid out—even his prize from the festival. On top of all the issues they'd had, the theft from the previous night seemed like something they couldn't come back from.

A knock sounded at the door. "Come in," Veron said.

His heart sank when the door opened to reveal Holden Merevail. Veron's six-week loan payment was due the previous week, but not having the money to pay it, he'd been avoiding the lending office.

"Veron, I was walking by and thought I'd pop in for a moment to say hello. What happened out there?" the old man asked while nodding his head toward the courtyard.

Veron's mind raced. The market looked like a disaster as the others worked on cleaning up. *I can't let him know how bad things are!* "Oh, we're just doing some reorganization. It's kind of a mess at the moment but should be clean soon," he told him. Veron saw the disorder as he looked past Holden through the doorway. *He's not going to believe we're reorganizing.*

"So, how are things going?" Holden asked.

"Great!" Veron said, forcing a smile. "Sales keep growing steadily as we add new customers each week."

"Good . . . Good." Holden's expression grew serious. The pleasant smile normally on the man's face was gone, replaced by a menacing look. "You missed your loan payment last week, Veron."

Veron tensed. He had hoped somehow to ignore the subject. "Yeah, I know, I'm so sorry. With this reorganization, things have been crazy here. I've been meaning to come by but haven't had the chance. I'll bring it to you this week."

Holden nodded and looked around the office for a moment. "I'm here now?"

Veron swallowed hard. He couldn't pay him now. He didn't have the money.

"I don't keep the money here. I'll have to go and get it, but I'll bring it to you."

"I don't mind going with you," Holden said with his jaw fixed and a rigid stare.

Veron's hands were sweating. "I can't right now. I've got to get back to work here." He motioned toward the courtyard. "I promise I'll have the payment to you by this Finday though."

"Very well," Holden said, standing up straight and looking down at Veron. "You've been good on your payments until now, but if you miss this week, you'll find my leniency gone."

The lender gave Veron a stern look before leaving the office and closing the door behind him. Veron breathed a sigh of relief, then put his face in his hands and growled a cry of frustration. *I feel like a failure. What am I going to do?* he thought.

Another knock sounded at the door before it opened again and Chloe stepped into the office. Veron sat up straighter and tried to compose himself.

"How are you, Veron?" she asked hesitantly.

Veron shook his head as he thought about the theft and the loan. "I want to do something good here, but we're having setback after setback. We can't make a profit, and I can't pay our bills," he said.

Chloe's forehead wrinkled. "Yeah, we've had some problems recently, but have you forgotten about last season? We made a profit!"

Veron hung his head and ran his hands through his hair. "No . . . We didn't. We should have made a profit, according to the books, but we were three sol short."

Chloe gasped. "What? Where'd it go?"

Veron rubbed the top of the desk absently. "I don't know. I wish I did. On top of that, we've been bleeding coins to deal with all of these problems, and this Finday, when I can't pay the loan, I'll probably be sold into slavery, and you'll all be on the streets."

"Oh!" Chloe said, putting her hand to her chest.

"I just need to think for a bit," Veron said as he looked down at the desk.

Chloe reached out and gently held Veron's cheek. "I still say what you've built here is good, no matter what happens." She smiled before turning to leave.

"Chloe! Don't say anything to the others . . . Please?"

She nodded and closed the door behind her.

* * *

Robert, the butcher, lay in bed, staring at the ceiling as a faint bit of light from the moon came through the window. Everyone at the market had gone to bed hours before and should have been long asleep. It was time.

The night was still while he made his way down the steps. He paused in the courtyard, listening. Snoring resonated from one of the rooms upstairs, and a cat yowled somewhere in the distance. Robert pulled a bottle from his pocket and walked to where Danyel kept the leftover baked goods from the day. He unscrewed the top of the bottle, revealing a fine powder inside, and prepared to sprinkle it over the bread.

"What are you doing out this late?" a voice said from the darkness of the stall next to him.

Robert jumped back and looked up. "I—I was making sure everything was all right down here," Robert said.

"Making sure everything was all right?" Veron emerged from behind the stall wall and walked toward him. "I was thinking about all the problems we've had recently, and I realized . . . no money ever went missing before I hired you, and none of the bad things we've experienced have impacted your meat supply."

Robert backed up toward the center of the courtyard.

"What's in that bottle?" Veron asked.

Robert made ready to turn and run when he hit something behind him.

"Hi, Robert, you're up late tonight." It was Morgan, without his usual smile. "I'll take that," he said as he snatched the bottle from Robert's hand. "I take it this isn't a sweetener to make the bread taste better?"

"So, what was the plan?" Veron asked. "If you poison the bread, the people who come here will get sick. Then once word spreads, no one will shop here?" He stepped closed. "It wasn't a wild animal that tore up the fabric, was it?"

Robert looked around frantically for a way out.

"Those bugs didn't randomly come to destroy my food, did they?" Morgan asked. "And Chloe didn't forget to blow out her candle, did she?"

Sweat covered Robert's forehead. He tried to form words, but nothing came out. Panicking, he pushed Morgan and ran for the door. He quickly unlocked the gate and fled into the night.

Veron wanted to pursue the butcher, to punish Robert for the grief he caused their group, but he had bigger things on his mind than revenge. Instead, he ran to Robert's room with his heart pounding. He didn't want to dare to hope, but he couldn't help it. Veron searched in and under the mattress and found nothing. He looked around, but there was nowhere to hide anything.

It's got to be here somewhere! Where would I hide it?

He got on the ground and felt the boards, one at a time. Against the wall, under the headboard of the bed, one was loose. His breath stopped. With his face pressed against the floor and his arm reached out, he pulled up the loose board and rummaged underneath it. His heart leaped as he felt the cold hard touch of coins. He grabbed what he could and pulled his arm back.

Sheer joy and immense relief flooded over him. A pile of coins filled his hand—his missing three sol. *I can pay the loan. We can survive!* Veron cried with relief as he lay sprawled on the floor.

As he stared at the coins, a nagging thought wouldn't go away. *Why would he do all of those things?* he thought. *What good would it do to sabotage us? Something doesn't make sense.*

* * *

The next day, Veron and Morgan relayed what happened to the rest of their team. Everyone was outraged and suggested various acts of vengeance. The betrayal hurt, but Veron simply looked forward to having things stable again.

That afternoon, just before closing, Veron helped Morgan restock newly purchased supplies when a commotion drew his attention. Eight men walked through the entrance with masks over their faces. All of them had some sort of weapon—a sword, club, or large knife on their belt—and two of them carried large torches. Veron and the rest of the market workers froze.

They're not here to shop, Veron thought.

It wasn't dark enough to need torches yet, and Veron was afraid he knew their purpose. He clenched his fists when he noticed a hooded figure in the back, dressed in the same clothes Robert wore the night before.

"Veron Stormbridge!" the man in front said.

Veron looked around at the rest of his people before stepping forward. "I'm Veron," he replied with a hard stare.

"You have until the end of the week to close this market," the man said.

Veron scoffed. "I'm sorry, but I don't answer to you. We pay our taxes and rent. We have every right to be here." He glanced up at the loft. *I wish I had my sword.*

"*We* have a right to *our* stores," the man replied. "We've worked in this town for years, and you have no place here. Your market is taking away the business we've built. Now, it's time for you to leave."

So that's what this is about? They're afraid of the competition? "What about *my* hard work?" Veron asked. "Do you think it was *easy* to build this place? You thought you'd send Robert to mess things up for us? You thought if we fell apart, we'd close?"

None of the men moved. Instead of answering, the man in front looked to his crew. The men with torches fanned out to the balconies on the right and left, holding the flames close to the dry wood.

Veron's breath quickened. *If they light the wood, there's no way we'd be able to put out the flames. The entire market would burn in a matter of minutes, and there's no chance we could recover from that.*

"No, I'm sure it wasn't easy. And I doubt you'd be interested in building it again, would you?" the man sneered. "If you push us, you *will* regret it."

Veron watched the men with torches, dreading any movement they made.

"You can work for the rest of the week," the man said. "But if you open your doors next Marketday, I promise it'll be the last time you ever do." With that, all eight men turned and left.

Veron looked up with his eyebrows raised as Morgan re-entered the courtyard from the street. "What'd they say?" he asked.

Morgan shook his head. "No luck."

"They're not gonna do anything?"

"They said that without knowing who all the people are, they couldn't do much."

Veron groaned in frustration. "So, what are the constables for if they can't do anything?"

"I mentioned Robert, but they needed more—more names, more proof."

The rest of the market team gathered around in the courtyard, trying to find a solution to their problem. "We should fight them!" young Brock suggested.

"Yeah, I'll fight!" Danyel said as he pumped his fist in the air.

"No, we're not going to fight," Veron said as he extended his arms and motioned for them to settle. Secretly, he wanted to do that exact thing but was concerned for his workers. "It's too dangerous. We could end up dead."

A few more ideas were suggested, but none held merit. Soon, the crowd settled into a quiet funk, having decided nothing.

With two days left to work, the workers slowly accepted their fate, and the atmosphere around the market grew somber. Veron tried to motivate everyone to keep up their good spirits, but it was no use. When he closed the gate on Finday, he knew it would be the last time. Some workers wanted to throw a party to pick their spirits up, but Veron wasn't in the mood. That evening, everyone sat around the courtyard and ate a meal in silence.

Not feeling hungry, Veron stood alone on the balcony, watching the last vestiges of sunlight flee along with his hopes and aspirations. *What do I do? I'd like to face them with my sword . . . but eight men is a lot to fight. How did I get myself into this mess? I should have just focused on training to be a shadow knight and forgotten the whole market idea.*

Morgan climbed the steps to join him. "Who do you think those guys are?" he asked.

"They're Robert's friends . . . or acquaintances," Veron said.

Morgan tilted his head. "What makes you say that?"

"They've been here before, coming at different times and only stopping at Robert's stand. They would talk quietly before leaving without buying anything. I thought it was odd, but it wasn't enough to get suspicious about."

"How can you know that? We couldn't even see their faces."

"I recognized the outfits . . . most of them at least."

Morgan chuckled softly as he shook his head and leaned on the railing. "Any idea what you're going to do next?"

Veron exhaled in frustration. "All I can think of is to start another market," he said before laughing at himself. "But that will just put me back in the same place with these guys as I am now."

"Yeah, I guess so."

"Maybe I'll go to Felting . . . start fresh," Veron said. "But I don't want to leave Karad. I love our team—these people . . ."

Veron choked up as he watched the people eating below him—Chloe, Jacob, Danyel, Henry, and the rest.

These people are my friends. I've never experienced anything like it before. Morgan stood patiently as Veron collected himself. "I'm not sad about losing the market, but I am sad about breaking up this community," Veron said. "And it's not fair for them. Everyone will have to go back to the docks or living on the street."

Suddenly, a thought hit Veron, and he looked at Morgan with wide eyes. Veron felt pale and weak. He stared blankly over the balcony, across the courtyard.

"What? What is it?" Morgan asked.

"I had been thinking the worst-case scenario was closing the market down, but I forgot about the loan. I still owe thirteen periods of loan payments! Closing the market means I won't be able to pay it back, and *that* means . . ." Veron's words faded, his chest hurting again as he felt the weight of his situation. *We can't close down. It's not an option.*

As he wrestled through the fear, an idea came to him. His heart raced with the faintest bit of hope. He turned to Morgan. "We can't leave. Don't go yet." Veron hurried down the steps where everyone finished up eating. "Don't leave yet!" he said to them. They looked at him as if he were crazy. "Stay here and be ready to open on Marketday."

Before even waiting for them to respond, he grabbed something from the office and ran out the door into the night.

* * *

When Veron woke on Marketday, his heart raced, and his chest ached with anticipation. *What happens today will determine the course of my future and for all the workers in the market. I've done all I can. Now, I have to wait and see how things play out,* he thought.

It started much like a typical day, but a strange and tense energy filled the air. Veron didn't tell the other market workers what he did on Weekterm, only that they should open up as usual and be ready. Every time someone came through the door, they all looked up anxiously to see who it was.

Late afternoon, just like before, the eight men were back with masks, weapons, and torches. This time, they did not intend to threaten. They would take action.

"You're back!" Veron said. "Why are you here?"

"You know why we're here," the masked leader said. "We warned you, and you didn't listen. Now, you'll have consequences."

He turned and nodded to the men with torches, who moved to light the nearest wooden structure.

"Wait, I'm sorry. What did you warn us about?" Veron asked.

The men stopped as their leader replied, "You had until today to close. Since you chose not to, the result is on you."

"But why do you want us to close?"

The leader shook with frustration. "Because you're taking all our business!" He nodded emphatically toward the men who angled the torches to the edge of the balcony. The sound of crackling grew as the wooden planks began to catch fire.

"That's enough!" a deep voice shouted from the back of one of the stalls.

The men snapped their heads in that direction as the sound of a whistle pierced the air. Danyel and Jacob emerged from second-floor rooms carrying water buckets, which they proceeded to pour onto the partially lit wood, dousing the flames and the men holding the torches below. Everyone watched while a dark-haired man made his way out from under the stall into the courtyard. Gareth Billings was there, holding a sword in one hand while steadying himself with a cane. Next to him stood Brixton Fiero.

"Anthony Tessingham, Nathan Farmer, Barrett Hershel, Willard Bettincourt, Martin Frash, Finley Merriton, Thatcher Young, and Robert Brighton," Brixton said, reading from a sheet of paper in a clear voice.

The eight men looked around at each other in confusion.

"My name is Brixton Fiero, and on behalf of the Karad Department of Commerce, due to unethical business practices involving coercion, intimidation, and destruction of property, your business licenses are hereby revoked. Additionally, you will no longer be authorized to operate a business within the city of Karad."

A few of the men tore their masks off and yelled in frustration.

"And my name is Gareth Billings, Lord of Defense for the city of Karad," Billings said in a low gravelly voice while he waved the sword in their direction. As he spoke, two dozen soldiers marched through the market entrance and fanned out around the men, holding swords to them. "And you are all under arrest."

The men looked desperately at each other as they brandished swords and clubs and faced the soldiers. For a tense moment, the two groups stared each other down, waiting for someone to make the first move. Finally, a short, hooded man with a club dropped his weapon, and the rest followed soon after.

Veron stood tall and watched with relief as the eight men were clasped in chains and led out the door. When the last man was dragged away, the market erupted into cheers. Veron wiped the sweat off his forehead as he turned to his rescuers.

"Lord Billings, Brixton, I can't thank you enough for your help," Veron said as he shook their hands.

"I have to be honest," Billings said, "I was hoping things might devolve into a fight. I would've loved to see you pull out a quarterstaff and wipe the floor with them."

All three of them laughed.

"So *now* will you tell us where you went and what you did?" Morgan asked as he approached.

The rest of the market looked to Veron expectantly. Veron stood tall and grinned. "Well, I knew where Robert's old butcher shop was, so that's where I went the night I left. I climbed the building across the street and watched. I got lucky when he came out a few hours later, so I followed as he led the way to Tessingham's shop in East

Fairren. Crouched under a window, I could hear them inside—a bunch of them. They had every intention of burning our market down and were prepared to kill us if we put up a fight."

Chloe and Mary exchanged wide-eyed glances.

"I took notes of all the names and shops I heard, and after they broke their meeting, I wandered the streets, trying to find the businesses. Most took daytime to locate, when I could ask other shopkeepers for help. Eventually, I tracked them all down, so my next stop was to see Brix." He nodded to his friend. "He reached out to bring Lord Billings in. We needed proof of a crime before they could do anything, so as soon as they arrived and made to torch our market, it was done."

"Why did you need all the names and shops?" Chloe asked. "Why couldn't you just get Brixton and Lord Billings to begin with?"

"We needed to know who they were," Veron said. "Without their shops or names, they were protected by their anonymity and could easily have fled. As soon as we proved we knew who they were and where they lived, they knew it was over. There was nowhere to hide."

"Why didn't you ask us to help you figure all of this out?" Morgan asked, looking hurt.

"I didn't want to pull any of you into it. I knew it might be dangerous and didn't want to risk it."

"But why did they care about us to begin with?" Danyel asked. "Robert's shop is on the opposite side of the city! You say Tessingham's is in East Fairren? We can't be taking much business away from them, right?"

"Apparently, they're an organized group," Veron said. "They've been doing this for a long time. Their shops are spread out all over the city, so if any of them are threatened, they all band together to intimidate as one group. Robert coming to work here was their attempt to tear us apart from the inside."

Lord Billings spoke up. "I heard from the Lord of Justice that they've been looking for an organized gang of shop owners. There have been several complaints over the years of this exact thing. No one was ever able to track them down before though."

"Nicely done, Veron," Brixton said, nodding in approval.

Veron felt a weight lift off his shoulders. All the stress and pressure he'd felt over their market problems and worry about paying their loan was now gone. *Now, I just hope things will go smoothly for a while. Maybe I can finally figure out this origine?*

39

Hunting

Veron sat on the stone wall and rubbed his hands together to stay warm. Wiether had arrived again, and the mornings grew cooler every day. It was early in the morning, at least an hour before the sun came up, and Veron waited for Brixton just outside of the gate to his house.

Over the last year, things had been steady at the market. Once they got rid of Robert and the problems that came with him, they started making steady profits. Each season grew better than the one before, and now there were only six weeks left until the loan would be paid off.

Veron had added a new butcher, Francis, and a cheesemaker named Mateo. Hesitant to add anyone after Robert's betrayal, Veron knew he had to take a chance on people. He did make sure to keep the money locked up safely though.

Veron and Brixton's friendship had grown during the last year as well. For only knowing each other almost two years, they had become close friends, but as time went on, Veron observed a subtle change in Brixton's demeanor. Ever since he became head clerk at the office, position and status seemed to dominate his thoughts, and his volatile temperament showed. Veron tried to overlook those moments and focus instead on the others—when his kindness was exhibited, like it had when they first met.

As he sat on the cold wall, a door opened behind him. He turned as Brixton exited his house and waved as he came through the gate. "Are you ready?" Brixton asked, loaded up with a large bundle on his back. Both of them were enveloped in cloaks to fight off the cold air.

"As ready as I'm going to be. You've got the gear, right?" Veron asked.

"Right here." Brixton indicated the bag on his back. "As well as plenty of food from the kitchen. Let's go!"

The young men walked up the street to the Royal Stables, where the Fieros kept their horses. "You take Mara, and I'll ride Windbreaker," Brixton said, indicating to the shorter horse for Veron to ride. Both were saddled and ready to go.

Veron had little experience riding, so he didn't want anything too wild and was thankful for the smaller horse. Once in the saddles, they trotted through the streets and left through the East Gate. They traveled for a while at an easy canter along the road that meandered through the countryside. The pace they moved at made Veron nervous, so he was relieved when Brixton brought Windbreaker to a walk and Mara followed suit.

"When I told you I didn't know anything about hunting deer, I wasn't exaggerating," Veron said as they rode side by side. "I'll need you to show me what to do."

"That's fine. I don't know much either, so we can figure it out together," Brixton said as he steered his horse around a deep rut in the road.

"You said you went hunting!"

"I said I had *been* hunting. I went once with my father when I was six and then again with my uncle when I was eight."

"You made me believe you knew what you were doing!" Veron looked forward again, nervous that he was going to lose his balance.

"I never *made* you believe anything. What you *chose* to believe was up to you. Growing up, we had servants that gathered and cooked all of our food, so we never really needed to hunt or do anything ourselves."

"Yeah, kind of the same for us," Veron said after a moment's pause. Faint light from the early morning started to fill the sky. Ahead of them, Veron began to see outlines of mountains. "So, what made you want to go today?"

"Today's my birthday, and I wanted to get out and do something fun," Brixton replied.

"Happy birthday! I had no idea it was today."

"Don't worry about it. Twenty years old. It sounds so old to say."

"So, what do you normally do for birthdays?" Veron asked as he adjusted himself in the saddle, trying unsuccessfully to make it more comfortable.

"Normally? Nothing. My parents usually have a nice dinner made, and both of them give me a gift. My mother's is usually a pair of shoes or a fancy belt or something, and my father always gives me a book on economics or trade tariff theory—something to remind me how he wishes I had more knowledge than I do. Generally, birthdays are pretty forgettable, so I wanted to do something different today."

I wish I even knew when my birthday was, Veron thought. Artimus celebrated each year on the first day of suether, but even he didn't know what day it was. The memory hit him suddenly. *Artimus. It seems like a lifetime ago since I lived with him. I owe him everything. My friends, the market, my abilities. I wish he could see me now.* Veron wiped the corners of his eyes, trying not to let Brixton notice.

"So, where's the best place to go?" Veron asked.

"It's been a long time since I've been here, but straight ahead will bring us into the forest. After a while, we'll leave the horses and proceed on foot," Brixton said.

By the time they arrived at the forest, the sun had come up over the horizon, and the glow of the Korob Mountains rising majestically over the plains shone behind them. The trees grew thicker as they proceeded. When Brixton declared they were far enough, they stopped and dismounted.

Each of them took a bow and a quiver of arrows from Brixton's bag of gear, and they left their horses lashed to a tree limb as they walked farther into the woods. After a bit, they came to a clearing with a stream, which Brixton decided would be a good place. They set their bows next to them, hid behind some brush, and waited.

"Did I tell you Hailey and I are to be married?" Brixton asked after a bit of silence.

"What!" Veron yelled.

"Shhh, you have to keep your voice down, or you'll scare everything away."

"Congratulations! That's great," Veron didn't particularly like Hailey. She was beautiful, but he found her a little too forward for his taste. She and Brixton seemed to be a good pair though. "When will the wedding be?"

"Next suether. I don't remember the date."

"I'm glad for you."

Quiet returned, and all Veron could think about was Chloe. She was older by five years and had been married before, but there was something about her. They had spent a lot of time together since the market began. He felt special when he was with her and missed her when they were apart. He smiled, thinking about her face and the way she laughed when they talked.

"I have someone I like. I think I could grow to love her," Veron said.

Brixton looked at him as if he wanted to laugh. "Love, ha! What a stupid sentiment. Who do you think you're in love with?" he asked.

Veron wished he could take it back, but it was too late. "I didn't say I was—" Veron cut himself off with a huff. "Chloe, at the market."

Brixton exploded in laughter. "You're joking, right? Chloe! That candle-making street urchin?"

Veron's face flushed with indignation from the insult. "She is *not* a street urchin! She's a good person."

"I'm sorry, a good person? Wow! You're really scraping the gutter, huh?"

Veron tried to stay in control but lost it as he found his fist balled up, punching Brixton in the face. Brixton rolled down an incline into the dirt, clutching his face where he was hit, yelling in pain. Veron stayed where he was and looked back across the clearing, shaking out his stinging hand.

Brixton pulled himself up and came back over, touching his face to make sure he wasn't bleeding. "Look, I'm sorry," Brixton said. "I just figured you'd have your sights on someone of a little higher station, that's all. But to each his own." He sat back down. "Man, that hurt!" Brixton pressed his hand against his face and held it there. "Honestly, I was always worried you had a thing for Hailey."

Veron jerked his head toward him. "Hailey? No!" He shook his head. "She's fine and all but . . . No."

Brixton eyed him with a suspicious glance. The two sat for a while, watching the woods. Two yellow birds rested on a branch at the edge of the clearing but soon flew off.

Eventually, Veron spoke up. "You said love is stupid. How do you feel about Hailey?"

Brixton scoffed. "Love seems so . . . I don't know . . . pointless."

"What do you mean?"

"I like Hailey fine. She's pretty for now, but she's going to get old. There'll be plenty more young women out there by then, you know?" Brixton poked him with his elbow, grinning crookedly.

No, I don't know, Veron thought. The comment burned him up. "Hailey will align me with the Billings family, and that's a good match. One day, I hope to be Lord of Commerce, like my father, or maybe even a high lord or baron or king one day! The more connections I can make now, the better."

Veron shuddered. *I can't imagine living like that. I have ambitions, but I don't want to use other people to achieve them.*

"You should tell her," Brixton said after a moment of silence. Veron looked at him, unsure of what he meant. "Chloe. You should tell her that you like her. I'm sorry for picking on you. Who am I to say who you should fall for?"

Veron smiled. "Thanks. I think I will."

"So...what about you? What goals do you have?" Brixton asked.

Becoming a shadow knight. Learning to use the origine. Stopping Bale. Veron wasn't going to share those thoughts with Brixton. "I want to pay off the market loan," Veron said. "I have only one payment to go, and then I'll be free from debt." He looked out into the woods. "All my life, I've wanted to have money. I wanted a roof over my head. I wanted to know where my next meal was coming from. But now, I want to make something. I've built this market from the ground up. And now I'm a mere six weeks away from fully owning it."

Brixton's head was tilted quizzically. "But you . . ." He sat, frozen in thought.

Veron held his breath. *I've said too much!* What he shared didn't fit with his wealthy merchant upbringing back-story, and he wasn't sure what to say to fix it. He stared back at Brixton with his mouth slightly opened, trying to think of an explanation.

A squirrel dropped to the ground, rustling the leaves directly in front of them, causing both of them to jump and then laugh. Veron sighed internally as the tension faded.

After the laughing settled, the look on Brixton's face changed. His head tilted down, and his eyebrows narrowed as he spoke in a low and measured voice. "You say you want to have money. What are you willing to do to make that a reality?"

A shiver ran up Veron's spine. He didn't like the inflection in which the question was asked. He felt as if he had stumbled into something he was going to get in trouble for. "Um . . . I'm not sure. Work hard I guess?"

"The longer I live in this city, the more I realize what it takes to be successful," Brixton said. "I've seen men with great minds and incredible talent end up broke and living on the streets. I've seen successful businesses collapse from the weight of a single bad decision. But I've also seen people rise. I've seen success come to people with little skill or ability. Do you know what I believe to be the issue that separates these people?"

Veron shook his head.

"Being able to set aside notions of what they're supposed to do and act when there is an opportunity," Brixton said. The breeze picked up, waving the branches around them. "Which group do you see yourself in, Veron?"

Veron swallowed hard. "Um . . . I guess the group that acts on an opportunity?"

"I thought you'd be." Brixton looked around as if he were making sure no one was listening in. "Keep your eyes open, Veron. You're going to have an opportunity to do something great very soon, provided you take it."

I have no idea what he's talking about. Clearly, he knows about something big coming soon, but I don't know if I like the sound of it. "Okay, I'll keep them open." They turned back to the clearing while the silence returned.

At midday, they shared some food. It was nice to have something to break up the monotony, but soon Veron was bored again. They saw a few rabbits and plenty more squirrels but no signs of deer.

"What do you know about Edmund Bale?" Veron asked, adjusting the way he sat to keep his leg from falling asleep.

"Bale? From up north?" Brixton said, nodding as he spoke. "I know a little. We talked about him at the Academy. I know he's been the king of Norshewa for fifteen or so years, and he's been warring with Rynor for much of that time. It took a two-year-long siege for his army to capture Bromhill. That must have been . . . five years ago, but they failed to take the rest of the country and were just recently pushed back into their own borders."

"I heard he wants to take over Terrenor," Veron said.

Brixton shuddered. "Yeah, I've heard that. That would be awful."

"What makes you say that?"

"He's brutal. When he takes over a city, it's laid to waste. Houses are burned. Women and children are killed for sport. I heard that Bromhill was utterly devastated after he took over. The people remaining weren't allowed to leave. Crops weren't cared for and fell to disease. Markets were barren. The people of the city starved and even resorted to eating leather and tree bark."

Veron swallowed hard, thinking of what Karad would look like after Bale ravaged it. *My market could be destroyed. My friends could be killed. I can't let that happen.*

"His own country even hates him," Brixton said. "His taxes are high because all he cares about is warring and building palaces. King Wesley is a fool, but he's far better than having Bale in charge."

The bushes rustled in the distance, and a small doe emerged at the edge of the clearing. The young men froze. Its short reddish-brown fur was motionless for a moment as the deer checked its surroundings. Not seeing a threat, it stepped to the stream to drink with a fawn following behind it. While the animals were distracted by the water, Brixton slowly picked up the bow and fit an arrow to the string.

"Let it be. It's just a mama and her baby," Veron whispered.

Brixton appeared not to care and pulled the string back farther as he took aim. Veron adjusted his position, and a small stick under his elbow snapped. The two deer stood up at alert as Brixton's arrow flew by where the mother's neck was moments before. The two deer bolted and were gone in seconds.

"Idiot!" Brixton yelled at Veron. "Why would you move?"

Veron held his hands out and shrugged his shoulders. "Sorry."

They sat for a while, looking out at the once again silent woods. Eventually, Veron's thoughts turned to King Wesley. *I wonder why Brixton thinks he's a fool?*

"I admire him though," Brixton said.

"Wesley?" Veron asked.

"No, Bale. He sets a goal and works toward it, even if it takes him years to get there. I want to be like that one day."

Veron's mouth dropped as he stared at Brixton. "He's murdered entire villages! He kills women and children!" *He killed my father!*

"Yeah, that's not ideal, but sometimes you have to make difficult choices to accomplish something great. I respect that."

How are we even friends? Our differences seem more apparent every day. "Well, I don't."

Brixton looked at him with an enigmatic stare but didn't say anything more. Veron turned back to the clearing, failing to notice the two people in the woods on the other side.

"Where'd it go?" Aleks whispered.

Chelci leaned around trees, trying to find the deer that was there moments ago. She held an arrow fitted to the string of her bow, trying to see where the animal went. "It came to this clearing just a moment ago . . . probably to drink from that stream," she said.

Aleks inched forward to the edge of the clearing.

"Wait," Chelci said softly. She indicated to the opposite end of the clearing where two people sat behind a bush. A low mumbling of speech carried across the field by the breeze. "Who do you think they are?"

"They can't be from Nasco," Aleks said. "No one comes this far north. It's the farthest I've been on a hunt before."

"They probably scared the deer off. Should we go and say hello?"

"No, let's leave them be. Who knows who they may be?"

The two of them inched back into the woods and continued their hunt in the opposite direction.

"Where have you been all day?" Raynor asked as Brixton walked into the room.

Brixton's father sat in his favorite chair with a stack of papers, as he always seemed to have. His mother looked up from her needlework.

"Why do you care?" Brixton said before he could stop himself.

Raynor stood and shook his finger at him. "As long as you live here, you'll answer my questions. And don't you *dare* speak back to me—"

"Raynor, please!" his mother interrupted.

Brixton hung his head out of habit. "I'm sorry, Father. I won't do it again. I was out hunting with Veron."

"Hunting! Ha! What do you know about hunting?" Raynor asked.

"I know as much as you taught me, Father." Again, as it passed his lips, he wished he could take it back. His father didn't seem to get angry about the pointed comment though.

"Raynor," Elenor said. "Isn't there something you'd like to say to your son *today*?"

He looked at his wife with puzzlement on his face before turning to Brixton. "I'll be out of town for the next few days. I need to head to Felting for a commerce meeting."

Good riddance, Brixton thought. *Maybe we can have a few days of peace at home.*

"No, Raynor," Elenor said. "His birthday?"

"Oh yes . . . Happy birthday, son."

The words carried no enthusiasm, but what bothered Brixton the most was the fact that his father didn't even look his way when he said them.

"Happy birthday, Brixton," his mother said. She walked to him and gave him a hug followed by a wrapped box.

"Thank you, Mother." He opened the box to find a brown leather belt with a shiny silver buckle and silver studs embedded along the length.

"It's from Felting. All the lords there are wearing them," she said.

"It's nice. Thanks."

Brixton and his mother both glanced at his father, who was still buried in his papers. "Raynor?" Elenor asked, causing him to look up. "Did you have anything?"

"No, I'm sorry, Brixton. I didn't get a chance to get anything. I've been really busy. I hope you understand."

"Sure," Brixton said. *The last thing I want is another reminder of my deficiencies.*

"Dinner should be ready shortly," Elenor said. "Brixton, we're having roasted pork, your favorite!"

It wasn't his favorite, but he didn't correct her.

"I wish you would have invited Veron to stay for dinner," Elenor added.

"Veron's quite an impressive young man. It's too bad he doesn't have a father around," Raynor said. "He's accomplished a great deal, and I'm sure it'd mean a lot to have a father appreciate it. Maybe I'll make a point of talking with him about it."

Brixton ground his teeth in frustration. *I've tried to accomplish things all my life. He is my father, and he's never said anything encouraging to me like that.* "I'm sure he'd love that," he said through a clenched jaw. *Veron, the perfect one. If only you had a son like Veron. Sometimes I wish he and I had never met.*

* * *

Brixton walked down the alley, hoping he wouldn't run into anyone who would recognize him. The lamps along the street fought off the darkness of the night, throwing long shadows on the walls as he passed.

Is this the right thing to do? Veron has always been kind to me. Father won't stop showing him attention though.

The image of his father reminded him of his words: *"Elevating yourself requires someone else to fall."*

As he wrestled with his thoughts, Brixton arrived at his destination. He paused with his hand held up before finally knocking on the plain door.

After a moment, the door opened to Charles Mortinson. "Yes?" the captain said.

"Captain Mortinson, I know you've helped my father with special tasks from time to time. I hoped you could help me with something." Mortinson opened the door wider allowing Brixton to enter. "I need you to look into Veron Stormbridge for me," Brixton said. "Supposedly, his family has run a market off River Street in Felting for many years. Something in his story doesn't add up though."

The captain stared fixedly at him. "I'm sure I could be *persuaded* to do that." Brixton exhaled and passed him a leather pouch. "Very good. I'll see what I can find," Mortinson said.

Brixton shuddered as the money exchanged hands. There was no turning back.

40

The Korob Mountains

King Bale tightened his wallum-skin cloak around his neck as he stopped to survey the army's progress. Ahead of him, a steady line of black shapes marched up the snow-covered slope. The snow was deep, which made progress slow, but they continued to move. The file of soldiers continued behind him, followed by a team of norsh bears loaded down with gear and tied in a row. Looking out into the valley behind them, Bale could see the foothills they came through over the last ten days since they left Daratill.

Nearly two years had passed since Bale made his plan to attack Feldor, and they were now finally advancing toward Karad. After conscripting every available man and boy between fifteen and fifty-two, their army had grown to over 10,000 men.

Ryker approached on the snowy path. "Tonight's gonna be cold," the commander said.

Bale nodded in agreement. "We'll be fine. Have them march until sundown then set up camp."

Since they arrived in the mountains, Bale had pushed them hard. The army marched almost nonstop from sunup to sundown. He would have kept them moving even after nightfall, if they had a moon to light the way, but the heavy clouds blocked out the sky completely. When a soldier moved, he wasn't as likely to feel the cold. Once he stopped, the danger set in.

They had another day, maybe two, until they crested the ridge. Until then, each day would get more challenging as they gained altitude. The soldiers had mostly kept their grumbling quiet, but now it was noticeable through the ranks. They were cold, and their bodies ached from the long, grueling marches. Many wanted to turn back, and a few tried—until they were caught and killed for desertion.

Soon, the army stopped to make camp. Whenever they did, the three priorities were erecting tents, cooking food, and securing the bears. If they didn't tie the bears down at night, the chance of them escaping was too great. Food was usually ready right about the time camp was set up, which allowed the soldiers to eat then get in their tents before they got too cold. At night, they covered themselves with their wallum skins, but even with the extra insulation, the temperature was brutal.

Bale had a tent to himself. While the rest of the camp slept, he sat up, poring over maps by candlelight. As he studied, he suddenly heard yelling. *What would that be? Most of the soldiers should be asleep,* he thought.

He left his tent and moved toward the commotion. The noise came from a part of the camp at the edge of a cliff. What sounded initially like yelling voices was drowned out by a deep, bellowing roar.

When he got near, the remains of a tent flew through the air. In the middle of a circle of soldiers with torches and swords was an angry norsh bear, neither tied nor blindfolded. Four men lay on the ground, bleeding out as the bear took swipes at those still standing. Another roar shook the ground, causing the men to shrink back again. The bear had several cuts in its thick hide and appeared to be favoring its left side. One of the soldiers rushed in and buried his sword deep into the bear's chest. It roared as it used the rest of its energy to knock the soldier away with a sharp claw. The effort was the last the bear had, for it collapsed to the ground amidst a round of cheers from the men.

While the bear stopped breathing, Bale stepped forward with his sword drawn. The men hushed as they recognized him. He inspected the wounded. Two appeared to be dead, and three had significant wounds they would likely not recover from.

"Who was responsible for tying down this bear?" Bale said. The wind whistled in response as it rushed through the mountain pass.

"I was, Your Majesty," a short boy said after a long moment as he bowed his head. "I tied the bear down with the help of some others." He looked around at the crowd to see if anyone else stood with him. "It was my knot across his back that we found undone. I'm sorry, My King."

Bale walked toward the boy. The crunch of the snow replaced the howl of the wind as the rest of the crowd waited. Heat crept up Bale's neck as his blood ran quickly.

"What is your name?" Bale asked.

"Eric, son of Urthgau, Your Majesty. In Thoring's battalion."

"How old are you?"

"Fifteen."

Bale stood before him with his sword still in his hand. His jaw clenched as he tightened his grip on the hilt of his weapon. "Where are you from?"

Eric trembled. "From Bryveld, Your Majesty."

The word caught him by surprise. "Bryveld?" His hand loosened as his shoulders relaxed and breathing slowed. Memories flooded into his head. "Did you know I was born there?"

Eric raised his head. He looked at the crowd around him then back at Bale as he shook his head.

"It's true. At the base of the large hill on the south side of town, there is an old house with a tree growing into the back wall. That's where I grew up."

"I know that house," Eric said. "It's down the street from where we live. My friend, Eli, and I like to play in the woods up on that hill."

Bale thought of himself, playing in those woods as a boy—hunting squirrels and climbing trees. He spent hours there, mostly because it kept him away from his house. He thought of the decaying building where he grew up, the meager meals they ate as a family, the flowers in a jar he picked for his mother from the field.

His mother.

He saw her cowering in the corner as his father beat on her, drawing blood and creating bruises. He tried to stop it, but his father turned on him next, yelling curses, saying he was worthless, stupid, that he would never amount to anything. Bale vividly recalled the day he turned fourteen. His mother lay unconscious on the floor, and his father sat in a drunken stupor on the rickety porch. That was the moment he decided he *was* going to amount to something. He *was* going to do great things. He walked to the counter and took the knife his mother had been using to chop onions. If he were going to prove he wasn't stupid, the first thing he needed to do was take care of his father.

A chilly gust of wind snapped Bale back to the present. The vision of his old house was gone, and Eric stood in front of him again, waiting. Taking a deep breath, he flexed his grip on the sword before relaxing once more.

Bale came alongside the boy and put his free arm around him.

411

"Eric, once we walk down the backside of this mountain, our army is going to have a big job to do, and I'm going to need all of my soldiers to do it. If we're going to be successful, we're going to need all of our supplies too, and to get those over the mountains, we're going to need our bears. Do you understand?" Bale said.

Eric nodded quickly.

"Are you going to be able to tie a correct knot next time?" Bale asked.

"Yes, Your Majesty, I will."

"Good. Because if you can't, I'm going to need to find someone else who will."

"I won't let you down."

"I'm sure you won't." Bale held Eric's gaze for a long moment before letting him go.

The king turned to the three wounded men on the ground, who moaned and writhed while holding their injuries as the snow stained red beneath them. A large bearded man with slashes through his wallum-skin cloak reached out an arm.

"Please, Your Majesty. Help me!"

Without speaking, Bale used his sword on the man's pale neck to put him and the other two out of their misery. A hushed gasp sounded in the dark around him.

"Toss the bodies over the cliff, but save the cloaks," he said to no one in particular. "Then, get some sleep. We have a long day of marching tomorrow."

He wiped his sword off in the snow and returned to his tent.

* * *

The next day, the army was up and marching as soon as it was light. As the day progressed, the top of the pass grew closer. Bale's scouts had found a flat area, large enough for a camp just past the ridge on the way down the backside of the mountain. At the pace they traveled, they would have just enough time to make it to the camp before dark.

They reached the crest of the rise not long before the sun set, and, despite the cold and wind, all the soldiers cheered. Downhill would be much easier to walk, and every step lower in altitude would bring warmer weather.

Bale stood on the ridge and took in the scene. Stunning cliffs and jagged rocks littered the way down the mountain. Eventually, the snow gave way to bare rock, and trees began to dot the slope. A green valley awaited them far below. The maze-like Kyrd Forest was off to the left of the valley, and in front of them, far off in the distance, stood the walls of Karad. Seeing the goal renewed his hope. The area where they were to set up camp sat just below them, no more than an hour's march away.

As Bale turned to look for Ryker, his hope shattered. His vision of resting peacefully in camp was gone. Unseen as they trudged up the mountain, an enormous wall of dark clouds pressed in from the north.

Ryker appeared, looking frantic. "What should we do?" he said.

"Where did these clouds come from?" Bale asked, his breath quickening. "At any moment, this storm is going to strike us, and we're exposed, in the worst place we could possibly be! How did we not see this?"

"The sky was clear only an hour ago. It must have blown in quickly," Ryker said.

We can't turn back to make camp. It would be hours before we found anywhere to stop, and the storm would be on us by then.

Bale turned back toward the way they were heading. He peered down the mountain as the wind whipped against his clothes. He sensed the storm advancing—the temperature dropping every second.

What are we going to do? His heart raced, but he couldn't think. No plan came to him. Ryker stared, patiently waiting. *Don't let them see you afraid,* Bale told himself. He swallowed hard and stood straight. "We've got to keep going. Immediately," Bale told him.

"We may not make it to the camp," Ryker said.

Bale stared at their destination. "It's our only option. We can't stay here. We have to make it." He turned to Ryker. "Go! Now!"

Ryker snapped into action. "Time to move!"

In a short time, 10,000 soldiers were on their way down the mountain at a brisk pace. Walking alongside the men, Bale was almost to camp when the storm arrived in full force. Visibility plummeted, and blinding snow hit from every side. When he stumbled into the location to make camp, Ryker was waiting, wrapped tightly in his wallum skin and barely staying on his feet.

"We can't set up camp! The tents and supplies will blow away! The storm is too strong!" Ryker yelled from an arm's length away.

Bale looked around, but all he saw was the blinding storm. To make visibility worse, the sun had just set, so only a faint amount of light remained.

"We can't stay here!" Ryker said. "We'll freeze to death! We need to keep marching!"

The sun is gone, and the storm will eliminate any light from the moon. If we continue, our whole army will end up lost or fallen off of a cliff. Freezing to death standing here doesn't sound right either. Bale shook his head. "No! We can't continue! Tie up the bears and horses, keeping each group of animals as close as possible! Then, have each battalion bundle up with as much warm clothing as possible and stand, huddled in a circle. Every five minutes, have the ones on the outside rotate in!"

Ryker nodded. "For how long?"

"All night, if necessary! We'll have to ride out the storm!"

Ryker went to work, shouting instructions at the captains who relayed them to the battalion sub-captains. Groups soon formed into circles as they desperately tried to find warmth and a modicum of safety in the punishing storm. Bale joined the battalion circle closest to him. The soldiers he stood next to were silent as they nervously avoided eye contact with their king.

When the last traces of sunlight had vanished, visibility was little worse than before, but the complete lack of vision took a toll on Bale mentally. Frozen bodies surrounded him, shivering and jostling against each other. The noise from the wind was deafening, but the heat of the crowd kept him alive.

As he took his turns on the outside of the circle, the bitterness of the wind and snow caused him to despair. *We're not going to survive this. We're going to freeze to death in this storm. It may never stop. All of our animals may die. Maybe I should have stayed in Daratill?*

He couldn't measure the passage of time. It could have been hours or minutes—it felt like days. Some soldiers could barely stand, but the others held them up. Eventually, the storm lessened, and a faint amount of daylight shone in from the east. Bale felt the slightest bit of hope, which increased as the storm abated.

Once the wind calmed enough, Bale ordered them to break ranks and set up camp. He didn't want to stay there long at such a high elevation, but his men needed rest after being up straight for a full day. He gave them a few hours to sleep.

The night in the storm was brutal. About one-third of the horses didn't survive, but thankfully, all the bears did. Out of the 10,000 soldiers, only eleven of them died in the harrowing night. After what they endured, Bale considered it a fortunate victory.

* * *

Three days later, five men on horseback approached a weathered wooden barn. Many of the side planks peeled off the structure, and most of the roof looked to have collapsed long ago. Bale was the first to dismount, followed by Ryker and the other three soldiers. All but Bale drew their swords as they entered the dilapidated building. Hay and cobwebs littered the old barn. Beams of light snuck through the rafters to illuminate the otherwise dark interior. It appeared to be empty.

"Maybe he's not coming," Ryker said.

"He'll come," Bale answered.

"Yes, he will," a new voice said from the deep shadow of one of the stalls.

A tall man with short hair stepped into the light. Bale's soldiers snapped to attention with their swords at the ready.

"Relax," the man said. "I'm unarmed."

He lifted his arms and spun, showing the lack of weapon on his hip. One of the soldiers approached the man and patted him down before looking back at Bale and nodding. Satisfied, the soldiers sheathed their swords but remained at attention.

"I am King Edmund Bale, ruler of Norshewa. You're the one I've been corresponding with?" Bale asked, peering intently.

"Indeed, Your Majesty. Thank you for trusting to meet with me," the man said.

"I hear you promise to make this meeting worth my while. I sure hope that is the case—for your sake."

"Of course. If you hear me out, I believe you'll find our interests align," the man said with a crooked grin.

"That remains to be seen," Bale replied.

"You and I both have aspirations. You desire to rule all of Terrenor.

While some may cry foul at this, it doesn't bother me. Someone is always in charge, and from my perspective, if it's not me, then I don't care who it is. All I care about is what my situation is under them."

Bale watched him carefully. "So, what do you propose?"

"A major step in ruling Terrenor is to control Feldor. The strategic position and the resources it gives makes conquering the other lands a mere formality. To control Feldor, you must take Felting, but you don't have the soldiers to do that."

Bale scoffed. *I think we do have the men. He's merely bluffing. Still, for victory to be assured, assistance would be useful.*

"You've come over the mountains and met with me. By sticking your neck out, you've shown a level of trust in me," the man said. "I've stuck my neck out by inviting my enemy to the doorstep of my city, which shows I'm trusting you. I have a plan to help both of us achieve what we want."

Crows took flight from the rafters of the barn suddenly, causing a few soldiers to jump.

The man continued, "You must conquer Karad first. Not only does that clear the path to Felting, but if you can make strategic alliances, it will make the goal even easier. You can't use a direct attack on Karad—the walls are too protected, and you can't come across the river because most of your men would drown in the fast current or die by Karad's army as they got to the shore. Even if you win by either of these methods, you'll lose too many men to be able to continue to Felting."

Bale was losing his patience. *He needs to get to the point soon.*

"How would you like to take Karad without losing a single man? And how would you like the soldiers of Karad to swear allegiance as they march on Felting side-by-side with you?" the man asked.

Bale looked at Ryker then back to the man. "How do you propose we do this?"

The man took a few steps forward but halted as Ryker and the other soldiers put their hands on their sword hilts. "The soldiers of Karad are fiercely loyal to the Lord of Defense, Gareth Billings. If you kill him, the soldiers will fight you to their deaths. However, if he's *with* you, they'll follow. As far as taking the city goes . . . I can get you in."

Bale stood tall and braced himself for what came next. "So, what do you require in return?" he asked.

A grin spread on the man's face. "When you take Felting and kill King Wesley, you'll need someone on your side to see to your interests in the land. If you're going to control all of Terrenor, you can't be everywhere at once. You wouldn't want to use one of your men from Norshewa because the people would reject them. You'd need someone from Feldor—someone people know—who'll willingly submit to your rule." He took one more step forward. "I will be that person. I'll give you Karad, and Billings will give you the army. Together, we'll take over Felting. In return, you set me to rule as regent in place of Wesley, and I will report to you. That is my price. Billings's price is thirty gold sol plus a position to command his men."

Bale looked to Ryker then paced the length of the barn in thought. When he returned to his place, he looked up and asked, "Who are you?"

"I am Lord Raynor Fiero of the Department of Commerce, and I speak on behalf of Lord Billings, which this letter will attest to." He handed Bale a letter folded and sealed with wax. "We can do what I say, and you have our loyalty."

Bale stood, unmoving, deep in thought as perspiration formed on Raynor's forehead. Finally, he nodded.

Raynor's shoulders relaxed as he exhaled. "Can you get your army to Karad by this Weekterm?" he asked.

"Why?" Bale said.

"It's the annual Merchant Awards Banquet, and the baron will be in attendance."

"We can. How are you going to be able to get us into the city?"

Raynor grinned. "That part is easy."

41

The Night Watch

Near the end of Chelci's two years of training, only seven candidates remained in the Academy. They kicked out Kohen and Reece at the midpoint evaluations for not showing enough progress. Arturo quit a few weeks later because he didn't think he had a shot of being chosen.

Village guard selection was in a week, and none of them knew who, if anyone, would be picked. Chelci had grown during her years of training. Initially the shortest of the group, she now met the height of several of the boys, and she felt good about her chances of being chosen. Her runs were strong. Her obstacle course time was down to under seven minutes. She was one of the top sword fighters in the class behind Aleks. Overall, Aleks was the most likely candidate to make it in the guard. The Furies were all doing well. Tate was a long shot to be selected, but Gael and Royce were solid.

Even though they still referred to them as the Furies, Gael, Royce, and Tate had mellowed out a great deal. As Chelci was able to prove she could hold her own, a grudging respect developed. They weren't overly friendly, but at least they didn't mock her anymore.

"So, what do you think we're going to have to do?" Chelci asked

Aleks as she swung idly on the rope in the training center, her long brown hair waving behind her.

"I have no idea. Maybe they want us to stay late and clean the hall?" Aleks said.

"Maybe they're going to take us somewhere we can sleep," Finley said, yawning loudly.

"I wish," Aleks said.

"They probably want us to stay so they can go ahead and kick you three losers out before you get your hopes up," Royce said to them from across the room, giving a small smile.

A year ago, that comment would have been malicious, but now, it was at least partially a joke.

Gael stifled a yawn as he sat on the floor.

The sun had set, and the seven candidates waited in the training hall, unsure of when their instructors would return and what they would have to do. Typically, they trained Marketday through Finday, and had one day off on Weekterm for rest. Each day was always a mixture of activities to keep their day balanced and interesting, but the instructors made sure to build in rest time.

The previous week had been anything but restful.

Starting Marketday, all candidates had to arrive at the training hall before sunrise. Instead of the expected balanced activities, the instructors hit them hard, going from activity to activity all day long—sword fights, wrestling matches, rope climbs, obstacle course runs, carrying heavy steel objects as a team through the village. Their reward for completing a task was to head off on another run. Instead of leaving in the afternoon, the candidates had to stay until well after the sun went down. This schedule continued every day for the entire week.

By the time Prefinday came, everyone was beyond exhausted. Chelci consoled herself that there was only one more day to go before the Weekterm break, but when it came time to leave, Russell announced they would not be going home and should be prepared to stay overnight. Groans erupted from the boys while Chelci fought to hold her tongue.

After the candidates waited in the training center for a while on their own, Russell and Bensen finally returned carrying bundles under their arms. "You don't get to keep these uniforms. They're yours to wear for tonight only," Russell said as they tossed a bundle to each candidate.

"Village guard uniforms. Nice!" Finley said as he put it on.

"Yes, these are village guard uniforms," Russell said. "Tonight, the night watch will be taking a break, and you all will take their places."

Chelci wanted to cheer but was conflicted. *This is what I've been working toward, but I don't know if I can do it after the week we've had,* she thought. A murmur from the crowd confirmed the others felt the same.

The uniform was a loose-fitting, mostly black piece of clothing that was worn over their clothes. It draped over the arms and had a slit running down each side. The front and back fell to around the knees. In silver thread, on the front of the uniform, was a symbol of a shield with a sword behind it. They also received metal helmets, which came to a point on the top and had a circular brim. Chelci felt invincible as she put the uniform on.

"Can we get something to eat first? I'm starving," Tate said.

"No, you don't get something to eat. A village guard is required to do what's needed, when it's called for. He's not given a chance to stop and take a snack break," Russell said as he glared at Tate. "Gael, Aleks, and David, you're with me. Royce, Elise, Tate, and Finley, you're with Bensen. Tonight, you'll patrol, and at some point, raiders will attack."

Chelci looked at Aleks in alarm.

"They'll come at least once—possibly two or three times," Russell said. "Don't worry, the raiders are members of the village guard, and they'll be testing you. Fight them off and defend the town, but don't injure anyone. Your swords are blunted, but theirs won't be. There are separate raider parties for each side of the town. If you hear an alert from the other group, you don't need to respond to it for tonight's exercise."

"But I can barely keep my eyes open," Gael said as he leaned against the wall.

"Then feel free to take a nap," Russell said. "We'll see how well that works defending the village. You all want to be part of the village guard? Tonight, you get a chance to prove how ready you are."

The two groups split. Russell took his group to the north side of town, and Bensen's stayed on the south. Night watch protocol dictated that each guard was responsible for an area of the perimeter. They patrolled their area and stopped where the next guard's began. This resulted in a long night of walking back and forth, so they changed patrol areas twice during the night.

Chelci's assigned post for her first watch period ran from just east of the Academy building to the far end of the town square. Finley had the next section, but she couldn't see Royce or Tate, who would be past him. Bensen planned to move between the four of them periodically to check on how they were doing.

Glancing around and seeing that no one was there to tell her to start, she began pacing. *I've trained almost two years for this. I feel strong, fast, and ready to fight off anyone who attacks.* Her arms shook in anticipation. *At any moment, raiders could come running through the woods to attack me and the village.* She knew it wouldn't be real, but the excitement of acting it out made her heart race.

Oil lanterns were lit nightly around the village, but the perimeter where they walked was kept dark. At first, she missed the comforting presence the lanterns gave, but her eyes adjusted to the dark much better without them. The moon was out, which helped with visibility. A cleared area between the path and the edge of the woods prevented anyone from lurking in the shadows.

Each watchman had a small bell, which they rang when needed to alert the others. *If someone runs at me with a sword, the last thing I want to do is pull out a bell and ring it in their face,* she had thought. Now that she was on watch, she realized its usefulness. *Even though a guard may not take time to grab it in an attack, there are plenty of situations where it would be useful. Voices or yells in the night could easily be confused and misunderstood, but no one would mistake the clear sound of a bell.*

As she walked, Chelci kept her eyes fixed on the woods, scanning up and down the line. She frequently spun around to make sure raiders weren't trying to sneak in behind her. Trees shook from the wind. Leaves rustled, and sticks snapped. Chelci jumped at every noise.

It's probably squirrels running around or a deer—maybe a garront scuffling along the ground.

As she paced, minutes slowly turned into hours. From time to time, Bensen wandered through her patrol area. He didn't say anything and didn't respond to her questions about when he thought they would attack. He merely watched before he moved along to observe the other candidates.

I'm glad to be walking because if I stood in one place, I'm sure I'd fall asleep. I can't believe we have to do this after this exhausting week.

After they'd been out for a couple of hours, she approached the far end of her section simultaneously with Finley.

"You seen anything yet?" he asked.

"I caught a few leaves trying to take over the village, but I stopped them cold," Chelci said.

Finley laughed. "I hope they show up soon. I need something to get my blood going again and distract me. My stomach is growling, and I'm about to fall asleep."

"Yeah, me too."

Carried across the village by the wind, the faint but frantic ringing of a bell caused Chelci to turn. It quickly stopped and was replaced by clashing swords and a yell. More bells followed. *The rest of the north patrol group are converging on the raiders*, she thought.

The swords sounded for a while longer, but they soon stopped. A cheer echoed off the trees, and silence followed.

"I guess they got their first attack," Finley said with a tinge of jealousy.

"Be on alert. That probably means our side will come soon," Chelci said, resting her hand on the hilt of her sword.

The two turned and walked in opposite directions, continuing their patrol. Chelci was again on high alert with her senses sharply tuned. Her fatigue was gone as she waited for the inevitable attack. She paced her route, watched the woods, and listened for bells. She saw nothing.

Around midnight, Bensen had them rotate positions. Chelci took Finley's place as he moved one spot over, and Royce covered where she had just left. While changing, she was extra vigilant, looking around for anything out of the ordinary. She had looked forward to changing sections, thinking the new one would be fresh and exciting again to help her stay focused. To her dismay, the new section was as monotonous as the old.

After a couple more hours, Chelci heard another shout, followed by frantic bell ringing across the village. The chorus of bells converged, followed by more clashing swords and shouts. After a minute, it ended in celebration again.

She found Finley again. His steps were disjointed as he looked around. "Something has to be wrong, right? Why would their side be attacked twice and ours not have anything yet?"

"They're just testing us," Chelci said in a firm voice. "They want to put us on edge, and then they'll attack when we're all frazzled. It'll probably happen at any time—just keep watching." *He's right though. It doesn't make sense. Could something be wrong?*

She soon met up with Royce, who waited for her on the opposite side of her patrol area.

"Have you seen anything?" Chelci asked.

"No," Royce said. "Nothing. It's not fair they've had two fights already, and we haven't had any! How are we supposed to prove ourselves if we don't get the chance?"

He doesn't seem concerned about something being wrong. Maybe it's just in my head?

Bensen had them switch up sections for the last time. They each moved down in the same direction as before, and she patrolled the area in front of Nevi and Russell's house.

"Bensen, something has to be wrong! How have we not been attacked yet? It'll be morning soon!" she said when the instructor came around next.

He didn't answer, but Chelci could tell he was on edge. Early in the night, he appeared calm and relaxed, but that facade was gone. He watched the woods with rapt attention as he moved.

"Just stay alert," he said before walking off.

Chelci froze. Her legs felt weak. *I've never heard him use that tone. He sounded urgent, almost desperate.*

She watched him walk away. Russell emerged from the village to meet him under a lantern where they spoke in hushed tones. She couldn't hear what was said, but it seemed like they were both upset. Bensen gestured toward the woods, and Russell shook his head. Soon, Russell returned to his side of the village, and Bensen continued his route.

Chelci turned back to her patrol section and kept a sharp eye out. The wind picked up, and the gusts chilled her under her uniform. A loud thump sounded in the woods. *What was that? It was too heavy to be a footfall. Could it have been a branch falling?* she thought.

Chelci froze for a moment to listen but didn't see or hear anything else. Glancing around, she saw Royce and Finley walking in the opposite direction with no sign of alarm.

I wish they were coming this way, Chelci thought, looking back at the woods. She took a deep breath then let it out. *I have to check it out.*

Chelci made her way down the slope and paused at the tree line. She tried to peer through the darkness but couldn't see anything from where she stood. She considered calling for Finley and Royce to come back her up but didn't want to make a big deal out of nothing. She kept going. Knowing roughly from where the noise came, she walked in that direction. The woods were so thick she could barely see where she moved. The lack of raider attacks had her on edge, and the darkness made her even more nervous. Her heart beat fast. Every rustle of a leaf spun her around.

The noise was somewhere around here. A strange odor lingered in the area as she walked. It was sweet and almost metallic, but she couldn't place it. *What's that smell?*

She circled the area and finally kicked her foot into something. Her breath caught as she froze. Chelci bent down. Her hand shook as it rested on a large tree limb. The edge of the branch was freshly broken, and the smell of dirt and splintered wood filled the air.

The thump was a branch knocked down by the wind.

Chelci laughed at how ridiculous it was. She spent the whole night expecting men to attack her at any moment, and she was most frightened by a stick in the woods.

I need to get back to my post. The last thing I want is for an attack to happen during the moment I'm off looking at branches. She left the limb behind and hurried back to the village.

After only a few steps, with her eyes focused on the clearing ahead, she tripped and fell head over heels onto the ground. It took her a moment to untangle herself from the uniform draped over her head. Embarrassed by her clumsiness and glad no one would be able to see, she stood up and tried to get her bearings again.

The smell! It's stronger here. She pressed the uniform against her legs to smooth it out and felt something wet and sticky. Chelci held her hand close to her face and found it coated with a dark liquid.

On the ground, a dark shape—the object she had tripped on—hid in the shadows. She bent down to see what it was and felt the cold hardened steel of a sword. Chelci jerked her hand back as a faint cry escaped her lips. Using both hands, she grabbed the shape and tried to roll the heavy weight toward her. She had to readjust her legs and use all of her body. The light was dim, but as the shape moved, she could see enough to make out the pale face of a man. The front of his clothes was sticky with blood where it had pooled underneath from the large slashes across his chest.

Chelci froze, staring. Her breath grew ragged. All night, she had been ready to battle at a moment's notice, but now that she faced actual danger, her fight training and conditioning meant nothing—she was a scared little girl again. She slowly stood up and backed away. Her hand shook as she took the bell out of her pocket and tried to ring it. The trembling resulted in a weak sound at first, but she persisted. As she emerged into the clearing, just past the tree line, the bell rang strongly, sending her distress call out into the night.

42

Code Black

"It's about time! Where are they?" Finley said as he bounded down the slope to meet Chelci. He held his sword drawn in one hand and rang his bell in the other.

Moments later, Royce arrived, putting his bell away as he approached. "I'm ready," he said as he peered into the forest and paced along the edge. "Come on out!"

Chelci remained staring at the woods and ringing her bell.

"Elise?" Finley said. "Are you okay? What is it?"

She heard her friend speaking but couldn't respond. Her face felt drained. *I may pass out.* Her bell continued.

"Elise!" Finley grabbed her hand to stop the ringing, causing her to stare at him in shock. "What's going on?"

"In the woods . . . I—I found him," she said.

"Him? Him, who?" Finley looked at her uniform. "Are you bleeding? What happened?"

Chelci looked down and saw the blood that smeared the front of her clothing. Two more bells approached behind her. She turned as Bensen arrived with Tate just behind. They stopped at the top of the rise, backlit by the lantern down the street.

"What is it?" Tate asked as he held his hands out in a shrug.

The presence of their instructor snapped Chelci back to reality. "There's a body in the woods. Grab that lantern and get down here. All of you, keep your eyes open."

Finley and Royce stepped back at her sudden change of demeanor. On the hill, Bensen grabbed the lantern behind him, and he and Tate ran down the incline. Chelci led the group into the woods.

"Lucian!" Bensen yelled as they arrived at the body. He bent over to feel the man's neck.

The scene was much more gruesome in the light. Chelci wished she would have been able to keep the other version in her memory, but it was too late now. The lifeless stare, the blood, the cuts—they would be forever etched in her memory. She couldn't stand the sight, and looked away.

"What'd you do, Elise?" Tate asked with disgust.

She wanted to punch him but restrained herself. "I found him like this."

"His face is already getting rigid. He's been dead at least five hours or so," Bensen said.

"Weren't you watching this section five hours ago, Tate?" Finley asked.

Tate shifted on his feet. The wind blew between the trees, causing the four candidates to look around. Chelci expected something to jump out at any moment.

"Uh . . . Bensen, l—l—look at this," Finley said, standing to the side, his voice shaking.

He pointed to the ground. Two large pools of blood stained the leaves and smeared away from the village as if something was killed then dragged into the woods.

"This must have been Tomas and Lachlan," Bensen said, inspecting the area. His jaw clenched, and he moved with purpose.

"We're gonna die!" Tate said in a panicked voice. "Someone's killing them, and we're gonna be next!"

"Bensen," Royce said in a quiet, calm voice.

The group turned to him in eerie silence. Royce stood next to Lucian's body and held an object up. Bensen extended the lantern, illuminating a sharp, black claw twice as long as his hand.

Chelci and Bensen locked eyes. *He knows what it is. Is this what happened to Russell's daughter years ago?*

Bensen spoke rapidly as he turned back to watch the woods. "Lucian, Tomas, and Lachlan were the three village guards who were supposed to raid our side during the night. This"—he pointed to Lucian's body—"explains why we hadn't seen them yet."

Suddenly, a howl pierced the night through the woods, and five heads snapped in its direction. It wasn't the high mournful howl of a wolf. It was low and scratchy. The sound sent chills down Chelci's spine. She had heard the sound once, many years before on the night she arrived in Nasco.

That's a howl that sends wolves running in fear.

"Finley, run across the village and get Russell," Bensen said. "Tell him we have a Code Black."

Finley turned to go but did a double-take, looking back at Bensen with fear in his eyes. "Code . . . what? Sir?"

"Black! Tell him Code Black—and run!"

Finley ran while Chelci's head spun.

"Royce, go and sound the village alert bell," Bensen said, but Royce was frozen in place, staring at him. "Now!"

Bensen turned to Chelci. "Elise, I—"

Another howl sounded, closer this time. Their group froze, silent. Bensen's sword scraped as he pulled it out of its scabbard, followed promptly by Tate and Chelci doing the same. Royce backed away before turning to run while the remaining three stood in a line with

Bensen holding the lantern out.

For several moments, no one spoke. No one breathed.

I wonder if whatever it was ran away?

Just as she was about to exhale in relief, she felt the ground move. She couldn't hear anything, but something was there. As she watched the darkness, a scent wafted through on the breeze. Chelci couldn't tell what direction it came from, but it smelled like death and decay. Its presence turned her stomach as she gagged on the rotten odor. Her legs felt weak, like they were made of water.

Tate shifted his weight, drawing her attention. A wet line ran down his pant leg. Finally, she heard it. It was soft at first but steadily grew louder and more apparent. A low, throaty growl rumbled in the darkness, but the lantern still couldn't penetrate far enough to reveal its source.

"We're gonna die. I know we're gonna die," Tate said as his sword shook in his hand.

"Shut up," Bensen said without taking his eyes off the woods.

Chelci chanced a look at the village to see if any backup was coming, but no one was there. She turned back toward the woods just as the most terrifying creature she'd ever seen emerged from behind a tree.

Its back was as tall as her chin, and the animal was double that in length. The hide looked thick and tough, and as the creature walked, muscles rippled through its body. A head the length of Chelci's arm attached to a short neck. Its eyes reflected the light from the lantern, looking like burning coals. A series of sharp-looking spines covered the back of its head and ran down its neck. Two jagged rows of teeth filled its mouth with long fangs on each side. The front feet had five digits, but the back legs ended with enormous claws—three on one but only two on the other.

That's where Royce's claw came from. Although Chelci had never seen one before, she knew without a doubt what it was—a valcor.

"Spread out," Bensen said.

Tate and Chelci shuffled a few steps in either direction without hesitation. The valcor stopped and looked back and forth between the spread-out trio. All three had their swords at the ready, and Bensen held the lantern aloft in his other hand.

Is it deciding who to attack?

Without warning, it reared up and stood on its hind legs, towering above them and unleashing a deafening roar. Chelci covered her ears with one free hand and a shoulder. As the sound faded, something rattled to her left. Tate's sword bounced on the dirt as he ran toward the village. Decisively, the valcor fell back down to the ground, and ran after Tate at a terrifying speed.

"No!" Bensen shouted.

As the valcor ran past him, Bensen lunged to stab it in the side. Chelci winced as the sword tip glanced harmlessly off the rough hide. The valcor paused for a moment and looked back at Bensen. It opened its mouth, bared its fangs at him, and roared before it turned to follow Tate.

"Tate, run!" Bensen yelled as he hurled the oil lantern at the beast.

The glass shattered on the animal's back, and the oil covered it in an explosion of flame. The valcor roared in anger. It stopped and thrashed about, rolling on the ground. The fire on its body quickly went out, but nearby bushes caught ablaze, illuminating the forest. The act was enough to turn the beast from Tate and focus its attention on Bensen.

It took a few cautious steps then lunged at the instructor. Bensen swung his sword in a flurry of strikes so fast Chelci could barely see them, but the sword still couldn't penetrate the valcor's hide. Chelci screamed as it grabbed Bensen with its front paw and swiped with one of its back legs. Blood sprayed through the air, the warm drops splattering across Chelci's face as Bensen's leg shredded. He screamed in pain as he collapsed to the ground, his sword falling from his grip.

Chelci froze, the nightmare playing out leaving her incapable of action. Her breathing was quick and ragged as she fought to keep her mind present. *Come on, Chelci! Pull it together!*

She wiped the blood off her face and looked directly at the animal focused on Bensen.

"Hey!" Chelci shouted. She stepped in and swung with her sword, but the blunted blade was even less effective than Bensen's.

The beast batted her away with its hand. The impact spun her around and knocked her down. She lost her sword and helmet and landed face-first in the dirt. Disoriented, she pushed herself up and looked in time to see the valcor disappear into the darkness. It headed deeper into the woods, dragging Bensen behind it.

She found her sword on the ground and looked back toward the village. *Russell or Finley or Aleks should be here by now. Maybe Tate had a change of heart? Coward.*

No one was there. No one was coming. Chelci took a deep breath and looked back toward where the beast disappeared moments ago. *This is what happened to those other village guards earlier tonight, and it's what happened to Madeline years ago. I can't stand by while Bensen meets the same fate, but if I go after him, it's going to kill me too.* She swallowed hard. *I can't abandon him.*

She followed the path of death into the awaiting darkness.

Deeper in the woods, the light from the burning bushes was gone. All Chelci could use to see was the moon as its glow snaked its way through the branches. Streaks of blood on bushes and rocks let her know she was on the right track as she ran. Behind her, the village alarm bell began to ring.

I can't wait. I might lose the trail, and every second counts if Bensen's going to have a chance to live.

After several minutes of scrambling up and down hills, Chelci worried she had lost the trail until the familiar scratchy howl summoned her forward. Soon an enormous tree's silhouette came into view with a dark shape climbing about halfway up the branches. One front limb held a body while the other grabbed limbs above it.

Chelci made her way to the base of the tree and started climbing as fast as she could. *It's a molopyr tree. Good. Easy to climb.* After climbing for a moment, the scraping and rustling above her quieted. *It's stopped moving. What am I going to do once I get there? I have no idea if Bensen will even still be alive, but I have to keep trying.*

Once she was a few branches under the animal, she could better see what was happening. It stopped on some sort of platform. From the ground, it merely looked like branches, but the sticks wove together to make a flat area bridging two large tree limbs.

I found its nest! Chelci thought. Bensen's body lay at the edge of the nest with one of his arms dangling over the side, but the valcor seemed preoccupied with something else. *Maybe there's still a chance to save him?*

Chelci moved to the backside of the tree to be able to climb higher without being seen. The sound of tearing and cracking came from the nest, giving her chills. She shuddered at the thought of what it was. As Chelci got up to the same height as the nest, a loud *whooshing* sound was followed by the tree shaking. A dark shape flew through the air out of the tree. Her heart skipped a beat.

Was that the valcor? Was it Bensen? She snuck a peek around the trunk and saw both the animal and her instructor remained. *At least it wasn't him.*

Chelci silently took her sword out of the scabbard and used her free hand to steady herself while she snuck around the tree. She stepped onto the edge of the nest behind the valcor, which was bent over, chewing at something and oblivious to her presence. She tried to wave to get Bensen's attention, but he was either passed out or dead. Her pulse thumped heavily in her ears.

While considering the most vulnerable place to attack the beast, a stick cracked under her foot. The valcor snapped its head back to her and snarled as it turned around to face her.

Her stomach dropped. *So much for the element of surprise.*

She jabbed with her sword, but it wasn't long enough to even make contact. The valcor advanced, and she scrambled backward. It snapped at her with its sharp teeth as she stumbled over branches, trying to keep space between them. Chelci jumped over a tree limb as the valcor lunged again. Its jaws stopped a hand's width away from her face as a branch blocked the rest of its body. Blood covered its teeth as it thrashed itself on the limb she hid behind, the rotten smell assaulting her senses.

Soon, Chelci was back on the opposite side of the tree while the valcor continued to advance. She waved her sword at its face, receiving hideous snarls in return. The beast stopped.

Maybe my small sword could actually be effective? she thought.

As she considered her options of what to do next, a searing pain jolted her body as something ripped into her side. She screamed in agony while she spun and fell onto the branch, barely holding onto her sword. The valcor was long enough to taunt her with its jaws on one side of the trunk and attack her with its back claws from the other. A large gash ripped across her side and bled freely. Merely looking at it made her feel dizzy.

She did her best to ignore the wound as she scrambled back on her feet. She held the sword toward the claws. They lashed out again, but she was able to block. After being rebuffed, the back legs disappeared from view. She spun around, expecting to see jaws about to bite her in half, but found nothing. The rushing in her ears and the beating of her own heart was so loud that it took her a minute to realize the snarling had stopped.

Chelci looked back and forth on each side of the trunk. She listened intently. Nothing. She made her way back around the tree to the nest. Bensen lay where he was before, but the valcor was gone.

She cautiously stepped on the nest as a raindrop fell. *Where did it go?* Chelci peered over the side, but the darkness below made it difficult to see much. More drops fell. *Something is wrong.*

The rain was thick and heavy, and it didn't fall in a regular rhythm. Her breath caught as she noticed her arm. It wasn't drops of water. It was drops of blood. A wave of terror swept through her as the low throaty growl rumbled above her.

Chelci slowly raised her head, and her heart stopped. An arm's length above her—with its jaws closed in a growl and blood dripping from its fangs—was the valcor. It opened its mouth wide and unleashed a roar. She shook from its force. The sound tried to push her body down, but she stood firm.

Before it had a chance to close its mouth, Chelci stabbed upward, piercing the animal in the upper part of the inside of its mouth. The sharp tip of her sword penetrated the soft upper palate and protruded from the other side.

The roar changed to a hideous shriek. The sound was unearthly. The valcor shook and thrashed its head as Chelci pulled the weapon out, nearly knocking her off her feet. It pawed frantically at its face, losing its grip on whatever it held. The beast shrieked as it fell, careening off the side of the nest. It flailed its limbs as it bounced off branches to the ground, where it landed with an earth-shaking boom.

Chelci watched over the side. At first, the animal was motionless, and she thought it must be dead. After a moment, it began to stir and slowly stood. It glanced up the tree before limping away and disappearing into the woods.

I did it! I can't believe it!

After the brief moment of celebration, she turned her attention to Bensen and hurried to where he lay. His chest moved. His eyes fluttered, and he muttered incomprehensible words.

He's alive! "Bensen! It's me, Elise! Can you hear me?" His delirium left him unresponsive. *He's lost a lot of blood. He may not be alive long.*

His arm revealed a deep puncture, and a shallow gash crossed his chest. Bensen's right leg was almost unrecognizable from the damage. His face was as pale as death and covered with sweat. His arm and chest had stopped bleeding, but his leg was in much worse shape.

Chelci winced as she took off her guard uniform, the pain reminding her of her own injury. Two slashes raked her side where the valcor's claws had ripped through her clothes. Blood ran down the gashes along her skin. It was difficult to breathe, so she probably had some broken ribs too. The loss of blood left her weak, and her hands felt clammy.

I may not be alive long either.

Using the rips the valcor started in her uniform, she hacked with her sword to tear it into pieces. She wrapped a torn portion around Bensen's leg, which elicited a groan. His body went limp, and for a moment, she thought he was dead.

Come on, Bensen. Don't die on me!

Chelci breathed a sigh of relief when his chest rose after a few moments. She used another piece of the uniform to tie around her waist. She cried out in pain as she tightened it to stop the bleeding on her side.

After the bandages were tied as best as she could, she looked around to determine how to climb down from the nest. Two disfigured lumps caught her eye to the side—what the valcor worked on when she arrived.

That must be the remains of Tomas and Lachlan, she thought. She didn't have time to run and get help. Bensen would bleed out by then, and there was the possibility of the valcor returning. The only option was to drag him back to the village herself. *If we were on the ground, it would be easy, but how am I supposed to get him down? Can I climb down with him on my shoulder?*

She tried to hoist him up by pulling his arms, but he was too heavy. She tried to grab underneath him and lift but was unable. "Bensen! Come on! I need you to snap out of this right now!" The rope coiled around his chest caught her eye. *That's it!*

After untangling it from around his body, she tied one end of the rope around his chest and looped the other over a branch just above them. She dragged his unconscious body to the edge of the nest and pulled the rope taut.

Can I do this? Am I strong enough to lower him down? She glanced over the side and felt dizzy, both from the height and the loss of blood. *I have to try.*

Pulling with all of her strength on her end of the rope, Chelci slowly pushed Bensen off the edge. The weight of his body leaving the platform was jarring. The force tried to rip the rope from her hands, but she held fast. Hand over hand, she steadily fed the line over the branch as his body inched toward the ground.

Chelci's side ached from the effort. Her ribs screamed, and her arms threatened to let go. *I can't hold this for long. I need to move quickly.*

Her shoulder soon went numb, and blood seeped through the bandage on her side. She felt weaker than ever but continued to feed the rope as it scraped along the limb above her. Chelci struggled to breathe. As her hands cramped, the rope began to slip, slowly sliding through them, burning her palms.

Suddenly the weight lessened, and she looked down. Bensen had made it to the ground and lay slumped on his side. She released the rest of the rope and scurried down after him. As she jumped to the ground, Chelci glanced around, hoping the valcor wasn't lying in wait. After deciding the coast was clear, she exhaled a loud sigh of relief.

We made it!

She staggered as the earth spun. Cold shivers ran through her body. Her hands looked ghostly from loss of blood. She shook her head to try to focus, expecting to blackout at any second. Bensen remained unconscious but breathing, and to her dismay, his bandages appeared to be as ineffective as hers.

How do we get back to the village from here? She tried holding his arms and dragging him behind her but couldn't hold on because of her bloody and sweaty hands. She found that if she faced him away from her and put her arms under his, she could lock her hands around his chest and walk backward while dragging him.

It seemed doable for the first ten steps or so, but she soon felt the pain. Her lower back was on fire. Her arms were tired and cramped. It hurt to breathe, and her legs felt like they were burning.

If I stop, I'll never get moving again. She kept going.

As she moved in a delirious haze, her mind wandered. *Nevi would be worried sick if she knew what I was doing. I bet my friends will miss me if I don't make it back. How did it come to this?* A pang of regret hit her suddenly. *I'm about to die, and my family will never know what happened to me. I wonder what Jackson is up to? How's Father's health? Has Mother ever gotten kinder? If I could, I'd really like to see them again.*

Chelci had no idea how far she dragged Bensen. Soon, she couldn't feel her arms or legs. Her vision was blurry, and the dizziness was overwhelming. Her body felt weak and tired. The blood from her side dripped down the left side of her body.

Maybe if I rest for a moment, I can build up my strength, she thought. *No! I can't stop. I have to keep going.*

Suddenly, Bensen's body no longer slid along the ground. It was as if Chelci had run into an invisible wall she couldn't pull him through. She strained under the weight, but he wouldn't budge. Faced with the thought of defeat, Chelci collapsed to the ground with Bensen's body leaning against her. She no longer cared about getting back—all she wanted to do was rest.

I need to keep moving though. She forced her eyes open. *Come on, Chelci! Get up!*

No, just sleep.

Her eyes were closed, and she lay on the ground when she remembered the bell in her pocket. She fumbled to grab it. Lifting it into the air, she rang it as hard as she could. She kept going as long as she was able, but soon, the effort was too much. Her arm fell, and she stopped fighting the need to rest.

I tried Bensen . . . I tried.

Before the darkness took over, as the cloud of exhaustion rendered her body useless, she heard something in the distance. It was weak and arrived to her carried by the wind, but the sound was unmistakable—the faint whisper of a bell.

43

Unexpected Surprises

ome on, just go over there! Veron thought as he tried to get himself to move. *She's just standing there. It's perfect.* He watched Chloe as she dipped candles across the courtyard, lost in her work.

Veron had been looking for an opportunity to talk with her all week since he got back from the hunting trip, but no time ever seemed right. It was Finday, and he still hadn't said anything.

Bracing himself with the courage he needed, Veron moved. "So, how are candle sales going?" he asked as he arrived at Chloe's workstation.

Chloe wore a simple, light blue dress with a gray shawl over it, but she looked radiant. A chill filled the air, so she also had a knitted green scarf wrapped around her neck, which Greta had made for her.

"Um . . . It's been good. My new scent is selling well. Have you smelled it?" She held a candle up to his nose. "Rosemouthe and peppermint."

Veron's eyebrows lifted. "Wow, that smells . . ." he tried to find the right word to express it, ". . . festive—like a party!" She smiled at his description. "After we close up the market in a few minutes, would you like to go for a walk with me?" Veron asked, kicking the dirt as he watched his feet.

"Sure! I'm low on wax anyway and need to pick some up from my supplier down by the river, if that's okay?"

Veron looked up quickly. "Sure. Yeah, I can help you carry it."

Chloe's attention drifted past his shoulder to the market entrance. Veron turned around and froze as his stomach twisted. Captain Mortinson stood in the courtyard, flanked by two soldiers.

"Veron Stormbridge," the captain said.

"Yes," Veron replied, his heart pounding.

"I need you to come with me."

Veron's mind raced, thinking through what he had done. *There's no way he found out about my childhood. He can't know about how I tricked the lending house, can he? Did he discover I'm not from a wealthy family in Felting?* He looked at Morgan, who shrugged. *I hope this isn't like what happened to Morgan!*

Not having any viable options, Veron left with the soldiers.

"I'm onto you," Mortinson said as they walked down the street with one soldier in front and one behind.

"What do you mean?" Veron asked, trying to appear casual.

"The quarter-staff competition. You're from Felting, right?" Mortinson asked.

"Yes," Veron said, staring at the captain.

"You trained under Salazar, didn't you?"

Veron wasn't sure if he should play along or if that might get him tied up in even more lies, so he decided the truth was best. "I don't know who that is."

The captain eyed him. "Your fighting style reminded me of him. My mistake."

Was that it? Am I in the clear? Veron sighed internally. *But where am I going?* Something about the exchange unsettled him, but he wasn't sure exactly what it was.

He mentally prepared himself for having to fight. He'd been continuing his physical training almost every day and felt ready for anything. The only thing that continued to frustrate him was his inability to tap into the origine. No matter what he tried, the extraordinary power source eluded him.

They continued walking in silence. As they crossed Karad Square, dark clouds approached the city from over the river, and thunder sounded ominously in the distance.

"Storm's gonna be here soon," the captain said to no one in particular.

I hope I can get back before then, Veron thought. *If I even get back at all.*

Soon, they arrived at the Department of Commerce. Veron cocked his head while Mortinson held the door open and motioned for him to enter.

Inside the office, Brixton talked with Hailey at his desk. As soon as he spotted Veron, he jumped up with a grin on his face. "Father, he's here!"

Heath sat at the desk next to him, and a third clerk Veron didn't know was at the other desk in the back corner. Raynor emerged from the office.

What's going on? he thought.

"Veron! Thanks for coming!" Raynor said before nodding to Mortinson and the soldiers. The captain stared Veron down one more time as he and his crew left. "Due to the impressive performance you've put together at North Karad Market, you've been selected as this year's Gold Crown License Award winner for the city of Karad!"

Veron's jaw hung slack as he played the words over in his mind.

The Gold Crown Award! Raynor, Brixton, Hailey, Heath, and the other man all clapped for him. Veron tried to say something but was speechless as he shook hands with each of them.

Never in my life did I imagine I'd receive this honor! My taxes will drop. My sales will increase. I can hire someone to handle the day-to-day work, and I can spend most of my time shadow knight training! I was doing great until now, but this is far beyond anything I've ever hoped for! Veron thought.

Raynor continued. "As you know, tomorrow night is the annual Merchant Awards Banquet, and there I will present you with the coveted golden seal."

"Thank you, Lord Fiero!" Veron said. "I—I don't know what to say. It's such an honor. I wasn't expecting this."

"You don't need to say anything. The results of your market speak loudly enough."

"Now, it's time to celebrate!" Brixton said, clapping Veron on the back. "You're coming out to Fenwick's with Hailey and me."

Brixton grabbed his cloak off the chair and headed for the door. Veron was too stunned to object.

The storm arrived soon after they entered the tavern. The heavy rain drummed above, but the downpour didn't dampen their spirits. "Did you know that your market is the youngest business ever to receive the gold crown?" Brixton asked. He sat behind his second pint of ale, which was already almost gone.

"No, I had no idea," Veron replied.

"You'll be making so much money now," Brixton said, shaking his head in disbelief. "Plus, you're about to finish paying your loan off, aren't you?"

"Yeah, only one more payment." *After the lack of loan payment, plus the reduction of tax, I should be making an extra . . . two argen each*

445

week! And that doesn't even consider any sales increase, Veron thought. *Whoa! I'm going to be rich!*

"You've done a great job, Veron," Hailey said, sitting next to Brixton and smiling at Veron in an odd way.

Veron fidgeted in his seat, feeling uncomfortable with her glance. Thankfully, Brixton was too interested in draining his mug to notice. Setting the drink down, Brixton flagged down the bartender who brought another pint for him and Hailey, who tipped her glass as she struggled to keep up.

"What are you doing, sipping on yours?" Brixton said, indicating to Veron's first drink, which was still mostly full.

"Leave me alone. I'm drinking it," he replied.

He seems to be back to his old self, Veron thought. *On the hunting trip, something was off, but I'm not sure what it was.*

Hailey saw a friend on the other side of the room and left to say hello. "So, are you ready?" Brixton asked in a hushed voice once they were alone.

Veron froze with a look of puzzlement. "Ready for what?"

"Ready for opportunity! I told you it would be coming soon, but to be successful, now you need to act on it."

"I'm sorry. I'm not sure what you mean. Act on what?"

Brixton scoffed. "The Gold Crown License Award, what else?"

Veron tilted his head. "Yeah, that's definitely an opportunity. I'm excited about it, but I'm not sure what you mean by acting on it," he said.

"You'll easily be making ten to fifteen percent higher profits now from doing absolutely nothing." Brixton leaned in across the table. "But people don't achieve success on their own. There's usually someone else they partner with to achieve mutually beneficial situations. You and I are going to be those partners."

"What do you mean? What are we going to do for each other?"

"I gave you the Gold Crown, and you're going to cut me in on a portion of your increased profits. I want three percent."

Veron was stunned. He looked around the room, searching for something to indicate it was all a joke. "What are you talking about? I *earned* the Gold Crown Award. Are you saying you want me to just . . . *give* you three percent?"

Brixton laughed. "Oh no, you didn't *earn* the award. I gave it to you. I've been padding your numbers and adjusting your tax receipts for the last year. Yeah, you've been doing great at the market, but it takes more than that to win the award. You needed to have help, and I was the one to be there for you. All I'm requiring is a tiny three percent." Brixton took a long drink from his mug.

Veron's mouth fell open. His stomach felt queasy. *Why would he do that? I don't want anything to do with this. I don't want padded numbers to get some prize I didn't earn.* "No! I'm sorry, but I don't want the award if that's what it takes to get it. Look, Brix, I appreciate you wanting to help me, but I can't take this. I'll tell your father that my numbers were wrong, and I didn't earn it."

Brixton sat back as if he'd been spit in the face. "Whoa, whoa! Don't be an idiot! You can't do that, Veron!" His voice rose, drawing attention from the tables around them. Brixton gathered his composure before continuing. "If you report that your numbers are wrong, what do you think is going to happen?"

"I don't know. I'll just make them right."

Brixton slid around the table to the chair next to Veron. "It's not that simple. What do you think happens to people who pad their sales and tax reports for a year?" he asked.

"But it wasn't me. It was you!" Veron said.

Brixton raised his eyebrows. "And what do you think is going to happen if you say *I've* been doing it? I'm not going to take the fall for your bad numbers. And whose side do you think my father will take?

His son? Or . . . the mysterious boy with no past and no references?"

Veron froze and stared at Brixton. *I know we're different, but I still thought we were friends. And now he's blackmailing me?*

"If you tell my father that I set it up, within a week, I'll see to it that you don't even *own* a market anymore." Brixton stared at him with hard eyes. "Accept the award, Veron. Don't be a fool. You'll get more money, and I'll get more money. What's the big deal?"

Hailey stumbled across the room and sat back down with them. "The big deal about what?" she asked.

"Nothing," Brixton said through heavy breaths as he moved back to his original chair and took another drink.

Veron stared at his mug as he fought to stay in control. He felt as if he'd been punched in the gut and was reeling from the blow.

"So, are you bringing someone to the banquet tomorrow?" Hailey asked Veron.

"Uh . . ." Veron looked at her, trying to focus on what she was saying. "I don't know."

"Oh, you have to bring someone!" she said. "Especially since you're winning an award."

I need to get out of here. I need to go somewhere to think, Veron thought. *Chloe! She's probably wondering what happened to me.* He stood up quickly. "I'm sorry, but I just remembered I have to be somewhere."

"Aww, come on! You haven't even finished your drink yet!" Brixton said with a friendly expression on his face.

Veron backed his way to the door. "I'm really sorry. Thank you both for your kind words." He moved to turn the knob of the tavern door.

"Veron!" Brixton called after him, causing him to turn around. "Remember what I said." The friendly expression was gone.

They stared at each other, frozen in the moment. Without another word, Veron left the tavern and stepped into the rain.

Veron shook off the water from his cloak as he entered the common room at the market. A shiver ran through him from the cold. The common room was the final project to build, which Jacob recently finished out of the open loft space. Everyone was there, engrossed in their own activities.

"What happened? Are you okay?" Morgan asked, running over when Veron entered.

So much had happened after Veron had left, escorted by soldiers. "Oh, that. Yeah, I'm fine," he said.

"What did they want?" Morgan asked.

Veron wasn't sure what to say. He felt trapped by Brixton and the situation he put him in. Veron sighed then flushed as he spoke. "We won the Gold Crown License Award."

Morgan's eyes lit up. He delivered a deep, hearty laugh and picked up Veron in a bear hug. "What! Veron, that's amazing! Did you hear that, everyone? Veron here won the Gold Crown Award!" Everyone in the room exploded into cheers.

Veron gave a weak smile, embarrassed by the attention, especially because he knew the story behind how it happened. Everyone took turns congratulating him on the achievement with a train of hugs and slaps on the back.

"I'm going to build a mount to go right over the gate where we can display the seal," Jacob said.

Veron noticed the one person he wanted to talk to the most wasn't there. "Morgan, where's Chloe?" he asked.

Morgan looked around the room for a moment then back at Veron and shrugged his shoulders. "She left earlier, a little after you did. Going to get wax, I think. I guess I haven't seen her since."

She should have been back long before now. With the storm outside, she wouldn't have stayed out any longer than was necessary, Veron thought.

He thought back through the afternoon, wondering where she

might have gone. He imagined her walking across Karad Square toward the wax shop as he pictured the scene he passed through earlier.

The clouds were dark. Few people milled about due to the impending storm. Shopkeepers brought in their goods. What was that? Veron remembered two figures on the far end of the square skulking against an alley wall almost hidden by shadow. *What were they doing? Why is Chloe not back? Something's wrong.* Without a word, Veron left the room.

He put the cold, soaking cloak back on as he ran down the steps with the rain falling on him. Immediately shivering, he paused at the bottom before turning around and heading back to his room. He took off his dripping outer layer and opened Artimus' chest. Inside, he found the black Shadow Knights cloak. He picked it up and ran his hand over the symbol on the chest, thinking of his father. The fabric was thick and well woven—and dry. He put it on and raised the hood. While he was there, he grabbed the ruby hilted sword and strapped it on his back too.

I don't know why, but I have a terrible feeling.

The rain fell steadily as Veron hurried through the city, thankful for the fresh cloak and the hood that kept the rain out of his face. The alley with the suspicious figures from before was empty, as was all of the city, so he continued down Market Street. He wasn't sure what he looked for or even where to go, but he walked toward the wax shop.

Veron turned down an alley just before the river. The sign for the supply store was visible ahead, but something on the ground caught his eye—a green scarf. His arm shook as he bent over to pick it up. It was Chloe's. His heart raced. A soggy note pinned to the soaked scarf simply read, "BENEVORRE LUMBER MILL – COME

ALONE."

The name itself sent flashbacks surging through Veron's mind. *Fend, Mortinson, the ill-fated robbery that went horribly wrong.* Now, he imagined Chloe, broken at the foot of that wall, run through with a sword.

Why would she be taken? Who would have done it? Why the lumber mill? Veron was thankful he'd grabbed the sword.

He considered going to get Morgan or Danyel to help or maybe alerting someone, but he decided to go alone. Veron ran through the alleys, reminding him of the night of the tailor's shop, six years before. He didn't even notice the pouring rain or the large puddles he splashed through. His dry cloak was soon soaked through, but he didn't care.

When he approached the ruins of the mill, he slowed, knowing that whoever had Chloe could be anywhere in a large area, and that it was better if they didn't see him coming. He skirted the mill on the right side and entered the collection of buildings by the river. Ducking behind walls, he scurried from dark corner to dark corner. With the rain covering any noise he made and the black hooded cloak, Veron was nearly undetectable.

As if something inside him directed his steps, Veron rounded the corner of a collapsed building and saw the place he headed toward—the place he had avoided for years—the alley where Fend died. He could feel the sensation of Fend slipping through his bloody grip. He could picture the sword entering his body as he lay by the wall. Veron's heart raced as emotion swelled in him. He breathed in short, shallow breaths as he moved and fought for control.

Suddenly, he stopped. His breath caught in his throat. Ahead of him, in the dim light where Fend died years ago, Chloe's body leaned against the wall.

Veron ran to her, but she didn't see him from the blindfold covering her eyes. A gag kept her from speaking, and her arms appeared tied behind her back. Blood ran down her face from a gash on her head, while water dripped off of the dress with its torn edges lying in the mud. She shivered, but other than the head wound, she seemed okay.

After looking around, he lowered his hood, allowing the rain to pelt his face and the top of his head as he crouched. "Chloe, it's me!"

She jerked at his voice. After Veron took her blindfold off, she blinked quickly. Veron saw recognition in her face just before her eyes widened.

"What happ—"

A *thud* resonated against the side of his head. The pain was searing, like an explosion of light, before he blacked out.

44

Pasts Collide

Veron's head throbbed and jaw ached even before he opened his eyes. He managed to force them open through much effort, revealing the dirt floor of an old building. A lantern hung on the wall, illuminating the space. To his left was the old wooden pushcart he remembered, unmoved and unchanged for years.

This is the room I watched from while Fend was murdered, Veron thought.

Veron froze when he saw her standing by the wall. Chloe's clothes were still damp. The gag covered her mouth, and her arms were still tied, but the blindfold was off. He would have run to her if it weren't for Bruiser standing behind her, holding a sword to her throat. Veron locked eyes with Chloe. She looked like a scared rabbit who was about to be killed. Veron reached for the sword on his back but found nothing. He paled as he noticed the ruby in the hilt of the one Bruiser held.

The sound of laughter jolted him as Veron became aware of the second man in the room. Standing to the side, smirking, and twirling a knife, stood Slash. "So, you thought you could steal from us and get away with it?" he said, walking toward Veron and crouching in front of his face. "You thought you could kill Coffin, and we wouldn't do anything about it?"

Veron gritted his teeth and stood up.

"Whoa, whoa, whoa!" Slash said as he backed up. Bruiser tightened the sword against Chloe's neck, causing Veron to stop moving. "You thought you could take our money and start a business on the other side of town where we wouldn't find you?"

Veron glared at them. "It was *my* money." His voice was calm but firm.

"Who can ever really know, right?" Slash flashed an evil grin.

"So, what do you want?" Veron asked. "Money? You let her go, and I'll give you my two and a half sol back."

Slash roared with laughter. "Oh, Veron, we've come so far since then, haven't we? You're no longer the street trash who ate other people's garbage and begged just to get by. Now, you have a Gold Crown License, and I think there's potential for a whole lot more."

Veron's eyes were wide. "How did you know that?"

"Oh, I have my sources." Slash paced back and forth, the knife still in hand. "No, I don't want two and a half sol. I want *three* sol . . . per half-season."

Three sol every fifteen weeks! Veron thought as he glanced at Chloe then back to Slash. "For how long?"

"Until I say so."

Veron paled. "You're not getting anything until you let her go."

Slash laughed again. "I think I'm not getting anything *if* I let her go. So, here's what we're gonna do. You're gonna leave here and bring your first payment back tonight. If you take longer than thirty minutes to get back or we see anyone besides you show up, we'll kill her. Then, every fifteen weeks, another payment is due. If at any point you stop paying—" Slash stopped and pointed the knife toward Chloe "—she'll die. As long as you pay, you can live a great life, and we'll leave you alone. You understand?"

Veron stared at Slash and didn't say a word for several moments. *Something about this whole thing doesn't make sense.* "Why did you bring me here?" Veron asked, motioning around him with his hands.

"I don't know. It seemed like a good out of the way place." Slash shuffled his feet, eyes darting.

Veron stared hard at him. "How did you know about Fend?"

Slash cocked his head. "Fend? What do you mean?"

Veron lowered his voice into a growl. "Where is he?" Slash looked unsure and glanced at Bruiser, who shrugged his shoulders. "Captain! You can come out!" Veron yelled into the night.

Slash and Bruiser didn't speak or move. For a long moment, they all stared at each other and listened to the patter of rain on the roof. Then, Veron heard it—the heavy steps and metal clanking of a soldier.

"It took me a while to figure it out," a deep voice said. Veron turned as Charles Mortinson emerged from the darkness and rain to enter the building. "You were never from Felting. I could spot that from the beginning. When we fought at the festival, I knew I recognized you from somewhere, but I couldn't quite place it. I made some inquiries and eventually discovered the connection. You worked at that grocery in Upper Sherry. I remember it—the one where we set up the owner with those phony tax documents."

Veron's eyes grew, and his breath caught, hands balling into fists.

"Oh, yes, you didn't know that, did you? Your grocer heard some things he shouldn't have."

Veron seethed as he listened.

"And before that"—Mortinson got in Veron's face—"you were street trash, taking what wasn't yours and ruining our city every day you were alive. I should have run you through by that wall the same

455

way we did your friend. Fend? Was that his name?"

Veron yelled as he pushed the captain, but he was stopped short by a scream from Chloe as the sword pressed deeper into her skin and a trickle of red ran down her pale neck. He took a step back from Mortinson, but his gaze could have melted steel.

"I don't know what lies you told to start your business, but we will happily keep your secret," Mortinson said. "And neither you nor your little friend here"—he walked over to Chloe—"need to get hurt. But that part's up to you. What do you say?"

Veron looked at the three men. "So, this is all about money? You despise me because I was once a thief, and now you're here to steal from me?"

Mortinson sniffed and stood straighter.

"Fine, I'll get it," Veron said.

Slash grabbed Chloe's hand and held the knife to her left pinky. "Don't take too long," he sneered. "It'd be a shame if you were too slow getting back and found her missing a finger."

The remaining color drained from Chloe's face as she stared wide-eyed at Veron.

Veron burned with anger. *Slash has tormented me all of my life, but now he's crossing a line.* He took a step toward them. "If you hurt a hair on her head, you'll be sorry!"

Slash dropped Chloe's hand and waved the knife at Veron. "You won't tell me what I can and can't do! You have *no* leverage here! I can kill her right now if I want to!"

Slash turned back to Chloe and slowly slid the knife down the side of her dress, causing it to tear, exposing her skin as well as a thin line of blood. Chloe whimpered.

"Who knows what I may decide to do," he said in an evil tone as he looked her in the face. She sobbed. "Quiet, you!" Slash shouted as he hit her in the side of her head with the butt of his knife, leaving a dark red gash. Her body slumped.

Veron's blood boiled. His heart beat wildly, and his mind raced. He fought to stay in control, but his body ached to act. *Clear your mind. Clear your mind.*

As he glared at Slash, the hatred faded, and something he didn't expect replaced it—purpose. He wanted them dead, not because he despised them or for revenge, but because he wanted to protect what was good. Chloe needed saving. He needed saving. His market and his workers' livelihood needed saving.

Before he had a chance to fill his mind with more worry, he perceived a strange sensation—a connection he'd never felt before. Veron sensed a warm tingling in the pit of his stomach as if he'd swallowed warm liquor. His arms and body felt weightless.

The origine!

Veron recognized it and pulled as much energy from inside him as he could. Immediately, time slowed down. Bruiser and his sword appeared frozen. Slash held his knife like a statue, and the rain outside seemed to have stopped. Veron heard his own heartbeat, but it was a fraction of its typical speed. His muscles felt strong, his body made of iron and capable of moving in any capacity he wanted. Awareness of everything around him filled his mind and body with power. He was invincible.

Veron reached out and grabbed his ruby sword from Bruiser's hand. The large man released it without a struggle. Without hesitating, Veron ran it through Bruiser's stomach with a loud yell. The thug's reaction was slow, as if it took him several seconds to feel the wound. His body fell in slow motion as Veron pulled the sword out and turned to Slash, whose eyes were widening. His mouth moved to say something, but Veron didn't wait to find out what it was.

Veron grabbed the knife from Slash's hand, turned it around, and stabbed him in the chest over his heart, shouting with every ounce of energy he had left in him. A thunderous roar shook the building's walls and roof, causing years of dirt and dust to float to the ground.

I did it! I tapped into the origine!

The excitement waned as he sobered from the thought of what he just did. Out of nowhere, his sharp focus drained away. Time felt like it sped up, leaving him feeling heavy and weak. At first, he thought it was the contrast from his heightened state to normalcy, but after a few moments, he realized he was utterly exhausted. He fell to his knees, his sword hitting the ground next to him.

This must be what Artimus meant about the origine depleting a person's energy quickly, he thought.

Bruiser lay on the ground. His arm moved slowly, but too much blood pooled on the dirt around him. He would be dead in moments. Slash lay next to him with his own knife sticking out of his chest. His eyes were already still and glazed over. Chloe appeared unconscious, her chest moving as she lay on the ground.

Good, she's alive. Veron kneeled in the dirt, panting, trying to catch his breath.

"What . . . was that?" Mortinson's voice brought a chill to his bones.

Veron had forgotten about the captain as he focused on the other two. The soldier stood at the other end of the room, limply holding his sword and trembling.

"H—H—How did you do that?" Mortinson asked. His eyes were wide, and his face ashen.

Veron grabbed his sword and stood with a great deal of effort. Mortinson looked confused and scared but lifted his own sword higher, trying to keep it steady.

"I did to them what I'm about to do to you," Veron said with feigned confidence. The captain stood up straighter.

Both men faced each other, neither wanting to make the first move. Veron couldn't fight in his weakened state. Luckily for him, Mortinson stood there immobile for what seemed like an eternity. After a long pause, the captain's face hardened, and he swung his sword.

Veron barely got his sword up in time to block as he stepped to the side. Mortinson paused for a moment before attacking again with another single strike that Veron parried away. *He's testing me.*

Veron tried to clear his mind again, but nothing happened. He struggled to focus but kept losing it as he had to defend himself from another swing of the sword.

"How did you move as you did?" Mortinson asked, moving more confidently.

"It's something a miserable wretch like you will never understand."

The captain swung a hard three-strike combo at him. Veron blocked the first two, then stepped to the right, dodging the last swing. His long cloak swayed with him as he moved. The grit of the dirt crunched underneath his feet.

"Tell me!" the captain yelled. Desire filled his eyes. "Forget the money and forget the girl. I'll walk away from this, and you can go back to your life if you teach me to do what you just did."

"Never!" Veron shouted, the sound echoing off the walls.

"Very well," Mortinson replied, the corners of his mouth turning up in a smirk. "Did you know this whole plot wasn't even my idea?"

"I don't care which one of you thought of it. Slash is done coming up with plans to abuse the people of this city."

Mortinson let out a deep laugh that unnerved Veron. "No, not Slash." He leaned in with a wicked smile. "And not Bruiser, either."

A chill ran through Veron. "What do you mean?"

"Oh, Veron, you have so much to learn."

Veron blanched as Mortinson's face hardened. He took a quick, deep breath. *Here it comes.*

The blow was hard and fast as the captain swung at his shoulder. Veron jumped back, feeling the air on his face from the blade that barely missed.

My strength's returning.

Mortinson followed with another hard swing from the opposite side, but that time, Veron stepped into it. He knocked the sword down and away and followed with a hard elbow to the captain's face. Mortinson staggered back, clutching his nose. Blood covered his hand when he pulled it away. He roared in anger and came at Veron, fueled by fury. Their swords clashed, side to side, as Veron parried the blows.

He's so much stronger than me. I can't hold him off for long, Veron thought.

With a loud yell, Mortinson delivered an overhead strike. Veron stepped to the side at the last second, and the captain stumbled past him. Muscles aching, Veron struck hard against Mortinson's back, but the sword glanced off chain mail.

Suddenly, Veron felt a sharp pain on the back of his leg as the captain's sword nicked him. He cried out through gritted teeth as he keeled over in the dirt, clutching his calf. Mortinson had fallen to the ground, but he turned around with a smug look as Veron grimaced in agony. The movement placed Mortinson closer to Chloe, and he looked behind him to see where she was.

Chloe! No! Veron stood up quickly. The pain was blinding—like a wild animal clawed at his leg—but he forced himself to ignore it.

Mortinson got to Chloe first, grabbing her hair and holding his sword tip to her neck. With a grin, he turned back to Veron. "Don't move or I—"

Veron saw it all in the blink of an eye—Fend screaming as the captain stood on his broken leg. Mortinson declaring they did nothing but contribute to the city's decay. The blood on Fend's lips as he died.

Mortinson's words were cut short as the sharp edge of Farrathan separated his head from his body in one smooth stroke. The captain's lifeless body crumpled to the ground. Six years of rage fueled the effort as Veron held his sword to the side and panted in a swirling pool of pain, anger, and relief.

It's done. He's gone. We're safe.

Veron turned his attention to Chloe, who was still unconscious. Untying her hands and the gag, he took the cloth and wrapped it around his own leg, pulling it as tight as he could and wincing in pain. After strapping the sword on his back, he picked Chloe up and carried her in his arms, using all the strength he had left.

He turned back once he was at the doorway to see the three bodies lying on the ground and their blood staining the dirt. The sight made him nauseous, but he pushed the thought of guilt away.

Outside, the rain fell steadily. Veron walked with a limp, dragging his injured leg, not even bothering to put his hood up. He cried most of the way back but wasn't even sure why.

45

Taking Risks

"Help! Can someone give me a hand!" Veron shouted as he entered the courtyard.

Morgan was the first to emerge from the common room, and he quickly rushed down the stairs. "Catherine! Mary! Get water and bandages!" he yelled back up the stairs. "What happened?"

"She was attacked," Veron said as Morgan took her body. Veron staggered after being relieved of the burden.

Veron followed Morgan as the older man carried Chloe upstairs to her room and laid her on the bed. Catherine and Mary showed up with a bowl of water, some cleaning agents, and various rags and bandages.

"What happened to her?" Catherine asked as she soaked rags and attended to Chloe's wounds.

"Some men attacked her," Veron said. "Luckily, I happened across them over by the wax shop and fought them off. She was hurt, and I got cut on the leg." He turned and extended his leg, showing the bloody rag wrapped around it.

"Oh my, let me look at that!" Mary said. She took off the soiled rag and cleaned the wound. "The cut is clean and not too deep. You got lucky on this one."

Veron didn't feel lucky as he cringed from the pain. She wrapped the freshly cleaned wound in a new bandage and had him prop his foot up.

"I don't get it," Morgan said. "Why would anyone attack her? She wouldn't have had much to steal."

Veron shook his head. "I have no idea. Some people are desperate, I guess."

"So, you fought them off? How did it happen?" Morgan asked.

"I . . . It's tough to say, for sure," Veron said. "It all happened so fast. I remember cutting one on the arm, which sent them running, but one got me in the leg. Chloe was knocked out by one of them as soon as I arrived."

"What did they look like?"

"It was so dark. I didn't get a good look. Average height, I'd say." Veron pictured the three dead bodies he left behind. *I know I can trust these people more than anyone in the world, but it's still best if they don't know everything.*

"I'll run by the constable's office in the morning to report it," Morgan said.

"No!" Veron shouted. The others jumped back at the outburst. "No, don't worry about it. I'm sure Chloe and I will heal fine, and I don't want anyone else worrying about a few people we won't be able to find anyway."

Morgan stared fixedly at Veron, but he didn't say anything further.

Catherine put the dirty rags in the bowl. "Well, that's about all I can do for now. Her cuts should heal fine, but she'll need some rest. And so will you, Veron," she said as she and Mary got up and left.

"Why don't I help you to your room so you can rest?" Morgan said. "I'll come back and watch over Chloe until she wakes."

Veron shook his head. "No, that's okay. I'd like to wait here."

463

Morgan nodded then lightly rustled the corner of Veron's cloak. "Nice outfit. Where'd you get this?"

Veron had forgotten he was wearing the cloak he had kept locked up for years. "It was Artimus."

The two sat in silence for a moment as Veron thought of Artimus and realized he had something he needed to tell Morgan.

"Morgan, when you lost your license . . . It was Captain Charles Mortinson who had that ledger planted," Veron said.

Morgan stared at him in surprise. "What?"

"Apparently, you heard something you shouldn't have. I think someone needed to discredit you or something like that."

Morgan breathed in deeply as he leaned back. "I figured that had something to do with it. I overheard the Lord of Commerce talking with some other guy about a plan to use out of circulation coins to pay for importing goods."

"The Lord of Commerce? Fiero?" Veron asked.

"Yeah. I don't know who the other guy was. I guess they recognized me and felt they needed to shut me up. No one would believe charges from a discredited ex-shopkeeper convicted of tax fraud. How'd you learn this?" Morgan asked.

Veron looked down at the floor. "I'd rather not say," he replied.

Morgan stared for a moment and then shrugged. "Well, I guess it worked out in the long run. If it hadn't happened, I wouldn't be here right now." He smiled and stood to leave. "Oh, Veron," he said, turning around in the doorway. "Whatever happened out there tonight, you may want to clean your sword off. If you only cut someone on the arm, it's going to be tough to explain why it's stained with blood to the hilt."

Veron looked at the sword leaning against the wall and shrank back as his friend left. *I know Morgan didn't buy my story, but I can't worry about that now. I just want to make sure Chloe's okay.*

The weight of all that had happened in the last several hours pressed on him like a heavy blanket.

I killed someone—three people. I can't believe I did that. Nausea turned his stomach as he remembered. He was behind Coffin dying a couple of years ago, but he never felt responsible for that.

What did Mortinson mean by it not being his idea? That doesn't make any sense. He must have been trying to unnerve me to gain an advantage. Veron tapped his fingers on his leg. *I don't think that's it though. Something about the way he said it felt genuine.* He sighed as he rested his face in his hands and rubbed his fingers through his hair. *At least I don't have to worry about them anymore.*

Looking down at his chest, Veron noticed the SK emblem on the cloak. A smile crept over his face.

The Shadow Knights. I did it! I worked hard for two years, and I finally learned how to use the origine. What does this mean? Am I a shadow knight now?

While Veron waited for Chloe to wake, he tested his connection to the origine again. It took him a few tries, but he found it. The energy was there, just waiting for him. He didn't draw from it but instead practiced finding and losing it over and over.

He grinned as he experimented with the energy, but it did nothing to help him with his Brixton problem. With all the things that happened that night, Veron had forgotten about his decision around the award.

Brixton! What am I going to do about that? I can't say something to Raynor. Apparently, he's corrupt. That would probably end with me in prison or at least stripped of my license. If I keep the award, I'll have to pay Brixton but will end up with more profit still. It feels wrong though. Veron shook his head. He had one more day to figure it out.

"Veron?"

Veron opened his eyes as he fought off the sleep that had taken over. He sat in the chair in Chloe's room, where he'd fallen asleep. Chloe lay in her bed, propped up on her elbows, looking at him.

"Chloe!" he said, moving to sit on the side of her bed. "Are you okay?"

"I feel okay. What happened?" she asked.

"What do you remember?"

She stared out into the distance. "Two men grabbed me near the wax shop. They tied me up and covered my eyes and mouth then carried me . . . somewhere. It was cold and rainy, then"—she looked at him—"you were there, and . . . What happened? How did we get away? Did you pay them?"

"Um . . . No, I didn't pay them, but you don't have to worry anymore. You're safe now."

Chloe's forehead wrinkled. "But they found me before. How do you know they can't just find me again?" she asked, trembling slightly.

Veron hesitated, trying to decide if the truth would help or hurt. "They won't be able to find you again . . . because I killed them."

Chloe breathed in sharply and put her hand to her chest. After a moment to breathe, she locked eyes with him. "I can't believe it," she said.

"I had to Chloe. They would have—"

"No, it's okay. I understand. You rescued me, Veron." She leaned forward and embraced him in a hug. "Thank you."

Veron had never rescued anyone before. For most of his life, he looked after no one but himself. When he was young, he would've been more likely to try to pick Chloe's pocket than even talk to her.

As the hug loosened, Veron decided it was time. He'd been trying to find a chance to tell her how he felt about her for a while, and no time was better than this. His heart beat fast. *Can she feel it?* "Chloe?"

he asked, pulling away, not sure of what the next words should be. "Yes?"

"Did you hear them mention the Gold Crown Award?"

Her eyes lit up. "Yes, I did. That's amazing!"

"The awards banquet is tomorrow night, and I can bring someone—if I want to. I know the timing isn't good after what just happened—and you probably couldn't go at this point—but I was *planning* to ask if you'd go with me."

Chloe tilted her head. "Why me? Why not Morgan? I only sell candles. You and he kind of started this place."

Veron laughed softly. "Yes, but that's not the idea. I wanted to bring someone that . . ." he looked down at the blanket on the bed, ". . . that I care about . . . that I could maybe see myself being with one day." *There's no going back now.*

He took her hands in his and looked up at her. His heart pounded as he looked in her eyes and waited for her response. Tears began to form at the corners of her eyes.

She's so moved by my feelings that she's crying with joy!

Chloe's face began to redden in splotches as the tears continued to grow. She pulled her hands away to cover her face.

This may not be good, Veron thought.

Soon she folded onto the bed as racking sobs filled the room.

"I'm so sorry, Chloe. I shouldn't have said anything." *This wasn't how I expected this moment to go.*

"No, it's not you," she managed to get out between sobs. "I'm the one who's sorry. It's all my fault." She broke down into another bout of tears. After a moment, she was able to calm down enough to speak. "You're a great guy, Veron, and I'm so thankful to have you as my friend."

There it is. She just wants to be my friend. He mentally kicked himself for getting carried away with his feelings.

467

"And I can never begin to repay you for what you did for me tonight. The thing is . . ." She stopped as tears started to well up again. Veron looked at her and waited as she choked back the tears. "The thing is . . . I'm married."

Veron felt like he'd been hit with a club. His body was numb. He blinked several times to bring him back to the present. "I thought your husband died in an accident at the docks?"

"I'm so sorry, I never meant for it to go this far," Chloe said, continuing to wipe away tears. "We grew up here in Karad. Patrick is a soldier in the army. When they stationed him in Karondir two years ago, we knew he'd have to travel around a lot, so I stayed here. I told people he died for sympathy . . . so I could sell more candles."

Veron was stunned. His soul felt crushed.

"When you and Morgan came along, I should have said something, but I didn't. Ever since then, I've been trapped in that lie, wishing I could get out of it, but I was afraid and didn't know how."

"You could have just *told* me!" Veron said in frustration. Veron felt as if his heart had been torn from his body, and he was left empty inside. *For two years, I fell for a girl who was already married.*

"I'm *really* sorry, Veron. If I had known how you felt, I would've said something."

His jaw clenched. He felt deceived and betrayed, but as he saw her grief, he slowly began to calm down. "It's okay," he said after a long pause. "That must have been difficult for you, and I can understand. It's not fair for me to put all the pressure on you without having said something before now. I'm thankful for you being here and will continue to be your friend. When Patrick returns . . ." he swallowed hard, "I'd love to meet him." He smiled at her reassuringly, but the words did little to soothe him.

Chloe smiled back at him as she sniffed. Her eyes were puffy, and her face was red. "Thank you. I really am sorry about it all."

He nodded. "Do you need anything?"

She shook her head. "No, I just need to rest for a while, I think."

Veron stood, favoring his uninjured leg. "Well, I'm going to go try to get some rest too then. The sun should be up soon, and I have a big day tomorrow." He stopped with his hand on the doorknob and turned back to her. "I told everyone else that I found strangers attacking you and I chased them off . . . and that was it. I didn't want to answer a bunch of questions about . . . you know . . ."

"I understand," Chloe said.

Veron opened the door and left.

Back in his room, Veron collapsed on his bed in a swirling pool of emotions. He barely noticed the throbbing pain in his leg. Chloe was the first girl he had ever cared about. He never imagined those feelings would end like that—empty and purposeless. Tears only eluded him because of his mental and physical exhaustion.

The decision over what to do about the award the next evening stressed him, but he was at least relieved that Slash and Mortinson weren't out waiting for him anymore.

46

Awards Banquet

Bale crept along the ground with a contingent of two-dozen soldiers, keeping to the darkness as best as they could. In front of them, the thick wall of Karad stood imposingly. Behind them, 10,000 Norshewan soldiers hid patiently in the woods. Lights illuminated the top of the castle over the fortification above them.

Bale stopped for a moment behind a large boulder and used his spyglass to scan the base of the rampart ahead. Most of the wall looked identical. Smooth stones stacked in rows to the top, but a darker section formed a small alcove ahead of them. Bale motioned for the rest to follow as he continued.

The opening itself was small—not even as high as his chin. Unless someone knew to look for it, it would be easy to miss. Bale had to crouch while turning sideways to fit. A body-length into the space, the path ended abruptly at a thick iron gate. It was so dark that Bale didn't even see it until he ran into it.

He fumbled in the dark until he found the thick lock that hung from the latch. As he turned it, the clasp swiveled easily. It was unlocked, just as he was promised it would be.

Veron walked through the gates of the castle for the second time in his life. The sky was dark, but the rooms and courtyards inside the walls were lit in festive anticipation of a banquet. He felt overly fancy in his blue and black puffy outfit. The only reason he wore it was because Henry and Greta worked on it all day, insisting he have nice, new clothes for the banquet. The white-striped sleeves looked like balloons. The high, itchy collar wouldn't stay, no matter how often he tried to push it down. He did like the black velvet pants though, which tucked into the high boots he recently purchased.

After a day of rest, the pain in his leg was practically gone. He tried to forget about Chloe as he approached the castle alone. Having a day to work through the disappointment helped, but seeing other merchants with their wives, dressed up and happy, made the hurt fresh. Veron tried to think the best about her, but he knew it would take a while to get past it.

Veron only saw the grounds outside the last time he was there, so getting to enter the castle itself was exciting. It did not disappoint. The grand foyer was intricately ornate, boasting elaborately curved gold and silver designs on the walls. Expensive, polished marble covered the floor, and a grand staircase ran up both sides of the room and met at the top.

He made his way through the castle, marveling at every doorway he came to, each opening to a new and exciting room. Following the other guests, Veron arrived at the castle's banquet hall, and his mouth dropped. The ceiling was easily six times his height. Four separate enormous tables spread throughout the room, each set for thirty to forty guests. Large paintings covered the wall, and a fire roared at both ends of the hall, keeping the large space warm.

A few dozen people mingled, but the room felt empty. *I guess not everyone arrives on time for these things*, Veron thought as he traded polite greetings with other guests. So far, he didn't know anyone.

471

While he waited, his curiosity led him out an open door to the side of the room into the hallway beyond. No guards stopped him, so he figured he was allowed to explore. The hallways were maze-like, connecting to other hallways that led to others. He had no idea where any of them went.

A sunny looking room with yellow walls caught his eye. Filled with expensive chairs and rugs, the space boasted a large window that spanned the entire wall and looked onto the castle courtyard below. The room was large and ornately decorated but felt intimate and inviting at the same time.

If I lived in the castle, I would spend most of my time here.

Veron followed a stone staircase up to see where it led. Each floor opened on a new and unexplored hallway. Three floors up, the stairs stopped, and he exited through the open doorway. A blast of wind hit him as he stepped outdoors atop a high structure.

I'm on the city wall! Veron thought as he walked to the edge of the battlement and set his hands on the thick stone.

In the darkness, little was visible as he gazed through the crenel out over the land. Spots of light dotted the area, identifying small villages or individual houses. Leaning through the opening over the edge, he looked down. At first, Veron thought he saw dark shapes on the ground at the base of the wall, disappearing into the structure. When he squinted to try to see better, he decided it was nothing.

Veron moved to the opposite edge of the wall, and the beauty of the city struck him. The towers of the castle rose high above him, but around them, he saw the entire wall of Karad with the river making up the far side. In the middle, like a bowl, rested the order and chaos that was Karad. The streetlamps and lights in windows made the city glow. He smiled at the grandeur.

A dark spot in the Bottoms next to the river indicated where the old mill was. *I wonder if anyone's found the bodies yet?* Veron pictured the gruesome scene. *Three people who were alive yesterday no longer live because of me. I only killed them in self-defense—no, that's not entirely true. I killed them because I wanted them dead.*

A rush of wind flowed over the wall, causing him to shiver, so he made his way back down the stairs to return to the banquet.

"There you are!" Brixton said as Veron reentered the banquet hall. "I was wondering if you decided to bail."

Veron cringed when he saw him, but knew it was pointless to avoid his friend. Standing with Hailey, Brixton appeared normal as if the conversation between them the day before had never happened.

"I like your outfit," Hailey said as she touched his puffy sleeves.

Veron noticed her own outfit was stunning. She wore a dark crimson gown, which matched her hair with long black elegant sleeves. The dress cascaded to the floor in an elaborate pattern of lace and fabric. What he noticed the most was her plunging neckline. It revealed much more of her chest than he felt he should see, which was accented by a glittering sapphire necklace. He had to force himself to keep his eyes on her face.

"I was here a little early, I guess, so I explored around a bit. I found my way up to the top of the wall. It was pretty neat," Veron said. "By the way, congratulations on your upcoming wedding, Hailey."

Hailey bit the side of her lip and looked down at the floor. "Thanks. Yeah, it should be nice."

That's odd. I would have thought she'd be more excited, he thought. A large amount of powder was on Hailey's cheek, appearing to cover a bruise. "Are you all right?" Veron asked, indicating to her cheek.

"She's fine," Brixton said as she opened her mouth to answer. "She hit it on a doorframe like an idiot."

Hailey looked at Brixton in an odd way. *Embarrassment? Fear? Anger?* Veron thought, unable to read her expression.

"Did you get a drink yet?" Brixton asked Veron.

"No, I hadn't."

Brixton threw back the rest of his glass and traded the empty one for two full glasses of red wine from a server's tray passing by. He handed one to Veron. "For you. Tonight is a big moment. You should be celebrating!"

Brixton lifted his glass in a toast with Veron and Hailey, and all three drank as Veron thought. *I know tonight is a big moment, one way or another, but it doesn't feel like a celebration.*

Baron Rycroft stood at the end of the room and raised his hands to collect everyone's attention. The crowd quieted. "Thank you all for being here tonight as we celebrate the merchants of our wonderful city," the baron said. "I'm personally thankful to all of you for your hard work and . . . for the taxes you bring in." The crowd laughed. "If you'd all find a seat, we'll begin with a feast, which will be followed by the awards ceremony."

Murmurs rose as the crowd resumed talking and began finding seats. The baron turned to engage in conversation with Lord Billings.

That's odd that the Lord of Defense would be here for a merchant banquet, Veron thought.

Veron, Brixton, and Hailey sat at the closest table, with Brixton in the middle. Bread and cheese arrived, but Veron didn't feel hungry. He nibbled on the bread as he stared distractedly across the table.

"Hey, are you there?" Brixton asked, bumping Veron to get his attention.

"I'm sorry? What?"

"I said, what happened to Chloe?" Brixton's tone attempted to be conversational, but it sounded like taunting to Veron.

"Sorry, I . . . My mind was wandering," Veron told him.

"So, you couldn't work up the courage to ask her to come?" Brixton asked. Both Hailey and Brixton watched him, waiting on his answer.

Veron hung his head. "Did you even ask?" Brixton said.

"Oh, I asked. Apparently, she's married."

Brixton laughed out loud. "Married! Oh, Veron, I told you not to mess with her. I can't believe you fell for a married woman. You're such a fool!"

Hailey glared at Brixton as Veron clenched his jaw.

"I'm really sorry, Veron," Hailey said across Brixton's body.

"So, how did *that* happen?" Brixton asked, continuing to laugh. "Did she have a husband hiding in her wardrobe or something?"

"I'd rather not talk about it," Veron said, racking his brain for another subject. "So, where's your father? I figured he'd be here."

Brixton looked around. "He's somewhere. We arrived together. Maybe he'll show up just before the awards." He grabbed a piece of cheese then leaned in close to Veron and spoke softly. "So, what've you decided about our deal?"

This is it—the moment I've been dreading. "I haven't decided yet." *Well, I have decided, but Brixton isn't going to like it. When they announce the award, I'll tell the truth in front of Raynor, the baron, and all the other merchants.* His mind was fixed, but the thought of it made his stomach feel upset. *Brixton will never forgive me.*

The servants brought out a course of roasted pork served over carrots and onions. The hall felt stuffy to Veron. The number of people, food, and noise in the room overwhelmed him, and he began to feel dizzy.

"I'll be back in a bit. I need to stretch my legs," Veron said as he stood abruptly and stumbled off.

Veron followed the winding passageways, not knowing exactly where he wanted to go. Eventually, he found himself back in the yellow room with the large window looking over the courtyard. He gazed outside at the torches lighting up the castle courtyard.

His thoughts turned to Chloe. *Before today, I expected us to fall in love. I pictured us married with kids, and growing old together, but now that's all gone—she's gone. I'm so alone. I wish I had someone I belonged with—someone who would love me back.*

"Veron?" He turned to find Hailey approaching. "Are you okay?" she asked.

Veron angled back to the window. "I'm fine. I just needed some space," he said.

Hailey arrived next to him. "I really am sorry about . . . what's her name?"

"Chloe."

"And I'm sorry about Brix. He can be insensitive at times," Hailey said. Her words were gentle and felt like a warm caress to his aching body.

Veron sighed. "I feel like a fool."

"It sounds like Chloe is the only one who's a fool here."

He laughed softly through his nose and turned back to her. Hailey was beautiful. Her skin was soft and smooth, and her lips were perfectly shaped. Tight curls of dark crimson hair cascaded down the sides of her face like a waterfall.

Veron narrowed his eyes and indicated to the side of her face by a subtle movement of his chin. "Is he hitting you?" he asked.

Hailey took a step back. She was about to protest but hung her head instead. "He gets angry sometimes."

"That's not right. I'm going to say something to him about it," Veron said, his voice growing in strength.

"No! Please don't!" Hailey reached out and grabbed his hand with both of hers. She paused, looking at their hands. Her words were soft and tender. "Not everyone's as kind as you are."

Veron squirmed and gently pulled his hand free. "It's not right."

She took a step closer and rested her hand on his upper arm. Her body pressed up against his, and she looked at him directly in the eyes. "Veron, I'm sure it must be difficult being rejected by a girl. If you ever need to talk with someone, someone who's not going to reject you, you can come to me anytime you like."

Veron started to sweat, and his throat felt dry. He craved distance and looked back out the window to try to create some space.

"Veron . . ."

He turned back to look at her as her hand found the back of his head and her fingers intertwined themselves in his hair. Before he realized what was happening, she pulled his head down gently, and her lips met his. Her kiss was soft but firm at the same time. Her other arm wrapped around his back and pulled him closer. Something inside of him fluttered, and his legs felt weak and tingly. He knew he needed to pull away but was so taken by the moment that he found himself kissing her back. The feeling of acceptance washed away the rejection and betrayal he had wallowed in as Veron wrapped his arms around her.

As they kissed, his mind soon brought him back to reality, and panic crept in. *What am I doing? No. No! NO!*

"I knew it!" shouted a voice filled with fury and disgust.

Veron pushed away, and he and Hailey turned to find Brixton standing in the room. "Brix!" Veron said. "I—I—" Fear covered his shame and embarrassment.

"I knew you two were seeing each other behind my back!"

"Brix, please—" Hailey started.

"Shut up, you!" Brixton yelled before turning to Veron and approaching. "I knew that street-girl love was a farce from the start. You've always had your eye on Hailey. I could tell from the beginning."

"No, I promise I never—"

"First, you steal the attention of my father! And now you steal my future wife!"

"I never intended to do any of that!"

"And you!" Brixton said, focusing on Hailey. "You were trash ever since you were a girl, but I was willing to marry you because I wanted to help you and your family."

Hailey dissolved into tears.

"I was going to give you *everything*! One day, I'll run this city. You could have been by my side, but you had to throw it all away with this . . ." Brixton paused and stared at Veron, spitting the last words out with disgust, ". . . peasant!"

Veron's breath caught. He stared at Brixton with a look of bewilderment. *Does he know? How can he know? Maybe he talked with Mortinson?* he thought.

Brixton glared at him. "Oh, that's right, I found out all about you. You lived on the streets most of your life in filth! The only way you could make anything with your life was to lie, cheat, and steal to get where you are now. I trusted you, Veron! I thought you were my friend, but it was all a lie! When my father finds out how you falsified your sales numbers and lied on your application, he's going to strip you of your license, and you'll rot in prison!"

Veron's mind reeled as he rubbed his head. *This can't be happening! Everything's falling apart.*

Brixton's expression changed. His voice became light and playful, taunting. "Or maybe it'd be better to let Lord Turnbill know about how you *murdered* a highly ranked army officer?"

The statement hit Veron in the gut, and he froze. *How does he know?*

"Captain Charles Mortinson was an upstanding servant of our city. I wonder how the Department of Justice will feel when they find out what you did?"

As if a lightning bolt struck him, the pieces suddenly came together for Veron. His shoulders slumped as he turned to Brixton with sadness in his eyes. "It was you. You had Chloe kidnapped to blackmail me," he said.

Brixton smirked. "Do you know what your weaknesses are, Veron? You care too much about other people and about being honest. I figured you might not go for my three percent plan, so I needed a backup. Mortinson proved valuable in helping me figure out who you really were. He was happy to help play out my idea. The street thugs were a regrettable but necessary addition to the team. It's a pity they were so inept."

Veron rested his hands on his knees as he leaned over. His head spun, and he felt nauseous.

Brixton turned back to Hailey with a look of revulsion and got in her face. His words were slow and deliberate. "Do you like how it feels to betray someone? Why don't we see how you like it on the other side?"

What does he mean? What's he going to do? Veron thought as a wave of fear flooded through him.

Before Veron or Hailey could react, Brixton pulled a knife from his sleeve. Hailey's hand flew to her chest, and her eyes widened in shock as she stepped back. Veron didn't even have a chance to yell before Brixton stabbed the blade deep into his fiancé's stomach.

A brief cry escaped Hailey's lips as she folded over and fell to the ground. Veron stood motionless, paralyzed, looking at Hailey as she lay with the knife sticking out of her. The blood spreading through her dress was barely visible against the crimson fabric.

Brixton ran, but Veron stood frozen, balancing on his weak legs. "Guards! Guards! He killed her! Come quickly!" Brixton's shouts echoed down the hall.

Veron snapped back into the moment. *I didn't do it. The guards can't arrest me.* He kneeled by Hailey's side. *Can they?*

479

Hailey's eyes frantically darted around. She tried to speak but could only sputter blood from her mouth as she gasped for air.

"Hailey, I'm so sorry," was all Veron could think to say.

Metal clanking and loud footsteps sounded up the hall, coming closer. Veron reluctantly got to his feet and backed away, holding Hailey's gaze.

"I'm so sorry," Veron repeated before turning and running down the hall in the opposite direction.

47

The Last Shadow Knight

Shouts and the sound of footsteps followed Veron as he tried to lose his pursuers in the maze of passages. He wanted to find the stairs that led to the wall but got turned around while the soldiers grew closer. Rounding a corner, he ducked behind a tapestry displayed in an alcove, hoping the soldiers didn't look too closely where his feet were visible. A few moments later, they ran by without even hesitating.

Veron breathed a sigh of relief but then realized he wasn't sure where to go. *Both directions now have people searching for me.*

A clash of steel and shouting echoed down the hall, but from his hiding place, he couldn't tell which direction it came from.

What would that be? Who else could be fighting? He came out of his hiding place and cautiously made his way in the direction he had been running.

Not knowing what might be waiting, he peered around the first corner to find nothing but a short, narrow hallway with a single lantern in the middle. When he checked the next corner, he discovered the stairwell he searched for at the end, but emerging from it was a group of soldiers in black and red uniforms.

Black and red uniforms? Who are they? he thought.

Not wanting to face this new group, Veron backpedaled in the other direction. As he peered around the last corner, he jumped back. Raynor Fiero just passed his old hiding place and was heading his way.

No, anyone but him! His breath came quickly. There were no other doors or paths to take to escape. The hallway was barely wide enough for two men to pass each other, much less provide a place to hide. *I wish I could disappear. Darkness!*

Veron ran to the lone lantern, lifted its door, and blew it out. While not completely dark, it was better. Veron braced his feet against the narrow walls and shimmied up as high as he could go. As soon as he got to the top, he froze as the soldiers came around the corner.

I'm not sure who these soldiers are, but Lord Fiero is about to run right into them.

Veron held his breath as the two parties met directly underneath him, oblivious to his presence.

"There you are," Raynor said, approaching the man in front. "You found the gate?"

The man Raynor spoke with was tall and menacing. His hair and beard were black and thick, and he had a scar on the right side of his face. "Yes, unlocked, as you promised. The rest of my men wait just out of sight of the walls," the man said, his resonant voice bouncing off the walls.

Who is that? Veron thought. *What are they talking about?* Veron's arms ached as he pushed with all his strength to remain wedged between the walls. His foot began to slide.

Raynor nodded. "Everyone is ready in the banquet hall."

"Good," the man said. "The baron?"

"Yes, he's there. Remember our agreement though."

"You'll be in charge, but *only* under my authority."

"Of course, Your Majesty," Raynor said.

Your Majesty? Who is this man? I don't think King Wesley is that tall. Veron's foot slipped again. *Just hold on a bit longer!*

Raynor continued, "Once the baron is gone, the army will follow Billings, and he's with us."

Drops of sweat dripped down Veron's face as he strained to keep his feet from moving. He gritted his teeth. His legs shook from the effort.

The man held up his finger in front of Raynor's face. "And if they *don't* follow, they will die."

"It won't be a problem."

The soldiers followed Raynor back down the hall he came from. Veron counted twenty-five in total. After the last one disappeared around the corner, Veron slid his way down the wall, relieved to be able to move his legs. He peered around the edge where they went. In the better light, he could see the uniform of the soldier in the rear more clearly. Across his back was an emblem of two swords crossing above a bear—the symbol of Norshewa.

The King . . . of Norshewa! Veron's blood felt like ice, and his stomach turned as bumps formed along his arms. He knew who the tall man with black hair was—the man he'd been waiting on for years—his destiny. Edmund Bale. *But I'm not ready to face him yet! I still have so much to learn! This can't be the time yet.* Fear battled anger inside of him, growing steadily. *Bale must be stopped. Who knows what he'll do to Karad? He killed my father.* Veron pictured his father, William, lying on the floor, riddled with arrows as he bled to death.

I know he needs to be stopped. I know I'm the one to do it, but I can't yet. I can't take on twenty-five soldiers. If I go after him, all that will happen is for me to get killed . . . just like the prophecy said. He paled. Veron turned and looked in the other direction down the hallway. Escape should be easy. He could get back to the market, take what money he could, and get out of the city. *Maybe my destiny is to confront Bale later when I'm better trained and ready to face him?*

Veron longed to be selfless. He wanted to stand up to him, fight against evil, and fulfill his destiny. Instead, he ran along the passage toward the wall, and away from Bale.

Bale entered the banquet hall ahead of his men. The tables were filled with people eating and talking, oblivious as to what was about to happen. Right away, he spotted Gareth Billings, who stood with a cane and gave him a solemn nod as he entered.

The man sitting next to him must be the baron, Bale thought.

As Bale's soldiers entered the room, conversations hushed, and everyone turned to stare.

Baron Rycroft stood, using his hand on the table to support his hefty body. His face was red from the intrusion. "Who are you? What is this?" he asked.

Bale's soldiers fanned around the room, and a murmur began. Without breaking stride, Bale walked to the baron, took a dagger from the sheath on his hip, and stabbed him through the neck. Rycroft flailed his arms and grabbed at his neck. Making no sound, he crumpled to the floor, dead.

Chaos erupted in the room. Women screamed. Chairs flipped over as people jumped to their feet. Shouting began in unison. Most tried to flee through one of the four doorways while some attempted to fight. The fighters didn't last long. When the dust settled, eight Karad merchants lay dead or dying on the floor.

Bale glared at Raynor as he entered the room after the people were gone. *Coward! He wants to align with me but is afraid of anyone knowing.* "Gareth, Raynor, assemble your men," Bale said. "I'd like to address them and have them swear allegiance as soon as possible."

Both men gave quick bows and left the room.

Bale turned to another of his soldiers. "Raise the signal to Ryker. Have him bring in two battalions."

"Yes, Your Majesty," the soldier said as he bowed quickly before hurrying to the door.

Suddenly, the soldier stopped mid-way across the hall. Bale followed his gaze to see a boy who couldn't be more than twenty years old standing in the doorway. He had a defiant look on his face as if he didn't plan to let anyone pass through the corridor. The boy held a sword over his head, and he looked like he intended to use it.

"Bale!" Veron yelled. "You will not take this city!"

He stood with a sword pointed toward the Norshewan ruler. Veron knew what he needed to do. He had a destiny to fulfill, and it couldn't wait—the people of Karad needed him, even if it cost him his life. He had picked up a sword from a fallen soldier as he made his way back through the castle to encounter his fate.

Bale looked at him curiously. "I'm sorry, but I'm not sure what you expect to do about it," he said in a thick Norshewan accent while nodding to his soldiers.

Dozens of soldiers converged on him, but Veron felt no fear. What he felt was the warm tingling sensation of the origine. The core of his body shuddered from the power as he pulled from his energy and met the soldiers head-on. Unlike the night before, when he used up the origine without control, he used only what he needed. His movements and strength were heightened, but only just enough.

Two soldiers' weapons flew from their hands as Veron knocked them away with a swift attack. Repeating the motion, he struck them both down with a blow to their chests. On his right, he jabbed an unsuspecting soldier in the stomach before he had a chance to react. Another was almost on top of him. He blocked the overhead strike with his sword and kicked out with his foot. The soldier flew across the room and fell unconscious after hitting the stone wall.

I didn't think I generated that much power. I guess I should conserve more, Veron thought.

He ducked under another slow-motion swing at his head then took out the soldier with a slice to the neck. Whirling around, Veron paled to find at least ten soldiers had him trapped from all sides with their swords drawn. Pushing as hard as he could, he leaped off the ground and flipped backward as he sailed over the soldiers below.

Veron struck down two as he landed then parried the attack of the next closest one. After knocking the soldier's sword out of the way, Veron grabbed him by the uniform and threw him at those on his other side. Soldiers flew from the impact. Veron dispatched several more with quick strikes one after another. He moved so quickly that the soldiers didn't even have a chance to swing at him, much less block his lightning-fast attacks. The tang of blood and sweat pervaded the air as the bodies piled around him.

"Stop him!" Bale shouted in a thick, unnatural sounding voice.

Veron's energy started to fade, and he began to worry. *I haven't done this enough to know how far is too far. I just need to hold on a little longer. If my energy gives out now, anyone remaining will kill me.* Veron struck another soldier down who tried to impale him with a spear, knocking it to the side before running the man through with his sword.

Four soldiers remained, circling him. Veron leaped into the air and spun, pulling his sword through the air in an arc with all of his strength. In one continuous motion, he removed the heads of all four soldiers before he landed hard on the stone floor, the impact echoing throughout the hall as the bodies fell.

Veron stopped. Terror flooded through him as he came to a horrifying realization. The origine was gone. His well was dry as he tried desperately to drink more. Around him lay the bodies of dead or incapacitated soldiers, but the one person he most needed his energy to face was the one person who remained.

I failed. I can't defeat him. Veron wanted to yell. He willed his body to fly with fury and strike him down, but he wasn't able. He pictured his father pierced by arrows and struck down by a sword. He tried to think through what to do, but he couldn't. His mind wouldn't work. The origine was empty, but he refused to let go of his hold on it. If he did, he would die.

He stood upright, his insides straining from the effort as he fought to keep his body from shaking. He stared coldly in front of him at the only other person moving in the room—Edmund Bale.

Bale's face was twisted in confusion. He held his sword, but it visibly shook as he stood hesitantly with one foot a half-step back. "But . . . the Shadow Knights were all dead," Bale said, barely above a whisper. "I—I had them killed. They were prophesied to defeat me, so I had them killed—you were all dead!" Bale's voice rose with agitation. He stared wildly at his sword before turning back to Veron. "Who are you?"

I only have one hope left. Veron steeled himself for his last act, drawing every ounce of energy he had left. "I am Veron Stormbridge," he said in a clear voice, moving into dragon stance. His face was like a stone, but everything in his body struggled with desperation. "I am the last shadow knight, and I have come to kill you."

Bale's face turned pale. His body swayed between advancing and retreating as the two locked eyes. His arm shook as he lowered his sword and took a step backward. One step became two, and soon, Bale turned and ran away through the closest doorway.

I did it! I stopped him! Relief flooded Veron as he released his hold on the expended origine and fell to the floor. His body convulsed, and he gasped for air. He rolled on the ground, trying to find relief, but his body hurt from exhaustion. He didn't even care that he lay in a pool of blood from the dozens of soldiers he just defeated.

"There he is!" someone yelled. The voice sounded distant and fuzzy.

Veron tried to look around, but the room spun. He was about to pass out.

"What happened here?" a cloudy voice said.

"Who are these soldiers?" said another. "They look Norshewan!"

Strong arms lifted Veron. His eyes were blurry and could barely make out Karad uniforms around him. *Bale! He went that way! You can catch him if you run!*

He wanted them to go after Bale but didn't have the strength to voice his thoughts or even point in the direction. His hazy mind jolted in surprise as chains attached to his wrists. Finally getting his eyes to focus, his heart sank. Brixton's face glared at him with narrowed eyes.

I forgot all about Brixton, he thought just before passing out.

48

Waking

"Guys, she's waking!"

The indistinct voice sounded muddled. Shuffling noises echoed vaguely in Chelci's head. She slowly opened her eyes and blinked away the fatigue to find six faces and one dog staring at her.

"Are you okay?" Aleks asked. "What happened?"

"What was it?" Finley added.

"How'd you get away?" asked Royce.

Aleks and Finley sat to either side of her bed. Russell stood at the foot while Royce and Tate stood by the door and Charlie rested his chin on her arm. They all leaned in eagerly, wanting answers.

"Out! Out! All of you!" Nevi told them as she pushed her way into the crowded room. "Give her room to breathe!" She shooed the younger boys out the door, but they didn't go far. All four of them peeked their heads around the doorway.

Chelci pushed her body to sit up, but the pain brought a grimace to her face. "Bensen?" she asked. "How is he? Is he going to live?"

Russell frowned. "We don't know for sure. He's alive, but he hasn't woken. He lost a lot of blood, and we had to take his leg," he replied.

Chelci let out a deep sigh. *At least he's still alive.*

"How are you feeling, Elise?" Nevi asked. "Are you in pain? You've been out for over a day."

She chuckled. *Pain . . . that's an understatement.* She nodded her head.

Chelci looked at her left side, covered in a bandage. A dull ache covered her entire body, but even the small movement of looking sent a sharp stab of agony through her side. She motioned with her hand to the bandaged area and swallowed hard. "Here's the worst. I think I'll live though."

Appearing content with the response, Nevi looked to Russell. "Elise," he said, "what was it that attacked you?"

Teeth dripping with blood and long sharp claws flashed into Chelci's mind. She remembered the foul odor and the sound of its growl. She shivered. Everyone in the room leaned forward in anticipation.

"It was a valcor," she said.

"No way!" Finley yelled.

Tate hit Royce on the chest. "I told you!"

"Wow!" Aleks added.

Russell motioned for the others to settle down. "Tell us what happened," he said to her.

"It killed the guards, Lucian and the others. I guess it was coming back for Lucian's body when it found us." Chelci looked at Tate and considered what to say about him running away. He hung his head and avoided looking at her. "It attacked Bensen and carried him off into the woods, so I ran after them."

"You *ran* into the woods after it!" Aleks said.

"I found them up in a molopyr tree and climbed after them. It had a sort of nest near the top, which was where the other guards' bodies were—what was left of them. I fought off the valcor and knocked it out of the tree. Then I brought Bensen down and carried him back as far as I could go."

"Wait? What! You *fought* it off?" Aleks asked.

Chelci looked at him, then around at the others. "Yeah, I stabbed it through the top of its mouth."

"Whoa!" Royce said.

"Awesome!" added Finley.

Chelci continued, "It fell from nearly the top of the tree. It probably broke some bones, but it didn't die—at least not right away. I saw it limp off. Then I lowered Bensen by his rope and dragged him as far as I could until I passed out."

"That's when we heard your bell," Russell said. "Elise, what you did was incredibly brave. You went above and beyond what anyone would ever have asked or expected of you."

"Foolish is what it was!" Nevi said, shaking her head. "I can't believe you—running after monsters in the dark. I don't want to hear any more of that from you, young lady." She turned to the boys. "I think there's been enough excitement for now. All of you need to leave, to let her get some rest."

The group shuffled out, wishing her to get better soon, and promising to be back to check on "the valcor slayer" soon. Nevi gave her some water, changed the bandage, and then left her alone.

Chelci lay in bed and stared up at the ceiling. *I'm glad to be alive. I can barely believe what happened. I'm pretty sure I have an excellent chance to be chosen for the village guard now, but I don't know if I want that anymore. Nevi and Russell feel like family, but . . . I miss my real family.*

* * *

Veron awoke to a stiff, cold floor, unsure of where he was or what had happened. He wrestled through the groggy feeling. His body hurt as he got up and found his arms and feet restrained by manacles and attached to the wall.

"Hello?" he yelled into the darkness, the sound echoing uselessly off the walls.

The stench of death and disease surrounded him in his cell of smooth, damp stone. The dank air rested heavily on his tongue as he breathed. The room's only door was against the far wall, which contained a small window with bars. Veron tried to get close enough to see out, but the chains restrained him just shy of it. He leaned forward, barely able to see out the bars.

"Hello? Is anyone there!" he shouted.

The only sound he heard in return was a dripping noise coming from somewhere unseen.

This must be the prison underneath the castle. He'd heard plenty about it—the torture that occurred, the people who died. In person, it was even worse than he imagined. *Why am I here? For murdering Hailey—which I didn't do? Maybe for lying when I started the market? Perhaps Bale has taken over, and they imprisoned me for how many of his men I killed?*

Veron still wore his clothes from earlier. The dried blood and grime covered much of the new fabric. *How can I get out of this? The origine! Maybe that can give me the strength to break the chains?* He cleared his mind and tried to tap into it—nothing.

Veron focused harder, doing the same things he'd done before, but nothing was there—no warm tingling sensation or well of energy to draw from. His frustration grew, making it tougher to concentrate.

Why isn't it working? He groaned in exasperation.

After several minutes of unsuccessful attempts, he gave up and sat back down on the ground, breathing heavily. The Shadow Knights medallion clung to his chest underneath his clothes. Its presence was heartening to him in his dire situation, reminding him of his worth and that he was destined for something great—the words Artimus spoke over him years ago.

Veron jolted awake at the clang of a heavy metal door somewhere outside of his cell. *I must have fallen asleep again.* He jumped up and ran to the cell door. "Hello? Please, I didn't do it! It was Brixton Fiero! He was jealous and killed Hailey Billings, then claimed it was me! Hello?"

Footsteps approached. Veron's face strained toward the bars, trying to see, but he shrank back when he recognized his visitor. Brixton.

"It was Brixton Fiero, was it?" he sneered. Veron didn't speak, and Brixton shook his head. "I accepted you as a friend. I gave you a chance. I tried to make you rich, and what did you do? You rejected my help and stabbed me in the back!"

"I didn't do it, I swear! There was never anything between Hailey and me. She came onto me out of nowhere. I didn't want her to kiss me. She . . . just *did,* and I couldn't stop her!" Veron said.

"Yeah, it looked like you were fighting really hard to stop her when I saw you."

He's right. I didn't try to stop her. "Brix . . . I'm sorry. I'm sorry about Hailey and your father's attention and lying to you about who I was. But my friendship was real, and I promise you there was nothing between Hailey and me. When you saw us, *she* kissed me. I—" Veron paused, trying to find the right words. "I know I should have stopped it immediately, but I was too surprised. I never did anything purposely to get her attention."

Brixton stared at him for a long moment and scratched his chin. "You're probably right."

Veron's hopes started to lift. *Maybe I'll be able to get out of this!*

"But it doesn't matter now," Brixton added.

Veron pulled at the chains, snapping them tight. His eyes were wide as he spoke, "What do you mean? Of course, it matters! I don't need to be here! I was going to accept the award! You and I were both going to get rich! Yes, I used to live on the streets. I admit I misled you when I started the market, but I've worked hard! Now, I own a great market that's thriving, and—"

"You *used* to own a market," Brixton said as he pulled a document from his pocket and waved it in the air. "You signed the license over to me yesterday."

Veron's mind reeled as he stared at the paper in Brixton's hands. "What?"

"Yes, apparently, after you killed my fiancé, you signed the market license over to me as a form of restitution. It was the least you could do."

Veron bent forward. He felt like he'd been kicked in the stomach and all the wind was knocked out of him. *How could he do this to me?* He stared at Brixton, hoping he would admit it was all some cruel joke. "Bale!" Veron yelled suddenly. "Did you know what's going on with Bale? He's trying to take over Karad and all of Felting!"

Brixton's gaze drifted away toward the floor.

"He killed the baron, and your father let him in!" Veron strained as he said the words.

Brixton didn't react as he remained silent, and Veron's accusation echoed uselessly through the space.

I don't believe it. "You knew? You knew your father was going to betray the city?"

Brixton straightened and spoke down his nose at Veron. "My father is now the baron of Karad after the death of Rycroft. King Wesley decreed it this morning after learning how my father and Lord Billings stopped the Norshewan king and ran him off. Under

494

my father's leadership, this city will prosper and thrive."

Veron shook his head in despair. *I've said everything I can think of, but he's not convinced,* he thought. The two stood in silence.

"No, I didn't know . . ." Brixton said, his voice softer, ". . . initially . . . about my father and Bale. I found out after the banquet." He shuffled his feet as he spoke.

"Please, Brix, let me go. I haven't done anything," Veron said.

Brixton nodded but didn't make eye contact. He leaned his head against the door as he held onto the bars. "I—" he stopped and exhaled. "I know you haven't done anything . . . but I can't let you go. I'm sorry."

Veron's body slumped as his gaze drifted to the floor. "What happened to Bale?"

"No one's seen him. All his men in the castle died, but no one knows where he went." Brixton looked at Veron. "Do you know what happened in that room?"

Veron swallowed as he returned the gaze and shook his head. *If anyone finds out what I can do, I'll be in even more trouble.* "They were dead when I got there."

Appearing to accept the answer, Brixton turned and started walking away.

"Brix! No! Don't leave me here!"

He stopped and turned halfway to Veron. "Out of respect for our friendship, I won't have you killed." He made as if to say something else but stopped, and after a pause, he left.

Veron waited at the door to see if someone else was coming or if something would happen, but all he discovered was silence. He returned to the end of the room and sat down on the cold floor. Staring at the chains holding him, his body began to tremble.

What are Morgan and the others going to think? Will they be okay? How did all of this happen? Tears fell down his cheeks. *Brixton betrayed me. I lost the market. The origine isn't working anymore. And now, I'm in chains.* Everything he had built and gained was lost. Veron curled up on the damp stones, weeping as his body shook. His cries echoed through the prison, but no one came to rescue him.

49

Graduation

helci walked along the village street slowly as Nevi held her arm. She didn't need the physical support, but it felt good knowing she was there. It had been a week since the night of the valcor attack, and her healing was progressing well.

Bensen had woken two days after the attack. They decided he was going to live but expected his recovery to take a while. Russell canceled the final week of Academy training out of respect for Bensen and Chelci's healing and the guards they lost. After a week of rest, it was time to gather for the village guard selection ceremony.

"No matter what happens today, I want you to know that I'm proud of you," Nevi said.

"Thank you, Nevi. I know you are," Chelci replied.

Since her favorite vest was torn from the night with the valcor, Chelci had to wear a different outfit—a light green dress Nevi had made for her. The feeling of a dress, which she had not worn in years, seemed foreign, yet familiar. It reminded her of home.

Chelci was the last to arrive at the training hall, where rows of chairs and a platform sat outside on the patio. Candidates, their families, existing guardsmen, and village leaders filled most of the seats. When she stepped through the doorway to the patio, the entire crowd stood and applauded. She blushed and waved timidly, finding a seat as the others settled and Russell walked to the platform.

"Today we conclude another village guard training class at the Academy," Russell said. "Twelve candidates started, but only seven remain after the grueling two years of hard work. Only a few nights ago, we were reminded of the danger we face in this job. I call on you to remember the service and sacrifice of the three men who gave their lives. Lucian Whitehurst, Tomas Maribold, and Lachlan Hornbert. May we all honor them with our memory."

The crowd was silent. Birds sang in the trees around them, and a light breeze blew. Several people cried.

After a moment, he continued. "The class we conclude today was exceptional. They worked hard from the beginning, pushing past physical and emotional limits to emerge stronger on the other side. We selected three candidates from this group to join our ranks and become part of the village guard."

A low murmur ran through the crowd at the mention of the high number.

"Our first selection showed incredible promise from day one. He brought his best effort every day, which continually kept him at the top of the class. His sword fighting skills were unmatched, and his teamwork and encouragement to others were worth emulating. Our first selection is Aleksander Bellingsworth."

Chelci squealed in excitement and gingerly stood to her feet along with the rest of the crowd. Aleks walked to the platform and shook Russell's hand as he handed him a brand new, folded village guard uniform. Aleks beamed as he faced the crowd and acknowledged their applause with a wave.

Aleks stood to the side as Russell continued. "Secondly, we have a young man who excelled all-around in most every category. He distinguished himself by his skill and strength. He also showed he could learn and adapt, using his time in the Academy to grow both his character and ability. Our second selection is Royce Black."

Chelci applauded. *I have to admit he's come a long way.* Royce reached the platform, accepted his uniform, and stood with Aleks. He didn't smile—as he rarely did.

"For our last selection, I'll turn over the stage to my assistant." Russell gestured to his right.

Chelci's eyebrows lifted as Bensen made his way to the stage using a pair of crutches and two men at his side to help. Bandages still wrapped his right leg, which had been cut off at mid-thigh, but he looked stronger than she expected. The crowd buzzed. Someone placed a stool for him to sit on.

As he sat, Bensen spoke in a clear voice. "Our third and final selection for this class is a surprising one. An underdog from day one, they had to fight for everything they earned, which included the respect of both their instructors and their fellow candidates. Through tireless effort and never giving up, they showed what it truly meant to excel—besting those who were bigger, stronger, and faster through hard work and perseverance.

"When I faced down the most fearsome enemy I'd ever encountered, only one candidate stood by my side—only one person came to rescue me. In the face of certain death, they thought nothing of self-preservation . . . but they survived. No one exemplifies what it means to be part of a team better, and there is no one I'd rather serve next to in the guard. For our last selection, I'm honored to recognize . . . Elise Barton."

Chelci's eyes watered, but she wiped the tears back. She blushed but cherished the attention at the same time. All around her stood a crowd of people, cheering and clapping. Even the remaining Furies—Gael and Tate—applauded wildly from the back row. Chelci made her way to the platform where Bensen and Russell waited on her with smiles on their faces. She held Bensen's hand.

"Thank you for your kind words," she said.

"No, thank *you* for not giving up on me," Bensen replied.

Chelci turned to Russell, who beamed. He handed her the uniform without saying anything and rested his hand on her shoulder. He was a man of few words, and that day was no exception.

She went down the line and shook Royce's hand. "I'm glad you made it," he said with a smirk. "You deserve it."

Aleks hugged her. "Third pick, huh? Maybe next time you can work on that first or second spot." His eyes twinkled as he shot her a crooked grin. She punched him playfully on the shoulder before standing at the end of the line.

Chelci looked back at the crowd who stood and applauded for all three. Never in her life had she felt so accomplished. As she watched the faces, tears started to fall down her cheeks. She didn't try to stop them anymore, and she didn't wipe them away. Chelci was afraid that if she wiped them away, her determination would disappear along with them. They were tears of sadness and loss—not loss of the guardsmen who died, but of her aspirations. After fighting and pushing herself for years, she had made it. She cried because it wasn't her objective anymore. She no longer wanted to be a guardsman.

It's time to go home, she thought.

That night after dinner, Chelci stood on the porch, leaning against the wooden rail. *Somewhere out there is a valcor—if it's still alive.* She wasn't afraid but would avoid going into the woods alone at night for a while.

Chelci tried to build up her courage all day to talk with Russell and Nevi, but she kept making excuses. She rehearsed the words over and over in her mind.

I don't want them to be mad, but I don't think they'll understand.

"Elise, there you are," Nevi said as she and Russell came outside to sit.

Well, I guess this is my time. Chelci swallowed hard as she turned to face them. She looked at each in the eye before speaking. Her heart beat fast. "My name isn't Elise. It's Chelci Marlow."

Russell and Nevi looked at each other. Chelci expected to see shock or hurt on their faces—at least some level of confusion—but instead, they smiled.

"Chelci's a beautiful name. I love it," Nevi said. "We knew it wasn't Elise."

Chelci stared with her head tilted. "What? How'd you know?" she asked.

"When you arrived here, it was obvious you were hiding something. You were running from something, somewhere. It must have been pretty bad to make you so desperate to flee on your own as a child with little food and no protection."

"We didn't know *who* you were," Russell added, "but we assumed Elise was a made-up name to leave behind whatever you ran from."

"We could tell you needed help, so we decided to accept you as you were and take care of you the best we could," Nevi said.

Chelci didn't know how to respond. Her carefully planned speech was ruined. "Thank you for caring for me. I'd never have made it without you. I grew up in Felting. My father is Darcius Marlow, High Lord of Commerce for Feldor."

Nevi's eyes widened. "I figured you came from a well-to-do family, but I had no idea!"

"My father was a kind man, but the cruelty of my mother, Luciana, overshadowed him. She hurt me—in many ways. She had a clear idea of who she wanted me to be, and if my wishes didn't conform to it, it wasn't acceptable. When I couldn't take it anymore, I ran

501

away. Saying it out loud makes me sound like a spoiled little girl, but I felt like who I was in my soul was being crushed. I was trapped and suffocating, like I was dying a slow death at my young age. I had to leave."

Chelci felt as if a weight lifted off of her. She had carried the burden of her childhood memories around for years, and being able to share them was freeing.

"I'm so sorry," Nevi said, rising from her chair to stand closer to Chelci.

"When you took me in, you were everything my mother wasn't. Life here in Nasco was everything my old life wasn't. It was filled with promise. I was able to hope again. I felt free. These six years have been the greatest of my life." Chelci looked to the ground, afraid to speak any more, but she had to. Her voice shook. "But now, I need to go home."

Again, she looked up, expecting to see shock, hurt, or confusion, but they only looked at each other, like before, and nodded.

"We know, dear," Nevi said.

"What! You couldn't have known! How?"

Nevi glanced at Russell before turning back to Chelci and smiling. "Have you ever had a Dream before?"

Chelci gasped and covered her chest with her hand. "No . . . did you have one?"

Nevi nodded. "Do you remember what I told you many years ago about Madeline, our daughter, and how she died?"

"Yes."

"My Dream showed me way back on the night after Madeline's disappearance, when Russell went into the woods to search for her. I Dreamed that he found her and brought her home." Nevi looked at Russell. "Wolves had attacked her, and he rescued her. We celebrated our daughter's return, but she was different. She left us a young girl and returned a warrior, always wanting to fight. Later in the Dream, she killed a valcor in the woods, and finally, she told us she was glad to have been with us, but it was time for her to leave."

A crease formed between Chelci's eyebrows. "I don't understand. Is your daughter supposed to come back?"

Nevi smiled as she rested her hand on Chelci's arm. "You are the girl from the Dream." Chelci's eyes widened. "I had that Dream six years ago, the *night before* you arrived here in Russell's arms."

Chelci's jaw dropped.

"From the day you arrived, rescued after being attacked by wolves, we knew we only had you for a while. We knew you were going to learn to be a warrior, one way or another. Russell tried to prevent it but realized he couldn't stop the inevitable. We decided to do everything we could to equip you as best as possible with the time we had. The valcor part seemed like a stretch, but after you lived through that, we knew you'd be leaving soon."

"But the village guard . . ." Chelci said. "I feel bad about abandoning them—"

"You don't worry about that, dear. They'll be fine," Nevi said as she smiled at Russell, who nodded.

"I'm so sorry. You've both been so good to me. There's no way I can thank you enough for everything you've done."

"So, tell me," Nevi said, "what drives you to want to go home after all these years?"

Chelci exhaled as she gathered her thoughts. "I ran away because I was afraid. I wasn't able to stand up for myself, and I couldn't bear the path my life was heading down. I felt that if I let my mother control me, she'd win. But now I'm a different person, and I realize that if I fail to face my fears and stay in hiding, I'm letting her control me in a different way. I want a chance to do it right. I want to be myself, but I don't want to give up hope that I can do it within the family I was born into."

"I understand." Nevi looked to her husband, who had been quiet most of the conversation. "Russell, don't you have anything to say?"

He looked at his wife, then back at Chelci. He sat quietly for a moment while moisture glistened at the corners of his eyes. He lowered his chin, fighting back his emotions as tears fell freely. "I'm just gonna miss you," he whispered.

"Oh, honey, I love you," Nevi said as she leaned over to kiss him on the cheek.

Chelci leaned in and wrapped them both up in her arms while all three of them cried. She cherished the moment. She loved them more than anything and was going to miss them.

50

Destination Unknown

Veron had no idea how long he stayed in the cell. It was at least a few days—possibly a week or more. Someone occasionally came to give him food and water. He tried to get answers from them, but they never spoke.

One day, three soldiers entered his cell. Veron backed up as two of them grabbed him by the upper arms, and the other replaced the chains holding his legs with a new set that allowed him to move.

"What are you doing? Where are you taking me?" Veron asked.

Without responding, they escorted him out of the cell and up two flights of stairs. Veron shuffled his way through several passageways before emerging into a stone courtyard at night. The soldiers walked him up to what looked like a carriage hitched to horses with no windows.

Veron struggled against the chains that held him, trying to tap into the origine, but he felt nothing. He kicked against the carriage as the men attempted to wrestle him into it. His resistance earned him a hit with a club on the back of his skull, searing his head with pain. He landed roughly on the floor of the carriage after the soldiers tossed him in. The door closed behind him, and the carriage started moving, jostling back and forth as his head throbbed.

Inside, the vehicle was completely dark. Veron had no way to measure the time, but it was many hours. He slept some, but the irregular and bumpy movement made it difficult. Light eventually crept through the cracks in the door, but they continued.

Finally, the carriage came to a halt, and the door opened. Veron covered his eyes to the harsh light as he exited into a small dirt courtyard with a closed gate. The building in front of him was a disordered structure of crumbling stone. The roof slanted, and most of the windows had rotted away.

Two men met him as he came out of the carriage. The older of the men was dirty and gaunt with crooked teeth. The other, a strong man who carried a sword, looked to be Morgan's age. An older woman exited the building to join them.

They removed his manacles but left the clasp on his left leg. Veron's heart sank as he noticed the metal ring that remained. *I know what that means.*

Inside the building, he had to disrobe and was forced to bathe. Worried about losing his medallion, he secretly removed it along with the key to Artimus' chest when he took off his shirt and placed it in the middle of his dirty clothes. Veron tried to cover himself awkwardly while the woman scrubbed his body in a tub with a coarse brush. The bristles hurt and left his skin red and irritated.

After cleaning, his captors gave him new undergarments and a plain gray shirt and pants to wear. Once Veron dressed, the older man pulled out a metal rod from some coals. "Pull up your shirt," he said.

What's he gonna do with that? Veron thought.

As Veron hesitated, the large man who had stood nearby stepped forward and pulled his sword halfway out of the sheath.

Maybe the origine will work now? I could grab that sword, kill them both, and escape before anyone knew what was happening. Veron tried to tap into it, but like before, it didn't work. He tried to clear his mind, but nothing happened. Sweat formed on his forehead, and he breathed heavily. *What am I doing wrong?*

Veron lifted his shirt, and the man pressed the metal against his side. Searing pain made his skin feel like it was on fire as his flesh sizzled. He doubled over in agony, trying to stifle a scream. Taking quick breaths, he groaned through his gritted teeth. Before the old man wrapped a bandage over the red area, Veron noticed the marking "24521."

I'm officially a slave, he thought. Veron felt numb. The mark merely confirmed what he'd been expecting.

Finished with their work, the men ushered him back into the same carriage he came in on.

"Where are we going? What are you doing with me?" Veron asked as the doors closed behind them.

The carriage rumbled through the streets, but the trip was much shorter, taking only ten minutes or so. When Veron exited again, he stood in front of an enormous building on an elaborate stone circular drive with a fountain in the middle. The building was three stories high and made of polished stone to where the exterior almost looked like flowing water rather than roughly hewn blocks. The steps leading up to the front door were split on the right and left by another smaller fountain in the middle. The purple and orange light from the setting sun gave the building a glowing look as if it were on fire.

A petite old lady in a black dress with white lace promptly walked out to meet them from the side of the house, her lively steps making up for her short stride. Her look was fierce with her chin held up proudly and her back straight.

After a cursory inspection of Veron, she handed a bag to the carriage driver and received an envelope in return.

"This way! This way!" she said to Veron, waving her hand for him to follow.

Veron glanced at the man with the sword, who kept his hand on the hilt as he stared Veron down. *What if I ran as fast as I could? I bet I could get away.* His stomach turned at the thought as he looked at the man's sword. *Something tells me it wouldn't end well.*

Reluctantly, he turned from the two men who delivered him and followed the lady around the side of the house through a smaller entrance at the basement level.

Upon entering the house, Veron discovered an enormous kitchen that looked large enough to feed an army. Several people ran back and forth, washing and cleaning while others moved things in and out of a nearby storage room. The lady motioned for him to follow her through the kitchen to a quieter place on the opposite side, where they stopped.

"My name is Tessa, and I am the house steward here. You will do what I say—always. Do you understand?" she said, glaring at Veron.

Although Tessa looked old and barely came up to the height of his shoulders, he sensed she was not one to mess with. Veron nodded.

"If you work hard and do what you're told, in time, you may find yourself with more freedom and living a life of comfort. If you give us trouble, you'll find trouble. Which path you travel on will be up to you."

Footsteps sounded on a spiral staircase behind Tessa just before a tall lady with sharp features emerged at the bottom. The dark gray dress she wore hugged her thin body, and a tightly woven bun of brown hair rested on the back of her head. The deep frown lines at the edges of her mouth indicated her scowl was likely a permanent expression.

"Lady Luciana!" Tessa said, bowing.

"This is the new one?" the woman asked.

"Yes, my lady."

The tall woman turned to address Veron. "My name is Luciana Marlow. You may call me nothing because you won't speak to me. You're fortunate enough to be in the service of one of the high lords of the kingdom of Feldor, so remember that things could be much worse. We have no interest in where you came from or why you're here. Your previous life is dead."

Veron swallowed hard and stared back at Luciana, refusing to avert his eyes from hers. "I haven't done anything wrong. I shouldn't be here," he said.

Luciana tilted her head as if amused and walked up to him. She was so close that Veron could feel the warmth of her breath and smell the scent of lilacs and peppermint. Suddenly, his face exploded with pain as she struck his cheek with a short whip he hadn't seen. Veron held his face as he shrank against the wall.

Luciana extended her hand to Tessa, who gave her the envelope. "Veron Stormbridge," she said in a slow, deliberate voice as she opened the envelope and reviewed the paper. "You're here to be a servant in our household."

"I was forced here against my will. Doesn't that make me a slave?" Veron asked with his teeth clenched.

Luciana lifted her hand with the whip and raised her eyebrows, causing Veron to shrink back again. "We don't employ slaves, but we do own the rights to your labor—purchased from the Department of Justice. According to them, you've lost your rights, so don't complain to me about it."

Veron peered at Luciana intently. "How will I be treated? Will I be paid? Am I free to come and go as I please?"

The edge of her mouth curled in a crooked grin. "How we treat you will depend on how you behave. You'll be paid in food, shelter, and clothing for your work, and you won't be restrained. You're free to come and go as you please."

Really? Veron thought. *As soon as I have the chance, I'm out of here. I can find my way back to Karad, meet up with Morgan, and figure something out. This may not be so bad . . . but how can it be that easy? Something doesn't add up.*

"Of course if you do abandon your post, or cause trouble while you're here"—she got back in his face and spoke softly in a low voice—"or displease me in any way . . . as the owner of your labor rights, I can invoke your collateral."

Veron's legs felt weak, and he paled at the mention of the word, remembering what Morgan told him years ago.

Luciana looked back at the paper she held. "I believe . . . Morgan Fenster, Chloe Washburn, and Danyel Barton will be very disappointed if you decide to cause trouble. It'd be a shame if something bad were to happen to them."

Veron held his breath from the shock of hearing their names. *No, she wouldn't dare do anything to them!* A sigh escaped his lips as he realized the trap that held him. For a moment, he wished to be back on the floor of the prison. Somehow, being curled up and alone had felt safer. He started to hang his head but caught himself. *No. I'm not going to let all of this defeat me. I've faced worse obstacles than this woman before.* His legs grew in strength as he thought through all he had done.

He used to be starving, living on the streets, and wearing rags, and yet he built one of the greatest markets in Karad from the ground up in under two years. He became a shadow knight and made Edmund Bale shake in his boots and run. He could build another market. He could figure out the origine again. He wasn't sure how he would get out of his situation without endangering Morgan and the others, but he would figure it out. *I know things will turn around soon, and for now, I can be the best at whatever awaits me here.*

Veron held his head up and stared back at Luciana. She was no longer a frightening master bent on subduing him. To him, she was a scared woman, trying to compensate for her shortcomings. A smirk crossed his face as he stood tall.

"What are you smiling about?" Luciana adjusted her stance and glanced at Tessa.

Veron shook his head, maintaining his wry grin. "You won't get any trouble from me. I'm going to be the best servant you've ever had."

51

A Fresh Start

Once she had told Russell and Nevi of her decision to leave, Chelci had to say goodbye to her friends. Finley was sad she was going, but the feeling didn't last long since he soon found out he got her spot on the village guard. Aleks was the toughest to leave. His friendship and encouragement over the years helped keep her going. As a parting gift, he gave her a new sword. It was sized and shaped like her practice one but made of real steel and had a sharp blade.

After a few days, when her side healed well enough, Russell saddled up two horses to ride with her to Felting.

"Thank you again, Nevi," Chelci said as she hugged the older woman tightly in front of their house. Both of them cried, not wanting to let go. Charlie whimpered by her side until Chelci released Nevi and bent down to pet him.

"Don't forget about us," Nevi said as Chelci joined Russell.

"I won't," Chelci said. "I promise."

Chelci and Russell spent one night in the woods, and in the afternoon of the second day, they arrived at the road just north of the city. Russell wanted to steer clear of any trouble with high lords for not having returned her years before, so Chelci dismounted at the gate to the city where they parted ways. Her greatest treasure was the rare hug he gave her when she left. His body was warm, and his face was kind. They both cried as she walked away, looking back over her shoulder.

Chelci walked the streets of Felting for the first time in six years. The last time she passed through them, she had been a scared, young, and impetuous girl. Now, she felt confident and unafraid of anything life had in store for her.

The city seems to have changed so little. Buildings look smaller than I remember, but it all feels familiar. A few people gave her funny looks as she walked. She looked down and smirked at the light-green dress she wore with a sword affixed to her waist. *What, have they never seen a girl with a sword before?* she thought.

She proceeded up the circular stone drive of the Marlow family house, marveling at the fountains out front and the size of the home she hadn't seen in years. Soon after she knocked on the heavy wooden door, it creaked open to reveal Jensen, the choreman.

"Hello, Jensen. It's good to see you again," she said, walking past him without pause.

"Excuse me! Can I help you?" he called after her.

Chelci ignored him as she continued down the hall, laughing to herself. *He doesn't recognize me.*

"Wait, you can't go in there!" the servant shouted.

Chelci burst through the double doors to the drawing-room without knocking. As expected, Darcius sat in his favorite chair, and Luciana lounged on her chaise. *Other than looking six years older, they're exactly as I remembered them.*

"Yes, can I help you?" her father asked, sitting up straight after the intrusion.

Her mother looked at her with a quizzical expression. Chelci took great pleasure in seeing the moment of realization. Her mother's eyes widened, and she put her hand to her chest. "Chelci?" she whispered.

"Yes, it's me, and I'm back," Chelci replied.

Her father gasped. "You're alive!" He quickly rose to his feet. "Are you okay? We thought you were taken!"

"I wasn't taken. I ran away."

The surprise in her mother's face changed quickly into a look of rage as she stood and stormed toward her. "You ungrateful little wretch! You—"

"No!" Chelci said, staring her mother down, and freezing her in her tracks. "You do *not* get to speak to me that way."

Her mother's mouth remained open, but no more words came out.

"I'm sorry if I caused you grief by leaving. I realize it was selfish of me, and I apologize for that. I know it was your job to help me grow and teach me the best way you knew how, but I am *not* a servant you can order around. I'm not a dog you can kick when you're angry, and you won't treat me like a piece of garbage. I'm choosing to come home and be part of this family because I want to be here—if you'll allow me back.

"I am your daughter by birth. As long as I live here, I'll respect your role as my mother, but only as far as you live up to what that role should be. I'm now a young woman and don't need your permission to have thoughts or feelings. You will *not* forbid my hopes, and you *will* respect my desires." Strength flowed through Chelci's veins as she stood tall and breathed steadily. "Is that all right?"

Her mother stared, suspended, appearing unable to voice a response. Her face looked bewildered with her eyebrows askew and her mouth gaping.

"Is that all right?" Chelci repeated.

"Yes," her mother replied in a shaky voice.

"Good. I'll be in my room getting settled."

Chelci closed the doors behind her with the lasting impression of her mother's incredulous look frozen in her mind. She breathed a sigh of relief as she walked toward the stairs.

It was late, but Veron couldn't sleep. The bed in his narrow room was comfortable enough, but his mind raced from everything that had happened. Tired of lying down and staring at the ceiling, he got up and opened his door.

She said I was free to come and go as long as I don't make trouble, he thought.

Tessa hadn't even shown him around the house before she had closed him in his room for the night, so he was keen to explore. Veron walked softly toward the stairs as he left the cramped third floor and traveled down two floors to get to the ground level of the house.

Exiting the stairwell revealed a large, open dining room. Light from the moon shone through the windows, illuminating the long table with many chairs.

As he entered the room, he froze when footsteps sounded back up the stairwell behind him. *I don't think I'm doing anything wrong, but I don't want to get caught wandering through the house alone on my first night!*

Veron flattened himself against the wall where it was dark. As soon as he stopped moving, a dark shape came out of the stairwell and proceeded out the opposite end of the dining room. He only saw the person wearing a dark cloak for a moment in the dim light, but he couldn't miss the glint of a sword as its edge caught the moonlight.

Is it a thief? A murderer? I don't want to get in trouble, but if I could stop someone who shouldn't be here, it may increase my chances of gaining favor with the Marlows. He slunk off the wall and followed the dark intruder into the next room, where a door opened at the back of the house.

Outside the door, Veron discovered a garden. Stone paths meandered between plants and flowers, and the silhouette of several large trees dotted the landscape. At the far end, the mysterious shadow moved furtively along the path, so he followed.

Just past the garden, another building stood separate from the main house. It was smaller, square-shaped, and made of wood, unlike the stone construction of the residence.

The person entered the smaller building ahead. *I can't just go in after them. There would be nowhere to hide. But . . .* A small window caught his eye on the roof of the building, and a tree grew directly next to it with its limbs hanging over.

Veron climbed the tree and stepped onto the roof of the building. He gently crept up the tiles to the window, but to his disappointment, he could hardly see anything. Directly beyond the window sat a loft, taking most of the view.

What are they doing in there? Are there valuables to steal?

Leaning against the window, Veron caught his breath when the pane moved. Testing it gingerly with his hand, he found the window pivoted smoothly, leaving a space large enough to climb through.

Cautiously, Veron stepped through the window into the loft, thankful the wood didn't creak as he moved his weight across it. Reaching the end of the small area, Veron rested his hands on the railing and peered down below. What he saw was the last thing he expected.

A girl, probably just younger than him, twirled and moved in the warm, gentle light from a lantern hanging on a stand. She held a sword, which danced and sang through the air as she spun. Her straight brown hair was pulled back behind her head. The cloak she wore a moment ago hung on the wall, leaving her with a white shirt and brown pants.

Pants? What girl wears pants? Who is she? She's not stealing anything or killing anyone.

As he leaned over the railing farther, the wood of the loft creaked, stopping his heart. The girl froze and looked up with panic in her eyes, matching what he felt, himself. They both stared at each other silently for a long moment. Veron's fear subsided when her face softened, and she motioned for him to come down.

The ladder at the side of the loft took only a moment to descend, and he soon stood in front of the mysterious girl. Getting to see her entirely took his breath away and gave him goosebumps on his arms. Her eyes were kind, and the skin on her face was soft and smooth. A few strands of her long brown hair had escaped the tie that held it back and dangled playfully across her face. Seeing her casual smile relaxed the tension in his shoulders. Even though she dressed like what Veron thought a man should wear and held her sword naturally like a warrior, she looked undeniably feminine. To Veron, she was beautiful in every way.

"Are you a servant here?" she asked in a gentle voice.

"Yes," he said with a catch in his voice before clearing it. "I'm new. I just arrived this evening."

"I arrived this evening too. Well . . . *returned,* at least. I've been gone a while. I'm Chelci Marlow, daughter of Darcius and Luciana."

Veron's chest tightened. *Perfect. The daughter of that vile woman. But . . . she seems nothing like her.* "Veron Stormbridge."

"I'm glad to meet you, Veron." She pointed with her sword up to the loft. "What were you doing? Following me in the middle of the night?" Chelci asked.

"I'm sorry. I couldn't sleep and was walking around. I saw you sneaking and thought you might be . . . I don't know . . . stealing or something," Veron said.

Chelci laughed. "That's honorable of you to defend the property of your new household."

"So, what are you doing here in the middle of the night? Can you not do this during the day?" he asked.

Chelci stared at him for a long while before responding. "My mother disapproves. I'm working on easing her in, but I'm not ready to push too hard. For now, it's simpler if she doesn't know."

Veron ran his hand through his hair absently, not caring that it stuck up. "Don't worry, your secret is safe with me," he said with a twinkle in his eye.

Chelci tilted her head as she focused intently and pursed her lips. "Have we met? You look somehow familiar, but I have no idea where it would be from."

Veron shrugged. "No . . . sorry. I'm pretty sure I would have remembered," he said as he smiled awkwardly.

Realizing he was staring, he averted his eyes to glance around the room. It was a large open space. A few swords were mounted on the wall, ready to be used. *It's an excellent room for training. Not as wide as the one Artimus had but plenty big.* "It's tough to sword fight on your own, isn't it?" Veron said.

"Yes, It's definitely better with two people. You don't know how to sword fight by chance, do you?"

Veron's breath stopped as he looked back at Chelci. *She's serious.* "Yes, actually, I do." His heart pounded with excitement.

"Grab one," she said, nodding to the wall. "Let's see what you've got."

Veron grinned as he took a sword off the wall. The grip felt right in his hand. The familiar feeling filled him with hope. *Things are already starting to turn around. Maybe being here won't be so bad after all.*

* * *

The wind whipped against the walls of the tent. Bale pulled his cloak tighter around him, not for the warmth it provided, but for the feeling of safety it gave. A pile of wax surrounded a candle on the table, burned down nearly to the base. He stared at the candle, his eyes unfocused, his mind lost in the depths of the flame.

The flap to his tent opened as Desmond entered, stepping gingerly. "Your Majesty, have you decided anything yet?" he asked.

Bale continued to watch the flickering candle without responding.

"Your men, they . . . they're starting to grow restless. Some wonder what your plan is." Desmond stood patiently but got no response except the whistle of the wind outside. "What happened, Your Majesty? It's been a week. You arrived back here without any of your men and haven't spoken a word. What's going on?"

Bale turned away from the candle to look at his advisor. "He was there," he said in a gravelly voice.

Desmond jumped at hearing him speak. "Who was there?"

"The shadow knight." Desmond's eyes widened. "He was there," Bale repeated as his eyes drifted to the wall of the tent. "He killed all of the men . . . like a flash of lightning. He would've killed me had I not . . ." Bale paused to swallow, ". . . had I not fought my way out. It was terrifying."

"I thought they were all dead."

"I did too. Apparently, he's the last one."

"So, what do we do now?" Desmond asked. "Do we attack again? Do we retreat home?"

Bale shot a scathing look of rebuke at his advisor. "We will not retreat," he said with confidence. "But before we can attack again, we need to find this . . . Veron Stormbridge. And we must kill him."

FREE BONUS CHAPTER to The Last Shadow Knight - "The Test" -
featuring Veron and Artimus.
Download today from michaelwebbnovels.com

Find out what happens next with Veron, Chelci, and Brixton in
Rise of the Shadow - The Shadow Knights Trilogy: Book 2 . . .
COMING 2022!

Please visit goodreads.com and amazon.com to leave a review with
your thoughts on the book!

Visit michaelwebbnovels.com for more information on the author
and upcoming books.

Acknowledgements

I'd like to thank everyone who helped make this story what it is. Eli, David, and Marilyn—my very first Alpha readers. You put up with some rough content and were a great start for me to fix some glaring errors. Thank you to my Beta readers: Jan, Sara, Amanda, and Nahusenay. You helped me smooth out the story and came up with some great ideas to bring it all together. A big thank you to my editor, Katie Andrews (sonderandmorii.com). You taught me an INCREDIBLE amount about writing. Thanks for sticking with me as I learned a lot of basics that must have been painful to put up with. Your guidance was pivotal in making this book the work it is now. Also, I want to recognize my proofreaders. You were able to catch a lot of mistakes that I missed after reading the same thing over and over. Finally, I want to thank Snuggs. You have supported and encouraged me since day one in this crazy idea I had to write a book. You always made me feel like I could do it!

www.ingramcontent.com/pod-product-compliance
Lightning Source LLC
Chambersburg PA
CBHW020226110726
47898CB00004B/1168